D0385451

DEATH OF A SIMPLE GIANT
and other modern Yugoslav stories

Death of a Simple Giant

and other modern Yugoslav stories

edited by *BRANKO LENSKI*

THE VANGUARD PRESS, INC.
NEW YORK

Manufactured in the United States of America by
H. Wolff, New York, N.Y.
Library of Congress Catalogue Card Number: 64-23319

All the stories in this volume are used with
the permission of the Yugoslav Authors' Agency
in Belgrade, Yugoslavia, with the following exceptions:
"The Story of a Bridge," "Miracle at Olovo," and "Neighbors" are printed
by permission of the Shirley Hector Literary Agency of New York, N.Y.
(on behalf of the Yugoslav Authors' Agency); the translation of "Miracle
at Olovo" is reprinted from Mademoiselle, ©, 1962, by the Condé Nast
Publications; the translation of "Neighbors" is reprinted by permission of
The Atlantic Monthly, ©, 1962, by The Atlantic Monthly Company;
"Hodorlahomor the Great" and "The Love of Marcel Faber-Fabriczy for
Miss Laura Warronigg" by Miroslav Krleža are reprinted by permission of
Stiasny Verlag, Graz, Austria; and "The Lovers" by Miodrag Bulatorić is
reprinted by permission of Mrs. Carlton Cole, literary agent, New York,
N.Y.

A Key to Pronunciation of Serbo-Croatian Proper Names

With few exceptions, the original spelling of Serbo-Croatian proper names has been retained throughout this volume. The following key will help the reader in pronouncing them:

c = ts   as in lots
č and ć = ch   as in change
š =sh   as in marsh
ž = s   as in pleasure
j = y   as in yes
lj = li   as in stallion
dj = j   as in major
i = ee   as in feet
e = e   as in net
u = oo   as in soon
a = a   as in father

BRANKO LENSKI

Foreword

Between 1941 and 1945, under the yoke of Nazi Fascism, 1,700,000 Yugoslavs were killed. Exposed to unprecedented terror, the Serbs, Croats, Slovenes, Macedonians, and Montenegrins, led by Tito, staged a remarkable resistance. From being bands of small, barely armed guerrillas, Tito's Partisans gradually developed into a regular army of nearly one million soldiers who, in the crucial days of World War II, held in Yugoslavia eighteen German divisions badly needed in France and Russia.

On March 27, 1941, two days after Yugoslavia had followed Hungary, Bulgaria, and Rumania in signing a pact with the Axis, a putsch, inspired by the slogans "Better a grave than a slave" and "Better war than a pact," ousted the Belgrade government responsible for the national shame. Hitler in his "finest hour" could not tolerate such an offense. To punish the Yugoslav heresy he postponed his attack on Russia for five weeks and thereby stood before Moscow's gates in icy winter instead of in autumnal sunshine.

On two other memorable occasions in the twentieth century the "Yugo-Slavs" (Southern Slavs) have played a significant role in world history. The assassination in 1914 of the Austrian crown prince Archduke Ferdinand at Sarajevo spurred the Southern Slavs within Austria-Hungary to rid themselves of their long Hapsburg tutelage. In 1948, Tito, the only satellite Communist leader who came to power without being installed by the Soviet army, refused to accept Stalin's domineering attitude toward "brotherly" Communist parties—a stand that resulted in Yugoslavia's famous breach with the Cominform and the coinage of the word "Titoism" to designate a rebellion within the Communist block.

Seven years later, a "rebellion within a rebellion" took place in Yugoslavia when Yugoslavia's second-ranking Communist, Milovan Djilas, turned against his former friends, a phenomenon reflected in the United States by the publication of Djilas' *The New Class*, an incisive analysis of contemporary Communist society, soon followed by *Anatomy of a Moral, Conversations with Stalin, Land without Justice*, and *Montenegro*.

Picturesque Montenegro, Djilas' native land, has given birth to a succession of proud rebels, from the *hajduci* in the fifteenth century, who relentlessly resisted the Turks when Montenegro fell under Turkish suzerainty, to Tito's Partisans, who fought off seven German offensives before driving the enemy out of their country. Through these centuries Montenegrin bards, the most famous among Yugoslav folk singers, have kept alive the old heroic sagas. Writers have followed the tradition of the minstrels. From the great nineteenth-century poet Njegoš to the 1961 Nobel Prize Winner for Literature Ivo Andrić, many Yugoslav writers have sought subject matter in the Yugoslav epos, that immense treasury of human suffering which now incorporates much of the history of our own days. Thus "The Shepherdess" by the Montenegrin Lalić consecrates the individual heroism of the Partisans who fought not only against the Germans, Italians, and the Royalist general Draža Mihailović and his Četnici, but also against the quislings—in Croatia, Pavelić and his Ustaši; in Serbia, Nedić and Ljotić; in Slovenia, Rupnik.

The second Montenegrin in this collection, Miodrag Bulatović, born in 1930, enjoys a considerable reputation in literary circles outside his own country as the leading avant-garde Yugoslav writer. His novel *The Red Cock Flies to Heaven* has been published in the United States. Like the history of his country, Bulatović's life reflects perpetual torment and deprivation. At eleven, while walking in the woods, he saw his father killed by a brother-in-law over a property dispute. At sixteen, he saw his first train and read his first book. Wandering from one secondary school to another, he snatched bits of education along the road between two sojourns in hospitals where he was treated for starvation and two stays in prisons where he was confined for vagrancy. A child of the war and the war's aftermath, he naturally turned to the war with his second novel, *Heroes on Donkeys*.

The broadest panorama of the Second World War on Yugoslav territory is the eight-hundred-page novel *The Crash*, which comes from the Serbian author Branko Ćopić, Yugoslavia's most popular writer. From his humorous short stories dealing with the adventures of Nikoletina Bursać we have extracted a sample, "An Awkward Companion." Nikoletina (Big Nick), the Yugoslav counterpart of the "good soldier Schweik," has become a part of the Serbo-Croatian language, denoting a "simple-minded, good-hearted colossus." Nikoletina fights his own war against Fascism. He is given all sorts of strange assignments for which he is somehow too awkward; nevertheless this giant, who knows how to destroy singlehandedly an enemy tank but cannot catch a squirrel with the help of an entire brigade, always acquits himself in his particular winning way.

The "simple-minded, good-hearted colossus" appears in another story, "Death of a Simple Giant," by Slovenia's major short-story writer Ciril Kosmač. Kosmač comes from a region that was Austrian before 1918 and Italian between the two World Wars, where at the time of Mussolini every non-Italian was considered second-rate and where a Slovene, at the whim of the local police, could wind up in prison for no other reason than to "pass an examination in survival." Then came the war and the Partisan movement organized by Tito; the "examination in survival" became harder than ever. In reprisal for the food and manpower given to Partisans, the Fascists burned entire villages. Exposed to the constant menace of unexpected Fascist raids, more men fled to join the Resistance. Many of those who hesitantly stayed behind were killed; still others collaborated with the Germans and the Italians. Kosmač's characters take shape against this background of terror. To pass their survival tests they possess a unique weapon: an extravagant optimism. In portraying the optimism of his "simple giant," Kosmač has probably touched upon the most outstanding characteristic of his country and his people.

Another Slovene, Prežihov Voranc, spent the better part of his existence in exile because of his opposition to the political system of old Yugoslavia. His life was a long succession of prisons and escapes, with hide-outs in different European capitals. Only after World War II, a survivor of Nazi concentration camps, did he permanently return to Yugoslavia to work and die there. Prežihov Voranc achieved prominence in contemporary Yugoslav letters for his depiction of the Slovenian village and its colorful characters.

Although there are no clearly defined literary schools in contemporary Yugoslav literature, two basic tendencies can be discerned. Ćopić and Lalić top the list of war-obsessed writers whose characters actively participate in the social changes in their country. If school there must be, these could be called members of the sociological school in contemporary Yugoslav writing. Opposite them are the "psychologists," headed by the Croats Marinković, Desnica, and Dončević, who are primarily concerned with the isolated individuals, the outsiders, the "derelicts in the sun," to quote the revealing title of one of Desnica's short story collections. In contrast to the village and the war-ridden no man's land of the "sociologists," their analytic gaze is centered on the small town. There, ensnared in the world of electrical gadgets, locks, and screws in a less civilized version of American suburbia, dwell Desnica's bourgeois neurotics in whose minds any trifle may acquire great significance and gradually develop into a hallucinating Kafkaesque nightmare. There, too, live Dončević's and Marinković's solitary lovelorn souls, dreamers at grips with an unsmiling reality. Dončević displays a keen insight into those purely contemplative and very Slavic natures—natures incapable of action yet that, because of some unknown, mysterious impulse, may suddenly do the completely unpredictable, to their own and the world's amazement. In Marinković's stories the reader occasionally encounters humorous and ironical allusions to certain political and social aspects of today's Yugoslavia. But these are never more than decorative bits of contemporary history, a colorful backdrop for Marinković's quixotic protagonists. To express his profound experience of war Marinković felt no need to describe battlefields; the symbol of "hands" sufficed. Whether they carve knives, sign death sentences, join in handshakes, write love letters, or collect keys, the hands in Marinković's world are but the lackeys of a dark subconscious that cannot be mastered by reason.

Two by now classic writers, whose first works, published just after the First World War, marked the advent of modernism in Yugoslav literature, occupy a place of special distinction in European letters: the Nobel Prize candidate Miroslav Krleža and the Nobel Prize Winner Ivo Andrić.

Krleža's Yoknapatawpha County lies between Vienna, Budapest, and Zagreb. A Proustian and Faulknerian atmosphere surrounds Krleža's saga of the rise, slow decay, and fall of two patrician families, the Glembays and the Fabriczys, a gallery of three hundred characters who marry, give birth, and die on the soil of Austria, Hungary, and Croatia between the days of Empress Maria-Theresa (1717-1780) and those of the Auschwitz, Buchenwald, and Jasenovac extermination camps (1941-1945).

Krleža's opus is impregnated with Croatian history. In the Middle Ages, under powerful kings, Croatia, like Serbia, Slovenia, and Montenegro, had its moment of glory. Then it lost its independence to Hungary and became, later, part of the Hapsburg empire. Turkish invasions followed. For a short while it was part of the Napoleonic empire and finally of the Austro-Hungarian empire until, in 1918, it became part of the Kingdom of the Serbs, Croats, and Slovenes, a name officially changed into the Kingdom of Yugoslavia in 1929. Between 1941 and 1945 it was nominally an independent state headed by a quisling. Since 1945 it has been one of the six republics of the Federal People's Republic of Yugoslavia.

How is one to live in the midst of such upheaval?

Other writers, caught in this historical momentum, did no more than bear witness to their times or follow a literary trend. Krleža rose to Olympian heights to gain total perspective over the geographic, historical, political, and social stage he was viewing. He rages against the feudal system with its hundreds of ways of torturing and exploiting the serf; he gives shattering examples of the methods employed by the early capitalists in the process of accumulating their initial fortunes, shows what underlies the veneer of social graces displayed by the Austro-Hungarian upper classes, portrays the confusion in the minds of his Fabriczys who do not know whether to defend Vienna against the Turks or march with the Turks against Vienna. Krleža's counterrevolutionaries have instinctive revolutionary leanings, just as his counterreformers pray in their secret hearts for the victory of the reform. In the dawn of Fascism and Communism, the last of the twentieth-century Glembays, heavily burdened with suicidal leanings, insanity, and alcoholism, try to solve their contradictions in flights abroad, only to end up as stewards on transatlantic steamers. There, between portholes, they hopelessly continue to dream of the golden lights in the vineyards where they once used to play games and where they first set eyes on their Lauras. How, according to Krleža, dreams of grand cosmopolitan escapes are likely to end, even when born in the head of an ordinary youth from Zagreb, is shown in "Hodorlahomor the Great."

Krleža has been compared in France to Malraux, Céline, and Sartre. His novels, short stories, plays, poems, and essays have recently been translated into German. He is recognized by Yugoslav officialdom as the man who pronounced the conclusive funeral oration over the dead body of a condemned system and who foreshadowed the revolutionary events to come. He is vice-president of the Yugoslav Academy of Arts and Sciences and editor-in-chief of the Yugoslav Encyclopedia.

Ivo Andrić needs less introduction to the American reader. His novel *The Bridge on the Drina* was published here even before he won the Nobel Prize for Literature. Other Andrić novels have since appeared in the United States: *The Devil's Courtyard,* three novellas under the title *The Vizier's Elephant,* and *Bosnian Chronicle.*

Andrić was awarded the Nobel Prize for the brilliant depiction of his country, in particular his native Bosnia, which for centuries stood on the crossroads between eastern and western civilization. Half Moslem and half Christian (Roman Catholic and Orthodox), situated between Croatia and Serbia, Bosnia served as an important Turkish military outpost against the Hapsburgs. In 1878, when Turkish power dwindled, Bosnia was occupied and later annexed by Austria until Yugoslavia came into being in 1918.

From the colorful history of Bosnia, where feudalism maintained a strong foothold until after the First World War, Andrić has drawn the subject matter for his novels and short stories. Inspired by the epic poetry of Yugoslavia and with a keen ear for legends kept alive among old Bosnian families and a flair for historical research, Andrić has turned his collected materials into a national chronicle. In his Bosnia come and go the viziers from Istanbul, the consuls from France, and the generals from Austria, while the good Bosnian people work for their daily bread and comment on the strange events around them, often with fear, sometimes with amusement, occasionally with incomprehension. With great love for humanity and subtle irony, Andrić shows how individual destinies decompose within the tissue of history. However, Andrić suggests, something always remains —a bridge, perhaps, proof that all was not in vain. "The Story of a Bridge" can be viewed as a seed of Andrić's major novel, *The Bridge on the Drina*.

Modern Yugoslavia is undergoing radical changes. From an agrarian country with an eighty percent peasant population before World War II, Yugoslavia has become industrialized to the point where today more people work in towns than on the land. The Adriatic coast and the Slovenian Alps are no longer invaded by conquering armies, but by swarms of tourists.

Yugoslav writers have long been obsessed by the idea of death and have manifested a particular fondness for dreams and dreamlike states as a means of escape from the pitfalls of their blood-drenched history. Lalić, Ćopić, and Kosmač seem unable to forget the countless unnamed Partisan tombs in the Yugoslav woods, many of them of teen-age boys and girls who fled home and school to fight Fascism. Marinković, Dončević, and Desnica show more understanding and sympathy for the troubled die-hard than for the rising "new class" hero. The hopeful socialistic Horatio Alger hailing from "agraria" toward industrialization and affluence needs yet to find his interpreters among the new young writers who are slowly and painstakingly breaking into the foreground.

May this collection of short stories provide the American reader with a new insight into the life and thought of contemporary Yugoslavia.

Branko Lenski

Contents

DEATH OF A SIMPLE GIANT
and other modern Yugoslav stories

IVO ANDRIĆ

The Story of a Bridge

In the fourth year of his term of office as grand vizier, Yusuf made a mistake and unexpectedly fell into disfavor. The struggle lasted a whole winter and spring. It was a wicked and cold spring, that refused to let the summer begin. But in May Yusuf emerged from banishment as the victor. And so life continued, glorious, peaceful, and even. But from those winter months when less than a hair's breadth divided life from death and glory from ruin, there remained in the victorious Vizier traces of oppression and preoccupation. It was something intangible, something that men of experience, those who have suffered, guard like hidden treasure and never reveal unless involuntarily, in look, movement, or speech.

While he was living, so to speak, in exile, all alone and in disgrace, the Vizier's memories of his origins and of his old country became clearer, for disappointment and pain always turn the mind back to the past. He recalled his mother and his father. (They had both died while he was still a modest assistant to the Sultan's Master of the Horse; he had since ordered their graves to be edged with stone coping and marked by white tombstones.) He recalled Bosnia and the village of Žepa, from which he had been taken when he was nine.

It was pleasant in his unhappiness to think of that distant country and the scattered village, where tales of his success and glory in Constantinople were told in every house and where nobody knew or even suspected the reverse side of the medal of glory, or the price at which success was attained.

That very summer he had had an opportunity to talk to people from Bosnia. He questioned them, and they told him what he wanted to know. After the revolts and wars there had been riots, scarcity, starvation, and all kinds of epidemics. He ordered considerable sums to be spent on material assistance to those of his people who were still at Žepa. At the same time he issued instructions for inquiries to be made about what they most needed in the way of construction. He was told that the Šetkićes still had four houses and were the wealthiest family in the village, but that the village and all the surrounding country had become impoverished, that the mosque had fallen into disrepair and finally been damaged by fire, that the spring drought had dried everything up, and, worst of all, that there was no bridge over the river Žepa. The village stands on a hill near where the Žepa joins the Drina, and the only way of getting to Višegrad was over the Žepa, about fifty yards above the confluence. Whatever kind of plank bridge was put up was always swept away by the water, for either the Žepa rose quickly and unexpectedly, like any other mountain stream, or else it was the Drina that rose suddenly, overflowing into the channel of the Žepa and checking its flow. Then the Žepa overflowed and lifted the bridge, which disappeared as if it had never been. Then again, in winter the planks became iced and slippery, so that both men and beasts were often injured. Thus, were anybody to build them a solid bridge, he would be doing the greatest service.

The Vizier gave six rugs for the mosque and enough money for a fountain with three pipes. At the same time he decided that a bridge should be built.

At that time an Italian master builder was living in Constantinople. This man had built a number of bridges near the city, and had made a name for himself. He was engaged by the Vizier's treasurer and sent to Bosnia with two men from the court.

They arrived at Višegrad before the snow had melted. For several days the amazed people of Višegrad watched the master builder, stooped and gray, but with a ruddy complexion and youthful face, inspecting the great stone bridge, knocking on it, crumbling the mortar and tasting it with his tongue. Then he went to spend a few days at Bania, whence the stone for the Višegrad bridge had come. He brought out hired hands to clear the quarry, which had been completely covered with earth and grown over with bushes and mare's-tail. They went on digging until they found a wide, deep vein of stone, which was stronger and whiter than that which had been used for the Višegrad bridge. Then the master builder went down the Drina as far as the Žepa and decided where to ferry the stones across. One of the Vizier's two men then returned to Constantinople with the accounts and plans.

The master builder remained behind to await his return, but he did not want to stay either in Višegrad or in any of the Christian houses overlooking the Žepa. He built himself a log cabin on a rise of ground in the triangle between the Drina and the Žepa (the remaining Vizier's man and a Višegrad clerk acted as his interpreters) and there he lodged. He cooked for himself, buying eggs, cream, onions, and dried fruit from the peasants. It was said that he never bought meat. All day long he would be busy constructing, drawing, investigating the various kinds of stone, and studying the course and direction of the Žepa.

Meanwhile, the other official returned from Constantinople with the Vizier's approval and a third of the necessary money.

Work began, and the people never ceased to wonder at the unusual spectacle. For what was being built in no way resembled a bridge. First, massive pine beams were laid slantwise across the Žepa and two rows of piles placed between them. These were then plaited together with brushwood and reinforced with clay, so that the whole thing looked like a trench. In this way the river was diverted and one half of the river bed was drained. But one day, just when this work was completed, a cloud burst somewhere in the mountains and in a short time the Žepa became troubled and rose. The same night it broke right through the middle of the newly finished dam. When the next day dawned, the water had already receded, but the wattle had been broken through, the piles torn out, and the beams displaced. Among the workers and the people it was whispered that the Žepa would not allow a bridge to be built across it. But the very next day the master builder ordered new piles to be driven in, deeper this time, and the remaining beams to be repaired and straightened. And then the stony river bed again resounded with the crash of tree trunks and the cries of the workers and their rhythmic blows.

Only when everything had been prepared and the stone delivered from Bania did the masons and builders arrive—men from Herzegovina and Dalmatia. Wooden huts had been built for them, and in front of these they chipped at the stone, becoming white as millers from the dust. The master builder went around, bent down over them, and constantly checked their work with a yellow iron set square and a green level.

When cuttings had been made in both steep, rocky banks, the money ran out. Dissatisfaction developed among the workers and the local people began to mutter that nothing would come of this bridge. Some who had just arrived from Constantinople reported that they had heard rumors that the Vizier had been ousted. Nobody could tell what was the matter with him, whether it was sickness or worry, but he was becoming more and more inaccessible and was forgetting or abandoning public works that he had begun in Constantinople itself. Yet a few days later the Vizier's man arrived with the remainder of the money, and the work went on.

A fortnight before St. Demetrius' Day, people crossing the Žepa by the plank bridge above the new works noticed a white, smooth wall of hewn stone, covered with scaffolding like spiders' webs, jutting out of the dark gray slate from both banks of the river. From then on it grew every day. But then the first frosts began and work was suspended. The masons went home for the winter, while the master builder spent that season in his log cabin, from which he hardly ever emerged. All day long he bent over his plans and accounts, going out from time to time only to inspect the bridge site. When, just before spring, the ice began to thaw, he was to be seen every few moments inspecting the scaffolding and dams with a worried look. Sometimes he would even do this at night, with a torch in his hand.

Before St. George's Day the workers returned and work was resumed. And exactly at midsummer the bridge was finished. Gaily workers took down the scaffolding, and from behind the structure of beams and boards there appeared a white, slender bridge, with only one arch spanning the distance between the granite banks.

Nothing was more inconceivable than such a wonderful structure in this impoverished and desolate region. It seemed as if the two banks had spurted petrified gushes of water toward each other, that they had met, forming an arch, and remained there, suspended for a moment above the chasm. Through the arch, at the farthest point of vision, one could see a small stretch of the blue Drina, and under it the now tamed and confined Žepa gurgled past. For a long time the eyes could not grow used to the well-proportioned slender line of that arch, which looked as if it were only resting a moment in this harsh, gloomy, and rocky desert with its old-man's-beard and its bramble, and that at the first opportunity it would continue its flight and disappear.

People flocked from the surrounding villages to see the bridge. Townsmen came from Višegrad and Rogatica to admire it, but to regret that it had been built in such a stony wilderness instead of in their own market-town.

"It's something to have produced a Vizier," the people of Žepa would say, slapping the parapet of the bridge. It was straight cut, with sharp edges, as if carved from cheese, not hewn from stone.

While the first travelers, dumb with amazement, were already crossing the bridge, the master builder paid off his men, packed and loaded his cases of tools and papers, and set off for Constantinople with the Vizier's two men.

Talk of him now spread through town and village. Selim, a gypsy, who, with his nag, had carted the master builder's things from Višegrad and was the only one ever to have entered the log cabin, would sit in the café and tell, nobody knew how many times, all he knew about the stranger.

"Truly, he is not a man as other men are. During the winter, when the work stopped, I did not go up to the cabin for about a fortnight. But when I went back everything was in a mess, just as I had seen it last time. He was sitting in the freezing cabin, dressed in a bearskin hat and so wrapped up that you could only see his hands, all blue from the cold. He would chip at a piece of stone and then write something down, and then chip again and make some more notes. I open the door and he looks at me with those green eyes of his and his eyebrows bristling, and you'd think he wanted to devour you. But not a word or a whisper out of him. I have never seen the likes of it. You wouldn't believe, lads, how that man took it out of himself during those eighteen months, and when it was all over, we took him across on the ferry and he trotted off on this very horse."

The townsfolk now questioned him with increasing interest

about the master builder and the life he had led, and the more they heard, the more they marveled. They could not forgive themselves for not having paid more attention to him when he was still to be seen in the streets and alleys of Višegrad.

Meanwhile the master builder was riding home, and he was but two nights' journey from Constantinople when he fell ill of the plague. He arrived in the city in a high fever, hardly able to keep his seat. He immediately went to the hospital of the Italian Franciscans, and at the same hour next day breathed his last in the arms of a monk.

The very next morning the Vizier was told of the death of the master builder, and given the remaining accounts and sketches of the bridge. The builder had received only a quarter of his pay. He had left neither debts nor ready money, neither will nor heir. After careful consideration the Vizier ordered that one third of the pay still due him should be paid to the hospital, and that the other two thirds should be used as an endowment to provide orphans with bread and soup.

Just when he was issuing instructions to this effect—it was a calm morning of late summer—a request was submitted to him by a young and learned teacher of the Koran who was by origin a Bosnian and wrote very polished verses, and whom the Vizier had from time to time patronized and assisted. This teacher had heard, the letter said, of the bridge that the Vizier had had built in Bosnia, and hoped that this—like all other public works—would bear an inscription stating when and on whose instructions it had been built. As always, he offered his services to the Vizier and begged to have the honor to submit the text for the inscription, which he hoped would be accepted—one that he had composed with great care and effort. Attached on stouter paper was the text, beautifully copied, with an initial in red and gold.

"When Lovely Skill went hand in hand
With Marvelous Administration,

This wondrous bridge was born, to cause
Vizier Yusuf's men delight,
And mankind lasting admiration."

Underneath was the Vizier's seal—oval, divided into two un-
equal fields: on the larger, *Yusuf Ibrahim, true servant of Allah;*
and on the smaller, his personal device: Safety in Silence.

The Vizier spent a long time considering this application, his
hands wide apart, one palm pressing down on the verse inscription, the other on the sketches and computations for the bridge.
Of late he had spent more and more time considering applica-
tions and official documents.

This summer it was two years since his fall and his banishment
from grace. At first, on his return to power, he had noticed no
changes in himself. He was at that age—the best of all—when a
man knows and feels the full value of life: he had vanquished
his opponents and was more powerful than ever; he was able to
measure the height of his strength by the depth of his recent fall.
Yet though at times he succeeded in dispelling his worries, he
was powerless to prevent dreams. At night recently he had
dreamed of prison, and from those nightmares, like a vague terror, the vision was carried over into the waking day, poisoning it.

He became more sensitive to the objects surrounding him.
Certain things, which till then he had never noticed, now began
to offend him. He ordered all velvet to be removed from the pal-
ace and replaced by bright cloth, smooth, soft, and rustling under the touch. He conceived something akin to hatred for
mother-of-pearl, for it was suggestive of a chill wilderness and
his own isolation. At the mere touch, or even the mere sight of
it, his teeth chattered and his skin froze. All furnishings and
weapons that contained any mother-of-pearl were removed from
his quarters.

This evil seethed within him, and there was no person to
whom he could even think of admitting or confiding it. And

when, in the end, the evil finally completed its work and broke through the surface, its secret would still be guarded and people would simply say: death. For people have no suspicion of how many of the great and powerful of this world die within themselves, silently, imperceptibly, but rapidly.

The Vizier began to regard everything with concealed, but deep, mistrust. Somehow the idea became fixed in his mind that every human action, every word, might lead to evil. This possibility seemed to him to be implicit in everything he heard, saw, said, or thought. The victorious Vizier had begun to fear life. Thus, without suspecting it, he entered into that state which is the first phase of dying, when a man begins to be more interested in the shadow thrown by things than in their substance.

That morning the Vizier was again tired from lack of sleep, but calm and collected. His eyelids were heavy and his face as if frozen in the freshness of the morning. He thought of the foreign master builder who had died, and of the orphans who would eat the man's earnings. He thought of the distant, mountainous, gloomy land of Bosnia (he could never think of Bosnia as anything but gloomy) that even the light of Islam had succeeded in illuminating only partially, and where life, lacking urbanity and polish, was miserable, brutish, and hard. How many such regions were there in this world of Allah? How many turbulent streams without bridge or ford? How many places without drinking water, how many mosques without decoration or beauty?

All the many forms of misery, poverty, and fear with which the world was filled occupied his thoughts.

The sun was gleaming on the tiles of the little summerhouse. The Vizier looked down on the teacher's verse inscription, raised his pencil slowly, and then crossed it out twice. Only a little was left now, and a moment later even less, for the Vizier now struck out the first half of the seal bearing his name. There remained only the device: *Safety in Silence.* He stood for some time gazing down on this, and then raised his hand again and struck that out, too. That was how the bridge came to have no name and no inscription.

There it is, in Bosnia, where it glints in the sun and glows in the light of the moon, and bears both men and cattle on its back. Little by little the circle of disturbed soil and scattered objects that surround every new structure vanished. People or the waters carried away the broken piles, the remaining fragments of scaffolding and construction, and the rains washed away the last traces of the work of the seasons. But still the country could not come to love the bridge, nor the bridge the country. Seen from the side, its bold white arch always appeared isolated and solitary, and startled travelers like some strange thought that had lost its way and was caught amid the rocks in this wilderness.

The teller of this story was the first to think of investigating the origins of the bridge. It was one evening, when he was returning from the mountains and, tired out, sat for a moment on the parapet. That was one summer season when there were sultry days with chilly nights. When he leaned against the stonework he noticed that it was still warm from the day's heat. He was perspiring, and a cold wind was blowing from the Drina. The feel of the warm hewn stone was pleasant and strange, and therefore a sympathetic link between the man and the bridge, and so there and then the man resolved to write its story.

Translated by Petar Mijušković

Miracle at Olovo

Everything that was born or lived in the Bademlić house was cheerful, feckless, and gay. The only exception was Kata Bademlić, the wife of the eldest of the Bademlić brothers. She was tall, bony, and blonde with blue eyes and a cold, penetrating regard. Brought to this rich and spacious house twenty-six years before, she had grown gloomier, duller, and more silent from year to year. She had not been happy with her husband, and she had had no luck with her children.

Her husband, Peter Bademlić, the eldest brother of this wealthy family, had married very late. All manner of stories were told of his younger days. Even when he had brought Kata home, although he was by then played out, there still remained in his way of talking and moving, and particularly in his way of smiling, something of his old wildness and dissoluteness. It was a broad, stupid, sensual smile that was stamped on all the swarthy Bademlić faces like a hallmark, impossible to conceal. There was something about that smile that during all these years had filled Kata, coming as she did from a fresh and healthy family in Livno, with terror and repulsion.

With her children it had been still worse. In the first twelve years she had borne nine children, and all had died, one after the other, just as they were entering their best years. The birth of the tenth child she barely survived. From then on she ceased to have children. This last child was a girl, and it lived. Up to her sixth year the child throve; she was small, but she was fair-haired and so pretty that people in church turned to look as she went by. In everything she took after her mother and her healthy Livno kinsmen.

But when she was about six, she began to waste away and grow ugly. She suddenly began to bend at the knees and to hunch over at the waist; her face coarsened and her eyelids grew puffy. In this condition, huddled up and with her mouth always half open, she crept from one divan to another and lay for years in the cold gloomy rooms of the Bademlićs' like a curse on the house and a judgment of God. Now she was nearing fifteen, but her bodily development was feeble, and her mental development even feebler. She was unable to straighten up, nor could she walk without someone to support her. She said little, only the most ordinary things, and then hoarsely and indistinctly. She got on best with her mother, and the old woman devotedly nursed the child; she would not let a single servant near her, but herself carried the girl from place to place, fed her, washed her, and changed her clothes.

She did everything she could to cure her daughter. After she had been the round of all the doctors and wise women with cures, and had tried all the medicines and everything anyone had ever mentioned to her, and had paid in vain for masses and prayers, she took a vow one day before the altar of the Virgin Mary that on the Blessed Virgin's Nativity she would go bare-

foot to Olovo and take her sick daughter to the monastery of Our
Lady of the Springs.

Like all people who have suffered much misfortune and seen
many deaths around them and who live apart and wholly within
themselves, she took account, in all her affairs, of the forces of
the invisible world and was closer and more intimate with them
than she was with the real world. When she had made her vow,
she continued praying for some time, and when she rose to her
feet, she repeated her prayer and her appeal to the Virgin Mary.

"I can bear it no longer. But grant that one of two things may
happen: either cure her for me or take her to Thyself, to
heaven, like the other nine."

A few days after this vow, the travelers set off before dawn
from the Bademlić house. The old woman took her sister-in-law,
a pockmarked old maid, and with them went two menservants
to carry the girl, since she was unable to stay on a horse. They
led two horses in halters for the return journey. It was light
when they came out on the first heights above Sarajevo. The
girl, who up to that point had complained, protested, and cried
a good deal, was now resting in a specially constructed shallow
wicker basket, which the menservants carried on two pitchforks
passed through the sides. Exhausted by the fresh air, she was
sleeping with her head on her right shoulder. Every now and
then, when jolted, she would open her eyes, but seeing green
branches, the sky, and a rosy glow overhead, she would shut
them again, thinking it was a dream, and smile, with that wan
smile that sick children have when they are beginning to get
better.

After a while they ceased to climb. They passed through thick
woods and the road became broader and easier. At this point
they began to meet people from other places. There were some
who were seriously ill, loaded onto horses like sacks, and moan-
ing hoarsely and rolling their eyes. There were crazy and possessed people, whom their relatives tried to restrain and calm
down.

The old Bademlić woman went ahead of her party, thrust her way through the crowd, paying no heed to anyone, and told her beads in a whisper. The bearers could hardly keep up with her. Twice they rested in a beech wood beside the road. At lunchtime they spread a dark-colored rug on the grass and laid the invalid on it. She stretched out her wasted legs and crumpled frame as much as she could. She was frightened when she saw her mother's feet beside her, bare, bruised, blue, and all bloody from their unaccustomed journey. The elder woman quickly drew her feet under her Turkish trousers, and the girl, joyful and excited by so many new sights around her, forgot at once. Everything was new, unusual, and cause for joy—the thick, dark forest grass, the heavy beeches with growths like shelves on their silvery bark, the birds that dived at the horses' nosebags, and the wide horizon with its bright sky and streaks of cloud drifting slowly along. Whenever a horse tossed its head and the birds fluttered around in alarm, the girl, tired and sleepy as she was, felt she had to laugh, long and quietly. She watched the servants eating slowly and seriously, and in that, too, there was something funny and amusing. She herself ate some preserves, then stretched out on the rug as far as she was able. Parting the cool grass with her hand, she looked at a flower called Grannie's Ear, a tiny bright red flower clinging close to the black earth as if lost. She gave a little cry of excitement. The old woman, who had dozed off from fatigue, started up and picked it for her. For a long while the girl looked at it and smelled it, holding it in her palm; then she pressed it to her cheek and closed her eyes in rapture when she felt how velvety and cool it was.

They reached Olovo at dusk. Around the ruins of the monastery and the vaulted pool, from which could be heard the muffled fall of the hot springs of Our Lady, it was as crowded as a fairground. Fires were burning and people roasted food and ate. Most of them slept on the ground, but there were places in a wooden hut for the wealthier and better class. Here the Bademlić family installed themselves. Both women quickly fell fast asleep, but the girl spent the whole night in a kind of reverie and gazed through the window at the stars over the black woods. She had never before in her life seen so many stars. She listened to voices, which murmured around the fires all night long, and in this way glided off to sleep. At times she would be awakened by the neighing of a horse or the fresh night air; and listening once again to the murmuring voices, she could not determine when she was asleep and when awake.

Early the next morning they went to the springs. First there was a low, almost dark room where one undressed. The floors were damp and slimy. Around the walls stood wooden benches on which the clothes were left. From there three wooden steps led down into a bigger and somewhat lighter chamber containing the pool. Everything was made of stone. The roof was of stone and vaulted, and high up at the top were small, round apertures through which shone beams of strange light. Footsteps made echoes, and the stone vault magnified and returned the slightest sound. The noise of water rebounded from the vaults and, thus multiplied and magnified, filled the whole place, so that it was necessary to shout when speaking. And this shouting in its turn broke and redoubled beneath the vaults. The steam made it hard to breathe. Water streamed from the walls and roof beams, to which green stalactites clung as in caves. The water fell in a thick jet from a stone conduit. It was warm, clear, and full of silvery bubbles; it spread out over the stone pool and there took on a greenish tinge from the gray slabs of stone.

Men and women took turns bathing. When it came to the women's turn, there was pushing, quarreling, and yelling. Some wore clothes and merely took off their shoes and paddled in the water, which came up above their knees; others had stripped down to their shifts. Childless women squatted up to their necks in water and prayed with eyes closed. Some caught water from the spout in their palms and rinsed their throats, ears, and nostrils. And all were so taken up with praying and thinking about a cure

that no one felt shy of anyone else; it was as if they did not see
one another. They pushed and squabbled a little for more room,
but a moment later they had again forgotten both their squab-
bles and one another.

Old Mrs. Bademlić and her sister-in-law led the girl into the
water. Although all the women were in a state of transport and
each was preoccupied with herself, they made way for the Bademlićs, since people of wealth and standing never lose their
pre-eminence anywhere.

Huddled up as she was, the girl trembled and was afraid of the
water and the people. But little by little she lowered herself
deeper and deeper into the pool, as if wishing to hide. If they
had not supported her under her arms, she would have gone to
the bottom. Even so, the water came up to her chin. Never in
her life had she seen so much water or heard so many voices or
strange cries. Only now and then, when she had dreamed that she
was well and that she could walk and run, had she imagined herself bathing with other children in water with countless tiny,
shining bubbles playing about her body, just as they were doing
now. She was carried away. She shut her eyes and quickly
breathed in the hot steam. She heard the voices of the women
around her from farther and farther away. She felt a kind of tickling in her eyes. She drew her brows down harder, but the tickling
did not stop. Finally, with an effort, she opened her eyes. A
beam of sunlight came down through one of the holes in the
vault and fell on her face. Into the light, steam from the pool
soared and hovered like fine dust, green, blue, and gold. The
sick girl followed it with her eyes. Suddenly she began to shud-
der and twitch, and then started with an effort to rise from the
water. Astounded, the mother and aunt began to let go of her,
loosening their hold little by little. And all at once the huddled,
crippled girl straightened up, as she had never done before, letting go of the hand that had supported her from either side,
and, although still stooping a little, she began slowly and un-
steadily to walk, like a small child. She spread out her hands.

Through her thin, wet shift her little breasts showed their dark rosy nipples. Drops of water sparkled on her heavy eyelashes. Her full lips parted in an oddly stupid, sensual smile. She raised her head and, looking up, high up, into that beam of light, she suddenly cried out in an unexpectedly clear and piercing voice: "There He is, coming down on the clouds! Jesus! Jesus! A-a-ah!"

There was something awesome and triumphant in that voice. All the women cowered beneath it. No one dared to raise her head and look at the sick girl or at her vision, but they all felt it above them. Some began to pray at the tops of their voices, and some started to cry, and their praying turned to weeping and loud sobbing. They could be heard beating their hands on their wet breasts. All their cries were strange and weird, like those that people utter only when they are in transports of pain or joy and when they forget human measure and shame. The ringing echoes magnified and prolonged their cries, and everything was mingled with the din of the water that fell with a continuous roar from above.

The only one who did not bow her head was old Mrs. Bademlić. She climbed onto the second step so that she was only ankle-deep in the water and from there sternly and intently looked at her daughter, her dreamlike movements, and the new smile on her face. Then suddenly, pushing her sister-in-law aside, she went up to the girl, seized her around the waist, gripped her beneath the knees with her other hand, and with great, angry strides, as if hiding something shameful, carried her out into the room where the clothes were.

Here it was dim and quiet. She put the child down. She looked around her. No one was there. The girl shivered from the sudden change and, bent once more, lay on the bare earth; but still there remained on her face that broad, unhealthy smile of sensual bliss.

From the pool came the sound of voices in prayer and exclamations at the miraculous cure. But the old woman stood motionless, thunderstruck, even sterner and grimmer than usual.

For she alone knew that this was the Bademlić smile, that there was no healing here, and that it had all been in vain. It was as if she could hardly wait to flee the world and be alone with the Virgin Mary, with whom she had a pact still unfulfilled. She did not even heed the girl who was shivering at her feet, but turned toward a dark corner and exclaimed several times in a sharp whisper: "Take her to Thyself! Take her to Thyself!"

Translated by Michael Scammell

I V O   A N D R I Ć

Neighbors

When it was time for me to move to that ancient Austrian university town for my studies, I entered the ranks of the chosen few who were deemed worthy to reside in the house of Miss Mariana. A doctor, a Czech who had come to our town as a general practitioner and who, during all the time he was a student, had lived at Miss Mariana's, had given me a written recommendation containing all the necessary data concerning me and my family.

Sixty-year-old Miss Mariana, the last member of an eminent and once-rich officer's family, lived in a comfortable apartment of four rooms. This comprised the entire upper story of an old two-storied house, which was separated from the street by a handsome garden and a courtyard paved with large slabs of hard stone. Both the rooms and all the accessory premises were extremely spacious, even though overcrowded with things that had come down from a larger, grander house. In fact, she and her elderly servant, Liza, did not need so much space. There-fore Miss Mariana used to rent one of the four rooms, which with its anteroom constituted a kind of tiny apartment in itself. She let the room because it helped her make her modest annuity go around, but even more in order that they should not be two old ladies completely alone. For Miss Mariana, like all old ladies, was afraid of burglars.

The renting of this apartment to "a single gentleman" was, in fact, the responsibility of Liza, a harsh, devout old spinster some-what younger than her mistress. Miss Mariana remained with-drawn and invisible in her rooms. But the question of whether the apartment was to be let or not—how, when, to whom, and under what conditions—was long debated by the two women. The conditions were neither easy nor simple. First, the price was considerably higher than that for similar apartments in the same district; second, whoever wanted to take Miss Mariana's apart-ment had to be recommended by a reliable party. And the whole manner of renting, payment, and soliciting was such that it in no way resembled the vulgar renting of students' apartments.

All this I knew in advance from the doctor who had recom-mended me.

When I arrived, I was received with distrust. I had to leave the letter and come again the next day. Then I was cautiously ques-tioned and my luggage examined. After this, Liza communicated everything to Miss Mariana. The recital of my good and bad points was not only long but also extremely loud, since Miss Mariana was evidently hard of hearing, so that I was able for the most part to hear it in the other room.

Finally, my good points carried the day; I was accepted and was able to move in. The furniture in my apartment was middling and the rugs cheap, but everything was tidy, the floor was pol-ished, there was not a speck of dust around, and the curtains had been laundered and the windows washed. The same soulless, monastic, and sanitary cleanliness reigned over everything. Ev-erything in those rooms was tidy, shining, and useful. Nothing was for luxury, the gratification of the senses, or idleness; everything was in the service of order, repose, health, and a long, God-fearing, dry, and barren life—the order and cleanliness of a pious world, devoid of imagination and of personal desires.

The whole house was dominated by a silence that fully corresponded to its order and cleanliness, a silence that was neither sad nor gay, but in which there moved people who spent the whole day doing the petty tasks of everyday living, while in their thoughts they took account only of the eternity of another world.

As I have already said, the arrangements for the apartment and my moving in were all completed with Liza, a spry, skinny, and hard-boiled old maid, whose green eyes gleamed out of her red face with a distrustful and energetic expression. During these conversations, Liza constantly invoked her "mistress," pronouncing her name with a special accent of almost pious respect. "My mistress does not like this—" "My mistress does not allow that—" Eventually I began to envisage Miss Mariana as the personification of strength, wisdom, and inaccessible authority.

Everything was done through Liza, but the money for the rent was handed personally to Miss Mariana. Thus I was for the first time led into her presence and introduced to her. My surprise was great. The spacious room with three windows was semidark from the heavy double drapes and a conglomeration of ponderous furniture. The floor was overflowing with Persian rugs of a subdued color, and the walls were covered with tapestries that had long since lost their freshness and with pictures in heavy frames of tarnished gilt by nineteenth-century German artists. In the corners were large indoor palms and green rubber plants, but they were all stiff and dark brown, as if made out of cardboard.

The large double doors leading into the next room were wide open, and through them could be seen just as spacious and dark a room, which was just as crowded with furniture, rugs, and pictures.

Between a small desk and a blackened but gleaming Biedermeier chest of drawers stood a diminutive woman dressed all in black. She remained completely motionless, as if she herself were part of this museum furniture. Light from the nearest window fell on her face. In contrast to the semidark room and the blackness of her dress, which came up to her chin and ended there in a narrow border of white embroidery, the woman's face was pale with the unhealthy pallor of closed rooms, and her hair, parted in the center and carefully combed back, was completely gray. The face and hair gleamed with a spectral whiteness, as if some ancient and dry dust had been falling for many years on the motionless woman; and even apart from this, she resembled those waxen images that fill children with fear and leave adults with a nagging awareness of man's futile struggle with the passage of time. In that dry, pale face the woman's lusterless eyes stood out like two black circles.

Miss Mariana spoke only a few words to me, enunciating each word extremely loudly, slowly, and distinctly, the way deaf people do. Then, with the movements of an ancient automaton, she took the money that I had placed on the little table, signed the receipt, and bade me farewell without offering her hand but accompanying me with an inflexible look from her extraordinary dark eyes, of which it was impossible to make out the pupils or to see either lashes or brows.

Now I knew what the room next to me was like, and also the appearance of Miss Mariana, whose name Liza pronounced with fear and reverence and whose will she invoked as the highest indisputable and irrevocable judgment. And from then on I was permitted on the first of every month to see her for several minutes in the presence of Liza, to pay my respects to her, and to receive a signed receipt.

Because I was very busy with the chores and still more with the distractions of student life, I did not think much about Miss Mariana. But although I did not have the opportunity to see her often, I could hear her almost every day. As I have already mentioned, the room in which Miss Mariana spent the day was next to mine. These two rooms had once been joined by doors, but now the doors were nailed up, stopped up with mattresses, and covered with a heavy rug, whose turbulent and not exactly tasteful colors filled my field of vision in the morning when I awoke and at night when I closed my eyes to go to sleep.

I do not know whether there has ever been or will be a student generation that slept less, or more irregularly, than the generation to which I belonged. The turning on of the electric light was for us the same as dawn. That is when our real life began, in the cafés, in the bars, in the parks, or in the rooms of other students. It did not matter where; the main thing was not to sleep. The most difficult and painful thing for us was parting, or the moment when we had to go home to bed. And even when we had begun to move homeward, still we accompanied one another home, often till dawn. I was among the students who had an aversion to sleeping at night and an unhealthy, inexplicable need to stay up. It is therefore understandable that I remained in bed till noon. But as early as the second week, Liza declared positively that her mistress considered my way of life worthless and that she could not in any case permit any room in her house to be tidied at noon instead of in the morning, as is done by all sensible and decent people. I do not know how or why, but I bowed to the will of the invisible Miss Mariana. I continued to come in in the small hours, slept for a total of three or four hours, and at eight o'clock got up and left the house. Of course, because of that I had to sleep for two or three hours after lunch. But it did not work out without difficulties. At about three in the afternoon almost every day a loud conversation would begin in the next room between Miss Mariana and an evidently older and extremely talkative man. His voice was hoarse, but strong and penetrating. Because of the woman's deafness, the man spoke in a still louder voice, pronouncing word by word and often repeating.

"My dear Mariana, you can't imagine, you just can't imagine how filthy the weather is outside; disgusting weather, I tell you."

"Is it cold?"

"Yes, very. Disastrous weather, as I told you."

With these words Miss Mariana's guest would usually awaken me from my postprandial slumbers. Slowly and brutally they would penetrate my sluggish consciousness, which still retained the echoes of individual sentences from the previous night's student discussions on the major issues of the world and the highest values in life.

No matter how tired and sleepy I might be, it was impossible to think any more about sleep. I was condemned to listen through my state of weary semiconsciousness to a conversation conducted in the next room by two old people without the slightest shame or consideration, not even thinking that they might interfere with anyone and not asking themselves whether anyone was listening or what might be thought of these conversations—conversations that moved in the lowest realms of banality. Most often they were concerned with the weather, with health and illnesses, with mutual acquaintances who were always mentioned by name, with stock values, with market prices, and with the news in the papers in general.

The old gentleman with the hoarse voice would bring a whole sackful of news, all from these lower regions of life, and would shake it out before the old lady, who would only occasionally become vocal and ask questions in that sharp voice typical of hopelessly deaf people.

"Today I met Agatha," the man would begin, but he would be interrupted by the woman.

"Who? Agatha? What did she want?"

"She didn't want anything. She has yellow jaundice."

"That was always her color," shrieks Miss Mariana.

"But she's ill with *yellow jaundice!* Do you understand? And he's home in bed; he has sciatica; she says he's got it all over."

"He's always had that."

The old man mutters and moves on to some more news: the Montana Company's shares have fallen noticeably. The woman receives this with an indignant exclamation.

"How far will it go? I don't understand anything any more."

"I understand everything," says the old man bitterly, more to himself, since the woman has difficulty in hearing him. "The world's been turned upside down for a long time now. Everything's gone downhill and is still going that way, headlong, as it passes."

"Who's passing?"

"No one's passing. I said everything's turned upside down."

"Well, what shall we do?"

"Nothing. We must wait. It would be the greatest madness to sell now, for that's what the Jews want; they want to drive everyone into a panic with this madness so that respectable people will get rid of their shares and then they can buy them up dirt cheap."

After a very short silence would come the conversation about the news in the morning papers. And it was always about the minor news on the back pages dealing with man's mundane material existence; about the prices of precious metals, about the stock exchange, about a new cure for cancer that had just been discovered by some German professor, about wages and salaries, about the harm done by tobacco to the human organism, and about the importance of animal droppings, feathers, hair, and bones for agriculture. Each individual piece of news served as an excuse for arguments of various lengths. The main discourse was conducted by the old man, while the woman participated only with brief questions and measured exclamations of surprise or approval. This provided the old man with a base for his long and loud speculations. Every day he made some of these news items an excuse to deliver complete speeches, in which other people and their faults were always condemned, while he himself was praised for his sagacity and farsightedness.

Once awake, I would have to listen to him for half an hour or sometimes for a whole hour, right up until teatime. Then I would hear Liza's voice, the tinkle of porcelain and small spoons, and coffee, or tea probably, being served. After that the conversation would slacken off and become milder.

Thus it was every day. Every day the subject of his conversation was different, but the indignation the same; there were the same sharp, ironical judgments of people and institutions, the same lauding of his own understanding and abilities. The subject was secondary and accidental, but his disdain for the world and esteem for himself were permanent and immutable. I quickly became accustomed to this and began to listen with a certain amount of curiosity to the old man's angry and arrogant voice, which sometimes rose to thunderous shouts and which also approached and retreated, since the old man evidently walked about the room while he spoke.

"Look, I ask you," he would begin loudly, the way you speak to deaf people, "look how in San Francisco they're getting over eighteen million dollars a year out of old rags, jam jars, and bones. Those are sensible and practical people. But as many as twenty-two years ago, in 1891 it was, I worked out a plan 'For the Utilization of Town Sweepings and Other Garbage.' And no one in this damned backward little dump would even read my plan or listen to me. The council chairman at that time was an ass, like the one we've got now. Even taking only the most modest achievements into consideration, from that time till now our council could have built a whole new quarter with the money that would have been raised on the basis of my plan. But no, you can't achieve anything with these Socialist dunderheads on our council. And nothing helps here, neither the best plans nor the most intelligent proposals. No one pays any attention to them. And I grasped the importance of this question twenty-two years before the Americans. Here, too, I penetrated to the essence of the thing, just as in so many other problems. I saw clearly what others didn't see and what the majority didn't even suspect, and what even today they cannot grasp or accept. But what's the good of it? With all those asses I have to live with here, it's no good at all. That's how they've been wasted, one by one, all my best plans, my greatest ideas, and my most useful proposals. You remember when, in 1895, in this very room, I explained to you my plan for the utilization of water power around our town? You must remember!"

"I remember, I remember," shouts the woman automatically.

"Well, look, since then it's been more than eighteen years. On those same principles, both Switzerland and Italy have electrified their railroads, while our streetcars even today use current that is supplied by coal. Expensive and difficult coal in place of free and simple water power. And even on the question of coal, when coal was left to do it, I had a plan fifteen years ago—yes, it was in 1897 or 1898—that I outlined here so many times. The plan was to cheapen and simplify the supply and transportation of coal. Do you remember?"

"I remember, I remember."

"But what's the use of talking to asses who are incapable of a single intelligent idea, but are capable of smothering every idea that crops up in heads far more intelligent than theirs?"

The next day the conversation was about some new methods for curing tuberculosis that were being used somewhere in Russia, according to the newspapers.

"Do you remember that as long ago as 1898 I was saying that our doctors kill their patients by sending them south or to the seaside, or cramming them with medicines? I had worked out a plan 'For a Work Colony of Sickly Children,' which was to prevent the spread of tuberculosis and reduce the number of the sick to a minimum. But what was the use when those asses at the university clinic and the general hospital and the municipal health department wouldn't even hear of it? Today our town would be famous for having the smallest number of TB patients in the world. My colonies would have been introduced into most of the civilized countries, and the world would have blessed me as a benefactor of mankind. But no, not even the greatest of intellects can do anything against the backwardness, conceit, and egotism of professional idiots. Do you know how it happened?"

"I know, I know," yells the old lady in parrot fashion.

On the day after that, the question of savings arose as the subject for the old man's passionate monologue.

"Ha, ha, ha!" he laughed lengthily, with rancor in his voice, and then continued wrathfully: "Look what this morning's newspapers are saying: 'SAVINGS WEEK. With the object of enabling all sections of the people, but particularly our youth, to get used to saving, the Municipal Savings Bank is opening a Savings Week,' et cetera, et cetera. But when I thought up a plan twelve years ago, in 1901—it was 'For Compulsory Saving in the Interests of the Community and Individuals'—no one wanted to listen to me or understand. At that time those gentlemen still had no idea about the principle of saving. Asses! You remember that project of mine! Do you remember that I explained it here in detail?"

"I remember, I remember," answers the old lady in an automatic voice.

Every afternoon I was forced to listen against my will to the conversation of this pair of deaf and elderly creatures and to learn one or two of the old gentleman's projects. In spite of my youth, normally so occupied with itself, I still wanted to become acquainted with the face of this speaker from the other room. Once I had to listen to him, it was only natural that I should also want to see him. It was not difficult. My window was directly over the front entrance, and after a few days I was able to wait for Miss Mariana's guest and to watch unobserved as he arrived or left.

I was not surprised by his appearance. Across the broad, handsome paving stones of the oblong, orderly courtyard he would come and go always at the same time of day—he came at three and left soon after six—a diminutive but erect and strutting old man, neat, buttoned up, and elaborate, dressed in the fashion of the eighteen eighties. On fine dry days he would be wearing a long black coat with velvet collar and cuffs, and sticking out from this blackness would be two white rounded shirt cuffs and an equally white high starched collar. On his feet would be narrow black button shoes, and on his head a black narrow-brimmed hat that was hopelessly out of fashion. When there was rain or snow, the old man wore a hunting costume. He would have on a brown and green cape and a suit of gray tweed with horn buttons and the same kind of hat with a green band and a short plume of wild-boar's bristle at the back. His long trousers would have green stripes down the sides. On his feet would be heavy tan shoes. In one hand there was always a walking stick and in the other, gloves. A black walking stick with a silver handle or a brown one with horn; brown pigskin gloves or gray deerskin, depending on whether he wore his black suit or the gray hunting one.

His face was narrow and delicate, his nose large and bent, his eyes set too close together and always lowered, his mustache trimmed and his sideburns worn long. His hair was completely gray, and he himself was somehow all gray, as if, sitting for long periods next to Miss Mariana, he too had been covered by that gray dust of pitiless and mortal time. He would step out with a resolute stride, and his whole appearance and bearing proclaimed him an irreproachably dressed Austrian gentleman in the style of the last century.

From a conversation with Liza I learned that the talker in the next room was a baron. But that was all I was able to learn, for the old spinster was just as thrifty with her words as she was with everything else, and she was shrinking and ingrown with her whole being.

As I listened in spite of myself to these extraordinary, senile conversations, I asked myself in vain what these two people meant to each other. Aged lovers? Close relations? Friends since

childhood? In my youthful inexperience and with scant knowledge of the world, I was not able even approximately to define
the nature of their relationship or the degree of their kinship.
Moreover, as soon as the afternoon conversations of the aged
pair in the next room came to an end, I forgot them, being completely taken up with the dreams and thoughts of my new student life, only to remember them again the next afternoon
when I was awakened by the baron's hoarse monologue in the
next room.

Finally I became accustomed to this waking and these conversations, just as one gets accustomed to any uniform and constant phenomenon of nature. When the old man's voice jerked
me from my sleep, I would rub my eyes, listen to the first few
sentences of whichever of the baron's tirades was on the program
for that day, and, listening thus to his boasting about some great
and unprecedented plan of his and to the old lady's mechanical,
birdlike assurances ("I know, I know," "I remember, I remember"), I would turn onto my other side and go to sleep again.
And when I awoke, my room would be filled with the red glow
of the setting sun and the silence would be absolute. And then
I would get ready to go out for another student session.

In this way, autumn, winter, and spring went by. The summer came with its short student nights, when dawn is early. On
one such July day, when I was again well behind with my sleep,
I came home immediately after lunch. A great sultriness lay over
the whole town, making it hard to breathe and causing one's
eyes to shut of their own accord. A thunderstorm was in the
offing, like a relief that could not seem to come. The rain, which
had been trying hard for several days, uniformly skirted the
town and broke on the hills surrounding it. I fell into a heavy
sleep.

I was aroused by voices from the next room. Only half awake,
I thought to myself: which of the baron's innumerable plans is
on the program for today? Then I laughed inwardly and turned
onto my other side in order to continue the sleep that was press-

ing me down into the bed like a lead weight. I was falling under
the weight of sleep, but nevertheless I was unable to doze off
again. I was suffocated by the sultriness of the gray day, with its
ashen sky before the storm and heavy air without a single breeze.
Thus, sluggish and bad-tempered, I listened to the voices coming from the next room. They seemed this time to be higher
and particularly sharp.

The baron was speaking with scorn and derision about some
news that had appeared in the morning newspapers concerning
a trust that had been created by the well-to-do citizens of
I-don't-know-which Italian town with the object of providing orphaned but good and deserving girls with a complete dowry,
thus enabling them to marry.

"Ha, ha, now they've remembered that this has to be done as
well. And the Italians at that, who are famous for their inability
to organize. Asses! And over twenty years ago, in 1892 it was—
do you remember?—I gave them a detailed plan for a state institution that would have secured to all marriageable girls from
the poorer sections of the population not a stupid dowry like this
—rags and swaddling clothes!—but a proper dowry as a solid
basis for future marriage. Everything was worked out: the organization of the institution, the manner of functioning, and
amortization. Do you remember? But none of these idiots of ours
wanted even to study the plans, or to consider my idea. You
know that?"

The baron's words came to me at times sharp and loud, as if
they had been spoken at my side, and at times muffled and distant, according to whether he was approaching or retreating in
his irate march about the neighboring room. I listened to him
talking as one listens to a familiar waterfall, which lulls one to
sleep equally as much as it keeps one awake. And I had already
begun to feel the sweet sensation of renewed sleep. Then I noticed that the baron's monologue was not being interrupted as
was usual with those loud expressions of approval ("I know, I
know," "I remember, I remember") which the old lady used to

interject with the high guttural voice of a bird that has been taught to speak. This aroused my attention and compelled me, instead of falling asleep again, to listen further to the voices from the next room.

But some kind of confusion seemed to have arisen in the elderly pair's conversation. At first there was a brief pause, several incomprehensible words, and then the baron's impatient and imperious voice:

"How is it that now all of a sudden you don't remember, when it was here that I explained my whole plan to you? It was— It could have been—"

"It never happened. Don't strain yourself trying to guess when it was."

"What? What's the matter with you, Mariana? What do you mean, it never happened?"

"Just what I said, it ne-ver hap-pened," reaffirmed the old lady loudly and resolutely, and she continued to speak fluently and consecutively as at no time previously. "By God, it never happened, just as nothing that you say here every day and that I confirm ever happened. Not one of all these fine, brave, rejected plans ever existed. You know that yourself. And as long as the conversation is about drains, hospitals, and all kinds of financial, military, and social institutions—I don't know the names of all those things!—as long as you talk about that, I can listen to you and support you, although I know very well, just as you do, that it occurs to you only now and you are speaking about it for the first time. But if I'm going to be told by you about some organization of yours for providing a dowry for unmarried girls who don't have one—you! Telling me! That's going too far; that I won't listen to."

"But, Mariana, please! What are you saying?"

"I'm talking about what I know and what you shouldn't even begin to speak about."

"But, dear Mariana, what did I begin to speak about, what did I say?"

"You began to speak about what you have no right to speak about."

The woman spoke in a wooden and shrill voice, as usual, but somehow collectedly and resolutely, while the baron had evidently lost his self-possession and was looking in vain for his customary elevated tone of boundless satisfaction with himself and deep contempt for the rest of the world. It could be felt through the wall, it seemed to me, how he had become perplexed and small. From his brief, hopeless words and pleading tone it was clear that all he wished for was to switch the conversation to a different topic and avoid a conflict.

"Please, Mariana, we're speaking now about general things, things en *général*. Isn't that it?"

"No, it's not, it's not," cried the woman, so that the room echoed, "it's not that at all. But now that you've raised this thing, I'll tell you how it is and what it's about. It's like this. The whole town, the whole region, I should think, from the highest to the lowest, everyone knows you are a nincompoop, a conceited ass, an idler, and a parasite."

"But, Mariana, please—I must remind you."

"Quiet, nincompoop! Nincompoop! Yes, you should be keeping quiet and be ashamed if you could, but instead of that, you are strutting about like a turkey cock. The world has no parallel of a man spending his life the way you have. You didn't want to go to school. You never wanted to do anything, not even a little bit, that was useful or intelligent. You've spent your life and grown old in stupidly and idiotically nursing your own person, in shaving, having your hair cut, bathing, being massaged, beautifying and titivating yourself, and taking cures. You've never even carried a letter as far as the post office, much less done anything else in your life. And for forty years or more I've listened to you ridiculing the whole world and boasting and blowing yourself up and lying to your own self, for you can't deceive anyone else with your plans that the world won't accept and can't understand. Consider how big a fool you are if you think someone would be mad enough, even for a moment, to believe that you really have something in your head, or that you are capable at all of inventing or understanding anything. Out of pity we've listened for years and years to your talking, and we are ashamed for your stupidity and impudence and—we keep quiet. But you misinterpret our silence and get even more stupid and impudent. And now it's come to the point where you talk to me of your inspired plans whose object is to settle orphaned girls and to bring happiness to mankind; you, who have eaten up my dowry and gambled it away and—"

"Mariana, for God's sake—"

"Quiet, nincompoop, I'm talking now! You know better than anyone else how you have exploited us all and squeezed us dry, both young and old, both near and far, in the family; you know what happened to me. You think that if I never speak of it and if I live alone like this—deaf, old, and ugly, cut off from the world—I must therefore be completely devoid of self-respect and of the last spark of reason in my head. For you forget yourself so much and are so infatuated with the sense of your own greatness that you think the whole world is a mere stand for your own divine activities, that other people's lives, property, and personalities are merely food for the insatiable appetites of your own exalted and inviolable personality. But in fact you are a parasite, a despicable, criminal parasite, without a soul, without a mind, without a reputation—"

"Mariana—"

"Without shame, without feelings, without—without limits and without cure. Ah!"

Here the woman's voice broke off. One could hear footsteps and a rustling. The baron endeavored to lead her into another room and calm her. It seems that he succeeded in this, for immediately there was absolute silence in the next room.

I was amazed and disturbed by what I had heard, and sleep was completely dispersed. The room was filled with an irritating and heavy sultriness. Outside one could see the darkened sky, full of billowing storm clouds and rain that had long been building up.

In the next room there was complete silence for several days. Miss Mariana was evidently keeping to her bedroom. Was she lying in bed ill? I don't know. Nothing could be read on Liza's immobile face. Nor did I see the baron come. The first feeling of disturbance aroused by the scene to which I had been an unwilling witness quickly subsided and was lost under the numerous and varied impressions of my night excursions. I got used to the silence just as I had got used to the old people's conversations. But the silence lasted only five or six days. One afternoon I had just dozed off when I was aroused by talking in the next room. Loudly and ceremoniously, just as before, the baron cried: "Good afternoon, my dear Mariana, good afternoon!"

In that same birdlike mechanical voice, Miss Mariana asked what it was like outside, and with the same solemnity the baron replied that it was better not to ask, for the heat was unprecedented and murderous.

Then, just as always before, one heard the nervous turning of pages and the rustle of a newspaper and the relaying and interpretation of the morning's news, both local and international. Hesitant and cautious at first, and then stronger and more self-confident, the baron's voice rose.

"That's nothing new or original. Do you remember that as early as 1901, I—"

"I remember, I remember."

"And you know how I worked out a plan in detail—"

"I know, I know."

I listened to them with youthful incomprehension, and waited only for Liza to bring them some tea before falling asleep again.

Translated by Michael Scammell

Hodorlahomor the Great

Pero Orlić was already dreaming about Paris when he was in primary school. Down the corridor, next to the Orlić kitchen, there lived a certain Frau Mayer, a German from Düsseldorf or Berlin. Her son, "her God," who was an upholsterer, had left for Paris at the turn of the century. Pero was a boy of three or four at the time, but his memory of the evening of the upholsterer's departure was so clear that nothing that subsequently happened could shake it loose. Unquestionably it was on that evening, when Franz Mayer took leave of his mother and father in the kitchen, that Pero's longing for Paris first took form. Pero was sitting at the large kitchen table playing with blocks; it was raining. Franz Mayer stood in the yellow light of a kerosene lamp in a striped waistcoat, a medallion of St. George banging away against its buttons. It was this golden St. George killing the dragon that, together with the yellow light of the kerosene lamp and the rain, impressed Pero so indelibly.

So this stout red man is going to Paris! This German is going to Paris!

The magic of this unknown word enchanted Pero, and that very night he had many fantasies about Paris. Paris became for him a life-force, and his fanciful childish stories were a sensation both in the Orlić household and in the entire neighborhood. The family would assemble—the usual group of aunts, the Roses and Lenas and Antonias and Rezas and Minas and Finas—and little Pero would tell the story of how, long before he appeared in this house on Potok, No. 76, he had lived in Paris as a man of the world. And Pero would tell his aunts of his baroque visions of brass bands, fountains, and churches, mixing the visions and molding them in the process, while his aunts would listen, nodding their heads in astonishment.

"He will either end up on the gallows or become a government minister!" was the general verdict after one of these literary evenings in the Orlić kitchen, filled with smoke, the smell of onions, tomatoes, and jam. At the time Frau Mayer went away, Pero was in the third grade and going through that intense religious crisis that occurs when an altar boy has his first doubts about afterlife. Frau Mayer's son, the upholsterer—that same Franz who had gone off to Paris—had meanwhile married an umbrella maker, bought two houses in the suburb of Villemomble, and was doing extremely well. So the mother decided to join her son. True, she was old and the journey was long. And in thirty-two years she had grown accustomed to Zagreb. But her son wrote of his good fortune (drinking red wine instead of water), and of his wife's pregnancy, and Frau Mayer decided to go after all.

She entrusted the grave of her late husband to Pero's mother and set off, all by herself, for Paris via Basel. Pero went with his father to the travel agency to buy the ticket for her "to Paris, via Basel." He was fascinated by the trials and tribulations involved in the great preparations for a journey "to Paris, via Basel." He studied the route carefully and went to the trouble of marking it on a map with a red pencil. But his effort was discarded as superfluous. Then Pero and his father went to the South Station to see old Frau Mayer off. What's more, they drove in a fiacre, and Pero cried all night with longing for Paris.

From time to time postcards and letters came from Paris. The old lady wrote that Paris was a big city, but that the water was not good, and that she did not understand a word, and was sorry that she had ever left Zagreb. And Pero read those German letters carefully, studied the awkward Gothic script, and filed these authentic Paris documents, these stamps and postcards, away in his schoolbooks. At school he would open his books and study the postcards, projecting himself into that small painted Parisian square and losing himself in it. The confusion of Paris would spread through the book and through the school. And Pero would disappear into the Paris streets.

For example, he looked at the Hôtel des Invalides.

The blue spring skies spread over the golden cupola, the distant roofs were covered in a silver mist, unreal red chimneys appeared as dreams appear when one dreams about Paris from Potok, No. 76.

Strange red omnibuses and ladies with parasols, and an officer in red breeches riding in the shade of tree-lined sweet-smelling streets. And then the Champs-Élysées. There had just been a warm spring rain; the omnibuses, carriages, and bicycles were reflected in the asphalt pavement, and the shadow of a guard officer, in formal uniform with a long red tail flowing from his bright shiny helmet, burst over the gray puddles, lost its shape, and vanished. Cars were screeching, porters yelling, and white horses in the marble frieze soared in the azure sky that was adorned with an orange glow and sprinkled with the aqua light of a May evening. Trees quivered in the twilight, and in the distance, far far in the distance, the contours of the gigantic Arc de Triomphe sank in the gray veil of the dusk so that the Champs-Élysées, with its procession of cars and riders and carriages, seemed to flow in a triumphal path above the city like a heavenly bridge!

Or the Trocadéro. Pero placed "Trocadéro" in his notebook, and as he looked at the Moorish towers and galleries and the fountains that bubbled like fairy tale fountains, he trembled as if confronted by a thousand-eyed beast. And those gray sooty palaces and bridges and golden cupolas and children with sailboats in fishponds inflamed little Orlić's imagination and danced with a fiery rhythm in his feverish mind. "Orlić! You lazy nincompoop! What are you staring at this time? What have you got there? You watch out, young man, or you'll be in the corner again."

Pero stiffened and, still half dreaming, looked around the room, at the blackboard and the map and the classroom and the teacher, all of which seemed strange, incomprehensible, wooden, and stupid.

Thus, a sick illusion was beginning to undermine little Pero, and as time passed its dimensions grew.

In those days, book salesmen—agents for the large publishing houses of Berlin, Leipzig, and Vienna—used to go from house to house selling stupid books to stupid people on the installment plan. Once Pero's mother ordered a large illustrated novel about the French Revolution entitled *Graf Axel von Ferson*. This book was about a well-known Swedish counterrevolutionary, one of Marie Antoinette's lovers. The novel was very bad and the illustrations grotesque. But little Pero studied it in detail and pondered for many an evening over those black crude drawings that still stank of machine oil. Noble ladies with wigs; the Trianon; and the waterfalls and parks; and those tense episodes connected with the seizure of the royal family at Varennes, when someone slipped a lamp under the very nose of the fat king; and then the innumerable court intrigues and affairs and crowds of armed men—such were the materials with which little Pero nursed his passion for Paris.

As time went on, certain symbols crystallized out of this huge chaos that, like visions, hovered in his inflamed imagination. At first the severed heads on stakes, the storming of the Bastille, the guillotines, the huge celebrations of the Republic, with torches smoking over monumental catafalques; and then, out of this torrent there emerged Danton, Marat, and Robespierre, and finally Napoleon himself. And afterwards Napoleon's empire liquidated the Revolution and established the great religious cult for the Corsican that burned in Pero like a sanctuary light, replacing Caesar in the boy's subconscious hierarchy.

In high school Pero devoured the entire Napoleonic literature and began writing a long novel of his own: *Napoleon, The Imperial Star.* In time Pero's Napoleon cult became identified with the Paris cult, and Pero stormed like a comet across the Lombardy plains from victory to victory, and then rushed off from the Danube to Moscow, across the whole of Europe, intoxicated by banners, artillery, and imperial eagles.

In Pero's fourth year of high school, a new idol, the poet Kranjčević, defeated Napoleon; once more the guillotine, the barricades, and the Revolution were in the forefront—that same horrible Jacobean revolution that had destroyed the aristocratic reptiles in their golden overcoats and white powdered wigs. And Pero dreamed of Paris, seeing before his very eyes the ruined palaces and the crowds of bloody sans-culottes singing the "Marseillaise," carrying aloft the severed heads of the French aristocracy.

It was in those days that the late journalist Matoš was writing his articles from Paris. In his shallow journalistic style Matoš had converted this bloody vision into a sweet cultural dream, full of poetry and harmony and the scents of gentle tranquillity—not too clear but, at any rate, modern. Matoš turned Paris into a sonnet that scanned well. The nostalgia of the age penetrated Pero painfully and sharply. The good old days when one read Matoš's articles in school! "Oh, if only I didn't have to do my Greek lesson! If only I were in Paris! I'm sure they perform *Hamlet* magnificently in Paris, and not in the sleepy way they do here!

"If I were in Paris I would go for a walk in the Bois de Boulogne, and not in this damned Zrinjevac.

"Zagreb is a village! Just one street, the Ilica! And look at Paris!"

That was young Orlić in the fourth year of high school, the young Orlić who had bought a torn Baedeker and was skimming through the maps and walking through the Paris streets and cursing Zagreb and fighting constantly over his marks, and living more on the Seine than on the Potok.

Orlić knew Paris by heart: the neighborhoods, the galleries, the museums. He knew the location of all the stations, cemeteries, boulevards; he knew when each bridge was built, to whom each monument was dedicated, where new streets had been laid out, and where and when famous people were born. He knew it all, in every detail. As he sat over his Latin or Mathematics homework, he would take out the red Baedeker, like a prayer book, and with a deep sigh bow to the "city of cities, the Babylon of Babylons, most holy Paris."

Later he got hold of Musset and Baudelaire. And in the Zagreb cafés he came upon the *Revue des Deux Mondes* and *Le Temps*, as well as other articles and reports, and it was no wonder that, at the first opportunity, when he found himself with a few extra crowns in his pocket, Pero Orlić rushed off to Paris.

It was a fever and a madness, this flight of his. Realizing that in a day or two he would see the city from a platform of the Gare de Lyon, Orlić trembled with a high fever and holy excitement.

"Babylon, Babylon," sang Orlić in his soul, and from the Swiss frontier onward he could not sit still. He trembled and shivered and shook and sniffed the air and flickered like a lamp.

"How good these French carriages smell!

"Even the seats are covered in lace and velvet, and not in worn old leather as at home.

"Everything smells of perfume! Even the third-class carriage smells of perfume!

"Look, look! These villages! How gentle they are! How warm! How pleasant! How sweet! And this famous ringing of bells! French bells! And these rivers, these French rivers!

"And these green canals and the glistening streams! What riches, what beauty! What solemn beauty!"

In his excitement, Orlić babbled and talked to himself. He placed his swollen feverish head on the cold glass of the windowpane, feeling the blood rushing into his eyes, thickening his veins.

"Babylon, Babylon," he exclaimed as the train cut across rich black fields, through long lines of poplars and mulberries, and the hamlets appeared one after another on the hills like distant ships on the green waves. The red bell towers, the park-enclosed mansions, the farms, and the wheels of the train, and the sweet-smelling earth that smoked after the spring rain, and the steeples in the small towns, and the tracks and railway crossings—together they thundered and sang, Babylon, Babylon!

It was a victorious, dashing flight across space, the flight of a happy, fiery soul that, like a burning spark, falls into a large hearth. And then it grew dark and night fell, and the train wound and rattled through the evening mist, thundering across iron tracks and bridges and rivers in which the last rays of the sun were reflected.

Orlić began to sense the nearness of the city, the City of Cities blossoming like a huge rose set in a plate bordered with blue. Houses sprang up in front of the window, first one isolated house, followed by two or three in a bunch, and then a café with a colorful sign out in front, and roads and viaducts and willow thickets and clearings filled with grunting pigs, and roads flowing parallel to the tracks, and carts laden with sacks and barrels crawling past in the mud.

The sad spring rain was dripping, and the drivers were covered with cheap blankets, and everything was sad and tearful.

The fat black horses steamed in the mist, and the small oil lamps along the way burned hopelessly as though they would go out at any minute.

Wreaths of red bulbs illuminated the road, and now and then a reddish light exposed a factory with its burning throat, and through gray dirty windows human shadows could be seen contorting and vibrating in the yellow light, as giant wheels rattled fiercely and black belts wound and crawled, appearing and disappearing miraculously. A forest of black chimneys gaped wide open, some standing out like gigantic tree trunks, and others vomiting up fireworks of glowing soot. But above the flame and dirt glowed the holy aura of the city, like a white line of magnesium or a wondrous polar light.

"Paris, Paris," whispered Orlić devoutly, watching the infinite white fan of light that spread above the black contours of buildings which disappeared one after another in the darkness. Advertisements flashed on the crystal panes, fragmented into shiny points of light like sunflowers springing up along the tracks at home. Wooden cows licking chocolate, geese with paté, and Negroes, and brightly lit villas, and five-story buildings, and factories and bridges thundering, and the burning sparks falling, and the people down there in the underpass walking indifferently, lifting their heads from time to time to glance at the train speeding across the dike in the forest of pillars, switches, and red and green lights on tall semaphores.

Two or three times the train raced through arched damp tunnels or sped above the yellow river on which a ship was pulling barges that cut red and blue lines in the troubled waters. Then sooty naked walls and gray buildings and black warehouses, and here and there bursts of yellow lights, and again walls and walls, and then suddenly the train came to a stop.

On all sides were other trains, speeding backwards in unknown directions. In the lighted cars people could be seen going to sleep, and waiters in white jackets hurried back and forth, waving napkins. For a long time the train stood and puffed with difficulty, and then slowly and pompously it crawled into the crystal throat of the great terminal to spew out of its insides the nervous and pale Pero Orlić.

Orlić felt that he had entered a temple. He had had much the same feeling when, as an altar boy, he had rung the bells in the cathedral during a great pontifical mass officiated over by the bishop himself. He had had the same feeling once when he had gone to confession three times, lest he should receive his first communion in a state of impurity and sin.

He paused and looked out at the noisy confusion, and it reminded him of holy things. So! He, Pero Orlić, was there! After fifteen years of longing, he was there at last, in Paris, by God! In Paris!

In front of Orlić were the famous boulevards flowing with carriages, buses, men and women, boulevards as straight as if drawn with a ruler, cut away from the rock like a great ravine.

The crowd danced, whirled, thundered, whistled, cried, and laughed, and Orlić flung himself headlong into the tide, swimming proudly across the current, just as he would in the River Sava.

As he threw himself into this swelling, unknown mass, Orlić completely forgot the plan on which he had worked so carefully for years and about which he had dreamed so many nights. The plan had been to cross the Seine, and then, following the river, to find his lodgings. And now he had forgotten this plan and had rushed straight down the street, in any direction, so long as he was in the heart of things! In the very nucleus! In the light! In Paris!

He forgot the fatigue of the journey, his hunger and thirst, and it was not until morning that, defeated and as though wounded, he found refuge in a modest hotel on a remote and disreputable street.

The street is called de l'Harpe, and it runs parallel to Boulevard St. Michel, and it was there that Orlić found a dirty, miserable little room with a gas lamp and a balcony, where everything smelled of burned sauces and the children were forever crying behind the wallpaper, and on the spiral staircase rats chased one another in the twilight. Across the street was a restaurant run by Hungarian gypsies, and some distance away a fountain gurgled and sprinkled by day and by night, and in Orlić's building, on the floor above his, a woman took her own life the very night Orlić rented his room.

That was the first thing that happened: this woman, her throat cut, and the bloody blanket and the pool of blood on the floor, and the police.

And then Paris with its mad rush and passionate drinking, animal-like, with both hands clutching the glass, intoxicating and teasing the nerves with the melody of dull indolence. Mad rushing through streets and water, galleries and towers, steeples and palaces and cathedrals and museums and parks, rushing in circles, every day ending in surfeit and defeat. When Orlić climbed the spiral staircase to his room he found he had already fallen asleep; that was the last straw.

And operas and ballets and stock exchanges and cemeteries and Rembrandts and Renaissance Italians and Cubists and Futurists and sculptors and painters and gardens and streets and restaurants whirled in Orlić's mad head.

He tried to embrace everything and was left with nothing. He wanted to grasp everything, and understood nothing. The only thing he did find was fatigue, the fatigue of the miserable Balkan rabble lost in the whirlpool. A poor animal, persecuted and whipped to death, yet aspiring to fresh adventure. Pero Orlić was still a child, just barely twenty, and he believed that he might come upon new adventures in the streets of Paris, like finding a louis d'or or a diamond pin. But he found neither the louis d'or nor the diamond pin, and as he walked wearily home one night, crossing a bridge illuminated with red lights, he said to himself:

"All this is a lie and a vacuum. An ugly vacuum. Paris does not exist. There is no Paris, there is no Paris.

"What is Paris? What is it, after all? Is Paris the lame Sarah

Bernhardt whom I saw this evening for twenty francs and who is a screaming parrot and stupid to boot, may God have mercy on her? Or is Paris that Spanish king with the long nose who takes rides in his carriage with his enormous entourage, and is greeted everywhere with fireworks by the Republic and given receptions to which I am not invited? Is that Paris?

"Who says they are freethinkers? Just fat burghers, as odious as our Zagreb butchers. Where is Paris? To hell with it!

"Is this Paris? This hunchbacked shoemaker, leaning over his work just as our shoemakers do on the Potok? He invents stupid patriotic phrases such as 'the great people,' 'the revolution,' just as our people talk about 'King Tomislav's fleet,' 'the Croatian Crown,' and 'Svačić.' It all amounts to the same thing, and it is all stupid. And someday these people will go to war for their 'great patriots,' those invisible gentlemen who live behind closed doors in their villas, feed monkeys and parrots and greyhounds, and sit on moneybags.

"Hey, Paris! Why don't you grab the moneybags from underneath those fat behinds? Why do they suck your blood and goad you like a horse? You blockheads of the Republic! Millions of blockheads in a heap! What do I care about kings and shoemakers and guillotines and skulls that do not exist? None of this exists! It is all dead! Buried! Paris is a cemetery!

"A phantom in a graveyard—this is what I believed in for so long! A dirty mass of stone, and my room full of cockroaches, and these shallow cretins who carry a woman in their hearts and on their lips, and those twenty people who commit suicide every day and die nameless and lie in greenish morgues and stare out at stupid black nothing! Is this the Paris about which I dreamed for so many black Balkan nights? There, in the mist, where Turkish fires still burn, where maidens are captured and revenge is celebrated! Where stakes are greasy with blood and women are silent and walk at a distance behind their men, where everything is rotten and cursed, and at the break of day the gendarmes' green roosters sing? Oh, there I had dreamed of Paris, and those dreams of mine were more Parisian than the whole of Paris. When I first listened to their songs, and felt the electrifying strength emanating from human words that have torn down prison walls, and saw the guns firing and the banners waving, my heart beat in my throat and I thought I had made a discovery! But I had discovered nothing. There is nothing to discover. It all amounts to the same thing! Budapest and Paris and Peking and Zagreb! Nothing but barracks and prisons and churches, barracks and prisons and churches—the eternal human stupidities —but there is no Paris. Paris is within us! Paris is in the poems of Kranjčević, that poor Sarajevo scholar who had more feeling for Paris than all of these fat cretins. Parisian, Parisian! You who know and feel Paris, where are you? Parisian, oh where are you?"

Thus, standing on a bridge over the Seine and waving his arms in the air, engulfed by a strange bloody emotion, Orlić cried out his sick fiery monologue, calling for a true Parisian to arise. He stared down at the yellow muddy water rolling past him, covered by layers of tar and slicks of oil. Lines of red lights trembled and vibrated on the water, and Paris murmured like an underground beast that has buried its snout in the darkness. Paris murmured and the vacuum was vast and black, and the Parisian did not respond.

"God only knows at what depths and in what pain the real Parisian now lives! If only I could see the flickering of his oil lamp, feel the avalanche of his thoughts, to know that there are Parisians in Paris!

"And so it goes! Nothing but the notorious 'red lights' burn in Paris! And black gendarmes and policemen and guard officers and detectives suspiciously watch everyone. And now they are watching me, those damned black dogs! Why is it? Isn't a man allowed to scream on a bridge?"

"My dear sir, it is forbidden to loiter on the bridge." The policeman seized Orlić.

"Leave me alone! I have no intention of drowning myself. I am only crying over Paris!"

"Forget the tears, sir, and show me your papers."

Orlić's papers were, of course, not in order, and he spent a night in the police station with a few drunkards.

The following morning Orlić was interviewed by a fool in white, well-pressed trousers. After his release Orlić took to drink, systematically, like a Croat, and soon became a drunkard himself.

He would get drunk in shady nightclubs, where soldiers played billiards in shirt sleeves and red trousers (perhaps they belonged to some colonial African regiment). Their sleeves rolled up, the soldiers drank and cursed, and Orlić drank too, some thick colored alcohol, squandering his money in holes and pigsties. And he gambled too, and won and lost. One night he won 520 francs, and then, in an instant, lost everything. He even gambled away the silver watch his grandfather had given him at confirmation. And with the loss of his silver watch he had nothing left. No money. No room. No illusions. Nothing. Not even those holy illusions that he had invented while still a boy in grade school. What was left of the city of the "Marseillaise," the barricades, and the guillotine? Of those café and Baedeker dreams, the articles of Matoš, oh, what was left?

What actually remained was Orlić's expulsion from his room and the confiscation of his raincoat. His revolver, which he had never used but which he put in his mouth two or three times every night (and then took out, of course), was not taken from him. The old woman laughed cynically and said that she spat on his Russian stupidity—that is, on the revolver. So she merely took his raincoat for the rent he owed her.

As a result the spring rains found Orlić in the street without so much as a raincoat.

And it rained and rained, and Orlić was hungry and roamed the streets like a bedraggled wolf, and that was Paris. He wandered through a cemetery arcade for days on end, and once spent two nights in a mortuary. He sat there, listening to the song of Paris, dully watching the corpse of a dead railway worker with a sharp nose on which the light of a candle danced. The man's name had been Victorien Hébrard. Just before dawn the mortuary was closed down and Orlić was locked out. He found a quiet spot near an imposing gate and there, for a short while, he was able to get away from his pointless and senseless wanderings. Unwashed and sooty, hungry, his shoes torn, Orlić walked whole mornings through museums. Oh, he cursed the classics, those endlessly stupid and superfluous lies. He came to hate them, and he scorned all of Europe from the bottom of his heart.

"God damn it! Why don't I tear into this Van Dyke with a knife? Those fat damned women of his! What do I care for Van Dyke? Or Van Gogh! Damn you, Van Gogh! So that's who you are? That's what you look like?"

With bloodshot eyes Orlić stared at the stretched canvas and flicked open the knife in his pocket, seized by the desire to rip everything to pieces. Then he watched children in the park as they ate biscuits and chocolate. He ingeniously stole a large box of candied fruit from a nurse, which lasted him for two days. One day Orlić remembered that he had intended to earn a living in Paris by writing articles. And he wanted to write, but each of his thoughts, and every line, turned into an ugly curse, directed not only at those who would read his articles and those who would print them, but at Paris, the world, everything. Only accusations, convulsions, curses, and protestations.

But nothing was as bad as those nightly walks in the streets. Exhausted from lack of sleep, heavy with hunger and fatigue, his knees would buckle and he would slump down on a bench, and the bitter and cruel struggle with sleep would begin. From one side sleep would approach with its warm, generous hand, caressing his brows and sprinkling them with a sweet balm; from the other side Orlić would be approached by the green squinting eyes of a demoniac policeman, who was everywhere at all times, crawling about like a beetle, leering at each new victim, grabbing him by the neck and tossing him into the hole of darkness. Into the police station, into filth, into Europe.

Yes, yes, an atrocity! A starving man! The streets! Night, rain, fatigue! And this is freedom, this is freedom, this is Paris!

And Orlić's heavy, too heavy, head swayed on his shoulders. Circles of divine sleep began to dance before his eyes and then, suddenly, the dance was interrupted by a jolt of fear, and the will was broken once again, and the wounded body tottered farther along, still farther, retreating to a more comfortable bench where the police might be forgotten.

As Orlić roamed the streets, everything seemed to be growling at him. He was pursued by black shadows, and bronze lions roared at him as he paused before a woman standing silently on a marble pedestal adorned with laurel.

"Oh, Mother Republic! All this is false and empty! I am hungry, I am hungry, Mother Republic, and you are made of stone and you are silent! These bastard sons of your Republic, they are terrible, and they do not understand you! And all this is false! And I am hungry, Republic! Republic, I am hungry!"

And so Orlić cried and yammered and wailed before the pedestal on which the huge marble Republic stood, and this must have been the eighth night of his wandering and hunger and suffering. The day before he had eaten two cakes and drunk a cup of coffee in a crowded bar, and then skillfully disappeared into the crowd. But since then he had had nothing. And now it was morning, and the hunger surged forth inexorably, wildly, powerfully.

His mouth was watering, his teeth grinding. A crowd of revelers walked past eating raisin-filled cakes, and when Orlić pleaded for a piece of cake they sneered at his barbaric pronunciation and kissed their scented women as though this hungry, fallen man were not even there. In his torment Orlić clenched his fists and buried his nails into the palms of his hands so as not to scream from pain and sorrow. And these drunkards were eating cake and kissing their women and laughing at him.

"Are there any people here? Is it only in Russian literature that people live? Is everyone a scoundrel, a villain in this cursed

Sodom?" And Orlić walked on, hoping to find someone, man or beast, from whom he could ask a crumb of bread. Only a crumb.

Nearby, at a construction site illuminated by a red flare, an old man was roasting bacon over a fire and sipping wine from a flask.

Orlić approached him gently, very gently. Inaudibly, like a slave. Orlić had withdrawn, reducing himself to the shape of a dog. He approached the old man as would a hungry dog wagging his tail, swaying his head obsequiously.

And the old man chased Orlić away, as though he were indeed a dog, telling him to go to the devil and waving a large stick.

As for Orlić, he wanted to bark, to jump at the old bastard, to bite the ugly monster's throat. And so, with the impulse of a healthy animal, Orlić threw himself on the old man, brought him to the ground, snatched the bacon and the rolls and the flask of wine, and started running.

Several men chased Orlić along the winding street and he barely got away. Orlić had a great deal to eat. Orlić had a lot of wine. Orlić was full. A comfortable lassitude spread through his body, and there, in front of him, stood a wall, a rampart, and some strange red barracks.

Dawn was approaching.

In the barracks the trumpets sounded and soldiers in rough blue uniforms scurried past, carrying cauldrons of hot coffee. A roll of drums was heard, officers mounted their horses, and a crude mustached sergeant slapped the face of a young boy. Strange shouts were heard and the earth resounded, as always when a battalion is on the move.

"Look at these men of the Republic!" thought Orlić as he peered through the grass and over the ramparts and into the large smelly barracks yard where soldiers were stamping the earth. And he, miserable, exhausted animal that he was, moving through the streets without bread or roof over his head, torn and tired, felt an indescribable sense of freedom. Stretching himself out in the damp grass, he fell asleep.

It was daylight when Orlić awoke, still on the ramparts of Paris. The skies were overcast and it was raining again. Wet through and exhausted, he walked along the gray dirty streets, back into the center of the city.

Quite by accident, Orlić found himself in front of the huge stone bulk of the sooty Louvre.

A thought struck him. He had spent a great deal of time at the Louvre of late, and knew all its corners, armchairs, and guards. He knew when each guard went outside for a smoke, and this enabled him to fall asleep in comfort, not fearing that his snores would be overheard and that he would be thrown out. You could snore to your heart's content, because the guard was smoking somewhere in the corridor, talking about his pension or God knows what. But today a particularly happy thought struck Orlić. Why shouldn't he sneak into the Egyptian or Babylonian gallery? Among the huge pile of rocks and sarcophagi, in some dark corner, there might be a spot where he could get some sleep. If only he could get some sleep! Then all should be well! He would beg for two or three sous, and that would give him a chance to put together his article at the café—a good article, by God! A sensational article about the Spanish king and the great maneuvers at which a hundred batteries fired and airplanes roared past. A long article of five hundred lines! Five hundred multiplied by four—five hundred times four—that will bring twenty crowns, by God! That will bring twenty crowns from the *Narodni List!* And then, quickly, another article! Three hundred lines. But what would he write about? The Russian ballet? Sarah Bernhardt? Expressionism? It doesn't matter! Three hundred lines in *Zagrebački Dnevnik*. They pay at the rate of seven filirs, and three hundred times seven is twenty-one crowns! And twenty plus twenty-one makes a total of forty-one crowns—a small fortune. And all this in no more than a week! By God, he must not allow himself to be ruined! He must have courage, he must survive. He must survive at any price, and again acquire a room. Then something will happen; something always does!

Thus refreshed with new speculations and encouraged by new illusions, Orlić stole into the Assyrian room of the Louvre. As a rule no one was there on rainy days. Who the devil cares for mummies anyway? The mob with red Baedekers lolled past on the floors above, and here it was nice and empty and quiet.

In fact, there was not a soul around: mummies and sarcophagi and the ruins of old temples were slumbering wisely, gloriously, and dumbly. Orlić caught sight of a beautiful marble sarcophagus that resembled a comfortable bed. A minute later, without knowing what he was doing, he lifted the glass top and slipped into the sarcophagus, covered himself comfortably, and fell asleep.

Outside, the warm spring rain was falling proudly, intoning a gentle lullaby. The strain of the last few days, the sleepless nights, and the hunger were now, like wounds, being dressed by balmy sleep. The fine bluish fluid in which the marble lions and winged bulls and heroes were swimming trickled down into Orlić's soul, and a gentle peace infiltrated his limbs and muscles.

Shadows vibrated on the old colorful mosaics and green bronzes, and outside the city was humming like a distant organ. From time to time he could hear the tooting of horns from the Rue de Rivoli, or the sound of boats on the Seine. Orlić dreamed about Babylon. Along with his passion for modern Europe, Orlić was consumed by a great love for the world of antiquity and the Orient. One half of his heart bled for Europe and the other half for the East. His eagerness to see Paris did not for a moment mean that he ignored the existence of the East. Oh, he loved Japan and China and India, and believed that his voice would someday be heard at the equator.

And now, in his general depression, these feelings were projected into the stones, into the bas-reliefs in which bearded men massacred birds and lions with bows and arrows.

"Any one of these old stones is worth more than the whole of Paris!" So ran his thoughts, and he dreamed about Babylon.

He dreamed that he was drinking wine on a marble terrace

ringed by curtains of gold and portals stiffened with red agate. The night was green, and the boatmen on the Tigris were singing, and the bright metal of their oars gleamed like the colors of the rainbow. The song of the boatmen sounded pleasantly, and Orlić felt precious life in his veins. He was sipping wine from a glass mug and listening to the parrots screeching; black slaves were waving above the red-hot coals, and a bluish smoke was rising into the skies.

In this way Orlić fled from the dirty "city of cities" where people live in dark holes and scream about everything and never tell the truth, fled from the mud and dirt, from the hunger and shame, the barracks and police stations—and found salvation on this Eastern shore of stories and legends. Then suddenly someone jabbed him in the ribs, throwing him into complete confusion.

"Hey, young man, don't think you are so light."

Orlić jumped into the air, and at first could not grasp what was happening. But then he remembered the money he had gambled away; strangely enough, he remembered the last banknote that he had won and immediately afterward lost, and he remembered that they had thrown him into the streets, and that he was hungry and had no room, and that he had sneaked into the Louvre and had come into the Assyrian gallery, Room No. 16, and had fallen asleep there. And now he had been awakened.

At first he could not credit his senses. He thought it was an apparition. But the eyes of the man who stood before him burned with a greenish light, and Orlić believed in this green fire, and collected himself.

"I'll be damned! It's a live man! He has beautiful healthy teeth. It is no apparition."

In front of Orlić stood a mummy from the sarcophagus, an Assyrian apparition, a man from the times of the dead. The folds of his cloak fell harmoniously, and his long black curly beard smelled of strange spices. Orlić, our miserable shabby Bohemian, felt shame before the bold dignity of this unknown man. He realized that while tossing in his sleep he had awakened the corpse in the sarcophagus. He always tossed in his sleep.

"I am Hodorlahomor," said the man in a deep voice, and Orlić shook in fear and anxiety.

"I am Hodorlahomor the Great! I chased innumerable herds of wingéd bulls, and loved a thousand women. My priests caught the stars with their hands. I listened to the poets wailing under the palm trees. We nailed them to the cross, to wail the more beautifully! I am Hodorlahomor the Great, and who, pray, are you?"

"I am, if you please, Orlić! Pero Orlić, that is. I have no specific bourgeois occupation. I live from day to day. I am a journalist for *Zagrebački Dnevnik.*"

"I defeated Lugašlagengur totally. And Lugašlagengur was a powerful king and had iron-plated cavalry. I defeated him totally and scratched out his eyes and pulled out his tongue, merely because he once had a bad dream about me. And you dare to touch me in my eternal peace! Speak up!"

"If you please, Your Majesty! I beg you humbly. It is not my fault. I did not know. I did not wish. . . ." Orlić became confused in his speech and was stammering nervously. "I have not slept in a long time! I am hungry! I live in the street! I never suspected that Your Majesty . . ."

"I defeated Lugašlagengur totally. I did! And I swear by all the lights of heaven that because of your sacrilege I will have you drawn and quartered. If only I felt better! And what are you, anyway? What is it you are talking about? Are you a beggar or a thief?"

"I am, if you please, a journalist for *Zagrebački Dnevnik,* seven filirs per line. I am from Zagreb. From the Balkans, if you please. And we are now in Paris, Your Majesty!"

"Zagreb? The Balkans? Paris? What on earth are you talking about? You must indeed be a madman. What is Paris?"

However, Orlić had already grasped the situation. It was not for nothing that he was a journalist for the *Zagrebački Dnevnik*, seven *filirs* per line. Instantly he perceived the proper angle by which he must approach His Majesty. My God! It was not His Majesty's fault that he is unacquainted with civilization's progress, as are we who have gotten good marks in school. His Majesty has been asleep for some time. Things must be explained to him. Nicely! Wittily! In the form of an article.

"The Balkans, if you please, are a peninsula of Europe. And Europe is, so to speak, an insignificant peninsula of Asia. A superfluous appendix, so to speak. Some sort of an appendix, if Your Majesty knows what that is. That appendix can be inflamed, and then you should see the trouble. You lived in the heart of the world, and not in its appendix where it is dark and smelly. You lived in the heart and we in this poor extremity. And you were right, Your Majesty! To concern oneself with Europe is not worth the effort. Since your day the earth has circled the sun nearly five thousand times. We discovered this only a few centuries ago. I mean, that the earth flies around the sun. It's like this: it turns, it turns like a bug on a needle. The poor headless thing turns and grows old, and we exist sadly. We haven't created anything, Your Majesty, during the past five thousand years. We still hog meat and butcher one another. At least you had an idea! You built a tower to bring God down to earth. You at Babylon! And we have done nothing! We are nervous, that's it! You played with the stars, and we perish in factories. You chased after wingéd bulls, and we wear boots and carry knapsacks and live in swarms. We build barracks, but still live off your wisdom. We are miserable, and our poets go hungry and homeless. I swear to God you would be better off in your sarcophagus. To tell the truth, this Babylon of ours is not worth a penny, Your Majesty, not a penny!"

But His Majesty, Hodorlahomor the Great, did not show the slightest inclination to return to his sarcophagus. On the contrary, his eyes brightened and he exhibited a dangerous greed for life.

"Listen, good man! I shall reward you royally if you show me this Babylon of yours. I should very much like to take a walk. Here! I have jewels and gold, I have everything! I shall reward you royally!"

Hodorlahomor's inlaid buttons glistened with jewels of yellow and red hues. And Orlić, who realized that he was being rescued in a moment of danger, could not resist the temptation.

Cautiously he walked into the hallway in which the guard, lulled by the warm spring rain, was dozing. Fighting to stay awake, the guard's head would fall against his chest as though severed, and he would bring it back up again with a jolt. As the guard was thus suffering, Orlić quietly removed a cloak from a closet, placed it on Hodorlahomor's shoulders, and the two of them sneaked out into the street and disappeared into the crowd.

Orlić sold one yellow jewel for next to nothing to a Jewish jeweler on Avenue de l'Opéra. He knew that he had sold it for a song, and the jeweler knew that he had bought it from a thief, so they were both pleased. Orlić had organized everything well. With those nine thousand francs he and Hodorlahomor acquired elegant luggage and wardrobe, as befitted Eastern princes. Dressed in this aristocratic clothing, Orlić boldly sold another two or three pieces of jewelry, assembling a small fortune, and the next day he and Hodorlahomor took possession of a nine-room apartment along with an entourage of uniformed servants. Hodorlahomor had his shiny, curly Assyrian beard shaved fashionably into an oval, Don Juan-like shape that appealed to women, and he looked quite dapper in his new black suit. His starched shirt front was as hard and as white as a breastplate, his tails like those of a penguin, and in his buttonhole there was a high international order in distinguished colors. These important trifles gave rise to the legend about which the whole of the Ritz was talking: the mystical Eastern prince who lived on the first floor.

"My God! Have you seen his alabaster teeth, Madame?"

"And those bronze muscles under his silk robe, Madame?"

"Not to say anything of that burning Eastern eye, Madame! Oh, my God! Oh, my God!"

This was the talk among titled ladies, marquises, baronesses, and whores in the dining hall, and when Hodorlahomor appeared in a sea of light between the draperies of yellow and purple silk, strutting like a tiger, he would hypnotize the whole hall with his monocle.

World renowned stars and the finest dancers supped with him, and golden cobwebs were being spun about this magnificent dark figure from whom money poured like rain. The evening newspapers printed photographs of the charming prince. His poor secretary, Orlić, was besieged by reporters and other flunkies of the great city seeking further information about His Asian Majesty. People melted like wax, their backbones bent like bows, when the prince and his secretary passed down the hall carpeted in red. White breasts of beautiful women burned with greed for the fantastic prince, in whose wake sequins dropped like beads. Paris overwhelmed Hodorlahomor. It overwhelmed him and defeated him. His face was burning passionately, and he sang a drunken hymn to Paris, as befits a barbarian charmed by its invisible splendor. And Orlić was just as disgusted by the pomp and splendor as he had been in the days when, still hungry, he peeped through the closed blinds of rich villas and watched countesses and marquises riding along shaded avenues. Now his stomach rose with disgust and he wanted to vomit. He scorned the Ritz, and the soirées, and the press, and the races, and the premiers, and the parades, and the women, and Hodorlahomor himself.

His contempt for Hodorlahomor grew each day. So this is the famous king of Babylon, the king of wingéd bulls and milky-skinned women! This ignorant barbarian, who is as primitive as a simple maid in the kitchen of a dirty village pub, and who, like a common soldier, takes pleasure in breastplates and armies and shows respect for bemedaled idiots and titled cavaliers. So this is the ideal that had acted as the antidote for Pero's disillusionment. And Orlić sang a dirge over the grave of this simpleton whose knowledge did not equal even that of a schoolgirl. Hodorlahomor knew nothing, nothing under the sun, and his greatest joy came in the evening when, after the rush of the day, he devoured chunks of raw meat in his room. He especially liked raw meat.

Paris seduced and overcame Hodorlahomor. Like sweet Delilah, he cut off those locks of fear and resistance and gave himself over to the mercy of pleasure. He sang a hymn to Paris, but what was even more base and ignoble, he destroyed Orlić's last illusions in an ugly, brutal peasant manner. He destroyed everything for Orlić, and Orlić treated Hodorlahomor like an open wound that stank. Hodorlahomor became unbearable to Orlić, and Orlić was obsessed by the idea of leaving this despicable mummy. As the days went by, this thought ripened within him and took definite shape in occasional instinctive outbursts climaxed by tasteless scenes.

In the morning they would stand in front of the stock exchange, where thousands were milling up and down the steps in top hats. Brokers yelled and automobiles tooted, and the morning panic was on, wild and powerful. And Hodorlahomor admired it all, gaping at the spectacle like a peasant, his legs spread wide.

"Oh, by the bloody moon, I never possessed such battalions, not even when Lugašlagengur strode across the desert. By God, this Babylon is beautiful! Excellent Babylon, heavenly Babylon!"

"Some heaven! They are all swine, all thieves and scoundrels, not people at all! They are animals! They drink the blood of millions!"

"Ah! That's an excellent thing! Human blood." Hodorlahomor smacked his lips enthusiastically. "If I really loved a woman, truly loved her, I would drink her blood. My men would slit her throat and I would sip warm female blood from a silver goblet! Ah, yes! From a silver goblet!"

Or they would be standing in front of a church. Hodorlahomor, his mouth wide open, his legs spread apart, would look in admiration at the Gothic steeple and the ornate façade.

"Ah, the stakes surrounding our camps were never so finely pointed, and in our temples there was a stink of smoke that filled our eyes with tears. You are much wiser than we were, and it is splendid that I am able to see it all. I had a madman killed because he prophesied the approach of a world full of wisdom. But it turned out that he was right; you are a wise people. How beautiful is this stained glass! And these musical instruments play so well! Ah, lovely, lovely! Your God is beautiful and noble. He lives much more splendidly than our gods."

And so he admired the stained glass and he greeted the cavalrymen in the streets and Orlić ground his teeth and watched this poor nomad who had lost his head. Hodorlahomor was as afraid of airplanes as he was of Jewish cherubs, and he bowed to the locomotive at the station with religious awe, trembling as if before a black god. And at night, after carousing and drinking, genuinely tragic scenes would unfold. Orlić would be asleep, and Hodorlahomor would timidly knock on the door, enter the room, stand reverently beside Orlić's bed, waiting for Orlić to awaken. Paris is beautiful and noisy, of course, and there are musicians and drums and women; but one cannot live on perfumed beans and boiled leaves and badly prepared beef drenched in colored water. There must be blood! Red, juicy meat with its heavenly smell to make one's mouth water! Ah! Meat, bloody, fresh meat! That's what Hodorlahomor did not have. And Orlić was the only one who could get it for him. Hodorlahomor was too awkward and shy, like every other mummy of an Assyrian king who might be walking the streets of Paris. One morning he started to eat in a butcher shop. But the butchers quickly spotted him and tried to seize him; he only barely made his escape.

So His Majesty Hodorlahomor the Great stood at Orlić's feet and waited, and Orlić, having some nightmare or other, suddenly woke up.

"Ah, it's you again! What is it you want now? Let me sleep! Didn't you hog enough yesterday, you beast?"

"I am hungry, my friend, I cannot live this way any longer. I shall die! When was yesterday? That was such a long time ago!"

"Die if you must! Die this minute! What do I care? What's the use of your living, you damned animal!"

Hodorlahomor and Orlić would quarrel through the night, and the following morning Orlić would go to the butcher shop and bring home a whole calf's leg to feed the animal. And Hodorlahomor drank royally, too.

One night, as he and Orlić were staggering home drunk, they paused on a bridge across the Seine. The red lights burned prettily and underneath flowed the yellow water, dirty with tar and oil.

And Hodorlahomor, intoxicated with life and Asiatic enthusiasm, exclaimed, "Ah, how beautiful it is! Not even the wisest among us could have dreamed of such things! We could never have built such towers and such cities! Like greyhounds, you charge into the path of fiery lions! You swim like whales and you create fires on the waters! You are fishes and you wave your fins and you eat fires, oh, you great and powerful people! You play with flames like hawks, and your women are beautiful! In comparison to you we were nothing, nothing! I spit! I spit a thousand times on that dirty village rotting in the damned muck. Our houses were made of reeds thatched together with mud, and our cows stank under the same roofs with our people, and pus flowed in the streets, and grasshoppers nibbled at us. And God trod on us as if we were sawdust, and annihilated us with plague and leprosy. And you have defeated God himself, and now you stand alone and victorious. Oh, I spit, I spit a thousand times on that village of mine!"

Thus cried Hodorlahomor the Great in his Asiatic enthusiasm, falling drunkenly on his knees before Orlić, kissing the tips of Orlić's patent leather shoes. And Orlić was disgusted by this accursed idiot, and he wanted to grab him and hurl him into the river.

However, he did not hurl him into the river.

This nightmare reached its climax one afternoon at the Eiffel Tower. It was a warm, bluish day, the sun piercing the canopy of heaven with innumerable shafts, and the May greenery spreading across the whole of Paris. The city sailed in an ethereal mist, and the distant lights could only be dimly seen. The blue dome of the Pantheon and the bright white basilica of Montmartre and the white boats on the water and the masses of houses all swelled in the May warmth. And above, on the Eiffel Tower, from the topmost gallery, everything glistened in the spring fire.

The two of them climbed up the tower and, overwhelmed by summer happiness, Hodorlahomor resumed his hymn in praise of life while Orlić winced in pain.

"What sense does this damned city make? Can its life be reduced to a single value? No, all of us—Hodorlahomor, myself, the whole of Paris—are nothing but a sick illusion. We would be better off if nothing at all existed."

While such sad thoughts were tormenting Orlić's soul, Hodorlahomor was bursting with capricious life, moving about buoyantly, like a colt. That very morning he had consumed one entire bloody calf's leg.

"Oh, Paris, Paris! Supreme joy of the world! Discovery of my life! Paris!"

As the exuberant Hodorlahomor was waving and shouting and laughing, he came across someone selling those horoscopes so popular with Russian emigrés, revolutionaries, and anarchists. Hodorlahomor picked one, and on this bluish slip of paper was the sign of a sorcerer with a skull and certain mystical hieroglyphs that Orlić could not decipher. But Hodorlahomor was so disturbed by the signs that he turned pale and began to tremble. Suddenly he realized that he was in fact a mummy, lying eternally in the dark. His was but a momentary walk in the May warmth to hear women laughing at the Ritz and see them dancing at the Opéra. The military bands, and the cavalry, and the dancing, the performances and the races, the sun and joy and Paris—all this would vanish and he would return to the sarcophagus at the Louvre in the Assyrian gallery, No. 16, to the right on the ground floor. Hodorlahomor was shaken by an indescribable fear: the premonition of death. And since Orlić was the only positive thing in his life, Hodorlahomor clutched him passionately, fell before him, and cried loudly.

"Oh, my only friend, I feel I am near death! Death is already sneering at me. You resurrected me, you saved me; save me once more!"

Hodorlahomor cried bitterly, his arms around Orlić's legs, and the scene grew increasingly embarrassing. Those fat German women in tourist uniform, with canes and eyeglasses, and those icy stiff English misses, and those dark Italian women, and gentlemen in checked caps and fine socks—this whole world of globe-trotting idlers sunning themselves that May afternoon on the Eiffel Tower—nervously milled around Orlić and Hodorlahomor, producing a most unpleasant tumult.

Hodorlahomor took no notice. He screamed even more desperately, and it was in vain that Orlić battered him on the head with his feet. Hodolahomor cried out more loudly than ever.

"Oh! Oh! I, Hodorlahomor the Great, Assyrian conqueror, beg you to save me. I beg with you and plead with you. Save me!"

The commotion grew. Old women selling medallions were dashing this way and that. They are madmen! They must be Africans! They are Croats! This man speaks Russian! What is a Croat? I think they are cannibals from some God-forsaken place. Hungarians! shouted the crowd, and from somewhere the police appeared, which frightened Orlić terribly. He remembered instantly that his papers were not in order. He had been afraid of the police ever since the Khuen demonstrations, when he had

broken some Zagreb shop windows. He was aware that a decisive step had to be taken at once. He grabbed Hodorlahomor
and tossed him over the railing.

People screamed, and the Eiffel Tower came down in a great
crash, and Orlić woke up.

It must have been late in the afternoon. Rested and desperate,
Orlić rubbed his eyes, and one thing was immediately clear to
him: he must leave Paris at once. For Paris was the most superfluous thing in this universe. In a provincial town he would get
work, not die of hunger, and write articles for *Zagrebački Dnevnik*, seven *filirs* per line.

And he started courageously on his way. When he was quite a
distance from the city, with only the dark contours of Babylon
still visible, and as the evening lights went on in the valley, he
removed his shoes and dusted them off.

And from his pocket he took out his revolver and, turning toward Paris, fired a round of six shots.

Translated by Drenka Willen

The Love of Marcel Faber-Fabriczy for Miss Laura Warronigg

Twenty years later, when all that was to happen had happened, when Laura and Marcel stood in life like two shipwrecked persons, there emerged in their conversations the old recollections of their Bukovec adventures, distant and faded as old English rubbings in half-darkened rooms. Marcel, who had just returned from Russia, was lingering for a while in Zagreb, anchorless in the mist of his Croatian homeland. He and Laura would meet in the front room of Laura's fashion shop, Mercure Galant. At that time Laura was already doomed to commit suicide, but the somber and sad conversations about all their past involvements were infused with the silent, golden light of the bygone days of Bukovec.

Their conversations about the Bukovec drawing room! Its enormous old-fashioned sofa in the corner with the oriental rugs, the sofa piled high with too many red, black, pale blue, and yellow cushions, and above, on the golden console, the gilded baroque saint with outstretched arms. The embroidered designs on the silk cushions, the vases and the jars in the Viennese glass cabinet, the clocks on alabaster pillars, and the tabouret where the old butler set the silver tea tray: all this stood before Marcel like the silent replica of an afternoon with sun shining through the green crests of linden trees under the balcony. . . .

The door of the balcony is open. One can sense the soft, warm, palpitating blue distance of the Maksimir and Dubrava horizon. The half silent movement of the leaves on the faded linden trees and laughter in the vineyard! Below on the lawn, near the fountain, under the yellow and red sunshade, Laura's friends are laughing: the Ballochanska and the Wagner girl, Melita Szlougan, some naval ensign and Laura's escort, Lieutenant Fabiani. They play crazy games in the vineyard, and all are impressed by Lieutenant Fabiani's fine talk about his recent admission to the Vienna Military Academy, while upstairs, in the drawing room, Marcel lies on the sofa and like a tired dog strains to hear Laura's voice! The mere echo of Laura's voice! The slightest quiver of air exhaled through her lips that would enter by the open balcony door and circle in perfumed incense-like whiffs around the drawing room. Silence. In the distance, somewhere on the Remete path, a girl sings. On the road an oxcart creaks. A bird flies from the tree. Marcel is in love; yet not for the first time.

Before Laura there was a certain Darinka, a girl two years older than he, a girl who had so overwhelmingly taken hold of his life, his existence, and his fifteen-year-old destiny that Marcel's wound did not heal for two entire years. Only when his cousin Laura Warronigg arrived in Zagreb from Vienna did he use Laura as an antidote to Darinka, thus creating new complications that were to follow him for many more years, throughout the haze and daze of puberty.

Darinka was approximately the thirtieth woman in his life. Marcel was as conscious of this gallery of female figures then as he was to remain faithful to their memory ten or twenty years later. At the time of Darinka, Marcel was a shy but perfect lover in whose eye Woman loomed more portentously than she would later, after all his sad experiences. He then sought in Woman a supernatural, spiritual mission; he thought that Woman's role should consist in making life easier for us in a "higher sense," in transporting us away from the futility of Latin and Greek and mathematical complexities. Naturally, "inferior as only an eleventh grader can be," Darinka could not have had the faintest idea of what storms were raging in the ninth-grader Marcel Faber, who waited for her like a faithful dog day after day near the tramway station to trudge behind her down the street named after a famous Dubrovnik writer of comedies on which she lived. As he was to find out later through experience, everything had been then as it would be with all women: the woman had not understood, and the woman would never understand, for the simple reason that woman is incapable of understanding. But in the case of Darinka (as so many times later in life), Marcel believed that this was not so and that it was possible that woman might understand after all; indeed, Darinka was not Marcel's first love experience, but she was his first entirely conscious encounter with frustration.

Between Miss Darinka and the dark, uncertain totterings preceding her, many bleeding and sorrowful loves had faded away. Miss Darinka was, in fact, only the first conscious climax in the rich love instrumentation that orchestrally accompanies every Godsent childhood—from fighting and quarreling over Karlsbad omelets, variegated marbles, red balloons, and punch cakes to hide-and-seek games in wine cellars where in the darkness girls' tresses smell like linden blossoms to boys. In the love history of Marcel Faber there existed prior to Darinka girls of inferior social standing, who smelled of humid scrubbed floors and bread soaked in creamy coffee. While Marcel Faber-Fabriczy walked about in his fine Kiel-made sailor suit with a red silk anchor on the left sleeve, these girls (daughters of charwomen, servants, and janitors), dressed in ordinary homespun, envied Marcel's little brass bells, lacquered hoops, and tennis balls in woolen nets. In his benevolent attitude toward the lower social strata, there was always something perversely merciful about Marcel's tender feelings for these "poor little ones" while, at the same time, he was attracted to them by his certainty of success; among these girls of his who admired his clothes and toys, great respect for the "upper social bracket" was noticeable at all times. The noble Fabriczy child, often spotted at his mother's side in the Glembay carriage, the doctor's son, the little gentleman and rich boy, was sure of a lordship's victory over these "miserable creatures." In a superior Don Juan-like manner, he mistreated the ugly, myopic cross-eyed girls with their thick glasses and greasy braids; being the only one in the group who had ever been to the gold rococo theater where musical comedy stars sang with heavenly voices amid violet lights and brocaded costumes, only he could fascinate the girls with tales of what love adventures unfolded on the stage. In the days before Darinka Marcel had taken much interest in the limping, tubercular widow of a suicide (said to have been deaf) who, day after day, locked in her attic room, embroidered gigantic, blooming La France roses on wool cushions and made covers for pocket watches. Servant girls and chambermaids in the service of his mother's friends in the city struck Marcel as mysterious beings, naked under their skirts like Titian's Venuses framed in green plush in Aunt Agatha's drawing room. . . .

Like an Impressionistic aquatint, its colors spilled from a most audacious palette, the enormous space in the interior of the cathedral seems permeated with light, perfume, organ music, and incense. At the altar of St. Jerome with the Lion Marcel assists the priest and Genoveva Rochard-Flieder stands in the second row among the girls of her class. A golden light shines upon all things. In the right nave, in front of the altar of St. Jerome, the entire school is assembled for the Holy Sunday Mass—the old director with his white waistcoat and gray umbrella, the teacher in her bell skirt tightened at the waist, falling in rich folds like a train and looking like the tube of some poisonous flower. The teacher's hat is enormous, like the nest of some unknown tropical bird, and under that hat, under the rich, black, Empress Elizabeth hair-do, next to that bell skirt, in the second row stands Genoveva Rochard-Flieder, a pale, anemic girl with an ebony prayer book, a rich girl for whom a carriage and an old top-hatted coachman are sent to school every day. . . .

Marcel was struggling through his paper on the Subject. For more than half a year now he had worked on this treatise based on Schopenhauer's epigraph, "The Subject, the Comprehending, never Comprehended," and when his work had attained sufficient clarity so that he had dared show it to Laura, she had returned his manuscript because "such things don't interest me; indeed, they truly bore me!" He had appended to his treatise several charts drawn in different colors of ink. The Table of Quantity, Quality, Relation, and Modality, the Table of Receptivity of Impression, and the Table of Observation. From the little Toldt Anatomical Atlas (from the library of his late father), Marcel had skillfully enlarged the anatomical cross section of the eye, colored the small brain in yellow, the lines of the *nervus facialis*, the *nervus opticus*, and the *nervus oculomotorius* in red, whereas the eyeball and lids he outlined like a symmetrical globe, in blue. The Table of Observation, with the red line of optical stimulation (from the pupil to the point of association), drawn in three colors on a double sheet of the finest cardboard, was a particularly decorative addition to Marcel's treatise on the Subject, and yet Laura had returned it all with the superficial observation that none of it "interests me in the least!"

The question of the difference between pure and empirical apprehension, the problem of pure Reason, the problems concerning the analysis of notions, the problem of Existence and of the Thing in Itself, these are naturally boring questions for Laura, but flirting with Fabiani, naturally, does not bore her.

With all the impassioned enthusiasm of his intelligence, Marcel defiantly skimmed through the leaves of his manuscript with a Copernican craving for beauty and with contempt for the unkind Laura who had no understanding whatsoever of all the pitfalls one stumbles across in reasoning and in the quest for truth. What is transcendentality of Space and Time to such a Viennese brat; what are all of Marcel's intellectual efforts when the only important questions for her are the Coronelli dance and the party at the Szlougans?

"The thinking of my Subject, the pure perception of my own inner consciousness and self-assertion, this transcendental inner power of mine, this heaven in me—this is what thinks in us. Our thinking must be like the finest yarn, covering everything that exists because it encompasses all that comes forth and appears to us, for otherwise, if something appeared to us of which we were unable to think, we would not be able to comprehend this unknown, and it would remain forever unimaginable and incomprehensible to us."

Marcel had copied his philosophical treatise for the ninth time and thought how unable we are to imagine a phenomenon without a category and how Schopenhauer approves of transcendentality in aesthetics but refuses to accept it in categories, how we encounter in notions something that is not a notion but something commonplace and sensual, how everything disintegrates into a mass of contradictions, how all thoughts evaporate like smoke, how nevertheless there remains beyond it all the terrible reality of Laura and the Idea of Laura. What are his tables and treatises when they don't interest Laura, why does he so persistently copy them when they lead nowhere and he should be working instead! Whenever he thought of his schoolwork, he was assailed with worries, feeling like the sleeping traveler who has no strength to awaken and to hasten despite the certainty that his ship is going to leave and that he will be late. This obsession with Laura was indeed a game played to the limits of endurance. Marcel knew how wise it would be to consult certain obscure chapters that he had ignored since the beginning of the semester, and yet, constantly torn between reality and illusion, he felt utterly powerless to resist his somber instincts and to confront facts. What did he care for the formula

$$\frac{x^2}{a^2} - \frac{y^2}{b^2} = 1,$$

when tomorrow in the concert hall some sort of Spanish virtuoso would perform and when in twenty hours he would see Laura. All right,

$$\cos x \, i = \frac{1}{2}(e^x + e^{-x}), \text{ or } \frac{x^2}{a^2} + \frac{y^2}{b^2} - \frac{z^2}{c^2} = 1.$$

To hell with all the hyperboloids and functions and written and oral work, when in twenty hours he will see her! Tomorrow Brenner, that disagreeable old man with fishy eyes and hairy hands, will stand at the back of the class and watch to see that nobody hides a book under the bench or copies from his neighbor. There he will stand, his back against the wall, drumming on the wall with his heavy butcher's hand. His fingernails are uncut, tough, black; his pockets reek with the stench of extinguished cigars. Then comes Latin. Cornelius Tacitus: "Whereas the worshipers of antiquity usually place the ones who were active before Cassius toward the end of the olden period and accuse Cassius of having abandoned the direct old style of expression, I claim that Cassius did not adopt such a style because of lack of talent or ignorance in matters of literature, but on purpose and in full cognizance of what he was doing . . ." (Tacitus, *Dialogus de oratoribus*, 19). And thirty-five other such idiocies; then physics with a dirty wet sponge, humid chalk breaking between one's fingers, superfluous formulas $\frac{h^1 - ho}{ho} = \frac{v^1 - vo}{vo}$. But all this is for tomorrow. It's all for tomorrow only, and until then there is plenty of time and it's all of no consequence when in twenty hours he will see Laura.

He last saw her on Sunday before Mass, in St. Catherine's Square. She was with her two intimate friends, Melita Szlougan and Blanka Balloczanska. They did not see him. He had shuddered and been unable to breathe. His throat and chest had tightened; a yellow mist blinded him. He was also with friends; then, noticing her hat (what redness, no young lady in town wears such a shade of red), his words stuck. He was talking with his friends of oil paints, of the Berlin blue tube and the shellac he had purchased for a good price at the stationer's in Duga Ulica, when he spotted her red hat and froze. He continued talking of yellow chrome and Berlin blue; he continued to walk erect; he moved forward mechanically, as one always continues to move, as if nothing has happened, when, in fact, the utmost of what can happen in life has happened: her red silk hat, with its ribbon and varnished cherries, was revealed to him. Tired, pale, exhausted, with trembling lips, listening to the voices of his friends as if they came from a distance, only seemingly present, Marcel Faber watched the red color of his cousin Laura Warronigg crossing St. Catherine's Square, and all those pigeons, telephone wires, closed blinds on the windows, and sunlight achieved a greater clarity, a tension deep as unconsciousness. This high-powered stimulation was surely bad for his health. Marcel spent an entire semester in desperate circumstances, with F's in Latin, Greek, and mathematics and two dubious D's in logic and physics. The unread material constantly grew in volume and there was no chance whatever that something could turn in his favor; in this already almost certainly lost game, in this compromised existence, in all this trouble, he sensed his slow sinking and ruination. But under the magic spell of a single thought of her, all that was black would change into a bewildering white light, and these thoughts of her would play over him like the vibrations of a bow on a fiddle. As Marcel thought of Laura, his gloomy moods brightened like a mirror in a darkened room suddenly hit by a ray of distant light. For more than half a year he was no more than a mirror of her as such. As he knew his

Handel by heart, so he knew by heart her walk in its every rhythm, the way her body was bent (in the hip, a little on the right), the tender pliability of her waist, the movement of her elbows, the scrubbed glow of the flesh on her bare arms, the curve of the nape of her neck, her Greek hair-do, and the non-chalant swaying of her hips from left to right, winding and rest-less. He knew her time schedule, the books she read, the expres-sions she used, and he knew Fabiani whom she adored, that goose, that eleventh-grader, that snob! On Sunday he had seen her for the last time in St. Catherine's Square, and on Monday he had waited for her for a whole hour in the rain in front of the house in which her piano teacher lived. On Monday from four to five; but she had not come. On Tuesday, Wednesday, and Thursday he had thought of her continuously, day and night, for twenty-four hours, of how on Friday at eight o'clock he would see her at the concert of the Spanish virtuoso. She would come in her new dress (of which Aunt Angelique Barboczy had talked last time at tea), in her splendid new dress and a Greek hair-do: clean, white, slender, with her oval face and dimples, her half profile (which Marcel was unable to draw). She, Laura, his cousin, accompanied by her mother and that chasseur Fabi-ani. He would stand in the concert hall, backed up against the wall so as not to collapse from fright, and for two and a half hours, as if hypnotized, he would watch her, her Person, among all those ladies, officers, chairs, and chandeliers, amid the warmth and scents of female bodies. He would watch Laura for two and a half hours—only her and no one else—with sweaty fingers, swallowing bitter lumps of terror, asking himself: would she perhaps after all turn around and honor him with a single look, kindly returning his greetings, openly, intimately, as is customary among relatives, the way eleventh-grade cousins are supposed to return greetings in concert halls when escorted by army officers facing promising careers? With this one single glance of hers he would go out into the midnight darkness, stroll through the streets and parks, and finally stand in front of old

Glembay's one-story house until the last light went out in that glorious room of hers next to the balcony. Her glance would be a sign that somewhere on earth one can begin living in different spheres, unlike the ones he has known thus far. From her Marcel, in fact, needs absolutely nothing—just to look at her, to contemplate in her the embodiment of some outer, more perfect world, some higher order that lies stretched out beyond his vain agonies and school entanglements. Her gaze suggests some sort of infinite possibility, a confident island that we are going to reach someday after all. Her gaze means the end of being hurt, and painful and difficult as this expectation is since last Sunday, it is nonetheless a grandiose event for Marcel, shining above, cold and green like a polar light.

Everything around Marcel is quite black. He is plunged into constant depression by the three F's, the clash with the religion teacher, the sixteen-hour detentions, the numerous warnings and unexplained absences; but above it all, like a glimmer of hope amid a dark shipwreck, are his thoughts of her. In them Marcel is totally immersed, lost in those fantastic regions as cold as a starlit night. It is bitter to dream about her and know that she does not understand. Her look, her conventional look, the look of a relative, of a Glembay, is vague and empty. In conversation and in touch with her beauty, in the too great nearness of real contact with her as a living person, in that passionate turmoil and hazard, Marcel suffered for nearly a year a hell of rapture and doubt. This is a vulnerable state, anatomically exposed to everyday, hairy, idiotic, logical school facts; yet compared with the heavy and repulsive smells of the classroom this state is a perfumed and other-worldly veil. At night Marcel would awaken, disturbed by a somewhat louder tick of the clock, and immediately his first thoughts would be: She, she, Laura, Laura, she is living together with him on the same planet, on the same continent, in the same city. She breathes the same air, she, Laura Warronigg. She exists, she is, she sleeps, great Lord, she is alive!

And side by side with this heavenly joy dimly bellows an entire complex of ruination and terror. In his nocturnal dialogues with her, Marcel has logically analyzed and discussed these things for hours. He is slipping downhill because of her, she does not understand him, he cannot concentrate on Greek or mathematics—she has totally hypnotized him. Yet when he meets her he blushes, sweats, panics, and with blood pounding in his brain, his heart in his throat, collapses in front of this cool, superior, rational eleventh-grade goose. He knows perfectly well that her horizon is compressed between the Szlougan party and the Coronelli dance, that her mother Olga Warronigg née Glembay is a lady who reads Kellermann, believing that Kellermann is a serious writer, that Laura seriously discusses Schopenhauer with Fabiani. But what? Where to? How? Pale, trembling, timidly sweating, Marcel knows and feels how truly unworthy of a man it is to sit silent, sad, and alone at parties, in a corner of the drawing room, while the pack of Glembay youth dances and rumbles through all the rooms of the apartment. But what is the use of all the reasoning power in him when he cannot stop dreaming of the slightest detail concerning her? They spent last summer in Rimske Toplice—his mother, Laura's grandmother, and Laura. Now, in the cold of winter, as he looks back on the sunny Rimske Toplice, Marcel comes close to choking with tears. The dawns and morning promenades. One can hear the first cocks and see the miners marching in the near darkness and the first light coming on in the mills. The icy morning air streams down from the brown chain of mountains, and poplars sway in the morning wind in the green and blue light of the forest. And Laura has come, still warm and transparent, in an orange-red sweater, in her hiking shoes, and has given him a bar of Suchard chocolate to store in the knapsack. The pine trees give off their scent, a superb silence reigns among the silver firs. And there, in the silver fir wood, Marcel first saw Laura's knee. In the company of boys and girls her age on excursion from Vienna (the children of generals and lawyers at court), she stopped to rest on an enormous tree that had been felled by lightning, and Marcel saw her knee.

He wakes up at night, sits up in bed, and thinks of that far-away afternoon, of Laura's knee, of her voice, of the colors in the wood, and of how strangely the flies buzzed in the stillness. As he remembers, his throat tightens and he sighs, sad and broken. Laura is a stupid Viennese general's daughter. She is limited; she reads stupid novels; she is more interested in the light cavalry officer Fabiani than in a student from Croatia who is flunking and who happens to be her cousin. She has no idea of what is going on within him, and even if she knew, she could not understand. She thoroughly enjoys Fabiani's jokes, and she does not know who Burckhardt is! He is tired of her; she bothers him; she is ruining his life, and it most certainly would be best for him if he could let it all drift away—let it evaporate and disappear!

In the course of his nocturnal meditations there come moments when he feels superior, proud and confident, strong enough to resist and to annihilate her in his thoughts, since it is only too clear to him that it makes no sense whatever to submit to her with such servility; after all, who is she and what has she given him? It's so simple! He should rid himself of this state of mind; it is all a phantasmagoria, and Laura knows nothing about it. In such moments of complete lucidity Marcel even senses hatred and scorn for that sweetly smiling Viennese doll; what a foolish and rotten way to suffer. But the next morning, when he would meet her, dewy, supple, and soft, her tan skin transparent in the sunlight, he would clearly understand that she is a shadow and that she does not really exist, but he knows also that should she order him to do so, he would unhesitatingly jump from the third floor.

Days went by in this debilitating fatigue and futile gloom.

As he thought about Laura, he became very frightened. He wished and desired to see her; yet he was somehow pleased when she was absent. Then he would spend two or three peaceful days in the negative delight of his ardent longing. In the passive lyricism of uninterrupted dreams there was more vivid happiness than in direct contemplation. This very afternoon he will ring the bell at the old Glembays, enter old Angelique Barboczy's open drawing room, and there, in the twilight, kiss his aunt's hand and learn that Laura is not at home, that "she is at the Szlougans." In the moments between his apprehension and the realization that he need not be afraid, since she is "not at home," he will fully perceive the vanity of his love. Then for a while it will seem as if his Laura had never existed, as if she were an optical illusion and no more. She would often vanish from his field of vision, and he would be unable to reconstruct her. Her dress yes, the knee too, also the left joint, the hair, the color of the cheeks, the movements, but not her. He saw her in the Glembay carriage, but was that really she? That was no more than her lingonberry red coat and peach-colored parasol. Frantically he tried to master her, to subdue her, to be the stronger, to overcome his obsession, but he could not. Instead, he found himself all the more entangled in these golden veils, and a merely superficial confrontation with the presence of her person sufficed to provoke a swelling throughout him that was like church bells ringing, and those bells would ring for days and nights. Indeed, Laura was not there. She was no more than his fancies! While she was absent, while she was only his Idea, while skyborne in his imagination, she was a glorious and unique feeling. As long as he feared that he might not see her, panicked that she might not be what he believed her to be, as long as he suspected her inferiority and thrilled over her existence, her incredibly beautiful eyes, the transparence of her hand, and the color of her voice, he floated upon the most sublime of waters. But when he saw her in the flesh at a party, all smiles for that idiotic Lieutenant Fabiani, talking in the clichés of a pseudo-fashionable education, a silk scarf from the Maison Chapeau d'Or more important to her than Schiller, then Marcel's sublime visions paled and only visions of death remained. She was inane and unintelligent, and there was really nothing beneath her Viennese veneer. On closer examination she really was rather short and her eyes were hazy, her voice weepy, and her spelling miserable, and there was no chance it would ever improve; so why should he lose time on such an eleventh-grader and such a goose? When she stood alive near him in the drawing room, under the lamp, surrounded by laughter, the clatter of plates, the click of spurs, and the piano, he looked at her and it struck him that Laura was a terrible carnivorous beast. Indeed, her teeth were strong, her incisors rapacious; she was unintelligent, unworthy of his sacrifice, too stupid and weak to understand and sustain the stream of yearning, dreams, desires, illusions, fever, and nightmares in which he reveled with increasing passion and lunacy. Laura was absent—the passionate, wild, sensual, grotesque, panicky feeling that Laura was absent!

Five days have passed since Sunday, since he last saw her, time enough to destroy himself on a number of counts. He has not worked at all; he has not read at all; he has thought of her the whole time. He has gone for walks in the streets, waited for her at street corners, looked at the passers-by as if they were a funeral procession; he has gone to the opera and visited the cemetery, and uninterruptedly, for five days and five nights, he has carried her in his every step and heartbeat, in mist and in rain. And finally, with her mother and Fabiani, she came to the recital of the Spanish virtuoso. During the entire concert Marcel stood in a solitary niche in the wall, deaf to all sounds. Laura did not turn once. Laura did not notice him. After the concert, the General's wife left first; Laura and Fabiani followed her. Fabiani bade good-by to the ladies in front of the carriage and was lost in the crowd. It was raining. Somehow Marcel managed to bring himself to the front of the one-story Glembay house, and there, tired and wet, he remained standing under the foliage of a tree like a dead man. In the quiet one could hear the rustle of rain drops among the leaves. At the end of the street a gas lamp gleamed, and there was Marcel looking into the apartment of old Glembay. His heart pounded as if it were jumping now to the left, now to the right. On the second floor of the house next Glembay's a woman in a nightgown moved the curtains aside and opened the window. In the green light of the room thus disclosed, Marcel saw a clock and a pendulum in a black frame and a potted palm on a chest of drawers. A bitter taste invaded his throat and tears came into his eyes. A frightful pain burned and hurt him all over; he felt like a dog on a heap of ashes. He was craving for her, but in fact she did not exist.

Translated by Branko Lenski

The Birdman

The old birdman pushed open the door to the porch and slowly, with a great effort, crossed the high doorstep. When he was finally outside, he stooped, tightened his worn-out overcoat, and glanced fearfully at the space in front of the hovel where the first pale gleams of the March sun were shining. His body shivered as if suspended in the wind, and his knees shook, so he leaned on a knotty walking stick that he grasped convulsively in the long, dirty fingers of his right hand. For some time he shuffled his feet as if he could not make up his mind, and then he began to move along the path that slanted off to the little town whose roofs were visible from the narrow valley below the hill.

The birdman was a strange creature. Nobody knew his real name and nobody cared. He was single, and for decades he had lived in a hovel overlooking the little town, drawing an insignificant pension from somewhere. He was well-known primarily because his face resembled that of certain hook-billed birds. At the end of an unusually long neck, in the middle of which was a large Adam's apple, perched a birdlike head. His narrow face consisted of a low, receding forehead from which, starting from the hairline, there jutted a powerful bone that curved to a pointed extension at its end. This extension, similar to the beak of a hawk, was the birdman's nose. Its expression definitely made his head look like that of a bird, although the other parts of his face contributed—such features as protruding lips, a thin, hardly visible beard, shallow eyes almost stuck to the nose, and ears sticking out like those of a bat.

It was known that the birdman's room was full of birds that screeched all day long, and that it looked just like an aviary—everything covered with a thick layer of birds' droppings and an unbearable smell. The birds flew freely about his room and nested wherever it suited them. The whole of his slender income was spent on their food. It was said that sometimes he was possessed by a strange passion and let his birds go to the point of starvation. The birds would scream despairingly while he sat motionless in a corner savoring the dying birds' screams. Some people were horrified at this and threatened to destroy the aviary and to bring the birds' torments to an end. But this never happened.

On this particular day the birdman had been driven out of his hovel by hunger. For two months he had languished in his aviary amidst a flock of birds including canaries, bullfinches, goldfinches, ortolans, wrens, jays, magpies, tomtits, sparrows, turtledoves, owls, thrushes, and hens. Since Christmas, thick snow had covered the ground so that he had been unable to find any kind of food for them outside. In autumn he had picked up roots, turnips, and potatoes in the fields, and plucked some grain from the wheat sheaves. But all that had already been used up and for the last ten days the aviary had lived on refuse and garbage.

The hungry rabble could hardly be kept under control now.

Day after day they screeched more and more desperately, attacked him, and made such horrible sounds that even he, who was used to them, could not get a wink of sleep for several nights. The more delicate birds even collapsed and were devoured, bones and all, by the others. Only the night before, the kite buzzard had been so overcome by hunger that he had gulped down a pedigree canary to the last feather. That was why he had to be put in the cage under the bench, where he looked as if he, too, were about to expire at any moment.

Three hens were huddled under the stove. One black, one white, and one speckled. Only a feeble flapping and cackling could still be heard from the dark corner. With wings spread and necks outstretched, the hens lay on the floor and watched their master with bloody, desperate eyes.

The birdman put his hand on his skinny knee and looked at them with eyes full of compassion. After a while he said in a hoarse voice:

"Little hens! Chickies! Don't be afraid! You're thin, so now you must pick up your strength . . . that's it . . . pick up your strength. . . . You over there, you black one . . ."

As soon as his eyes were satisfied, he got up, caught the larger birds that might gobble up the others in his absence, and locked them in their cages. The birds submitted, offering no resistance. When he had finished, he put on his overcoat, which was completely covered with birds' droppings, put a basket on his arm, picked up his stick, stood in the middle of the room, and said aloud:

"Quiet! Today you are going to get something to eat!"

From all sides, from the walls, from under the bench and the table, from underneath the cupboard, some ten feeble voices began to croak and to squawk, as if the birds wished to show they had understood. Only from under the stove were no voices heard at all.

The birdman noticed this; his birdlike face twisted a little and then he walked out of the hovel.

The birdman approached the houses of the little town with feeble step. As soon as he reached the first house, he met a crowd of children sliding along a frozen shady path like a deep gutter. The birdman was always an interesting sight for the children and they surrounded him immediately.

"Here's the birdman, here's the birdman!" shouted the children on the slippery path.

The old man, who seemed hardly able to stand, appeared to pluck up courage. He suddenly strengthened himself and stared at the children, who made faces of unutterable hatred at him. They withdrew a little and began to shout from a distance, "The birdman, the birdman!"

Then the old man raised his stick as if he were going to chase the toddlers nearest him. But they skipped off in time. A few of the boldest burst into malicious laughter and began to shout: "A duck, a duck! The birdman, the duck, the duck!"

These words seemed to strike the birdman like a thunderbolt. He stumbled, and it seemed that he would fall full length to the ground. But he still had enough strength to keep on his feet. He crouched like a hedgehog; his eyes, which had been watching the children with a hostile look, withdrew behind the red swollen lids and grew fearful and puzzled. As though through a distant mist he discerned the contours of the first house of the town before him. Full of fright and confusion, he dashed toward it.

"Duck, duck!" shouted the children after the fleeing old man.

In a flash the birdman succeeded in reaching the entrance of the house. He leaned against the door with his whole weight and pushed it open, so that he almost fell across the threshold; then he slammed it behind him with such violence that the whole house trembled. He was shaking all over. Thus frightened, and in a cold sweat, he dropped on a chest just behind the door and almost fainted.

Then the door to the kitchen opened and two women dashed out.

"What's the matter?" cried the first of the two. But as soon as she spoke she noticed the old man sitting on the chest and leaning against the wall.

"Oh, it's the birdman!" They both recovered at the same time.

"And what are you doing here?" asked the first woman.

The old man gave a little start, but he was so frightened that he could not utter a single word. He only directed his vague, lost look toward the front door. Outside, the voices of those arrogant children could still be heard shouting: "Duck, duck!"

Then the women looked at each other, blushed a little, and smiled. The older one soothed the old man: "Those are only children's jokes, you old birdman! That's nothing! Now, then, you had better come over here where it is warm."

The old man looked at her gratefully, gathered his strength, and, tottering slowly, followed the women into the kitchen where they indicated that he should sit down on a low stool near the coalbox. He twisted about, put his palms between his thin, trembling knees, lowered his head on his hands, and remained silent.

The women left him in peace so that he might warm himself. In the meantime they looked at each other suspiciously and wrinkled their noses at the unpleasant smell that soon pervaded the whole kitchen. Despite this discomfort, they could not hide the smile that fluttered across their faces.

To tell the truth, the birdman had the reputation throughout the district of being not only queer, but even mad. Besides, everybody knew that in spite of his passion for birds, he despised all birds with large beaks, such as ducks. Never had any bird that had the slightest kinship with a duck entered his aviary—neither a duck, nor a goose, nor a woodcock, nor a heron. His entire birds' paradise consisted of crooked-beaked and pointed-beaked kinds. Whenever he caught sight of a wide-beaked monster, he almost had an epileptic fit. Malicious grownups and children, knowing this weakness, made him angry by calling "duck," while the peasants chased him from their sheaves when the wheat was drying and he tried to pick off a few ears for his birds as he passed by.

For a while the two women watched the shivering old man silently and with a strange, uncomfortable feeling. They looked in disgust at his sharp, birdlike features, his bloodshot, red-rimmed eyes, his dried-up body. They were particularly horrified at the sight of his hands, with their long fingers like claws and sickeningly long nails. Then they remembered that the birdman had never cared for women; people said he adored birds instead, particularly hens. . . . In recalling this, everybody, both old and young, shuddered.

As they watched the birdman, the women forgot for a time that they had a hungry man in the house. Then they made a pot of tea and added a good dollop of rum. The younger one cut a big slice of bread.

"Here, have a bite and something to drink!" they invited him.

By now the birdman was quiet. He was still shivering from exhaustion, since he had not eaten anything hot for a week. He finished his tea before the women even noticed it, but he did not touch the bread.

"Why don't you take some bread?" asked the older woman almost reproachfully.

The birdman kept silent; he only raised his eyes imploringly. The woman understood.

"Oh, I see!" she said, and then added in a good-natured voice: "You just eat that bread. And as for the birds, I shall give you something else to take to them."

She poured him more tea, and only then did the old man snatch up his bread and eat it.

The women took his basket, which he had placed near his feet, and prepared some food for the birds—a mixture of potatoes, beets, and grain.

"Have you got hens too?" asked the younger one meaningfully.

"Yes, I have,'"the birdman replied in a low voice.

The woman put some extra grain for the hens in his basket. "That's for your hens!"

The birdman thanked the women and slowly walked out of the house. The older woman saw him to the door, warned the children to leave the old man in peace, and quickly returned to the kitchen, where she promptly washed her hands to clean them of contact with the old man's basket. The younger did the same.

The old man did not start directly for home, but waddled to the little town. He went to the merchant where he had left the last few pence of his pension, and where he could still buy some trifles on credit. From the merchant he went to the butcher, who sometimes gave him refuse for the carnivorous birds. He did not go there in vain. The butcher put in some stinking, yellowish offal. When the birdman had stuffed it all in his basket on top of the other things and was about to leave, the butcher asked him to wait a bit. He disappeared, and quickly returned with a big mousetrap in which was a live young rat.

"This might do for the hawks and the fowls," he said, pointing to the mousetrap. "Our cat has so many, it is already sick of them."

The old man blushed. The animal was rushing about excitedly in the narrow space. When the old man looked at it, it stopped immediately and remained motionless. The animal did not move even when the old man put his long fingers into the mousetrap, but yielded without resistance and let itself be pushed into a separate compartment of the basket.

From the butcher's the birdman went to the baker's, where he bought some bread and where something more found its way into the basket for his birds to drink. It was already dark when he disappeared past the last houses, on his way back to his hovel.

When he entered the room, he was welcomed by an earsplitting, hellish screeching released from desperate starved throats and beaks. All the croaking, whistling, cooing, and crowing was drowned by the cawing of two crows, accompanied by and mingled with a feverish rattling and fluttering of wings. The birds dashed themselves against the walls and ceiling, fell on the floor and dragged themselves into the corners, while those that were in cages hit themselves against the wire netting.

This was the usual scene whenever the old man returned home with a full basket. The carnivors had smelled the offal, and the granivorous birds, the grain.

It was almost dark in the room: the two little windows, which were blocked with rags, pots, and bottles, let the last feeble rays into the narrow aviary. But soon they disappeared, and the hovel was wrapped in darkness.

The birdman sat on the bed, put the basket on the table, and remained motionless, sitting in the dark. Although there was no fire, the room was not too cold, warmed as it was by a whole flock of winged creatures. For a common villager, perhaps, it might have been cold, but the birdman was warmed by his own nature, which was akin to that of the birds. He felt happiest in that atmosphere, in that cauldron of smells and stinks.

Then it began. . . .

Perfectly still, he listened to the sick screaming and desperate fluttering of the starved birds, reminding him of death, which excited him and provoked a mysterious, morbid passion. The stronger and louder the birds' shrilling, the more intense his passion grew.

Half an hour or more passed. The old man still sat on the bed motionless, with his legs crossed, as if he were afraid of something distant and strange; listening to his own wild blood. Had the room not been so dark, one could have seen how his bird-like face glowed with a secret self-satisfaction, how his lips trembled.

He tried to distinguish the separate sounds. That feeble sipping . . . oh, that was the canary. He is angry not only because he is hungry, but because he has lost his little mate, eaten up by the vile kite. Now there was another voice that squeaked tensely, as if the narrow bird's chest were letting out its last breath . . . the finch. She was already exhausted, but she could drag herself on for another day or two. . . . Yes, she could. But the Hartzer would certainly die. The devil would likewise have taken the bullfinch and goldfinches. Those tiny birds have no resistance. . . . Behind the cupboard a titmouse twittered . . . tsvr . . . tsvr, so feebly that it was hardly audible. Its tiny eyes already had in them the true glitter of death. Two magpies screeched on the wardrobe. There was only one owl in the house, but she screamed as much as five other beaks together. She was still fairly strong. In the cage above the bed small wings fluttered constantly. A baby bird had got entangled in the net and one could hear the tiny body hopping up, falling back to the bottom of the cage, resuming its flight, and flapping down once more. . . . That was the bullfinch; his mate, however, was quiet. Next to him the thin voice of a goldfinch was twittering, hardly audible, at its last gasp. Two buzzards, shut up under the bench, croaked restlessly; but the most annoying of all was the kite, which in fact was less hungry, having swallowed the canary; but that bite had very likely only quickened his appetite. Everything was in motion, shrieking, screaming. . . . The owl alone crouched motionless in her corner. She had started squawking once, quite feebly, as if in panic, but now she was quiet; just two bright eyes glittered from the small corner. . . .

The birdman listened to the sobbing in the aviary.

Suddenly his body jerked; he shook his head, rose, and shouted: "Oh, you've been suffering, haven't you, my little birds? I've also been tormented, they tortured me so much that they drove me mad. . . ."

At first his voice brought complete silence, but afterward such a cawing and croaking broke out that the hovel's foundations trembled. There was a harrowing shriek of dying creatures. One could hear the straining of the muscles of the wide-open beaks, narrow chests inflating, wings spread with the last scrap of strength, flapping with hope.

The birdman laughed with satisfaction. He was less excited now, and the strength that had abandoned him earlier gradually returned to his exhausted muscles.

The squalling did not abate. The birds suspected that the end of their suffering was now approaching, and that surmise elated them.

The birdman put his right hand into a drawer, took out a match, and lit the lamp on which there was no glass because it long ago had been broken by the birds. The reddish flame soon illuminated the place faintly. The magpie sat on the old man's head, the crow on one shoulder, the owl on the other, while other birds hung down his sleeves, chest, and back. The birdman did not drive them off; but, looking thus ridiculous, he began to fuss about the room, talking to the birds in a mild, plaintive voice: "Chickies, birdies . . . now you're going to get something to eat; just in a minute—now you'll get something."

Then he bent over the basket and began with the utmost care and gentleness to feed the birds. Every kind of bird had its own small trough in one of the corners into which he poured seeds, grain, or crumbs. Now he could release the birds of prey from the cages because they were no longer dangerous. The owl stood on his wrist, perching determinedly. Not until she had grabbed a semi-rotten beef rib did she relax her grip and fly to her corner.

The basket was well filled and the birdman poured the drink and cut the food generously. The hungry beaks devoured and gulped, the wings fluttered greedily, and the sharp claws scratched enviously.

The birdman waddled from one corner to the other, pouring more maize. That was for the hens. But whereas the other birds swallowed their food with savage fury, the hens did not appear at all.

The old man's dried lips twisted, distorting his face into a grimace.

"Now, now!" he said in a loathsome voice. "You are on strike, little hens, aren't you?"

He crouched in front of the stove and started to stir a heap of wheat with his clawlike fingers, pretending to peck.

"Little hens, little hens, my chickies! Don't be afraid, just come, come on," he murmured, continually stirring the small heap of grain.

Some time passed before the hens moved from under the stove. The black hen was the first to crawl up to him. Peeping sideways at the heap of wheat, she began to approach, as if distrusting the master's invitation. Finally she drew near the heap with the utmost caution. The birdman knew he must withdraw if the hen was to begin pecking, so he got up and moved away. But the black hen did not start eating at once, but continued to watch to see what was going to happen. Finally she went up to the food and slowly began to peck at the grain.

Only then did the other two come out from under the stove and peck at the supper with the same hesitation and lack of enthusiasm as the first. Their appetite, however, gradually increased, and soon they were swallowing their food greedily.

At the sight, the birdman's birdlike face lit up. With the tip of his tongue he licked his thin, almost invisible lips, and murmured in a sleepy tone: "I knew it, my chicks. I knew it. . . ."

All the birds were eating except the kite under the bench, who was the last to take his turn. Although his cage had already been opened, he did not obtrude himself, but remained crouching on the earth, swaying his body forward as if he wanted to start flying in a certain direction. In the meantime his gullet kept him warm by its noises.

The birdman turned his eyes toward him. The kite considered the old man's look calmly. They kept on like this for some time, like two adversaries estimating each other, both reluctant to be the first to give way. The kite, however, was the first to yield. He bent his neck and waddled forward as if his legs were about to collapse.

The birdman was moved; aware of his superiority, he addressed him generously: "You, glutton, you are going to get something too!"

The kite nodded with satisfaction; the old man returned to the basket, put his long fingers into the separate compartment, and produced the rat. Holding it by its long tail, he swung it high in the air above the head of the kite, who now slowly hopped toward him. He stopped in the middle of the room and raised his head toward the prey.

The animal was quite stiff and swung in the air with his legs stuck together. Crouching on his claws, the kite swung to and fro with the movement of the animal.

Finally the old man let go the rat's tail. What followed could rather be guessed than seen: the buzzard caught the body as it fell and his claws sank into it. One could hear the bird's feathers cracking as they rose, the squeak of the prey before death, the brief struggle, the immediate devouring of the rat, and finally the fluttering of wings.

"Have you eaten it up already?" asked the birdman in an almost compassionate voice. For another moment he watched the feeble efforts of the greedy little bird, then he sat down on the bed.

The old man slowly bent toward the lamp and extinguished the wick with two fingers. The room was wrapped in darkness. The birds were quiet; they had eaten and drunk, so they all went to their resting places. Only now and then was heard a thin voice or a light fluttering of wings, but there was an atmosphere of satiety and drowsiness that overcame the bird inhabitants.

Amidst this peace the birdman remained sitting silent and

motionless for almost an hour. He gazed at the darkness without wishing to see anything through it. His whole body and soul derived pleasure from the impenetrable silence and looked forward to the occasion when something heavy, sweet, and inevitable would emerge in his callous limbs.

Gradually, the old man was pervaded by a pleasant warmth. He rose to his feet and cautiously, as if afraid that some of the birds might hear him, stood by the bed. And in fact nothing moved—every creature was fed, calm, and at rest. He made one step, then another, and listened again, feeling his blood pulsating, every single nerve tingling.

He was by the stove.

He stood there for at least five minutes and, holding his breath, listened for any possible sounds. Then he bent down, quick as lightning, put his hand under the stove, and grabbed the first hen he could feel.

"Gra, gra!" cackled the frightened bird wildly. She stretched her neck as if she would die at that very moment.

Her cackle woke all the inhabitants of the aviary and was immediately answered by countless cacklings, cawings, screechings, cooings, and squawkings. As if bewitched, the old man remained standing, rooted to the spot. It seemed as if he felt ashamed at the awakened bird world. He stood there motionless for a time, until the birds slowly calmed down. With the utmost caution he then grasped the hen with the other hand. Although it was pitch dark in the room, he immediately recognized which hen he was holding in his hands. He immediately fell into a rage.

"You get back under the stove, you white one!" he said, and chased the fowl back to its place. The hen's body fell heavily to the earthen floor and lay there as it had fallen. He bent again slowly and grabbed another hen. Just like the rejected white one, this one burst into a desperate screeching—the room again resounded with its dreadful, frightened squawks.

But by now the birdman was a little bolder; his icy body was imbued with warmth. He did not wait for the screeches to abate, but promptly grasped the hen in both hands. But, again, it was the wrong one.

"I don't want you either!" he said impatiently, and put it back under the stove.

He bent down for the third time and finally dragged out the black hen. This one screeched even more loudly than the first two, and her cries were accompanied by the violent squawking of the rest of the birds.

The old man pressed the hen closely to his breast and began talking to her: "My little pullet, my tiny black one, don't screech, don't!"

The warmth of the hen's body, which he could feel, excited his stomach. So he pressed her even more closely to him, then took two hasty steps up to the edge of his bed and sat down on the straw.

When, after a long time, the hen fell to the floor and blindly flew under the stove, the birdman remained sitting there motionless. The cold began to creep through his veins. His hand lay on his knees devoid of any strength, but his eyes, as if blinded, blinked at the corner behind the door.

A few uneasy moments passed.

All of a sudden the birdman's body went down, his eyes protruded like those of a madman; he gaped, and an inhuman shriek resounded: "A duck!"

The old man's eyes sought the corner and stared at a yellow phantom, with a gaping beak and unutterably disgusting appearance—they fell on the apparition of a real, genuine duck. . . .

The shriek was so hideous that instantly all the birds went mad. They abandoned their corners and perches where, until now, they had been asleep. There was a frightful, pathetic screeching; the fowls kept flying at one another, hid themselves behind the furniture, clung to the walls with fluttering wings, and then fell to the floor.

The birdman jumped to his feet, and his legs began to tremble with horror. He stretched out his arms and covered his eyes to ward off the specter, which laughed sardonically. But the more he defended himself and tried to hide, the more visible the specter grew, emerging more and more horrifying from the corner.

"Oh . . . a duck, a duck . . ." The old man groaned helplessly, and stretched out his hands in despair.

"Oh!" echoed the frightened dark room, full of confusion and the fluttering of wings; around him the big burning eyes of the birds glittered from the darkness, and the fluttering wings touched him fearfully.

But the old man was completely deaf and blind to all the commotion. In his despair he began to defend himself furiously. He snatched an old shoe and flung it at the phantom.

"There you are, damn you—you filth!"

The shoe was thrown into the corner and it fell on the floor with a loud bang.

But the phantom remained untouched. Moreover, its beak jutted out even more persistently than before from its duck-yellow throat. . . .

Now the old man took the lamp from the table and threw it at the yellow apparition. The lamp broke and the birds flew off in every direction.

But the duck still crouched untouched in the corner. The birdman was ready to faint. Whatever he could get hold of in the dark, he flung at it: bottles, clothes, the basket, straw. A hellish screeching filled the hovel. The birdman foamed at the mouth.

"Aren't you ever going away?" he groaned, and began to retreat slowly to the opposite corner. His eyes desperately sought a way out, but they could not find one—behind the door was the grinning phantom and the windows were barred.

He shuffled toward the bench where the hawk usually crouched by the moor buzzard. But the birdman's trembling fingers groped in the dark in vain: there was no hawk there. The awareness of a deadly struggle for existence had sobered him for the moment. He whistled, knowing that the bird would answer this invitation. The next moment the hawk replied with a moribund but greedy screech and sat on his shoulder, so that he could feel the thin feathers against his cheek.

"You've come!" wheezed the old man gratefully.

He removed the bird from his shoulder, took it around the breast in both hands, and began to push it like a shield in the direction of the phantom.

"Here, jump . . . catch hold of it . . . gobble it up!" he panted.

And feeling confident that he was holding a safe weapon in his hands, he drew near the apparition.

But the buzzard, frightened to death and strangling in the old man's fingers, did not jump at the duck, since its eyes could not discern it; and as soon as the old man's grip relaxed, it flung itself on the old man's chest and clung to him desperately, gripping him with its claws.

The old man was so startled by the hawk's abrupt movement that he almost fell on his back: he was only halted by the edge of the bed. Suddenly a voice full of hatred came from his chest: "Go away!" he shouted, and began to tear the buzzard away from his chest. But the bird refused to leave him. The more the old man tried to get rid of it, the more firmly the buzzard clung to him. Finally the old man succeeded in tearing it off, not knowing that the bird's merciless claws had torn away bits of his clothing and flesh.

Relieved of his burden, the birdman took an exhausted and panting breath and leaned against the bed, gazing into the darkness. He was obsessed by a dreadful awareness; he grew stiff, and in spite of his excitement he was in a cold sweat.

"I've lost the battle!" His voice grew silent, calm, sorrowful. He toppled down on the bed and burst into bitter tears.

The hens started to cry with him so bitterly that even the fainting birdman was almost aware of it.

"You, my dear birds, you are crying too, my little creatures, you are crying because of me, because of my miserable, bitter life."

And the birds actually cried.

"The duck, the duck!" he yelled with a last effort, and fell down on his back.

At that moment the duck's apparition disappeared before his eyes. The room resounded with the last screeching of his faithful bird-companions, but he could no longer hear their greeting.

A fortnight later the people from the little town broke into the hovel. The lonely old man had not made his appearance all that time, nor was there any smoke coming out of the chimney. Nobody was worried about this, as there was nothing unusual about it. But it seemed strange to the passers-by that none of the birds' voices could be heard from the hovel, and that was why they finally forced the door.

They saw a dreadful sight: all the furniture was broken into pieces and scattered about the floor, while the floor itself was thickly covered with various kinds of birds' feathers and gnawed white bones. Of all the birds that had for so many years shared that narrow, stinking place with the birdman, all that was left were the two hawks, the owl, and the two crows.

At the foot of the bed, on the bare boards, was the dead birdman, lying on his back. The two hawks were standing, calmly pecking, one from each of the eye sockets. The owl was perched on his chest, deepening an open wound with its beak. The two crows strutted at his sides.

After the birdman's death, the birds were left alone, silently watching their master, who could not move. When they grew ravenous, the hawks began to strangle the other birds, and soon they finished their work. They first attacked the small singing birds, then the forest birds, and finally the hens. When the last scrap was devoured, the carnivorous birds turned to the dead birdman and demolished him, bit by bit.

Translated by Zora Depolo

Luck

As far back as I can remember, the people in our village never concerned themselves much with the question of luck. If they longed for it, they did so secretly, and they did not mention it aloud. Even the word "luck" was used only in connection with bad luck. If someone's barn burned down, the neighbors would say, "He really had luck. It was so windy his house might have been burned to the ground." If someone fell and broke a leg, his friends consoled him and added sagely, "He was lucky. He might have fallen on his head and broken his neck or cracked his skull. Then he would have been killed on the spot."

Luck of this kind visited our village often and distributed her gifts with both hands. I was about seven years old when I experienced this kind of luck for the first time. There were six spinning wheels in our attic, left over from bygone days when grandmother was alive and used to spin. Every Sunday the children from the neighborhood gathered together, climbed up to the attic, and played soldiers there. We were little Garibaldis, Loudons, Radetskys, and other generals we had learned about from our grandfathers' tales and from the book *Our Emperor*, written by the old empire teacher, Josip Apih. We fought great battles, waving our swords, which somehow resembled pea-stakes seen along the edges of the meadows, and spinning the old wheels—our cannon. In one such battle, two of the cannons came too close together and struck each other, and the old worm-eaten wheels were shattered. A piece of one hit me on the forehead and my right eye was adorned with a bloody gash. I began to howl and raced to the stairs. My mother ran to us, and when she saw the mess and the blood on my face, she screamed in terror. She grabbed me and led me to the tap where she carefully washed my face. Fearfully and cautiously, she lifted the bruised skin hanging over my eye. When she saw the eye itself had not been damaged, she clasped her hands, looked heavenward, and cried thankfully, "Thank God and Saint Lucia, he might have been blinded!"

The neighbors came over, wringing their hands and wagging their tongues, and tried to prove to me how lucky I really had been. All afternoon I lay at the back of the barn, underneath the boxwood tree, pressing a compress to the swelling and thinking about the luck still waiting for me. In the evening it came—I was given a sound thrashing "to teach me not to tempt Providence unnecessarily again." The next day my mother lit the stove to bake bread and when the fire was blazing, all our cannons—the spinning wheels—went up in flames.

Luck of any other kind rarely came to us. I do not believe that our people ever knew or heard about the other kind. They did not waste their time talking about luck in love: they got drunk on brandy, cursed and wept, or took it out on their enemies. If someone started wandering gloomily about the streets and fields, sighing unhappily because of the tortures of love or some similar misfortune, the people laughed at him, waved their hands, and said, "Be patient and don't take it too much to heart. Sooner or later luck will come to you too, as Strežek says."

Strežek was a tiny figure of a man whom no one took altogether seriously. Some people even said that the wheels in his head were not turning in the right direction and advised him jokingly to go to the watchmaker's to have them fixed. But Strežek only smiled broadly at such remarks and declared that sooner or later luck would shine on him too.

"God knows why things are as they are," he said, repeating the words of his pious mother.

Strežek's cottage, which was the cleanest house in the parish, was in the center of the village. It was beautifully whitewashed inside and out. The windows gleamed, the floors were scrubbed, and the window boxes bloomed with all kinds of flowers. Strežek's mother looked after the house. She was one of those really miraculous women who know how to make life comfortable on nothing, to make life rich in a small way, as one might say. She had no garden, no farm or fields, yet each year she fattened a pig such as any farmer might be proud to own. Besides that, she raised twelve chickens, six rabbits, and two ducks, which were the only ones of their kind in the village. And she took care of Strežek just as well as she looked after the house. She saw to it that he was well-fed, well-dressed, and clean. She let him go to work as assistant to the road mender so that the workers in the village would not poke fun at him; she took him to country fairs and to Mass on Sundays, as though he were a child; and a child he remained until she passed away.

He had reached the age of forty when it happened. He was left alone and felt lost. He roamed sadly about the village sighing deeply. For a time the peasants pitied him and gave him food. But soon he began to get on their nerves and they tried to convince him he should marry a woman to take the place of his mother, but he only giggled at the idea. Finally he was talked to by two traveling salesmen from the border region near Beneška known as the fat and the thin Matelić brothers. He had a great deal of respect for these two men, who spent the night with the Strežek family whenever their travels took them to the valley of Idrija. Their long cigars and their trade, which they described as "walking after their stomachs," aroused his admiration. The advice they gave him, therefore, seemed worth considering. When they promised to look out for a bride for him, he simply smiled and nodded his head as if to say that he, too, would have luck someday.

So it happened that during Shrovetide of the same year, Strežek married a plump woman, some ten years younger than he, brought to him by the traveling salesmen from the border of Beneška. He was terribly proud of his marriage. He strutted around the village like a cock of the walk, explaining to everyone he met the charms and virtues of his Katarina.

"Didn't I tell you," he would say, "that sooner or later I'd have luck too?"

In the fall Katarina gave birth to a daughter. Right away, people started hinting that the baby was premature, that it did not belong to Strežek but to the traveling salesmen from Beneška, who had been especially persistent in making their rounds in the valley of Idrija that year. These suspicions were confirmed by the traveling salesmen themselves. The slim Matelić brother stood godfather to the child and presented Katarina with several pieces of printed fabric. The stout Matelić, who came two weeks later, gave Strežek some velvet for a pair of trousers. He could not very well be godfather since the child had already been christened. Some claimed that the father of the child was the thin one, others asserted it was the stout one, while Mrs. Uranjkar simply combined both opinions with her long tongue.

"I wouldn't be surprised if they were both the father," she said, loudly blowing her bulbous nose on her colored apron. "Those two rogues wished this piece of luck on Strežek just so they could have a sort of home in our valley."

Strežek was rather upset by the gossip. One day he came home from Mass with his ears ringing with it, and he spoke harshly to Katarina, as he himself admitted later. But she looked at him so sweetly that the tears came to his eyes. From then on he stood at the crib for hours admiring Tinka, who sucked her rosy little fingers and regarded him with tiny, ever so slightly crossed eyes. He smiled down at her and went off to the village, his step youthful, his eyes happy.

"Dear Lord," he murmured to himself, nodding his head, "she's only three months old and already she can smile. Ah, that child will have great luck." And then he smiled gaily in the middle of the deserted afternoon street.

Tinka grew and could raise herself up. She rarely cried, but often laughed with a clear, bell-like sound. Soon she left her crib and went crawling around the house and then toddling out into the street, trotting about the village in her colored skirt with two big red flowers front and back. All day long she chewed chocolates or sucked the candy brought to her by the traveling salesmen from the border of Beneška. When she was six years old, she started going to school. She sat in the first row and kept turning around like a pinwheel in the wind. She did her homework badly and could barely manage arithmetic, but she loved learning rhymes by heart. When the teacher called her name, she would jump quickly to her feet and look him right in the eye, as if she were listening attentively to his questions. But the dimples would soon deepen in her cheeks, hinting that laughter was near. When the teacher asked his questions, followed by the "Well?" with which he encouraged her, she had difficulty in controlling her red lips, which were slowly widening into a hearty smile. But that smile was not quite enough for the gentle schoolmaster, who was otherwise satisfied with very little. He pinched Tinka's curving cheek and said, "Why are you grinning as if God knows what luck has just come to you?"

"Ha, ha, ha," all the children in the class laughed loudly, "she's Strežek's daughter!"

Strežek's "luck" was not unknown to the teacher, so he smiled and forgave her. Tinka also smiled, and sat down.

Unlike Tinka, I was always frightened in school, and for the first three years I cried almost every day. As soon as my name was called, the tears came to my eyes. The teacher, who was an old man and knew a great deal about home remedies and cures, told my father that my crying was a sickness and that was why he did not call my name often.

At the end of the third school year, the dean from Tolmin visited our classroom to see how well we knew our catechism.

He called my name and asked me to recite the creed. I rose and—I do not know how it happened—looked right at the first row where I met Tinka's eyes. She grinned, mockingly wiped her eyes with her rose-colored pinafore, and meowed out loud. The parish priest made a threatening gesture in her direction and whispered something in the ear of the amazed dean. He smiled and nodded. I recited the creed through a flood of tears. During recess, I grabbed Tinka while we were going downstairs. With righteous rage I tugged at her pigtails, mercilessly, and gave her a good beating. The old schoolmaster simply gaped at us silently. That was the first time I fought and the last time I cried in school.

The next day was Sunday. I knelt in front of the altar but my eyes wandered constantly in the direction of the communion rail where the little girls were kneeling. Among them was Tinka in a pretty white dress and a broad-brimmed straw hat with three glass strawberries on the ribbon. Through the stained-glass window the sun's rays broke and scattered, making the three glass strawberries gleam. Our eyes met several times. She dimpled and I blushed. When I left the altar after Mass, the priest in the sacristy struck me over the head with the Bible. My aunt, who was waiting for me in front of the church, pulled my hair and shouted, "What were you gaping at during Mass?"

When she asked me that, for the first time in my life I blushed at something I did not understand. I did not feel her blows or hear her resounding words. In front of the church door stood Tinka, looking at me and smiling. I wished the ground would swallow me up. Next to my aunt was the storekeeper, Pavla, a jolly woman. She liked children and often gave them pieces of candy and joked with them.

"He's in love for sure," she said smiling. "If I'm not mistaken, he was staring at Strežek's daughter all the time. She's going to be his girl."

I reddened and could have screamed with rage. But it was no good—from that day on thoughts of Tinka followed me everywhere. Pavla, the storekeeper, did not keep quiet about the matter, but told everything to my uncle, who, like her, was a great joker. For a few days they all teased me about having a girl; even Mother did so when she was in a good mood.

The next year I attended the morning class at the school. In those days school children were still strictly divided into those who went in the morning and those who went in the afternoon. The former were the "goods," the latter the lowest of the low. The children who were in the morning session were even more strictly separated into "boys" and "girls." This separation of souls was terrible and uncompromising. When we played "Catch" we played apart. Once in a while we pulled one another's hair and I would wrestle with Tinka. I would grab her hair or hands, or seize her round the waist, and it always seemed to me that Tinka liked to fight that way. . . .

And so passed four years of quiet love, expressed in rude words and fierce hostility. I finished school and when I was fourteen years old my father suddenly remembered I "had a good head on my shoulders" and sent me to school in Gorizia.

There I attended high school. Among the other useless things they stuffed into my head was mythology, but I must admit that despite its uselessness it fascinated me. I was slowly maturing, and in *Stories from the Bible* the ones I liked best were those about the forbidden fruit, the drunken Noah and his daughters, and the pure Susanna beset by two lecherous old men while bathing. I liked reading about exciting lives and looking at the statues of naked gods and demi-goddesses. And thus it was that I learned about mythological luck.

"Luck," the professor used to say, "was, in the opinion of some scholars, the daughter of Zeus and the sister of Fate and, in the opinion of others, the daughter of Oceanus and the sister of the three Parcae. She has been portrayed as a maiden standing blindfold on an ever-turning wheel, handing out good and evil at will."

But this interpretation seemed too brief and unsatisfactory to the young professor, who was very learned and self-important, like all professors who had polished off their philosophical studies in four short years during which they learned everything there is to know about the material and the spiritual life. He felt it his duty to take us on short walks through the fields of philosophy. He tried to prove to us that it was necessary to distinguish between various forms of luck and happiness as such; that general happiness was impossible because what was lucky for one man was unlucky for another; that luck also brought evil with it, and so sometimes good luck was really bad luck; happiness as such was an internal harmony, the fulfillment of all wishes; wishes were desires and if all our wishes were fulfilled we would be without desire; desire was happiness, and a man without desire was unhappy . . . and there the professor lost himself somewhere at the obscure crossroads of the spiritual life that he had studied so well. He waved his hands, fidgeted in his chair, and stammered. As we gazed at him coldly, he raised his voice and said that we Slovene barbarians were lucky that a cultured state had liberated us, at such great sacrifice, from the yoke of the Austrian barbarians. My tongue itched and I could barely refrain from asking if this was a case of luck, or of happiness as such.

Then I remembered Strežek, his luck, and Tinka. During the day I strolled deep in thought through the deserted courtyard of the school. At night I lay back on my bed listening to the breathing of my neighbor and made the firm and daring decision to walk out with Tinka during vacation time.

Meanwhile Tinka had grown up. She was a big girl now, with a slender body and well-developed breasts. "Well, and I can say," declared Strežek with a shake of his head when he saw the eyes of young men lighting up as they looked at her, "that child will have luck." And she did.

In the spring the gendarmes fired their old serving woman and cook, Jara. Tinka went to work in their barracks. The old women's tongues grew sharp, but Stržek just shook his head and said, "Well, didn't I tell you? What a piece of luck! She gets thirty lira a month and doesn't have to hire herself out somewhere where she'd dirty her hands. Tinka was not made for heavy work."

During the summer vacation I did not go down into the village often, but stayed chiefly at home. Our house was out of the way, a twenty-minute walk from the village. I was not greatly interested in the affairs of others and they said I was conceited, that I wore "knickerbockers" and went around without a hat. I worked in the fields, sat with my mother, who was ill, and on Sundays I wandered among the willows along the river, sunning myself and fishing.

That was how I met Tinka one day. It was afternoon, and the oblique rays of the sun were beating down on me. I was squatting at the edge of a burning hot sand bar, teasing an eel I had caught and put in a hole, when soft hands covered my eyes. I was taken unaware and wanted to jump up, but the hands held me down firmly. In the throbbing summer stillness I heard first a ringing laugh, and then a low voice that said, "Guess who it is."

The whole thing annoyed me and I tried to break free. But I had to exert almost all my strength, for the hands held me tight, and I felt the warm body of a young girl pressed close to me. The fight lasted quite a long time, both of us breathing hard and struggling on the hot round stones of the sand bar. When I finally freed myself in a fury, Tinka stood before me. She was wearing a short, print skirt and a white silk blouse, out of whose low neckline rose a big carnation. She was breathing deeply and her nostrils quivered; her cheeks were red. She looked me straight in the eyes with her slightly crossed glance and said in a hoarse, soft voice, "Are you angry? I only wanted to ask you how your mother was, and as you were squatting there so nicely, I just couldn't resist taking you by surprise."

Her face started to dimple, hinting at the laughter to follow.

"She isn't well," I told her carelessly, "and you didn't frighten me."

The hint of laughter disappeared.

"That's too bad," she said. "Four years is a long time to be sick. And we haven't seen each other for a long time."

"I haven't been at home. And how are you?"

I stared at her. She felt my gaze like a touch, straightened up, and looked at the deep cut of her blouse.

"This blouse is too tight on me," she said. "And you have grown too. . . . Everything is too tight on me, everything I wear just bursts. . . . When Matelić comes I'll get a new skirt. And a blouse too," she laughed. "I can't sleep at night. I lie on my back and when there is moonlight I leave the house and walk about on the dewy grass." She waited silently to see what I would say. Since I said nothing, she asked, "Do you wrestle at school there in Gorizia the way we used to? I would still wrestle like that if I were going to school."

She drew the carnation from the deep cut of her tight blouse and whirled it in her damp hands. The sun was shining on them and they gleamed with little beads of perspiration, the way grains of sand shine under the noonday sun.

"I'm at the high school there," I said.

Silence.

"That's what I thought. Did you buy those in Gorizia?" She pointed at my swimming trunks with her carnation.

"No, Mother made them for me."

"She can still sew. Yes, I can see now, the trunks are made from an old umbrella. Now we don't swim naked any more."

Again silence.

"I'm going now," she said and took a step backward, beginning to pluck at the carnation.

"And I have to go home to Mother because she's alone," I said, turning to go.

When I looked around after taking a few steps, I saw her jumping slowly from stone to stone, swaying and balancing herself with outspread arms; then she plucked the carnation and the red petals fell on the white, glowing stones like drops of blood left in its tracks by a frightened wounded animal as it flees. The summer stillness throbbed and my heart beat hard and seemed to want to jump into my throat.

That was my last meeting with Tinka.

A few days before I was to leave for Gorizia again in the autumn, there was talk all over town that Tinka was pregnant. People whispered all sorts of queer things and those that ascribed Tinka's state to the gendarmes could be numbered among the good and intelligent. The parish priest spoke of it openly from the pulpit. During the sermon he flourished the Bible in his hands twice, and in a solemn bass voice read the passages about the corruption of the young, the millstone around the neck, and the drowning at the bottom of the sea. The sermon seemed to set the tongues of the village gossips wagging even more. They began counting all the new dresses, blouses, and aprons Tinka had worn that year. To their great surprise, they also established that the visits of the traveling salesmen from Beneška to Strežek's house had doubled, if not tripled, that year. They folded their hands under their aprons, rocked back and forth, and could not, of course, agree as to what had taken place. Mrs. Uranjkar had the last word. She spoke of unheard-of things, about lewd old men, and she referred to the Bible story of Susanna and the two repulsive ancients who sat on her while she was bathing. But the story seemed too remote for her, since no one had been personally acquainted with Susanna or the old men. So she found an example from the valley behind Tolmin and told a true story about a seventy-year-old sinner who lived three hours' walking distance from the rest of the world and had a child by his own daughter: she had seen it with her own eyes.

Tinka gave birth to her child in the late spring. When the midwife came to the house, Strežek fled to the cellar, sat in a corner, and covered his ears. Nevertheless it seemed to him he could still hear the rending cries of the girl in childbirth. Tinka had a daughter, alive and healthy, but an idiot. From her mother she inherited only her small crossed eyes and black hair. Strežek's wife wrung her hands in despair and Strežek wandered sorrowfully through the village. When they asked him about Tinka, he shook his head and said, "Well, she's lucky. She is very young to bear a child. She might have died. It's a real wonder."

There was a lot of talk about Tinka's child, as a birth of that kind was a big event in the village.

"Well, now, luck has smiled on her! Alive, christened, and crazy into the bargain," said Cestar's servant, who was well-known for his venomous tongue. He had taken to drink of late because he himself had had an eye on Tinka.

After that, Tinka's child was called Luck in the village and no one knew her by any other name. No one even mentioned her Christian name.

That summer I spent my vacation with a friend in Brda. I came home only three times and then stayed a few days with my mother. I did not see Tinka at all, but they told me she never left the house and was secretly making ready to go out into the world.

"And what else can she do?" they asked.

In the autumn she disappeared without a word of warning. Even the best gossips learned about her flight only a week later, to their great astonishment.

"Ah, now she will probably have some luck," declared Strežek. "She has suffered so much till now."

But Mrs. Strežek would not be consoled. She was taken with asthma and coughed throughout the whole winter. All the healing herbs of Jera Pajntar and all the medicines and advice of the two traveling salesmen from Beneška did not help her, and in the spring she was gone. Strežek shed a few tears as befitted the occasion, and after the death of his wife he whitewashed the rooms himself and looked after little Luck. He made no money, and indeed what job could he have held with little Luck to take care of, poor fellow? Sometimes he helped the peasants with their work to earn his daily bread. He had to take Luck with him, wrapping her in a white woolen scarf belonging to his late wife. He would set her in the young grass in the spring sun at the edge of the meadow while he worked. When he mowed hay, he placed her in the shade of one of the rare bushes in the field. And actually the peasants showed much more commiseration and goodness of heart than their words indicated. At Christmas Tinka sent some money and Strežek went from house to house showing it to everybody. Oh, now everything was going well with Tinka—that was what she wrote. She had had luck at last. In the spring she would come to visit him.

But Strežek waited in vain. Tinka did not come, either in the spring or in the autumn, though she sent money every month.

Luck grew bigger and bigger. She could stand by herself and she learned to walk. But day by day, she became more and more unruly, and Strežek could hardly manage her. Whenever she could, she ran out into the street, tearing off her clothes, running around the village, butting into people, all the time laughing her cold, empty laugh. Her only human and attractive features were the two little dimples just like Tinka's. Strežek had great difficulty in controlling her, and when he went somewhere he wrapped her in broad bands and tied her to the bed. But that was while she was still little and could not tear them. When she grew bigger, he had to make a coop for her, and with tears in his eyes he locked her in it. His life with Luck was reflected both in his body and in his soul. He withdrew into his shell and became queer. He talked to himself aloud and his hands began to tremble. He was now rather deaf, and when anyone shouted something in his ear, he always mumbled back, "Yes, things are fine now. She has had luck. She is coming back in the spring."

After that I came home and stayed two years, but I used to go down to the neighboring village and not ours. The wealthier people in our place did not approve of my father having sent me to school. Then my mother died, and when I was nineteen I went to jail, where I spent a year passing an examination in survival for the simple reason that I was young and not an Italian. When I was released from prison, on my twentieth birthday, and went to register at the police station, I saw Luck for the first time with my own eyes. It was already dusk and the village was unusually quiet. At the crossroads in the middle of the village crouched a dirty, half-naked, but well-developed child, cooing the way the doves used to coo on the roof of the jail. She was scooping up dust from the street and putting it in her mouth. When she saw me, she jumped up and her jaw dropped, showing me her firm white teeth. Then she grunted and butted into me. So this was Luck. My heart froze. I shook myself free and went off. From Strežek's house, which was no longer the cleanest in the parish, emerged a small, stooped old man who looked at me sadly from lashless, bloodshot eyes. He grabbed the child and disappeared, like animals do with their young.

At home I asked about Tinka and they told me they knew nothing of her whereabouts. Some people in the village declared that she was living in Trieste, others said Milan, and still others, Padua. But no one knew exactly where. She sent money less and less frequently now. In the neighboring parish was a young man who had been in the army in Milan, and he said that Tinka was there "serving the regiment." He himself had been with her because she was not in an expensive house.

Strežek always went on hoping she would return. Whenever she sent him money she promised to come for a visit, and so whenever anyone shouted something in his ear, he repeated over and over again, "Yes, yes, in the spring, yes, yes, she is coming."

The next time I stayed at home only four months and then I escaped across the border, where I had so many troubles of my own that I forgot all about Tinka.

About a week ago I received a long letter from my father. First he excused himself for his long silence, and then he complained about the hard life he led, his oppressive debts, the taxes he could not pay, the interest he could barely meet. The harvest was poor. The potatoes were rotting, although they had been planted in sandy soil. The wheat was full of blight. The cornfields had been flooded. He then went on to say that it was a good and fine thing that I had devoted myself to writing. He was also working for the people; he was teaching them to sing, and had founded an educational society. He was very proud of me, he wrote. He asked nothing of me because he knew that literary bread was so thin that a man could see a church on a far-off hill through it. But still he would be happy if I would send him something once in a while if I could. He was in trouble now because they were threatening to sell his effects at a public auction.

As usual, his letter ended with a chronicle of events in the village.

"Peter's house has burned down and it was not insured. I do not know what he will do. The youngest Venćek set it on fire. Krivec has died unexpectedly. He was still strong although he was seventy years old. All Sunday afternoon he wandered around the woods looking for a bear that had, they say, lost its way from the forest of Trn. In the evening he jumped from the top of the stove and hurt himself in the chest. After that he complained of a pain there. He fell down near his carpenter's bench and died. He left no will. The two Čargo boys are still in jail in Rome. Franz is seriously ill. He has T.B. and they say he will not last long. They cannot send him anything. But why should I write to you about that, you know what it is like in prison.

"And now I have one more startling piece of news for you that caused a great deal of excitement here. You probably remember Strežek's daughter, Tinka, she went to school with you, and your uncle even used to tease you by saying she was your girl. And you remember Luck. Well, both of them are gone now. Luck grew too big and got more and more violent as the days went by. She attacked people and, if she could, scratched and bit them. Too much luck is sometimes bad luck, the old folks say. We can see that is true when we look at the Cestar family. They have as much money as there are stones on the common but they are not happy. The doctor has had his proposals of marriage turned down three times already, and all the girls are still sitting at home although they are nearing forty. But to return to Luck. She was already nine years old and she howled and barked like a dog. It sounds terrible as I write it, but it was even worse to hear. Especially at night. We trembled at the sound. They kept her locked up, but Strežek was so weak that he could no longer control her. The man is old and helpless, and stone deaf as well. They say it is the result of Luck's howling. And he went on waiting for Tinka. When folks yelled in his ear, he laughed and nodded, "Yes, yes, she's coming in the spring. It's time for her to come now. I can't take care of Luck alone any more." And about a month ago she really did come. The old women, who gossiped about her a great deal, were all curious to see her and they visited Strežek's house in a regular procession. But they did not come empty-handed. All of them brought something under their aprons, not because they wanted to give her a gift but because they needed an excuse. They hinted that Tinka already had another piece of luck under her heart. And Mrs. Uranjkar even blurted out something about a repulsive and probably incurable disease that infected women who lived the way Tinka supposedly did. And she was really expecting another baby, as I said before. During the recent flood that carried away part of our farmland, they both disappeared one night. Strežek was stricken by the event. He roamed the streets, stopping everyone, local people and even strangers, shouting at them and asking if they had not seen a young woman with Luck. All of them regarded him in amazement. Poor man, everyone took pity on him. They had to force him to go home, and they could hardly persuade him to eat. It seemed as if he were going mad. Tinka and Luck were found five days later somewhere downriver in Podsela. The water had carried them far away. Tinka's dead body was, they say, quite eaten away. Some parts had been nibbled by fish and Luck's tooth marks were found on others. As I said, Luck was very strong, and when they were drowning she probably clutched at her mother convulsively, biting her. Strežek went to Podsela. They say he came across the two traveling salesmen from the border of Beneška. They purchased a coffin for Tinka and Luck and paid for the funeral. There was no priest. Strežek returned home a beaten man. But he is quieter now, and it looks as if he will get better. Otherwise he has not changed. He even allows himself to be consoled. He nods his head and says humbly, "That was the only luck she ever had, her dying."

Yesterday I wrote my father a long letter in answer to his. I told him about my difficulties and tried to comfort him. Before I sealed the letter I read it once more, and I saw that I had told him to be patient and not allow himself to grieve too much about his hard life, because sooner or later luck comes to all of us.

Translated by Cordia Kveder

CIRIL KOSMAČ

Death of a Simple Giant

The day before, Mata Hotejec had followed his usual custom of throwing rocks to test his strength, strength that still welled up in him even though he was nearing fifty. He always did this at the Domin ridge, half an hour away from the village, near the lonely Temnikar homestead. The day before, during the silent summer noon hour, once again his well-known cry had suddenly echoed through the valley.

"Ho-ooo-hoy!"

"Mata!" yelled the Temnikar children, and ran out of the house.

"Don't go too near!" their mother shouted after them as she churned butter on the porch.

"Only as far as the cherry tree!" promised the children. They raced through the orchard and really did stop under the cherry tree on the slope. From there they had a good view of Domin's ridge, a high rock shelf rising steeply out of the deep water on the other side of the river. Mata was standing straddle-legged on the rock shelf next to a pile of boulders. Picking up one rock after the other, he would raise it high above his head and throw it down into the water with a thunderous yell of "Ho-ooo-hoy!" The children stood silently, watching the white rocks falling with surprising slowness and then loudly hitting the water that foamed and sprayed upward. After Mata had hurled the last one, all of them chorused "Ho-ooo-hoy!" and ran home.

"Ho-ooo-hoy! He's finished throwing them!" they cried. Imitating Mata, they jumped all over the yard to the accompaniment of their mother's usual threats:

"Just you wait, you devils, until Mata sharpens a good, long switch!"

"Ho-ooo-hoy! He'll never get it sharpened!" the children howled in unison, for they knew well the story of Mata's switch.

"Oh yes he will!" said Mrs. Temnikar, pouring the milk into a ten-quart jug. "You won't even see or hear him when he comes. That's the way Mata comes: you don't see him anywhere and when you turn around, there he is, standing on the porch drinking milk."

"Ho-ooo-hoy! He won't come today!" answered the children.

"Why not? He'll be thirsty. He's always thirsty. And he can smell the milk a half hour away."

Mrs. Temnikar took the butter to the cool pantry while the children rushed to the kitchen for ladles to drink the milk with. No sooner had they turned their backs than Mata appeared on the porch. First they saw his gargantuan legs and broad bare feet, the long fat big toes sticking up like two blunt rhinoceros horns. They looked up. Mata really was a giant; the top of his head touched the smoke-blackened roof. He was holding the ten-quart jug to his lips and drinking with a barely audible, stifled gulping. Under his arm was a white switch.

"Mata!" yelled Mrs. Temnikar.

Mata slowly and carefully set the jug down on a box. With the back of his hand he wiped his mustache dripping with milk. Then he put his head to one side, his big clouded eyes blinking, and mumbled pleadingly in a deep voice:

"Anice, I only took a little taste."

"A taste!" Mrs. Temnikar raised a hand. "Now you may as well taste it down to the very bottom. You've messed it all up."

Mata stooped down, his hands on his knees, and peered into the jug. His brownish, tobacco-stained spittle was swimming on top of the milk.

"There, do you see?" asked Mrs. Temnikar.

"I see," admitted Mata, repentance in his tone.

"And you have nothing to say?"

"There's nothing wrong with tobacco. It's healthy for you. . . ." grunted Mata.

"I'll show you how healthy it is!" threatened Mrs. Temnikar, turning aside to hide a smile.

"Are you angry at me?" asked Mata after a short pause.

"Yes, I am angry!" replied Mrs. Temnikar with exaggerated severity. "But so what if I'm angry! Wait till you see how angry the Partisans will be!"

"What?" Mata's big eyes widened.

"That milk was for the Partisans."

"For the Partisans?"

"For the Partisans. Or maybe you think that Partisans don't get thirsty. And what am I to tell them when they come, eh?"

Mata's gigantic bulk stood motionless. His only movements were the blinking of his eyes and his deep breathing. From his broad, flat nose came a whistling sound, and his thick mustache fluttered up and down at equal intervals, moved by the powerful breath.

"So, what should I tell them?" repeated Mrs. Temnikar, spreading her hands out. " 'Mata has already messed up the milk for you,' that's what I'll say."

Mata flinched and reiterated his only excuse:

"But tobacco is healthy, quite healthy. . . ."

Mrs. Temnikar dropped her arms with a sigh. Wiping her face with her apron, she pointed to the jug and ordered curtly:

"Drink it!"

"Drink it!" Mata repeated aloud, and raised a finger as if to fix the command in his memory. Then he grabbed the jug, spread his legs wide apart, and began to drink and drink. The children did not show any particular signs of astonishment because they knew that Mata went from house to house begging for milk and that he could drink as much of it as a thirsty cow could water. But nevertheless they gazed at him with respect and awe. Mata drank more than half. Then he drew the jug from his lips, took a deep breath, looked at Mrs. Temnikar, and asked in a hoarse and frightened voice:

"All of it?"

"Ah, you, you sinful creature, you!" shrieked Mrs. Temnikar, taking the jug from his hands and spilling the rest of the milk into the trough.

Mata wiped his dripping mustache, sighed loudly a few times, whistled through his nose, and asked in a booming voice:

"Anice, are you still angry?"

"Yes, I am!" Mrs. Temnikar shook her head, her lips tight.

"And are you going to tell the Partisans, 'Mata has messed up the milk'?"

"No! I won't say anything to the Partisans."

"Aaah!" Mata heaved a sigh of relief.

"Don't worry about it!"

"Then I don't have to worry about it," repeated Mata as he drew his switch from under his arm.

"Now, then, what about the switch?" asked Mrs. Temnikar in a friendly tone. "Have you finished it yet?"

"No, not yet, not yet!" answered Mata, showing her the hazel switch, a good three feet long and as thick as a thumb. "You see, it is still a bit too thick at this end."

"Well, then, whittle it down some more!"

"That's what I'm going to do."

"But hurry along with it, hurry," said Mrs. Temnikar, who was already wishing she were rid of Mata.

"Hurry!" repeated Mata, and raised a finger to help him memorize the command. He then turned on his bare heel and went silently toward the door. As he bent over to push his enormous body through the doorway, the porch grew dark.

Mata disappeared behind the house. The children ran to the kitchen window and pressed their noses to the pane to see him once again as he went through the orchard. But he did not take the orchard path. Rising about sixty feet from the steep slope was a rather high straight bluff. Mata climbed up on it, sat on the edge, and lowered his long legs into the void, swinging them to and fro a few times to make sure his heels would not knock against the rock. Then he drew some pieces of broken glass from his pocket, selected one that seemed the sharpest, laid his switch across his knees, and began swinging his legs and whittling. The curly white shavings that flew from under his clumsy hands were carried away by the light afternoon breeze and finally fell to the green fields below. Mata became completely absorbed in his work while his broad feet swung in the air as if kicking at something. Actually, it looked as though Mata were not sitting still at all, but sailing over the valley together with the rock he was sitting on. It was a clear, quiet day. Far in the distance, gray, broad-backed Krn Mountain rose motionless. But Mata was even mightier than the mountain, or so it seemed. He shut out the view with his huge body while his head, rising above the mountaintop, swayed against the background of the blue sky. At times that gargantuan head rose to the height of the white clouds themselves. Every once in a while Mata would straighten himself to have a better look at his switch and to ascertain at which end it was "still a little thicker." When he saw which end it was, he stretched. Slowly he raised his arms, shook his fist at the heavens thrice, and waved his arms as an eagle would its wings. In his left hand he held the white switch, and in his right, the piece of broken glass that reflected the sun's rays, making it seem as though lightning were flashing through his fingers. He looked up at the sky and around at the peaks, blew his nose through his fingers, and scratched his bushy mane. While he made these movements the glass glittered in the sunlight so that the flashes of lightning seemed to be coming first from his nose and then from the top of his head.

The Temnikar children stood in the kitchen watching Mata a long time. Little by little they gathered up their courage, left the house, and drew closer and closer to him. Finally they sat down on the grass only a few feet away, watching him whittling without a word. He whittled and whittled, first one end and then the other, until the switch became so thin that it snapped in two. This did not upset Mata at all. He threw the pieces into the bushes, cut off a new switch, first peeled it with his knife, and then began scraping it with the piece of glass.

The sun was setting and shadows descended down the slopes into the valley. A shadow reached Mata and covered him, covered the house, covered the river, and began to spread to the other bank over Modrijan's broad meadow. Evening was drawing near.

Mrs. Temnikar came around the corner of the house and disappeared into the chicken coop. She counted the chickens and then lowered the bolt on the door. Turning toward the slope, she yelled:

"Mata, aren't you going to go to bed?"

"To bed!" thundered Mata. Swiftly he put the piece of glass in his pocket, scrambled down the rock, and descended to the road. The children tagged after him.

"Well, have you finished whittling it?" asked Mrs. Temnikar, pointing to the switch.

"No, not yet, not yet!" Mata shook his head, drawing the switch from under his arm to explain: "You see, it's still a little thicker at one end. . . ."

"It doesn't matter. You'll whittle it down tomorrow," said

Mrs. Temnikar. "But look at your hand! Don't you see it's bloody? You've cut yourself again! Let me see!"

Mata stretched out his hand slowly and showed her his broad, bleeding palm.

"Oh, that's nothing at all," he mumbled. "It always heals up again."

"Of course it heals up," Mrs. Temnikar shook her head. "But that doesn't mean that you should go on cutting yourself."

Mata hid his hand behind his back, tucked the switch back under his arm, and remained standing there.

Mrs. Temnikar remembered what he must be waiting for and asked:

"Do you know where you're to eat tomorrow?"

"No, I don't know yet," answered Mata, hanging his head.

"Where did you eat today?"

"At Jure's on Kobilnik."

"Didn't Jure tell you where you were supposed to go tomorrow?"

"No, he didn't say," Mata shook his head and looked at Mrs. Temnikar expectantly while she held her chin thoughtfully.

"You're to go to Lazne," she said after a moment's hesitation.

"To Lazne," repeated Mata, and raised his finger to memorize the order.

"I'll bet you like to go to Lazne," said Mrs. Temnikar.

"I do like to go there," replied Mata.

"It's really nice there. You can see the whole village below. And you'll have a good meal."

"Yes, I'll have a good meal."

"And then afterward you can sit the whole day long at Laznar's bend and whittle your switch."

"At Laznar's bend," repeated Mata with satisfaction, and raised his finger.

"So now, you may as well go!" Mrs. Temnikar said, looking him up and down as though hoping to spirit him away. But her look had the opposite effect, riveting him to the spot. "Phew, what a fellow you are!" she exclaimed in disgust, and twisted her mouth in revulsion. "Ugly! You're as shaggy as a bear. Even worse. You're as bristly as a porcupine."

"A porcupine?" Mata's eyes bulged as he scratched his beard, which really did consist of straggly, long, hard needles.

"You'll see!" threatened Mrs. Temnikar. "All the girls will run away from you."

"Run away?" trembled Mata.

"Naturally, they'll run away. And you still care about them, don't you?" she asked.

"I still do," mumbled Mata, hanging his head and turning over the gravel on the road with his long blunt toe.

Mrs. Temnikar crossed her arms on her chest as though preparing to continue the conversation and asked:

"And which one has caught your eye now?"

"Tilka Kokošar."

"Oho!" clucked Mrs. Temnikar enthusiastically. "You do have a good eye. Who would ever think you had such a good eye? Tilka is really pretty."

"She is pretty," agreed Mata.

"Are you fond of her?"

"I am fond of her," admitted Mata, and again turned over the gravel on the road with his big toe.

"And what does Tilka say?"

"Nothing. She's going to give me a flower."

"She's going to give you a flower?"

"A sunflower."

"A sunflower?" Mrs. Temnikar clapped her hands. "She's really giving you a sunflower?"

"Yes, a sunflower," Mata answered proudly.

"And when is she going to give it to you?"

Mata grew confused, blinked, looked aside, and then mumbled:

"She didn't say."

"And why don't you go after it yourself? The sunflowers are in bloom right now."

"Old Mrs. Kokošar is angry about it," said Mata, justifying himself.

"She's a crazy old hag!" shouted Mrs. Temnikar, more for her own benefit than Mata's. "Mata, you just go after that sunflower, if Tilka really told you she was going to give you one."

"She did tell me."

"Well, then tomorrow go and get it."

"Should I?" asked Mata, and again scratched his untidy beard.

"Go, when I tell you!" said Mrs. Temnikar. "But first go to Loputnik's and get a shave."

"First go to Loputnik's and get a shave," repeated Mata, and raised his finger to remember.

"And then for the sunflower afterward."

"And then for the sunflower afterward."

"And then to Lazne to eat."

"And then to Lazne."

"That's right. And now off with you. It's time for bed," said Mrs. Temnikar with determination. "And where are you going to sleep?"

"In Plesnikar's hayloft."

"Fine. But mind you don't snore too much," she warned.

"Snore," said Mata blinking. "I never heard myself snore."

"Of course you didn't hear it. If you had, you'd know that you snore like a bear. You snore so loud you might even bring the hayloft down."

"Bring the hayloft down?" Mata's eyes bulged and blinked even more fearfully. "Do you think I shouldn't go into the hayloft?"

"Ah, what a big baby you are," laughed Mrs. Temnikar. "For goodness' sake, of course go into the hayloft. And snore as much as you like, my poor dear. And now good night."

"Good night," repeated Mata, turning and leaping from the road to the bank.

Mrs. Temnikar went into the house while the children remained outside looking after Mata, who was wading into the river. He waded across and got out on the other side, disappearing into the dark thicket. He snatched at the shrubs as though he wanted to reach the sun disappearing over the top of the ridge. He crossed the state road and started climbing along the mown hayfield that spread out like a soft, deep cover in the evening sun.

Before the First World War, around our part of the country you could still hear people say "God's child" or "a child of God." These expressions, which grew up out of the relationships and sentiments of the time, are no longer in use. They have been lost in the vortex of tumultuous modern times that have penetrated even to the remotest spots, turning human relations inside out and inciting new passions, carrying away forever from human speech the expressions that have dried up for lack of the juice of life. The expression "God's child" was sometimes used to designate an illegitimate child because it had been "God-given," meaning that no one knew who the real father was. "Child of God" was used to describe the wretches who were born with a clouded mind and who later, when they grew up, were not dangerous enough to be sent to an asylum, remaining little children and living out their lives quietly.

Mata Hotejec was both "God's child" and "a child of God," therefore a "God's child of God" because he had been both "God-given" and had been born with a cloud over his mind, remaining childlike until his death.

Actually, Mata's name was not Hotejec but Lužnik. Pepa Lužnik had brought him, still unborn, from Egypt where she had served in the homes of the rich, or so her mother claimed. Old Mrs. Lužnik was a lazy, sloppy, malicious crone. She lived alone in a tumbledown shack and eked out a living by working from time to time as a charwoman and by making frequent visits to homes in the village. All the livelong day she would wag her tongue in one village home after another and get a good meal in the bargain. Coming home in the evening, she would lock up her three chickens, brew a pot of coffee, sit on the doorstep, and drink it noisily. Taking a bit of snuff, she would remain seated in the soft, quiet darkness to get her breath back after the whole day's gossiping. Slowly and sensuously the sharp teeth of her malice would digest in peace the intrigues she had swallowed in a hurry during the day. She would then select the house she would visit the next day, gaze at the evening stars, sigh contentedly at a day's work done, rise, bolt the door, go into the shack, lie down, sigh again, and mumble a prayer for a peaceful night. Then she would fall asleep and sleep soundly, at peace with God. She lived thus well and quietly, so it was quite natural that she did not feel too happy about the return of her Pepa when the latter waddled up to the hut one evening. A sharp glance over the bloated body of her illegitimate daughter, whom she had not seen for seven years, told her all she had to know, and she greeted her daughter thus:

"Well, you haven't sent me a farthing, so I thought that one day you'd turn up yourself and bring me what you had earned."

"And you haven't waited in vain. I've brought you all that I've earned!" retorted Pepa quickly, proving herself her mother's true daughter.

Old Mrs. Lužnik did not expect such an answer. She was silent for a moment, wondering whether to choose another approach. Instinct, however, told her she was now on an equal footing with her daughter so she thought it best to continue in the same vein.

"That you could have earned at home just as well," she spat out scornfully. "For that you really didn't have to go to Egypt."

"Right you are," agreed the daughter in a flash. "That type of thing is not lacking at home either."

"You seem to have lacked it if you had to go dragging yourself all over the world for it."

"So what, so I lacked it," shrugged Pepa.

"I see that among the big shots everything goes in a big way. They even do their sinning in a big way."

"Nobody is stingy with that type of thing, even in shacks. You weren't stingy with it. If you had been, I never would have seen the light of day."

"Is that so?" old Mrs. Lužnik raised her head and gave her daughter a sharp look. "So you want to start that, do you?"

"No, I want to finish it," answered Pepa decisively. "I'll have the child and then go back to Egypt to work as a wet nurse. I'll earn more and I'll be able to send you more so that you can take care of the child."

"You'll send me fiddlesticks," burst out her mother, waving a pot in the air.

"Well, then, fiddlesticks," shrugged Pepa.

Mrs. Lužnik did not answer. The conversation was over. Pepa bent down and picked up her bundle. Her mother took some snuff and silently moved to the side of the doorstep, drawing up her knees. Pepa passed by her mother without a word and went into the shack, put down her bundle, and began making the bed.

Less than two months later Pepa gave birth. The women waited impatiently for the midwife, Polona, to come back from Luža where Mrs. Lužnik lived. When she arrived in the village, they gathered around her asking:

"Well, what was in the cards?"

"A boy."

"A boy . . . what's he like?"

Polona was quiet at first. She looked up at the sky with her sly gray eyes, shrugged her shoulders, and answered brusquely:

"Like that . . ."

The answer encouraged the women to ask about his color.

"Is he . . . black?" they queried.

"No, he isn't black," said Polona, nodding her tiny head. "But he is a little dark."

"A little dark," slowly reiterated the women, looking at each other in disappointment—or wasn't Egypt in Africa and didn't blacks live in Africa and shouldn't the child therefore be black?

"He's like what he's like," Polona gestured. She smoothed out her apron and sighed deeply:

"Well, we've got one more Arnejc!"

"So that's it," the women said. "Has Arnejc Hotejec ever been in Luža?"

"No, he hasn't. But he'll go, don't worry."

Jernej Hotejec, or Arnejc, as he was called, was a rather wealthy and good-natured middle-aged peasant. He had had no offspring of his own and so took to acting as godfather to almost all the illegitimate children in the neighborhood. He never waited to be asked, but offered his services himself. The unfortunate mothers would then repay his goodness by giving the children his name. This had become so much the custom that in the village they no longer used the word "illegitimate child" or "bastard," but said "Arnejc" instead. Old Mrs. Lužnik, however, would not have been herself had she followed the custom and thus showed even a grain of gratitude. When Mr. and Mrs. Hotejec came to take the baby for christening and asked what name to give him, she flung over her shoulder:

"Why ask? You know as well as I do!"

Although Hotejec had expected a tongue-lashing from Mrs. Lužnik, the words nevertheless made him uneasy. He scowled and said:

"You say what name it should be."

"Don't think I won't. You know very well all such orphans have your name. All of them are called Arnejc."

"I never asked for it."

"Whether you asked for it or not, I can tell you I think all your goodness is not worth a bag of beans," she hissed venomously.

"Arnejc, let's leave the child and go," said Mrs. Hotejec who, probably because of her own barrenness, was timid and, in contrast to her determined husband, rarely opened her mouth.

"What are you talking about? This has nothing to do with the child," said Hotejec, giving his wife a reprimanding look and taking the baby from her arms. He turned to Mrs. Lužnik and said sharply:

"Bag of beans or not, that is my affair. It's your business to choose a name for the child."

"I know it's my business but I'm not going to do it," burst out Mrs. Lužnik. "Let the parish priest look up a name in his calendar."

Some of the parish priests in those days used to select names for illegitimate children according to their own inclination, to say nothing of their malice. When the parish priest heard that the child was not going to be named after Jernej Hotejec, and that no one at home had chosen a name for him, he opened his calendar with satisfaction and began to thumb the pages searching for something "suitable" for the child, but also for Mrs. Lužnik, who had been a fly in his ointment for some time now. He kept on turning the pages of the calendar, smiling with malice all the while, until Hotejec began to boil with rage.

"Stop turning those pages," he said savagely. "Although the child is from Luža, and may be part Egyptian, or so they say, you're not going to stick any old name on him. Today is St. Matija's Day, so let his name be Matija."

"Right! Why look any further? Let his name be Matija!" the cunning parish priest quickly agreed, for he knew that an argument with this well-to-do peasant could cost him something when he went around making his collection.

So they christened the child Matija, which meant that by custom he would be called Mata. Pepa stayed with him only a month and then returned to Egypt and never sent either money or letters. While she was still at home, the women neighbors had not come to visit her at Luža. The minute she arrived she had shut herself up and stated in no uncertain terms that "she did not wish to see a living soul and especially none of the female sex." So the women waited until she had left and then went to Luža to see the "little Egyptian." The child was not black at all and, truth to tell, could hardly even be called dark. If the women had not known that Pepa had brought him back with her from Egypt, they would probably never have claimed that his skin was "just a little dark" or his lips "just a trifle thick" or his nose "just a bit flat" or his forehead "just a mite low." His eyes were blue and very large so that the women turned to Mrs. Lužnik exclaiming loudly:

"He has the Lužnik eyes."

"Not only Lužnik eyes but Luža eyes," retorted Mrs. Lužnik in such an odd tone of voice that the women stared and asked:

"What do you mean, Luža eyes?"

"Why pretend?" she burst out. "You can see very well that there is no light in his eyes."

"What? No light in his eyes?" slowly repeated the women and observed the child again.

"Really, his eyes do seem a bit clouded," Mrs. Vogrič was the first to admit.

"Yes, I'd say so too," nodded Mrs. Zagrič.

"You think so?" protected Mrs. Usadar. "That's probably only because his skin is a little darker."

"You crazy women, you. You know that light shows up even more in the dark," replied Mrs. Lužnik scornfully. "His eyes are not clear and that's all there is to it," she snapped. "Anyway," she added in her venomous, provoking tone, "how could he have clear eyes when he's from Luža?"

"Oh, now why say that?" Mrs. Usadar continued, protesting. "The child does not even see yet. When he begins to see, his eyes will clear up."

"Like the devil they will," again snapped Mrs. Lužnik, waving an arm and adding with the same venomous scorn, "In any case, the crazier he is, the easier he'll live."

"Well, that's the truth," the women agreed with a sigh, and began lamenting the trials and tribulations that constantly embittered the life of the average man.

Mrs. Lužnik went to her char duties rarely now, but paid more and more frequent visits to various village homes. Now she not only had a meal herself but collected food for Mata as well—"for that unfortunate worm who would eat day and night if he could." The women were more than generous with her so that she was able to bring up the child. She took care of him after a fashion but she did not bend over backwards to do so. The truth is that she fed him rather poorly and then prayed to God to take the child unto Himself, as it would be better for him that way and even better for that "rat" Pepa if she ever came back.

But Mata would not die. He lived on and grew. He spent his first two years rolling about in his cradle. Old Mrs. Lužnik did not want to take him out into the sun because she half hoped that he would slowly wither away in the semidarkness and the room's stifling air. But Mata did not wither away. On the contrary, one day he rolled himself out of the cradle and onto the threshold of the hut.

"Go on, stay there if you like!" rasped old Mrs. Lužnik, hoping that if death had not come for him in the hut it might do so outside. But death, although passing by the hut every day, did not take Mata from the front doorstep. He neither rolled down the steep slope nor drowned in a puddle nor caught any disease. Every night when she came back from her visiting, old Mrs. Lužnik found him on the threshold, alive and healthy.

"Death doesn't want you, it seems," she would throw out at him.

"Theems, theems," lisped Mata in repetition, blinking his big cloudy eyes with fright.

"It just doesn't want you, it doesn't!" concluded old Mrs. Lužnik vehemently, dragging him into the hut to feed him.

Mata ate and slept, lived and grew. He began to walk by himself, but naturally did not begin to talk. This, however, did not seem too strange—even if he had not been mentally defective, he could not have learned to talk, being alone all day as he was and having no one to talk to him. At night his grandmother only grumbled and snapped.

From time to time the women remembered the unfortunate tyke.

"Well, is he getting any better?" they would ask.

"How can he get better in Luža?" the grandmother retorted scornfully.

"And growing, is he growing?"

"Why shouldn't he grow? He's living in Luža, and 'luža' means swamp. So he gets plenty of moisture to grow on."

And Mata really was growing like a swamp reed. When his grandmother finally came to the conclusion that God was not thinking of taking the child unto Himself at all, she began taking him with her on her visits. In the homes of others Mata heard laughter for the first time and slowly began learning how to talk. His grandmother dragged him from house to house and instructed him in what he should say in each one. Like the sly old crone she was, she knew that her health would fail some day and hoped that Mata would at least have enough sense to go scrounging about the village and bring her something to eat.

She never had a chance to see whether he would have the sense or not, for she caught pneumonia and never rose from her bed again. Mata was then fifteen years old but he had the mind of a small child. He went from house to house by himself but this was not so easy now. While he was with his grandmother, the village urchins had left him alone, but now they attacked him from all sides. They chased him with switches, howling:

"Egyptian!"

"Nigger!"

"African!"

"Turk from Luža!"

Mata ran away from them as fast as his legs could carry him, but one day he fought back.

The village urchins surrounded him at the watering trough and began throwing mud at him. Mata ran to and fro for a long time to try to get out of the circle and then backed up against the trough, waving his arms and defending himself as best as he knew how. First he laughed, then his big cloudy eyes started blinking with fright. The children were coming closer, pricking him with the switches and teasing him:

"Here, take it!"

"Hold it!"

"Hold it if you dare!"

"Take it and hit me!"

"Hold it, you swamp rat!"

"Hit with it!"

"I dare you! I dare you!"

Mata defended himself for a long time and then all of a sudden leaped, grabbed the stick from one of the boys, and hit him with all his might across the back. After that he began hitting out furiously at everyone. The children let out a savage cry and scattered in all directions. One of the men nearby, Ustinar, who was bringing his cattle to the trough, ran toward Mata, grabbed him, and started pummeling and kicking him. Hotejec, who happened to be passing, intervened immediately. He extracted Mata from the grip of the other man and said sharply:

"Have you lost your mind?"

"Lost my mind?" yelled Ustinar. "That lunatic has lost his mind! He went wild for no reason at all and almost killed my child!"

Mata instinctively drew closer to Hotejec, trembling like a leaf. He was so frightened he could not even wipe the mud from his face.

Hotejec took the stick, broke it over his knee with a snap, showed both ends to Mata, and threatened him in severe tones:

"Mata, don't let me see you hitting anyone again!"

"Hitting anyone again!" repeated Mata, raising his finger to help him memorize the command.

Hotejec threw the stick into the bushes, turned to Ustinar, and asked:

"Who threw mud at him?"

"Why do you ask that?" rasped Ustinar. "Boys will be boys."

"That may be so, but Mata is a child of God!"

"He's a beast, and not a child of God!"

"Even a beast defends itself! You ought to know that by now. And there is something else you ought to know. The man who beats a lunatic is not very bright himself!"

"There you go again, acting the wise guy!" burst out Ustinar. "Anyway, what do you care about Mata? Could it be that he is a Hotejec?"

Hotejec fell silent, and then said seriously and determinedly:

"So be it, Mata, from today onward, you can consider yourself a Hotejec."

And so it was. Hotejec looked after the child so well that soon everyone began calling him Mata Hotejec. No one touched him again, nor did Mata ever hit anyone again. Hotejec tried to teach him to work, but his efforts were in vain. Mata was not only incapable of doing any work but could not stay in any one place for long because he had been so accustomed to going from house to house for years. The peasants decided among themselves that Mata could live the way the district beggars of the time lived, going from one house to the next. But since Mata could not read the house numbers, whenever he ate in one house the master of the household would tell him where to go the next day. Mata would go, eat his fill, and then hang around the village. His favorite pastime was sitting next to old Vogrič, the shepherd, watching him for hours and whittling and carving all kinds of sticks and whips. The shepherd, who was deaf, paid no attention to him, chewed his tobacco, spat the brown sputum all around him, and loudly praised his own work.

Mata was obsessed by this whittling. One day, Hotejec found him at the Laznar bend. He was sitting on a high stone fence, swinging his long legs, chewing tobacco, deeply immersed in what he was doing. He had taken a piece of broken glass and was whittling a switch a yard long and as thick as a thumb.

"Mata, what are you whittling?" asked Hotejec in surprise, for he had never seen Mata doing anything with interest before.

"A switch!" answered Mata brusquely.

"So," nodded Hotejec. "And will anything come of it?"

"It will," answered Mata, and showed him the switch. "You see, this end is still a little thicker."

"Yes, you'll have to whittle it down a bit more."

"Have to whittle it down a bit more!" repeated Mata. Then he closed his left eye, looked down along the switch, spat, nodded his head, and said: "You see, again this end is a bit thicker."

"Yes, yes, but it doesn't matter, you'll whittle it down some more."

"Whittle it down some more," repeated Mata, and went on whittling, closing one eye, looking down the switch, and nodding. "You see, now again this end is a little thicker."

"Well, it seems that one end is always a little thicker."

"Always a little thicker," concluded Mata, and began whittling again.

"Who taught you that?" asked Hotejec.

"Old man Vogrič."

"Yes, yes, I see," nodded Hotejec, looking at Mata whittling the switch first at one end and then the other so that the shavings flew. The switch got thinner and thinner and finally broke in his hands. Mata quickly threw away both ends, leaped to the bushes, cut off another switch, peeled it with his knife, and again began whittling it with the piece of glass.

"So, so," nodded Hotejec thoughtfully. "Mata, you just go on whittling. When it's finished, bring it to us to see."

That night Mata came to Hotejec not with a finished switch but with a gaping cut on his palm. He was blinking with fear and looking at the thick blood oozing from his big fingers.

"I'm going to die," he sighed.

"Did you cut yourself with the knife?" asked Hotejec.

"With the knife."

Hotejec examined the cut and then laughed carelessly.

"It's nothing, Mata."

"It's nothing," Mata sighed deeply.

"Nothing at all," confirmed Hotejec, washing out Mata's cut with brandy and bandaging his hand. "Don't worry, the skin is not like a shirt."

"The skin is not like a shirt," repeated Mata.

"No, it's not like a shirt. Skin always heals by itself, and a shirt won't."

"A shirt won't," repeated Mata.

"No, a shirt won't. Ever. And trousers won't heal either. Or shoes. That's the way it is. When they get torn, or cut, they're no longer good for anything."

"No longer good for anything."

"That's right. You can throw them on the garbage heap."

"You can throw them on the garbage heap," repeated Mata, blinking.

"That's the way it is," nodded Hotejec. "But you can always use your skin. It heals by itself. So you don't need to worry. You'll be able to whittle your switches again."

"Whittle your switches again," happily repeated Mata, and left. He cut off a switch from the bushes behind the barn and set off for the village.

The next morning Ustinar and Vogrič brought Mata back minus his shirt and trousers.

"Now what's happened?" asked Hotejec in astonishment.

"How do we know?" answered the peasants. "That's the way he was wandering along the road. If we understood him right, he threw his trousers and shirt on a garbage heap because, he says, they're good for nothing because they're torn and won't ever heal up."

"So that's it," nodded Hotejec.

"Well, now you show him that his trousers are still good even if they won't sew themselves up," said the peasants. "We're not the ones who put these ideas into his head so don't you act smart or think we're fools. And another thing. This Mata has to be taught a lesson. You teach it to him, with a whip or without it, but he's not to go around the village naked any more. He's too big a rascal for that."

"All right, all right. I'll explain it to him," said Hotejec, and dragged Mata off to the house. He knew very well he himself was to blame, so he did not take the whip to Mata. First he dressed him and then tried various ways of explaining to him with threats that he must not go about undressed.

"You must always have your trousers and shirt on," he said severely, shaking a finger at Mata. "Always."

"Always!" repeated the frightened Mata, blinking.

"If you get undressed once more and throw your rags on the garbage heap, the policemen will catch you and take you to jail."

"Catch you and take you to jail," Mata blinked while repeating, his fright increasing.

"Yes, that's right. And they'll take your knife away from you."

"Take your knife away from you." Mata suddenly thrust his hand into his pocket.

"And you'll never see it again. And then tell me—how will you be able to whittle your switch?"

Mata was so frightened that he did not even repeat Hotejec's words.

"So you see, that's why you must always wear a shirt and trousers," concluded Hotejec. "Always, both day and night."

"And night," repeated Mata, and raised a finger to memorize the order.

And he really did remember. Never again did he come into the village undressed. Even at night he kept his shirt and trousers on and behaved properly. He sat about on the rocks or fences and whittled his switch, going from house to house, eating and growing until he had reached gigantic proportions. He would stop in front of women, swallowing them with his eyes, smiling softly and breathing loudly. The young girls gave him a wide berth if they happened to come upon him while alone. If there were more than one, they joked with him.

"They say you're going to marry Katra," they would tease.

"Katra?" Mata gaped in astonishment.

"Don't you like her?"

"No," he would answer right away.

"Why?"

"Katra is ugly."

"And you're handsome. But you would be even more handsome if you didn't let your beard get so shaggy."

"Get so shaggy?" repeated Mata, scratching his thin, curling beard.

"You really could start shaving, you know."

"Shaving?" blinked Mata in surprise.

"Naturally, but not by yourself. You might cut yourself. Go to Loputnik and ask him to shave you."

"To Loputnik to shave you," said Mata, raising a finger and taking off in the direction of Loputnik's house. Loputnik was a shoemaker but he also worked as a barber, meaning that he cut hair and shaved invalids, the sick, and the dead.

The girls were only joking with the harmless giant, but the wandering Katra, a clumsy forty-year-old woman who was a little mad herself, really feared him. From day to day, from dawn until dusk, she waddled along cart roads and village paths carrying her baskets from one lonely homestead to another, buying eggs, butter, and chickens. In the village she had angry exchanges with the girls who had been trying to persuade Mata to marry her. But on the lonely roads she would often tremble for fear that Mata might assault her.

"Whenever he sees me sees me, he always stops me stops me, and looks at me looks at me," she complained to Hotejec, tears in her eyes. Her way of talking was to repeat half the words in every sentence.

"I've heard, I've heard that he has an eye on you," said Hotejec, who liked to joke with Katra.

"That means that you heard him, you heard him," nodded the clumsy peddler woman. "He looks at me looks at me like a crazy ox."

"Really, Katra, you've nothing to fear," laughed Hotejec, waving an arm. "An ox isn't dangerous. Especially not a crazy one."

"What are you saying, you saying—he's not dangerous," the peddler woman said slowly, insulted, her swollen, watery eyes popping. "You you can laugh since you're not a woman you. If you were a woman were, you'd also tremble."

"Of course I'd tremble," nodded Hotejec. "Every real woman trembles a little."

"I don't tremble a little a little," groaned Katra. "I tremble all over I."

"Well, that's going a bit too far," laughed Hotejec.

"Nothing is going too far nothing," Katra rebelled, offended again. "I tremble from head to foot head to foot, and you would tremble if he attacked you you."

"Attacked?" Hotejec asked.

"And he attacked me me," said Katra tearfully, bending and taking up her apron with her hands.

"Who attacked you?" asked Hotejec seriously.

"Mata attacked me attacked me," said Katra slowly, raising her apron.

"What?" Hotejec straightened. "And just when did he attack you?"

Katra did not reply, but bent even lower and began wiping her swollen watery eyes with her apron.

"Where did he attack you?" asked Hotejec severely.

Katra was silent, bent down again, and blew her nose loudly in her underskirt.

"Why are you trumpeting with that nose of yours? Open your trap!" yelled Hotejec. "Are you lying?"

"No, I'm not lying at all at all!" answered Katra, taking offense. "He assaulted me in Žlebe in Žlebe—I was passing by Štruklj's hayloft, I was already past it past it, and turned around

around and saw him saw him. He was standing under the roof and giggling. . . ."

"And he rushed at you?"

"He rushed. . . . I began to run, and I heard him yell 'Ho-ooo-hoy,' and he ran out from under the roof under the roof. I ran myself myself but couldn't seem to get away. My feet were like were like lead. . . . And he was already after me after me and was already breathing down my neck breathing. . . ."

"And he grabbed you?"

Katra did not reply, only nodded her head and wiped her swollen bleary eyes.

"So," Hotejec breathed a sigh of relief. "That means that he didn't grab you."

"He didn't grab me," admitted Katra, and added, "but he would have grabbed me would have if I hadn't awakened from fear. . . ."

"What?" Hotejec gave a start. "Awakened? What are you talking about?"

Katra sucked in her breath audibly and then said quite slowly:

"But he didn't really assault me assault me. . . . I only dreamed that he did he did . . . and I was all wet with sweat wet when I woke up. . . ."

Hotejec's mouth grew taut as he rolled his eyes upward. He bit his mustache and looked at the mad woman, for he really did not know whether to burst into rage or laugh.

"Why are you looking at me like that like that?" asked the peddler woman fearfully.

"You nitwit! Is Mata to blame if you dream of these things?"

"Why isn't he to blame to blame?" Katra was offended again and her swollen, bleary eyes seemed about to pop from their sockets. "If I wasn't afraid of him afraid, he wouldn't pursue me pursue me in my sleep."

Hotejec was silent, thought a while, then nodded his head:

"You crazy woman you, from your point of view, you're right."

"There, you see you see. Are you going to teach him teach him a lesson now?"

Hotejec was thinking and did not answer.

"If you're not going to teach him a lesson a lesson, I'll go to the police go to," threatened Katra.

"You nitwit!" Hotejec leaped up. "I knew you were batty, but that you were quite as dim-witted as all that I couldn't imagine."

"I may be dim-witted, but I am a woman a woman. . . ." Again the weeping woman took offense and blew her nose with gusto. Then she took up her bundle and again threatened: "I'll go to the police go."

"Get along with you! Go on!" said Hotejec as if bored. He wanted to be rid of her and to have some peace to think the matter over. Katra was, after all, only Katra, and her empty babbling was just that and nothing more. But other normal women had discussed this with Hotejec a number of times, women who were afraid that Mata's blood might reach boiling point someday and that he might go berserk. So, they claimed, it was necessary to put the fear of God into him before an accident happened. Hotejec usually laughed and calmed them down because he considered Mata a child. He even thought it would not be a good idea to call Mata's attention to these matters. And yet he knew that nature, being what it was, would ask its due. Often he had racked his brains wondering how to tell Mata these things.

But before he could give him a lecture, an accident happened that was, truth to tell, no misfortune at all. Nevertheless it served to teach Mata a lesson. Brandy was being made at the Robar homestead and the young men there got Mata drunk "for a joke" and then sent him off to Katra "to flirt." The drunken giant wended his way to the peddler woman's home. When she saw him, she flew out of the house and began yelling at the top of her lungs.

"Oh, Holy Mary, oh, purest Virgin, Mata is Mata is . . ."

People gathered around her immediately to hear what had happened but it turned out that Mata had merely "dragged himself to her hut, giggled, breathed heavily, and looked at her like a moonstruck calf."

"And just for that you're howling as though you were being flayed alive?" Ustinar burst out.

"You'd howl howl if you were a woman were," said Katra, bridling. "And what would have happened have happened if I had not had not fled, eh? I could have been a martyr now."

"But since you escaped, you aren't," retorted Ustinar, who had a sharp and poisonous tongue. "See now what a dumbbell you are. You've lost such a wonderful chance to become a saint! Maybe they'd even put your picture in the calendar. A fat woman with two baskets: St. Katra, virgin and martyr, patron saint of the peddlers."

The men laughed derisively. Katra's eyes bulged and in her excitement and anger she could not find the words she wanted. The women, however, started discussing the case seriously and wondered what would have happened if Katra had not run off. They put up such a fuss that the policemen had to search out the unhappy Mata, drag him off to jail, douse him with cold water, and throw him into a cell.

Hotejec was satisfied with this cloud that had a silver lining. First he went to the Robar house and gave them all a piece of his mind. Then for two days he cooled his heels in the jailhouse office until he managed to get Mata released.

The harmless giant was so frightened and so hungry that he shook like a leaf. Hotejec took him home, gave him a good meal, and then a lecture.

"Mata, you're never to drink brandy again!" he ordered sternly, striking the table with his bony hand.

Mata winced but raised his finger and repeated, trembling like a frightened child:

"Never drink brandy again!"

"If you even so much as taste it, the police will shut you up in jail again."

"Shut up in jail again . . . ," repeated Mata, shaking.

"That's right!" confirmed Hotejec. "So watch out! Brandy isn't for you. You're a child—drink milk!"

"Drink milk," repeated Mata, raising his finger to memorize the order.

"And you're never to go to Katra again!" said Hotejec, pounding his fist on the table.

Mata seemed to reel. He opened his big cloudy eyes wide.

"Never go to Katra's again," he repeated, frightened. He obviously did not even recall his visit to the peddler woman but in spite of this he raised his finger to remember this order, too.

"And you're never to touch any woman! Even like this!" said Hotejec sharply, touching Mata's hand with his forefinger.

"Not even like this," repeated Mata, blinking and raising his finger.

"If you even so much as touch one, the police will shut you up in jail and give you a sound thrashing."

"A thrashing," trembled Mata.

"And not only a thrashing. They'll kill you."

"Kill you!" Mata shrank back in terror.

"They'll kill you," said Hotejec. "So watch out. Don't be a fool. Drink milk and whittle your switch."

"Whittle your switch," repeated Mata. He thrust his hand into his pocket and groaned.

"What's the matter?" asked Hotejec.

"I don't have my knife," said Mata desperately.

"You see. Didn't I tell you they'd take your knife away?"

Mata only blinked and sat still with a downcast look.

Hotejec went into the kitchen and returned with an old penknife that he gave to Mata, who grasped it eagerly and examined with true childlike curiosity.

In the meantime Hotejec was gazing thoughtfully at the

harmless giant. He looked at his bare feet with their enormous big toes sticking up like blunt horns, at the long legs, the huge trunk, and finally at the large head planted firmly on the thick neck.

"Ah, Mata, Mata," he sighed. "How did a mountain like you ever choose such an easy job for himself? You should be moving boulders around."

"Boulders around," repeated Mata by habit, still examining the knife.

Hotejec grabbed him by the shoulders, shook him, looked into his big, bleary eyes, and said seriously and slowly:

"You know, Mata, you ought to go to the Domin ridge once in a while."

"To the Domin ridge," repeated Mata, blinking.

"And all day long carry the boulders from the river bank to the road."

"From the river bank to the road."

"And at night throw all the boulders into the whirlpool."

"All the boulders into the whirlpool!" Mata wagged his head with obvious satisfaction and raised a finger to memorize the command.

The next day he set out for the Domin ridge and did exactly what Hotejec had told him to do. All day long he carried boulders from the river bank to the road that was cut into the rock about fifty yards above the water. In the evening, yelling "Ho-ooo-hoy!" he would throw all the boulders down into the river below.

And that was how Mata overcame the last temptation worth mentioning. Hotejec knew that he would be quieter and wiser now. He never tasted brandy again but drank milk the way an alcoholic drinks liquor. He would glide secretively into a house and many a housewife would find traces of his tobacco-stained spittle in her milk afterward. In the beginning some of them complained about it to Hotejec, but they stopped when that good man said, after listening to their story:

"My dear woman, if you resent his taking a bit of milk, why, just lock it up!"

Mata never touched a woman and especially avoided Katra. The girls, who were still fond of teasing the harmless giant, had to do a good deal of persuading to even get him to talk to them again in the fields. Now they no longer teased him about Katra, but discussed all the girls one by one and decided that the prettiest was to be his girl.

Mata then went to have a look at the prettiest girl who had been chosen for him and, if she had her wits about her, she usually gave him a flower. When she got married, Mata did not mourn very much because the girls would select another sweetheart for him, again the prettiest, of course. This became such a custom that when a young girl started flowering into a beauty, the village people no longer said, as of old, that the tidings of her beauty would reach nine hills away, but that she would be Mata's sweetheart.

Mata was peaceful and happy. He continued going from house to house, sitting on the rocks, whittling his switches, and tirelessly swinging his legs as though sailing back and forth over the green valley. Sometimes he would visit his sweetheart to get a flower. Once a week he went to the Domin ridge to carry the heavy boulders from the bank to the path and then throw them into the river.

Thus he lived another twenty years until the day of his death.

The summer morning had already spread out through the valley when Mata woke up in Plesnikar's hayloft after sleeping long and soundly. He pulled his long body out of the hay with a feeling of satisfaction, stood up, and went out on the porch to stretch his arms and legs that had had a good rest but were still stiff from the loads of heavy boulders. After stretching, he spread out his arms, yelled "Ho-ooo-hoy!" and jumped from the porch to the grass. He blew his nose and thrust his hand inside his shirt to scratch his back. But since he could not reach the place that itched, he went up to an apple tree and gave himself such a hard scratching on the rough tree bark that the dew fell from the tree, sprinkling him. This felt so nice that he smiled and looked gratefully upward into the green branches spreading out above him. He gazed at them, blinking his big clouded eyes, once again scratched himself against the tree, and was again sprinkled with dew. He snorted with satisfaction, wiped his face with his broad hand, and looked into the valley to see what the weather would be like. The morning mist was already disappearing, the sky was clear. Krn Mountain blazed under the first rays of the sun. Mata again snorted with delight, stood up straight, and, with his finger raised, repeated Hotejec's order in severe tones:

"And give yourself a wash every morning, do you hear?"

"Hear," he nodded humbly and went off toward the river. A few steps from the bank he stopped and stared into the water's rippling surface. He saw a distorted image of his face that spread out one minute and narrowed down the next, making Mata laugh first and then cry. But then he smiled again, for it was not like him to cry. He bent down and started splashing water into his face. After he had had a good splash, he straightened up, raised a finger, and seriously acted out last night's conversation with Mrs. Temnikar.

"Go to Loputnik tomorrow so he can give you a shave," she had said strictly.

"To Loputnik's to get a shave," he repeated, and felt a pleasant shiver run up and down his spine at the thought of how Loputnik's bristly brush would tickle him. Then he grew serious again and said in the same severe tone:

"And only then can you go to Tilka's to get the sunflower."

"And only then can you go to Tilka's to get the sunflower," he repeated, lowering his eyes bashfully.

"You will lunch at Lazne."

"You will lunch at Lazne."

"And you'll whittle your stick at the Laznar bend."

"At the Laznar bend."

He sighed happily as he saw his day spread out before him, carefree as the sky above. Not a cloud in the blue up there and not a worry down here until suppertime, which was still far away somewhere beyond the nine hills.

He wiped his wet whiskers again and waded happily to the other side of the river. In the middle, he stopped once again to have a look at the valley. It seemed to him that he was viewing the earth from afar. To his mind, water was not really a part of the earth, which was firm and unmoving, like the firmament. The only difference between the earth and sky was that he could easily reach the earth from the water but he could not reach the sky where the birds soared without a care in the world. He liked to stand in the middle of the river, in the middle of that fluid element, and from it—from afar—look at the earth, at his valley that was like a huge green cradle covered by the blue arch of the transparent sky. Today, too, he turned lightly on his heel, looked about, and listened. Everything was green and washed, everything was peaceful and quiet. The birds no longer sang, for the day was already well on its way; not a sound could be heard from anywhere. Only the lone eagle, winging his way from Vranjek and seemingly tied by an invisible thread to the rocks, sometimes cried shrilly and angrily. It was always quiet at this end of the valley, but today the silence was so complete that Mata stretched his neck, sniffed the air, and pricked up his ears like an animal sensing danger. All of a sudden he winced as though death had brushed past him.

He stood still and then once again slowly turned around, looking at the meadows, fields, mountaintops, and sky with his watery, clouded gaze. There was nothing out of the ordinary anywhere. The sun was already up. It had stopped to rest a bit behind one of the hilltops before beginning its climb heavenward. The glittering morning light divided the valley lengthward into two halves: the sunny and the shadowed. The line of the shadow stretched out straight along Modrijan's fields. Mata waded across the river, arrived at the line between sun and shadow, and started walking along it. He swayed first right and then left, as though picking his way along the edge of a precipice. His powerful bare feet sank deep into the dewy grass that came up to his knees and was so lush that he had to bend forward as though wading through water. The grass should have been cut long ago, but Modrijan, who was on the enemy's side, could not find mowers. The Partisans had threatened they would shoot down anyone on his field with a machine gun.

Mata plowed through the grass as far as the Tiha swamp when all of a sudden he heard the whir of an airplane. He looked up but the plane was already upon him. It was flying so low that Mata threw himself on the ground out of fear; the air around him whistled and he could see the grass wave. When he stood up, there was no sign of the airplane. Perhaps he had only imagined it. He scratched his head and winced again, as though death had passed by him.

He stood motionless until he was brought back to reality by a detachment of Partisans pouring out over the field. They ran across the road and in single file hurried off in the direction of the river.

"Ho-ooo-hoy!" yelled Mata happily, waving his arms.

But the Partisans did not stop, nor did they laugh or wave their rifles or wait for Mata to start talking to them about what his switch was going to be like and how pretty his sweetheart was.

"Probably Mrs. Temnikar told them I messed up the milk!" thought Mata. He stood as if rooted to the spot and watched the Partisans running swiftly through the tall grass and disappearing, one by one, into the gray-green willow bushes. The splashing of water could be heard, meaning that the Partisans had gone into the water with their clothes on. Mata sighed with relief as he realized that Mrs. Temnikar had not told them about the milk after all. Then he began to tremble because he knew the Fascists would be coming to the village now. He blanched with fear and then began to move slowly forward. Carved deep into his subconscious as though on a rock were his instructions for the day: go to Loputnik's, then to Tilka's, to Lazne for lunch, and then to the Laznar bend to sit out the day.

At the entrance to the village Mata met four peasants taking their cattle with them, each one leading a calf on a tether. They were making for safety in the neighboring village, which was on liberated territory where the enemy would probably not go.

"Mata, come along with us. Help us get the cattle there!" rasped Ustinar, holding a big, strong calf by the tether and tail and prancing unwillingly along the road with it.

"I'm going to Loputnik's for a shave," said Mata slowly.

"Watch out, or it's the Fascists who will give you a shave!" snorted Ustinar angrily, fully aware that it would be like beating his head against a stone wall trying to persuade Mata to do what he wanted.

Mata blinked in fright and moved on. He found Loputnik in front of his house. Loputnik was usually a gay, waggish fellow but today he looked as glum as a rainy day. He was looking with scorn at his tiny wife, who was swaying to and fro on the threshold, tears streaming from her eyes from the smoke curling out of the kitchen, and groaning:

"Will you or won't you tell me whether to let the chickens go or leave them in the coop?"

"You nitwit!" Loputnik burst out. "Slaughter them and pick out the feathers so that everything is ready. Then, when they come, all you have to do is ask, 'Would you like them boiled or roasted?'"

"Oh, Luka," sighed the woman desperately, raising her eyes heavenward. "Will you be serious for a change? This is no joke. Tell me, will you, should I let them out or should they stay in the coop?"

Now it was Loputnik's turn to raise his eyes to the heavens and fold his hands in front of him in mock prayer, exclaiming:

"Dear God, give her some sense!" Then he stormed: "Did I or didn't I tell you to let them go! At least the enemy will have to run for them if he wants them. And maybe one of them will manage to hide away so something will be left!"

"That means you want me to let them go?" asked the wife, without moving from the doorstep.

"You know what?" Loputnik bent his head to one side and looked his wife up and down. "Go and ask them. The chickens are smarter than you are and they'll know which is better."

"Ah, Luka, all you care about is making jokes," sighed his **wife,** shaking her head at her husband's lightheadedness and **slowly** waddling behind the house to her chickens.

"Well, she finally caught on. What a woman!" Loputnik shook his head and turned to Mata.

"Finally caught on," repeated Mata from habit, and smiled.

"But you haven't caught on. Today there is really no joking and no shaving!" said Loputnik darkly, and he disappeared into the house.

Mata followed him silently and stood in the middle of the room, as unmoving as a statue. Loputnik searched his drawers and shelves for something. Then he collected a pile of papers, twisted them together, and stuck them into an old boot that he then thrust into the midst of a pile of shoddy footwear. Mata was still standing motionless in the middle of the room. Loputnik knew he would not budge until he had had his shave. So he had one more look in the drawers and on the shelves and then without a word sat Mata down on the three-legged stool and threw a dirty shoemaker's apron over him. But before he began to lather Mata with his rough, bristly brush, he looked at the wall clock and peered behind all the pictures hanging on the walls. While doing so, Loputnik appeared so serious and thoughtful that Mata blinked in fright. Finally Loputnik stopped searching the room and took up the brush. He had hardly started the lathering when he put a finger to his forehead, quickly grabbed the shoemaker's knife, leaped to the furnace, opened the door, and peered inside to see if anything was there. He sighed with relief and returned to Mata. For a long time he lathered him silently, shrugging his shoulders and mumbling.

"Oh, anything can happen," he finally snorted angrily as though arguing with someone.

"Anything can happen," repeated Mata as was his wont, enjoying the lathering with the stiff brush.

"Anything, anything!" nodded Loputnik thoughtfully. "But you don't need to worry," he waved his hand. And because his waggish tongue gave him no peace he added with a bitter laugh: "And if anything does happen to you, at least you'll go to heaven with a smooth shave."

"I don't want to go to heaven," quickly answered Mata.

"Then where will you go?" laughed Loputnik.

"To Kokošar's," answered Mata.

"To the Kokošars? And what will you do there?"

"Get a sunflower."

"What kind of sunflower?"

"Tilka told me she would give me a sunflower," said Mata in confusion, scraping the floor with his bare feet.

"Tilka?" Loputnik straightened and pondered a moment. "You know what, Mata? Let's hurry and see if Tilka is still at home. And if she's still there, tell her to get away immediately."

"Where should she go?" asked Mata, blinking.

"All you have to do is say 'Tilka, Loputnik said to clear out!' "

"Tilka, Loputnik said to clear out," repeated Mata, raising a finger.

"And don't go hanging about the village," warned Loputnik after he had shaved him and was sending him off. "Go straight to Tilka's place."

"Go straight to Tilka's place," repeated Mata, raising a finger and going off toward the village.

He crossed the bridge but there were no children about to run after him and ask him at which end the switch was thicker now. The road glistened in the bright noonday sun. At the

Usadar bend, a column of dust was rising as though a storm were threatening. Everything was still and there was nobody about. Only Modrijan and the parish priest were standing in front of the café. Modrijan was unfastening the traveling bag from the parish priest's motorcycle and the priest was pulling off his gray coat like a big black insect shedding its skin.

"Why the rush, Mata?" asked the priest, raising a short, fleshy finger to stop him.

Mata stopped but did not reply. He did not like Modrijan and he feared the parish priest. Even though his mind was clouded, he could see that of late people had begun avoiding both of them. The priest and Modrijan exchanged glances as though to say, "Look at that! Even this 'child of God' is against us!"

All at once there was a great roar. Mata raised his eyes and saw a big plane flying over the road, the same one that had flown over Modrijan's field this morning. Modrijan and the priest exchanged glances and smiled, while Mata winced as though death had touched him.

"Mata, go on, be off with you, in the name of God," said the priest, waving his plump hand.

Mata sighed with relief, quickly rounded the corner, and went toward the Žuželj hut. Mrs. Žuželj, who was pulling a stubborn calf with all her might out of a half-darkened barn, was happy to see him.

"Help me, Mata," she said breathlessly.

Mata yanked the calf over the threshold with one pull.

"Oh, Mata, take the calf with you," begged the exhausted housewife. "And at night, when the Fascists go, bring it back."

"I'm going to Tilka's. She's going to give me a sunflower."

"Oh, my poor fool!" shrieked Mrs. Žuželj, grabbing her copper-red thatch of thick hair with all ten calloused fingers. "A horde has invaded the village, and he's going for a sunflower. . . ."

"Mrs. Temnikar told me," blinked Mata, trying to explain.

"Sure, Mrs. Temnikar can say whatever she wants since her

house is far off," said the desperate peasant woman. Then she threw the tether over her shoulder and began pulling the calf toward the river with both hands.

Mata went straight to the Kokošar house. Even at the front of the garden he could hear Kokošar's angry grumbling and was afraid to come up to the house. He hid behind the corn crib and gazed around the yard. The doors of the porch opened wide and Tilka appeared. She had on boots and trousers, a blanket slung over her shoulder, and a knapsack on her back. Mrs. Kokošar came out on the threshold and shouted in a voice that both pleaded and threatened:

"I tell you for the last time—stay here!"

"And I'm telling you for the last time—I'm off!" said Tilka quietly but determinedly and started walking along the cart road that went past the corn crib.

Mrs. Kokošar strode after her. Tilka heard her heavy footsteps, turned around, straightened up, raised her hand high, and fixed her blue eyes on her mother. Mrs. Kokošar stopped short and stood still as though paralyzed. Angry, frightened, and astonished, she opened her eyes and mouth. Then she gave a start, as though wishing to say something, but her daughter waved a hand so suddenly and authoritatively that her mother stopped again. They remained that way for a few seconds. Then Tilka, still keeping her eyes fixed on Mrs. Kokošar, lowered her hand easily, turned around slowly, and went off quickly without saying a word.

Mata stood still. When Tilka was in front of the corn crib, he came to his senses and stepped out on the road. Tilka gave a soft cry and backed up instinctively, although she recognized the harmless giant at once.

"Mata," she cried, frightened. "Why are you going around scaring people?"

"I came for the sunflower," he said slowly and bashfully, his big clouded eyes blinking.

"The sunflower?" she said, puzzled, wrinkling her forehead in surprise. Then she smiled. "Of course," she said kindly. "I promised you a sunflower."

"Promised," repeated Mata and shifted his feet.

"Give me a knife," she said. There were sunflowers growing along the garden fence and she cut off the biggest one, attaching it to Mata's shirt. Her fingers fondled the still dewy petals and like the real sun the flower shone brightly on Mata's tanned chest.

"That is really the flower for you," she said, standing on tiptoe and touching his broad face. "If you lose it, I'll be angry with you."

"I won't lose it," promised Mata, and then, impelled by God knows what indiscernible laws of emotion, stood aside to let Tilka pass along the road.

She smiled at him, nodded her head, and made off. After walking a few steps she turned around, waved her hand, and said:

"Good-by, Mata."

This seemed so strange to Mata that he could not find his tongue, but her voice put his huge body into motion. He walked along the road and held his chin high so as not to press down the flower that shone on his chest. He followed mutely after Tilka, who ran like a deer in front of him. She could not hear his footsteps but the sound of his heavy breathing followed her and she turned around to ask:

"Where are you going now?"

"To Lazne," he said slowly.

"Oh, you're going to have lunch there?"

"To have lunch."

"Oh," she nodded, and stepped off the road. They walked over the dewy grass that swished around Mata's bare feet.

At Lazne they stopped at the porch of the house to which Mata was going.

"So, Mata, now it is really good-by," said Tilka, extending her hand.

Mata did not shake hands with her but blinked in fright, hid both his fists behind his back, and even retreated a step with a gentlemanly gesture.

"Oh, you poor, dear fool," she smiled. "You're afraid to touch me. Well, I'll touch you then."

"Touch you," he repeated, then sighed and extended his hand.

"That's right," said Tilka, firmly shaking the outstretched hand.

Mata stiffened from the unknown feeling of pleasure and from a mindless fear. A strange warmth flowed from Tilka's hand into his. The warmth spread rapidly through his body, welled up in his veins, and struck savagely at his heart, which began to beat with fright in a chest that now seemed too small for it. Mata closed his eyes, thinking something would burst inside him.

"Good-by," repeated Tilka, shaking his hand once more. Then she turned and left.

Mata stood there with his hand outstretched, watching Tilka swiftly climbing uphill.

He opened his eyes and mouth wide, gasping for air. This lasted quite some time until he got back his breath enough to stammer, "Tilka!"

The fear was so strong in his voice that Tilka turned around immediately.

"What is it?" she asked in a worried tone.

Mata straightened, raised a finger, and said slowly, as though stifling:

"Tilka, Loputnik said 'Clear out of here!' "

She wrinkled her forehead and asked seriously:

"When did he say that?"

"This morning."

"So," she nodded thoughtfully.

"Are you angry?" blinked Mata with fright.

"Why should I be angry?" Tilka asked in surprise.

"Because I forgot about Loputnik," said Mata repentantly, lowering his eyes since he could not lower his head because of the sunflower on his chest.

"Oh, Mata, Mata," smiled Tilka. "You can see that I'm going. Can't you see?" She slapped her blanket and knapsack with her hand.

"You see," sighed Mata and nodded.

"You tell Loputnik that I have gone."

"Have gone," repeated Mata.

"And if I come back, I'll come back with the Partisans."

"With the Partisans," Mata straightened, blinking his big clouded eyes.

"That's right. And now, once again, good-by. No, not good-by, but so long," she said determinedly, and waved.

Mata remained motionless, looking at the valley until Laznar hit him on the back and said angrily:

"Get out of the way, you oaf!"

It was only then that Mata noticed people milling all about him. They were running to and fro, carrying bags and baskets, pails and buckets, and shouting at each other impatiently. Mata seemed to be in everybody's way so he seated himself on a stone table under a tree. He sat up straight as a ramrod with the bright sunflower on his chest, looking somewhat like a tribal chieftain viewing with a superior air the sufferings of his subjects. After the noise had subsided, Mrs. Laznar came out of the house with the maid. She held a bowl of holy water and an olive branch while the servant girl carried an old, long-handled frying pan in which olive leaves were smoking on coals. They moved along the cart path toward the road, swinging the incense and sprinkling the holy water around them.

Laznar, who was just emerging from the barn, stood rooted to the ground. Then he threw down his hat with all his might and cursed with all his soul:

"What in thunderation? Have you gone crazy?"

Mrs. Laznar showed acute embarrassment at her husband's

discovery of what she had been doing, for she had been keeping her quasi-religious activities a secret from him.

"Oh, Toma, just turn your head the other way," she said, not looking at him. "I'm going to sprinkle and burn incense so the devils won't enter the house."

"You dimwit!" her husband snorted scornfully, for he had been a freethinker for a long time. "The Pope has blessed them and burned incense over them and it's he who has sent them on their way here. If you don't believe it, go to the priest and ask him to burn incense here at our place. Do you think he would come?"

Mrs. Laznar's eyes widened and she slowly nodded.

"So," Laznar spread out his hands. He picked his hat up from the floor, struck his knee with it to shake off the dust, and said thoughtfully:

"Go on, get rid of that junk of yours. You'd do better to burn incense after they've left . . . unless they do the burning themselves. . . ."

"What do you mean, 'do the burning themselves'?"

"What do I mean? Just remember Rupar!"

"Oh, my God!" Mrs. Laznar gasped in terror and looked toward the next hill where the fire-blackened walls of Rupar's house stood out against the green background.

"Never mind about God now. Give that man something to eat," Laznar said darkly, and pointed at Mata still seated on the stone table, his bleary, clouded eyes blinking in surprise. The women went into the house. The servant girl returned quickly with a bowl of porridge and put it in front of Mata.

"Oh ho," she said, putting her hands on her hips and feigning surprise. "Well, Mata, now that's what I call a flower."

Mata smiled proudly and began eating. He grabbed the spoon and ate clumsily because he could not bend his head over the bowl with the sunflower under his chin.

"Oh, Mata, you'll never finish that way," smiled the servant girl, drawing the sunflower from his shirt.

"Tilka gave it to me," said the frightened Mata hoarsely, putting out his hand.

"Well, I'm not going to eat it," retorted the girl, putting it down on the table. "When you finish eating, call me and I'll fix it for you again."

Mata gulped down the porridge and stuck the flower in his shirt himself.

"Where are you going now?" asked Laznar, who was walking nervously to and fro around the house.

"I'm going to sit at the bend," said Mata, pointing to the road curving in and out of the cliff side.

"Oh," mumbled Laznar carelessly, "at our bend," he repeated, and the thought seemed to please him. "Sure, sure, just you go and sit there, just sit there. Sit there all day, and if they come . . . if they come . . . so what if they come . . . what I wanted to say was . . . if you're thirsty come here to get some milk."

"Milk to drink," repeated Mata and went off with his head raised high. He cut a switch from the first bush and went toward the bend in the road. There he sat on the edge of the stone fence, on the very same stone where he had sat so many times. He let his feet hang down, peeled the switch with his knife, took a piece of broken glass from his pocket, and began to whittle. He whittled, swung his legs, and sometimes looked off to the valley. He saw the red roofs, the blue smoke rising from the chimneys, the river dashing over a cliff in a broad waterfall and then flowing on, blue and quiet, under the bridge. The village was unusually silent. Not a voice could be heard, only an occasional bark or cockcrow.

The sun was rising higher and higher. Mata whittled faster and faster, swinging his legs with increased momentum as though about to rise and float over the valley. He examined the switch closely to see "at which end it was still a little thicker," blinking and scratching his thick mane of hair. While he was making these movements, the sun's rays were reflected from the piece of glass in his hand as though lightning were flashing from it.

After he had whittled the first switch down to nothing he threw it away, went over to the bushes, and cut off a new one. It was then that he heard a roar. He looked at the sky but it was a clear blue. He looked at the white road curving from the village and saw three trucks slowly rumbling from Hlip's house, as though coming from the Hlip barns.

"They're coming," sighed Mata, and jumped up on the fence again. At that moment, just as suddenly as it had done that morning on the meadow and later near Modrijan's café, the airplane thundered overhead. It flew so low and was already so close that Mata could see the two men in it clearly. He wanted to throw himself on the ground, but instead—for what reason nobody knows; maybe because of the sunflower under his chin —he straightened up. The airplane was already upon him and the next moment it was gone. Mata winced as though death had brushed past him—but it had not gone past. He saw the burst of flame from the plane and the next minute he seemed to be caught in a whirlpool that picked him up and cast him down from the bend.

When Mata regained consciousness, he saw that everything around him was yellow. He blinked in surprise and quite some time passed before he realized that he was lying on his back in the middle of Laznar's wheat field. He couldn't remember anything, nor did he wonder how he got there, but moved as though to stand up. Then he groaned and remained motionless on the ground, a sharp pain shooting through his body. He blinked, put his hand to his chest, and started feeling downward. When he came to his stomach, he felt something moist. The pain seemed to be coming from there, burning through him as though a cauldron of boiling oil had been poured on him.

Mata then recalled the flame bursting from the airplane and winced again, as though death were passing by.

"They've killed me," it dawned on him. He opened his eyes, raised himself up on his elbows, and looked at himself. An enormous wound gaped open on his stomach. He trembled but was not afraid.

"Skin always heals itself," he mumbled as he had mumbled so many times before. He grasped his stomach firmly with both hands, turned over on his hip, and slowly got to his knees. Then he saw the sunflower in front of him.

"If you lose it, I'll be angry," he heard Tilka's voice. He crawled over to the sunflower, picked it up, and stuck it in his shirt. Then he took the half-whittled switch and tucked it under his arm. And now to get to his feet! He took a deep breath, gritted his teeth, and stood up with one effort. He groaned and staggered but stayed on his feet, then slowly left the field and leaned on the trunk of an old pear tree.

The sun was already setting. It had settled on Marnovsko Hill and seemed swollen, tired, and blood-red now. It looked strange to Mata so that he blinked at it a long time. Then his clouded gaze traveled over the hill. It stopped at Loputnik's cottage, which no longer existed. From the charred ruins a curling wisp of white smoke rose lazily. Mata squinted disbelievingly, but no matter how he focused his eyes all he saw was four bare walls. And even they were very low and narrow and had a mournful look. He did not think of Loputnik or his wife. All he thought of was the shaving brush.

"Who's going to shave me now?" he worried. But he did not answer the question because he was surprised by the grunting of pigs. His gaze wandered over the village and stopped in front of Modrijan's house. The three big trucks that had been rumbling along Hlip's bend were standing there now. In the first truck were some soldiers drinking from a bottle; in the second some calves and pigs; and in the third more soldiers. Also among them Mata could clearly see Loputnik, Laznar, Rudi Oblažar, and Mrs. Žuželj, the latter pulling at her copper-red mane with both hands and swaying back and forth. Mata opened his eyes wide as if to ask when all this could have happened but he did not have a chance because the trucks made off, leaving the village. He looked in surprise at them going down the white road until they disappeared behind Hlip's bend.

The village came to life. People moved out on to the road, going from one house to the other. Mata also began to move.

"To Hotejec" flashed through his mind. Mata wanted to go to Hotejec to show him his wound because nothing like this had ever happened to him before. Just the shadow of a look of pride crossed his face, now bathed in the cold sweat of pain. He gritted his teeth, held his stomach even more firmly with his hands as though carrying it in a bread trough, and began slowly descending into the valley. His first steps were painful but astonishment and pride surmounted the pain.

Never had the road been so long, but Mata finally arrived in the village and with him came silence. He walked down the middle of the road because something had happened to him making it right for him to walk down the middle of the road. He walked slowly and straight, his broad feet treading silently on the dusty road as though it were covered with flour. Under his arm he held the switch and on his chest the sunflower shone—shone even though it was already wilted. Sweat was pouring down his face in rivulets, his eyes were moist and open wide. The drooping mustache hid a strange smile that had stiffened as though frozen.

Keeping a distance that bespoke deep respect, the children followed Mata, joined later by the women, who were also silent. Then the men started gathering behind them without speaking. No one uttered a word, as though afraid that the slightest sound would send Mata crashing to the ground.

Hotejec was standing on his threshold. He was gazing at the evening sun so that the group approaching him seemed to be in a black shadow.

Mata stopped two feet in front of him and, without saying a word, fixed his big clouded eyes on Hotejec. The children quietly formed a semicircle around him. Behind them stood the mute men and women. It was the silence that staggered Hotejec.

"Mata!" he yelled into the silence, then strode quickly to him and grabbed him with both hands as though fearing Mata would collapse. His eyes appealed to the people nearest him who came up and carefully took Mata into the house.

"He must lie on something flat, on something flat," said Hotejec.

Some of the men put two tables together, raised Mata slowly, and put him down on his back. Hotejec took his dark red pillow out of the chimney corner and put it gently under Mata's head.

"Mata, what happened?" he asked.

"Shooting," gasped Mata.

"Where?"

"At Laznar's bend . . ."

"How?"

"From above—airplane . . ." groaned Mata, and blinked with fright.

The men looked at one another and shook their heads. Then they drew closer and leaned over him.

"Look, it almost sawed him in two," whispered Ustinar, and shook his head.

"Sawed in two," repeated Mata, a hardly discernible smile of pride playing about his lips despite the pain.

The men drew back without a word, obviously convinced that nothing could be done.

Mata focused on Hotejec and said quietly:

"Skin always heals."

"Always, Mata, always!" Hotejec quickly agreed, putting his bony hand on the moist forehead.

"Always!" murmured the men, pulling their hats down over their eyes and drawing back even further.

"The skin is not a shirt," continued Mata.

"No, it's not a shirt," nodded Hotejec.

"And it's not like trousers."

"Nor like trousers."

"The skin can always be used."

"Always, always," nodded Hotejec, wiping the perspiration from Mata's brow.

Mata smiled as though to say: we two understand each other. Then he trembled, closed his eyes, and groaned aloud.

"Give him some brandy," Robar spoke up.

"Brandy?" said Mata hoarsely, raising himself on his elbows and looking at Hotejec with fear in his eyes. What was this now? Hotejec had ordered him never to drink brandy.

"Never mind, Mata," said Hotejec, putting Mata's head back on the pillow. "You can have a little brandy. You're old enough now. And you're smart, too. Brandy is very good for such big cuts."

"For big cuts," repeated Mata, and the fear in his eyes faded. But he still looked with disbelief at Hotejec, who was pouring out the brandy.

"Now then," said Hotejec. "Now we'll clink our glasses together."

Mata did not put out his hand. Hotejec raised the drooping mustache and poured the brandy into his mouth. Mata grunted, coughed, and then grabbed his throat. He trembled again and raised himself on his elbows. He looked at his chest, opened his eyes wide, and groaned miserably.

"Lost . . ."

"What have you lost?" asked Hotejec.

"The sunflower. Tilka will be angry," sighed Mata, blinking with fright.

Hotejec looked around him inquiringly. The women found the sunflower, straightened it out, and put it on the pillow next to Mata's head. Mata grew quiet and closed his eyes.

The house was already full of people. The men were in the room, the women were crowded together in the kitchen and on the porch, and children peeped out of every corner. They were silent. All at once Modrijan's rasping voice was heard in the kitchen:

"For God's sake, let's call the priest, let's call the priest!"

The words burned into Hotejec. Suddenly he straightened his eighty-year-old body and went to the kitchen threshold.

"So, it's you!" he said slowly, piercing Modrijan with his gray eyes. "I thought you'd run away."

"Run away?" gaped Modrijan.

"Well, if you haven't left the village, you're going to leave my house this very minute!" Hotejec grated through his teeth and raised a bony hand.

"Je-e-ernej! Don't think about politics now. Think of his soul!"

"Of course. You also buy and sell souls."

"Je-e-ernej, death is not a business!"

"You're right—it's not!" agreed Hotejec. "That's exactly why I want you out of here!" Pointing a bony finger, he stormed, "Out!"

Modrijan disappeared and Mrs. Temnikar started lamenting: "It's my fault! . . . I sent him to the village!"

"Stop it, Anice!" ordered Hotejec quietly. "How could you know that those swine would invade the village today?"

"I didn't know . . ."

"Well, then, it was his destiny," concluded Hotejec, and turned to go back into the room. But as he turned, the peddler woman, Katra, who was now seventy years old, spoke up.

"Is he going to die?" she moaned, her swollen, watery eyes bulging.

Hotejec turned around again but Katra had already dissolved in tears. She fell to her knees, clasped her hands in front of her, and began praying in a sad voice:

"Our Father who art in heaven . . ."

"Take her out of here," ordered Hotejec quietly but sternly, and closed the kitchen door behind him.

The commotion upset Mata. He raised himself on his elbows

and looked at the kitchen with fear in his eyes. The peasants had to use all their strength to keep him on the table. Hotejec was able to calm him down again. He put his hand on Mata's forehead and slowly pressed him backward to the pillow. Mata closed his eyes but soon raised himself again and groaned:

"Thirsty . . ."

"Oh!" whispered Mrs. Usadar, and put her head in her hands. "Milk!" she whispered again and went to the door. The women began murmuring. After some pushing and shoving, and though the men tried to wave them away and nodded their heads in negation, they brought a great quantity of milk. Soon each woman was holding a pitcher in her hands. And Mata drank.

"That'll be enough, Mata!" Hotejec stopped him, and pressed his head back to the pillow. "Rest . . . you've got to rest with such a big cut."

"Rest," repeated Mata, and looked at Hotejec with his moist eyes.

"To rest and to sleep . . . to sleep, so that the skin can heal up again easily."

"Heal up again easily," repeated Mata, and closed his eyes. He lay motionless for a long time, breathing audibly. Then the fever began shaking him, and the table under him.

"Give him some more brandy," said Robar.

They gave him brandy. Now almost every peasant in the room had a flask in his hands and was offering it to Hotejec.

It grew dark and Mata became more quiet. He breathed evenly. Hotejec moved away a little and whispered to the people:

"He's sleeping."

"Do you really think he will fall asleep?" asked old Rejec.

Hotejec nodded.

"Oh, why doesn't it come?" sighed Vogrič.

"Who?" asked Čargo in surprise, since he never in his life had understood any conversation.

"What who?" Ustinar looked at him scornfully. "Death."

"Aaahhh . . . ," said Čargo at length.

"It's already here," nodded Hotejec. "But Mata isn't like a blade of grass. Mata is an oak. And it isn't easy to cut an oak down with a scythe."

The men nodded thoughtfully and looked at Mata's huge body. The room again sank into silence. The small sound of a bell broke the stillness. Suddenly unrest swept the room, for the clanging of the bell was getting louder and louder until the noise seemed almost unbearable. Over the heads of the women appeared the long arm of the sexton ringing the bell; behind it came Modrijan's head, and behind Modrijan's, the priest's. The women moved to one side and in the doorway stood the solid-looking priest in his white robes.

Hotejec quickly strode to Mata's side, placed his left hand to his forehead, and with the right one pointed so swiftly at the priest that the latter gave a start and threw his head backward. He took a deep breath and opened his mouth as if to say something, but saw that Hotejec was trembling with rage. Hotejec pointed his hand at him once more with such force that the elbow joint cracked. The priest looked at Modrijan, turned around, and disappeared onto the dark porch.

That was Mata's last temptation, but it passed him by. The fever racked him the whole night through. Before dawn he grew quiet. His breathing became more shallow. He sighed once more as his powerful chest heaved. Then he exhaled and his mustache fluttered over his red lips. He was still.

Hotejec struck a match and his bony, shaking hand brought it slowly to Mata's lips. The flame did not go out and the silence was so profound that you could hear the slight crackling of a hair from the drooping mustache.

"It's over," said Hotejec loudly, and winced. All of them winced with him, as though Death, which had finished its work here, had flown past them out of the room. They stood a few moments, motionless and still. Then they gave a start and began to talk. And their talk got louder and louder.

Translated by Cordia Kveder

The Shepherdess

On a late spring Monday in 1942, on the eve of a large-scale operation, they were captured by Četnik sentinels right at the entrance to Kolašin. First came Veko Brujić, a decrepit old man, the father of an executed Partisan. Either he was recognized or else someone had given him away—but the fact was that they took him by surprise so that he did not even have time to pull his revolver out of his vest pocket. After they disarmed him, the old man no longer concealed his purpose—that he had come to kill Commander Minić and thus avenge his son's death. In the afternoon he was shot along with Selić, Zečević, and Lakičević. Bent over and exhausted, at the last moment of his life, scornfully he straightened himself, saying: "I am glad to die with such company, with such good honest people and with heroes representing two great Montenegrin tribes." Shot in an upright position, he was buried deep in the earth, and because of the fame of those who had fallen with him, his own reputation was forgotten so that practically nothing was either mentioned or known about him later.

Another person was more interesting from the very start: a girl of medium stature, a healthy peasant whose beauty was hidden under her rough clothes, sunburned and with a sturdy look in her silvery-gray eyes and black eyebrows. Her name was Djurdja Vlahović, a shepherdess from the small village of Trebaljevo. On that day she was leading about twenty lambs to be exchanged with those of her relatives. At other times this might have been nothing unusual, because at the end of spring, lambs are separated from their mothers and given to other sheep so that they can forget about milk and learn how to live exclusively on grass. But that spring, when everything had changed and there was continuous fighting in different parts of the Tara valley, both shepherds and lambs, as well as anything alive and mobile, seemed suspicious to the Četniks.

The girl walked along calmly, knitting stockings and concentrating on her work as she passed the sentinels, pretending not to see them. Her composure was an insult to the sentinels and it did not increase their suspicion so much as it heightened their eagerness to see her face and to arouse her fears, as they were accustomed to doing. The commander of the guard, an ex-policeman whose beard sometimes covered the soiled collar of his buttoned-up jacket, cleared his throat and asked maliciously: "Well, where are you coming from, my pretty one?"

She stopped and turned around as if she had not noticed them before. She shook her head slightly, but her look became all the more resolute, cold, and angry. She replied without haste: "I? I'm from right there, from the mountain."

"Which mountain? There's more than one mountain around here."

"Well, I'm from that one over there, Mount Biograd," the girl said, looking at her stocking as she knitted. She wanted to proceed, but one of the men dashed in front of her.

"Wait, wait a minute: why don't you say you're coming from the zone controlled by the Partisans? Give me your pass!"

She had no pass and even pretended that she did not know what the pass was or why it was important. They took her to an inn to see whether the innkeeper could recognize her and to search her belongings. Milena Tutova, a fat widow who had helped the Četnik movement in many ways, was the innkeeper. She could not recognize the girl; she did not know the peasant-folk, especially the women. The shepherdess said that she belonged to the Vlahović family of Trebaljevo, but that did not mean very much because Vlahovićs, like all the other families, were separated as they fought each other in deadly combat, some favoring the Četniks and others the Partisans. The girl tried to prevent them from searching her on the excuse that she had to catch up with the lambs, but the sentinels were not at all interested in her lambs. They kept her at the inn by force, and with a sly look the innkeeper unbuttoned the girl's blouse and discovered a package of leaflets concealed beneath it. The leaflets contained an appeal, calling upon the people to join in the struggle against the invader and his mercenaries. As soon as they heard the paper rattling, the sentinels knew what the matter was even without looking at the text of the leaflets. They began to beat the shepherdess. Her face began to bleed; her eye was injured, her hair was disheveled, and three times her white kerchief was pulled off her head. She was totally silent but grabbed her kerchief again and again to cover her head because, according to the strict custom of her village, women's hair was not supposed to be exposed to men's eyes.

Then the sentinels took her to security headquarters. They could not beat her in the street in front of the people, but they could scream and curse, thus giving vent to their hatred and showing their devotion to duty and authority, as well as attracting people's attention to their big catch and success. Suddenly it seemed to them as if they had grown bigger, that they were a foot taller than the other passers-by—the startled and frightened townspeople who with uneasy curiosity frequently stopped, turned, and attached themselves to the enraged, screaming group. And thus the quiet procession grew ever longer and in it each individual silently wondered what had driven that unknown shepherdess of Trebaljevo to choose a martyr's path, what had brought her to the Četnik's Kolašin, and who had given her away to the murderers. What was going to happen to her? No one asked the question because everybody knew the answer. All heads were bent because of the weight of that heavy thought. No one paid any attention to the abandoned lambs, which now lagged behind, sniffing and grazing the dusty grass along the fences in the street in that sordid place where they knew only the shepherdess; and then they rushed to catch up with her. But she had obviously forgotten about her lambs as she was pushed along at the head of the procession.

In front of headquarters the group came to a stop. The girl was taken inside and the crowd stayed for a while staring at the dark black square gap leading to the corridor. In silence they stared at one another questioningly, but no one either asked or said anything. They dispersed to tell what had happened, and by using this as an example to frighten their families, they tried to put a check on daring—that evil, unfortunate quality of young and able people who are punished in this manner or even more drastically simply because of it.

The area in front of the headquarters building was soon deserted. For a little while only the lambs lingered, involved in their innocent play, but then, attracted by the green grass, they, too, ran away to the meadow below the dam. The guard, who did not know whose lambs they were and how they had gotten there, mentally selected the fattest one for himself, imagining a barbecue and fire and licking his lips in anticipation.

He watched them sadly as they went away and soon forgot about them as they disappeared out of sight.

Puzzled by their sudden freedom, the lambs stopped a while to think, and called their mothers and the shepherdess by their feeble bleating, and then again forgot everything in their play. They advanced, passing through slanting fences and uncultivated gardens and fields, across the hard and dusty road that did not appeal to them, and then across the barren fallow land where many Partisans were buried without tombstones. And so they reached the sandy woods near the Tara and gazed with their frightened little eyes at the skinny, molting, and ugly coachman's horse grazing there. The big animal, with his calmness, made them feel confident. Hesitating to approach him very closely, the lambs remained in his vicinity all day, grazing and skipping over the natural green carpet and playing like butterflies. In the evening the coachman came and took the horse away. The abandoned lambs, although frightened and startled, hopefully ran after him at a distance. They stopped in front of the stable and spent the night there, alone, frightened, and huddled together in a warm little group.

In the meantime the shepherdess was interrogated at police headquarters.

She was questioned by Božanić, the illegitimate son of a laundress, who had previously served at police headquarters. The laundress had not lived long enough to see the authority and fame of her illegitimate offspring. Before the war Božanić had been a small police agent in Belgrade, a homeless spy who had long forgotten and completely dismissed Kolašin. In the second year of the war, he returned to his "native town" with the identity papers of Nedić's intelligence officer. He alleged that he had escaped from Nedić, who maintained close ties with the Germans, to serve Draža, because he trusted the English more than the Germans. He boasted how he had machine-gunned handcuffed Communists at Banjica and how he had skillfully captured them in various Serbian villages. The people there believed the former statement, but they doubted the latter. Četnik officers, mostly conceited higher-class people, did not, in spite of everything, accept him as one of their own kind; remembering his low origin and obscure birth, they believed that the laundress's bastard had escaped from Serbia because he had been caught as a thief. On the other hand, other more cautious people tried to guess whether Božanić was a Nedić or a Gestapo spy, sent to Kolašin to control Draža's headquarters; therefore they were very careful not to offend him.

Božanić interrogated the girl "in the Belgrade fashion": that is, he would tie the victim's hands and legs and bind them both together behind the victim's back, thus tightly arching the body; he would then hang that living bundle on a horizontal stick whose ends rested on two especially arranged little tables. The stick was called the bridge and the victim was called the bell clapper. When the assistants hung the victim to oscillate under the bridge, Božanić would grab a whip and skillfully begin a bastinado.

That day he had difficulty. He had to hang the obstinate girl three times, and three times he had to let the fainted girl go. At intervals, when his assistants sprinkled water on her to make her come to her senses, he scratched his small ugly head furiously as locks of his colorless hair stuck to his sweaty fingers. Everything was in vain. In the beginning it seemed as if the girl had accepted the torture as something necessary and compulsory. The torturers did their best to explain to her that the length of the torture depended on her own confessions, and that she could put a stop to it as soon as she made up her mind to talk. But she was very stubborn and persistent and refused to accept the explanations. She remained as mute as a fish and thus she did not even try either to confirm or deny her original statement. That first statement was: that she had found the leaflets tucked in a haystack and had taken them to give them to her mother and brother as cigarette paper. This explanation was given prior to the bastinado and was obviously false, and Božanić even refused to put it down. Tired and angry, his face twisted because of a severe toothache, he ordered that the girl be put into prison and he himself dashed out of his gloomy office, rushing headlong down the stairs across the dam to the nearest café.

The girl was brought before the court the next day.

The Četnik court of Kolašin was formed for purely formal reasons—to amuse the public and to create an impression that capital punishment was meted out there on the basis of evidence. In fact, that punishment was decided prior to the court trial itself and outside the courtroom at Četnik headquarters, where no evidence was taken very seriously. Marko Milović-Čoro, a drunkard and quarreler, was the pillar of the court; his face was pale and bloated because of drinking. Before the war he had been a lawyer and an admirer of the notorious Fascist Ljotić; he himself liked to tell how, as a candidate for parliamentary office on Ljotić's list, he had not received a single vote, and so from that time on he had begun to hate the human race. He would wink with his left eye for a long time and when asked to explain this action he said: "This way I can see fewer loathsome people in this world."

Milović's assistant, Vule Vlahović, was seated to the right; Vlahović was a very tall man with hazy eyes, suffering from tuberculosis, who, on principle, asked capital punishment for every accused Communist. Vuksanović, the third judge, crouched on the left-hand side of Milović. Vuksanović was scared to death day and night, he could neither eat, drink, nor smoke, and, as Milović put it, "fear constituted his only food and sustenance." However, despite that fear, or perhaps because of it, Vuksanović sometimes was courageous enough to disapprove a death penalty, but that, of course, was not even taken into consideration.

When they brought the girl in, they could see that she was limping and this incited Milović's first remark, which was meant to puzzle the defendant and to amuse the public.

"Bent-backed one," he addressed her, "what kind of change is this? Yesterday you did not limp, while today you do."

She stopped, as if wondering whether she had heard him correctly. Although her face was covered with black and blue marks, still the insult brought a blush to her face. Lifting her head, she frowned and stared: "You, too, have changed," she said. "Last year you were a Montenegrin, whereas this year you are an Italian. You'd become a Turk and change nine creeds to avoid suffering only half the tortures I have gone through."

Milović grabbed one of the sheets of paper in front of him and furiously crumpled it.

"You have a sharp tongue," he said, throwing the small white ball into one of the corners of the courtroom. "You've been well trained, sleeping with Partisans."

"Partisans are my brothers, and it would not have mattered even if I had slept with them," the girl said, watching a malicious smile come on the judge's lips. "But do you know the loathsome people with whom your wives and daughters sleep?"

Milović, pale and with bulging eyes, rose to his feet, banging on the desk: "Do you know where you are?" he screamed in a hoarse voice.

"I do: in front of executioners!" the girl replied almost simultaneously.

Judge Vuksanović's pencil slipped out of his hand and rolled down on the floor. He bent down to pick it up and in the terrible silence one could hear the squeaking of his chair and the rattling of the pencil in his trembling hand. Milović said, "Hm," his head dropping over a pile of documents. He closed his eyes, meaning that he had surrendered his position in the court to Judge Vule Vlahović. The people in the courtroom, a major part of whom came mostly to have a good time listening to Milović cursing the defendants, were instantly disappointed and lost interest in the trial. Vlahović's interrogation was dull, he spoke with a grave-like voice, had a literary accent, and did not conceal the fact that what was taking place was a mere comedy and not a court trial; the decisive sentence had been irrevocably passed in advance.

He calmly took the usual data of names and dates, and then grimly asked: "This means . . . you've brought the lambs . . . Well, but where are they now?"

The girl said she could not tell exactly where they were, but that they had most probably been prepared as food for the Četniks.

"All right, all right," the judge waved his hand, and asked another question: "To whom should you have delivered those leaflets?"

The girl frowned again, as if trying to find the right answer. Looking him straight in the eyes, she said: "You'll die before you know."

"I see," the tubercular tall man admitted bitterly as he smiled spitefully. "That's . . . that means, how long have you been a Party member?"

"That, too, you are never going to know!" the girl replied scornfully, staring at Milović's bristling beard.

Obviously tired, Vlahović looked at Judge Vuksanović observing the girl's composed face covered with blue marks, her resolute eyebrows on which all her spite seemed to have accumulated. He waved his hand; he had no more questions to ask.

They took her back to prison and during the last two hours of life the girl washed her face, combed her hair, and straightened her clothes. At lunch she could not eat at all but, to mislead and encourage the others to eat, she plucked and chewed a single bite for a long time and crumbled a small ball of corn bread with her fingers.

In the afternoon they called her name out and informed her that she was sentenced to death by hanging and that the sentence was to be carried out immediately. She was asked to get ready. Listening to all this, she did not even blink: it was as if she had known her fate long ago and did nothing else than to make ready for it. And really, she was prepared for it—she knew that in Četnik's Kolašin, women, being unworthy of a death by shooting, were as a rule sentenced to death by hanging. Ruža Rip, a "Partisan doctor," had also ended her life hanging from a snare, while Djurdja Vlahović did not doubt for a moment that she could get anything better from the Četniks. People talked about how Ruža had faced her death quietly and how she gathered her long, thick hair and pushed it through the snare with her small, almost childlike hands. That story showed the girl that even such a humiliating death chosen for a woman and a Jew had some traits of beauty and sadness and was also human.

Before she shook hands with her comrades in the women's prison, Djurdja crossed the yard to the men's prison and went from one cell to another taking leave of the comrades she had not even had time to get to know. Resolute and composed, she deceived many prisoners by her cheerfulness, so they thought she was going home and only later regretted that she was no longer among them and that they had not seen more of her while she was there. As she walked along the pebbled path across the yard on her way back to the women's prison, drum-beating resounded in the street in front of the prison gate, and then the shrill voice of the town crier was heard inviting the townspeople of Kolašin not to miss the opportunity to attend the execution of the Communist organizer, Djurdja Vlahović. The girl stopped in front of the open gate of the women's prison and, looking pale and smiling, said bitterly: "He's calling together my wedding guests, have you heard him? Mother, my poor mother, can you imagine what my wedding will be like. . . ."

Frowning and terrified as a result of the tension, the guards, with their faces hidden in their woolly beards, escorted the girl beyond the locked gate. Out on the street she started to run and the guards ran after her. By the time she reached the dam overlooking the meadow, the girl noticed the assembled crowd and became aware of the hundreds of people staring at her. This was the moment she dreaded most: isolation and loneliness before such a glare of eyes. Her head drooped and her legs began to tremble under their burden. But the next moment she straightened herself up and began to walk resolutely through the huge crowd, which made room for her to advance, and soon she reached the wooden poles of the gallows, surrounded by armed men and hordes of people whispering in admiration.

This admiration redoubled her strength and spite. In a wink she jumped to the stool beneath the gallows. Looking down from that height, it seemed to her as if the crowd was silenced by her appearance. She looked around for the face of an acquaintance, but among the first she saw was the bloodless face with its goat beard of Commander Minić, slyly smiling. She addressed him with her hoarse, biting voice that rang as cold and sharp as metal itself: "Are you pleased, Ljubo Minić, commander of the macaroni? Laugh, you sly fox, but remember: your fate will not be a lucky one either!"

Taken by surprise, Minić did not hear her first words and knew in advance that he would not be able to give her the right answer. He only muttered: "Well, you magpie, Mehmed will now baptize you, since the first baptism did not help you!"

Besides the blacksmith Jogaz, Mehmed was the only Moslem who could have survived under the Četnik rule in Kolašin. This insane and timid streetcleaner and domestic servant would perform any humiliating task out of fear; he had also consented to hang the condemned Partisan women since no one else wanted to do so. Short, ugly, and stumpy in his filthy, ragged clothes, he stood on the stool waiting for a sign, gazing stupidly, listening with pricked ears to what the girl was saying but unable to trust his own ears.

"Pull it, what are you gaping at?" screamed Minić to Mehmed.

"Hey, fool! You're listening to a speech, ah, Turkish rogue!" Minić's commander of the guards added, ready to assume the executioner's role.

Mehmed was puzzled. He tried to catch the swaying snare but the girl pushed him abruptly and vigorously with her elbow. Surprised, he clutched his chest and fell from the shaken stool.

"Ah," the people sighed with admiration, approval, and congratulations along with a dozen forbidden, dangerous, and suppressed feelings and desires.

The girl stood firm and pulled the snare around her thin white neck.

She pulled off her white kerchief and uncovered her hair, which was divided into two fair braids. She threw the braids across the snare and let them fall on her bosom, reaching as far as her waist. Framed by her pale forehead, her shining hair and eyes made her face more beautiful. For a few seconds in these last moments her great beauty radiated forth.

"I know how to hang myself unaided," she said in the dead silence, and with an almost invisible gesture pushed and turned the stool under her feet.

She jerked and hung down, stretched out straight and stiff, hung by the snare.

Women began to scream and cover their eyes so as not to see what they had come to watch. The citizens realized that they had fulfilled their despicable duties and rushed to the dam. Mehmed was the last to leave. He felt dizzy, his legs trembled, something urged him to turn around, but he lacked the courage to do so.

The hanged girl remained alone. The first to approach her were her lambs. Fewer in number, huddled together, gone wild by the chase, they had descended along the river and followed the trampled grass on the meadow. Below the gallows they came to a stop and one after the other lifted their heads. They stared at the shepherdess, astonished and sad—as if imploring her to come down and protect them. A mild wind blowing from the summits of Mount Ključ swayed the hanged girl's body, and her shadow moved over the grass as if she were alive, frightening the lambs. Huddled together, alone and abandoned, they rushed in terror in the direction of the Tara and its muddy waters, which have never recorded a worse spring than that one.

Translated by Zora Depolo

BRANKO ĆOPIĆ

An Awkward Companion

Squad commander Nikoletina was setting out from his brigade headquarters to the rear command. They gave him some mail to carry, a sum of about three million lire, and then they tagged on to this a little Jewish girl about six years old. He was to deliver her to the command and they would settle her in one of the villages deep in the heart of liberated territory.

"For heaven's sake, men," grumbled Nikoletina with a sour glance at the little girl. "What do I do with this? I don't know how to handle kids. I'm no good at it."

"Listen to him talk! She's not a land mine," scolded the secretary of the brigade headquarters.

"I know she isn't . . . but suppose the tanks raise the dust under my feet while we're on the road? How can this little thing retreat?"

"Ho, ho! And you call yourself a man!" the secretary retorted good-naturedly. "Up to now you've retreated and advanced a dozen times with that big machine gun, and now you think it would be hard to clasp the kid under one arm and then run for it. See how light she is—like a feather."

"Hm! a feather! A machine gun's one thing and a living creature's another."

"Just listen to him," frowned the secretary. "We snatched the kid a few days ago, under gunfire, from an Ustaši truck, and now you talk like that. What do you want us to do, throw her away? Or what?"

"Go to the devil, who said anything of the sort?" retorted the ruffled young man.

When they set out, the child immediately followed the squad commander, meekly and trustingly.

Pleased with the way she showed no fear of him, Nick asked her, still frowning:

"Afraid of me, little girl?"

"No," she replied, looking squarely at him with big, dark, frank eyes, so that he drew his away in slight confusion and mumbled:

"How freely she looks at you, just like a grownup. Trust a female not to be squeamish about anything."

He looked at the child again stealthily and wondered: What nationality can she be? Such red hair! A Jewess, was it, somebody said last night?

"Look here, what's your name?"

"Erna."

Erna! What species would that be? Some sort of Turkish name, or maybe German? Perhaps she was a little Jewess after all. Who's to say? Oh, Nick, Nick! there's no end to the nationalities you'll be leading around in this uprising.

The squad commander slowed his pace and asked:

"Hey, little one, what are you?"

"Beg pardon, sir?"

"I'm no bishop, that you should be begging my pardon! I said, what are you?"

"A little girl."

"You don't say! Well, I thought you were the commander of the anti-Četnik battalion!" Nikoletina stopped short and his eyes looked questioningly at the child.

"I meant, what are you—you know: Serbian, Croat, Moslem?"

The little girl also halted, looked at the glowering, big-stepping soldier with the automatic rifle astride in the middle of the road, and suddenly began to tremble, her eyes widening and never leaving Nikoletina's face.

"Well, what is it now, what is it?" the squad commander glowered.

"Sir, you're going to kill me," mumbled the child.

"Why? You little goose! Come now, what's wrong?"

"Because I'm a Jew," whispered the little girl.

"The devil, you say!" retorted the squad commander angrily. "Do I look like a Fascist? Do I? Where did you learn that propaganda?"

Erna continued to stare at Nikoletina. One could expect almost anything from such a huge and clumsy soldier.

"Well, come on now, what's wrong? Why have you got a face as long as a fiddle? Afraid of me?"

"Yes," whispered the little girl.

"Afraid, afraid! In that case, what's to be done? Here, how would you like to hold the automatic, seeing as you're afraid I'm going to kill you with it. Here, take it!"

Nikoletina hung the automatic rifle about the child's neck and muttered through his teeth:

"What the devil made me take you along? Now I've got to waste time convincing you I'm not a killer. Come on, little girl, still afraid of me?"

The child lowered her eyes, fluttered her lids, and said hesitatingly:

"Yes, I am."

"There's the devil for you," and he slapped his thighs. "Now, by all that's mighty, tell me why you're afraid—why, just tell me that. Look, I'm a Jew too. Yes, I am, by St. Nicholas! You don't think they chased us any less than they did you! By heaven, they didn't!"

The little girl was silent, her eyes lowered to the ground, her face shadowed by her long lashes. Only her thick copper hair shone in the light. Well, what was a man to do now?

"Look, what do you still want of me?" the squad commander spread his hands. "You've disarmed me, I've changed my faith because of you, I've capitulated like the old Yugoslavia, and you still . . . would you like me to jump into that brook there?"

Nikoletina approached a small wooden bridge and leaned over across a narrow stream full of frog spawn.

It would serve you right, he thought, to leap into that.

The little girl was sadly eying the Partisan and shifting her weight from one foot to the other.

"Well, let's get going, shall we?" asked Nikoletina.

"Yes," said the little girl disconsolately.

With the rifle around her neck, the child was lagging behind Nikoletina. After a short while she spoke up timidly:

"Sir, the rifle's too heavy for me."

"Of course it is. Come, let me carry it for you."

In the course of the march, the little girl began thawing out a bit. She even started asking a question or two.

"Sir, what street are we going to now?"

"What did you say?"

"What street are we going to now?"

"What on earth are you talking about? Street? I can't make you out at all!"

"Oh, sir, you are silly!"

"Your old man's silly, not me!"

Nikoletina turned about to stare glumly at the child and muttered:

"Look at her, used to streets, isn't she! No streets here! It's the forest we're going to, dear heart!"

"The forest? That's where the bandits are," said the child gravely.

"O-ho, the bandits! So you've fallen for their propaganda too! The bandits are in the towns, child. In those streets of yours."

They were now climbing slowly up a sparse birch-covered hill. Suddenly the child grabbed Nikoletina's sleeve and cried out in fright:

"Sir, there's a wolf!"

Nikoletina's eyes darted swiftly in the direction of her glance and then he burst out derisively:

"Ha, ha, a fine wolf, that! Don't you see it's somebody's donkey?" He looked at the beast as though it were to blame for something:

"Don't you know the difference between a wolf and a donkey? Just think of it. And which of us is silly now?"

Having nearly arrived at the edge of the oak forest, Nikoletina stopped, loosed his belt with the heavy loader, and looked at the little girl:

"Child, are you tired? Shall we sit down a while?"

He sat down beneath the first row of oaks, stretched his body out along the ground, the bag with the millions under his head, and murmured contentedly:

"I'll wager the bourgeoisie knew how to live: millions under their heads, then a rest in the shade, and let the devil take the hindmost."

He was already rolling off into sleep when the child's scream startled him:

"Oh, what's that? Look, sir, look!"

Still lying down and half asleep, Nikoletina looked toward the forest. A faint shadow was darting up a nearby tree trunk and then disappeared among the branches.

"What is it now? That, over there? Why, it's only a squirrel. Why the panic, child, for heaven's sake! Only a squirrel, poor kid, and you afraid of it . . . I almost thought it was the enemy reconnaissance."

With her eyes still glued to the tree, the little girl came closer to Nikoletina.

"Uncle, I'm afraid."

"Dear me, dear me!" the squad commander waved his hand. "I knew I'd have trouble with you. And what is it going to be like on the road if the tanks start coming? What will you do then? You'll reveal us with your screams, and then we're lost!"

Erna looked at him intelligently and gravely:

"Uncle, I'm not afraid of tanks."

"Oho! Listen to this!" cried the squad commander. "You so scary and not afraid of tanks, eh?"

"No, I'm not. They used to pass down our street every day. The tiny, little ones and the big ones, too. The grownups were afraid, but we children—not a bit."

"You don't say!"

"Are you afraid of tanks, Uncle?"

Nikoletina coughed and cleared his throat and, looking round him as if anxious not to be overheard, said:

"Well, it's like this . . . hm . . . listen to her! Well, if you're not afraid, there's no reason why I should be. To tell the truth . . . it's downright ugly to see one of them growling uphill, but otherwise . . . hm. . . ."

"The devil's face is painted on them too," said the child cheerily, raising her brows.

"I don't doubt it," admitted the Partisan thoughtfully.

The child took a few steps to and fro, observing the Partisan carefully, and then softly touched his arm with one finger:

"Uncle, you're afraid of something."

"Nonsense, child. What could I be afraid of!" replied Nick, touched to his very heart by the child's solicitous statement. To conceal his emotion, he frowned ridiculously and grumbled scoldingly:

"Why are you uncle-ing me all the time? My name's Nikola, Uncle Nikola to you."

The squad commander hoisted the mail pouch over his shoulder, took the rifle, tightened his belt, and said in a businesslike tone:

"Shall we start, Comrade Erna?"

"Let's go, Uncle Nikola."

Translated by Vida Janković

RANKO MARINKOVIĆ

The Hands

I contemplated them, interlocked behind his back, the left hand lying snugly in the palm of the defter, stronger, wiser, more serious right. I might add "older," had I not known that they were conceived together and born of one mother (indeed, of one father, too), and now left by their parents to knead a clod of soil into a crust of bread.

They were the offspring of desire, of strange ramblings in the dead of one night, in the blackout of reason, and now they roved here and there in their embrace, full of love for each other, inseparable. The right hand hugged the left, carrying it with care and solicitude, as a bitch her pups between her teeth. The left lay snug in the embrace of the right, amusing itself at its leisure, its thumb tripping from fingertip to fingertip to the soft tune of do-re-mi-fa . . . fa-mi-re-do . . . , and then to another strain drummed in march rhythm.

"What are you doing?" asked the right hand.

"What do you think? Singing," said the left hand.

"What are you singing?"

"Do-re-mi-fa and 'Onward Christian Soldiers' . . ."

" 'Onward Christian Soldiers?!' Nonsense!" retorted the right hand with an unconcealed smile of contempt. "You're not a soldier."

"It isn't only soldiers that sing 'Onward Christian Soldiers' . . . Children sing it too."

"But you're not a child."

"I'm neither a soldier nor a child. But why is it nonsense to sing?" asked the left hand with a flash of irritation in its voice. "I will sing if I want to," and then burst out with,

> "Every letter, big and small,
> I can read and write them all;
> Numbers also—one, two, three,
> Won't you come and read with me?"

"Do you mean to say you can write?" asked the right hand in an exasperated voice.

"Oh, dammit, I can't go about silent, or only counting on my fingers like a moneylender!"

"Are you saying I'm a moneylender?"

"You don't count on your fingers."

"What do I do then?"

"You work and act, as an illiterate fool has already observed before me."

"How do you know those were the words of an illiterate fool? You can't read."

"Neither can you."

"But I can write."

"You can't read, though."

"At least I can turn the pages of a book; you can't even do that much. All you can do is hold the book while I turn the pages. He reads, I turn the pages, you hold the book like a bookstand. That's all you can do. You've never looked in a book. You know books from their weight, but you haven't got the faintest idea of what's in them."

"I can turn the pages too. And if he were lefthanded, I could write."

"Write; yes, but how?"

"Like you do. And maybe even better. If he were lefthanded, I'd be able to do everything you do, and perhaps even better than you!"

"Would you know how to pull puppet strings?"

"Yes."

"And paint?"

"And paint."

"And draw three hares on the nail of my little finger?"

"And draw three hares on the nail of your little finger. And two chicks as well! By the way, why on your nail? I'd draw them on my own."

"Drivel! Even I can't do that. No one can."

"I could, though."

"It means you'd be able to cut your own nails?"

"Of course. I cut yours, don't I?"

"Yes, you cut mine, but I'm talking about yours. No one can do that."

"Stop saying, 'No one can do that!' I could!"

"All you do is boast, but you couldn't even catch a flea."

"Rot! As if I never caught a flea!"

"Would you sew?"

"I'd sew too."

"But how about threading the needle? I'd have to do that for you."

"I'd thread the needle. I'd do everything myself."

"And tie a tie?"

"And tie a tie."

"And drop drops in his eye?"

"And drop drops in his eye."

"And shave him?"

"And shave him."

"But he wouldn't let you shave him."

"Why not? I'd shave him better than you do."

"You'd cut his throat."

"I'm not a murderer! You might do that. Anyway, you did try to do it once."

Silence. The right hand was at a loss as to what to say. It shook at those words, as though an odious memory coursed through its veins.

"But I thought he was serious about it," came the meek voice with a hint of guilt in it. "I only wanted to do what he said. . . ."

"Do what he said? He didn't ask you to kill him, surely?"

"His every wish is my command. I thought it was really his wish."

"Aha, you mean he is insincere? Who told you he wished to do that?"

"I thought he did. . . . He was in trouble. He hadn't slept a wink all night. I'd wiped his moist forehead, lit cigarette after cigarette for him, and wrote his good-by letter. He groaned, sighed, wrestled with his pillow . . . and then whispered, 'I must end it all, I can't go on like this!' And then he took me to his razor."

"And straight off you took that to mean he wanted to cut my wrist!"

"Don't torment me! What else could I do when he kept saying . . ."

"What did he keep saying? That he couldn't go on like that, that he must end it all. . . . But those are only words! Words aren't fathered by wishes but by the tongue. It's easy for the tongue to play the fool, and harm comes of it only in those books whose pages you turn. The tongue splutters forth its words (always the same, by the way, and known for ever so long) and they melt away like smoke. Nothing happens: the earth keeps on spinning, people eat, smoke, and sleep, and speak the words again, and still nothing happens. People like to talk, but their words do not show their wishes; in fact, words even hide them. Words are a screen. So that proves he didn't mean what he said!"

"How can we know what he means, if not from his words?"

"Least of all from his words. He said, 'I must end it all,' but he didn't mean it. Even I knew that much."

"Where did you get that from?"

"Oh, you know: I'm clumsy, weak, and a fool. Yes, and fickle. And words are as strange to me as light is to the ear and sound to the eye, and I don't know one from the other, or sweet from bitter, they're all the same to me, and I don't believe any of them.

"I don't know how to follow words, I can't keep my balance along the circles and ellipses, parabolas and spirals of words; I can't twist and turn and swing like a teetotum and slide over the ice of conversation, drawing fancy figures, turning somersaults, doing monkey business like a monkey in the circus, and pat shoulders and diplomatically shake the right hand of a diplomatic enemy, and raise another gallantly to his lips to kiss. I'm neither a *preziosa* nor a *cicisbeo*, I'm neither a lady nor high society, I'm neither an academy nor a buffoon: I'm Molière."

"Molière? And what else?"

"A fig in the pocket. Or out of the pocket—whichever you wish. Because I'm as insolent as Figaro. I'm your lackey: while you prostitute yourself naked in all sorts of handshakes, I hold your glove like a Roman slave. I'm supposed to bear your train, to trot and trip after you while you carry on conversations, broaden horizons, build worlds. For you are a mason, a genius, a Demiurge; you're his pride, his strength, wisdom, skill: a Hand, in a word!"

"And what are you?"

"I? I'm only a holder. I'm still a kind of walker, a foreleg, a feeler, a pseudopodium, or something like that. I keep him in touch with the earth, like a foot, but still I know how to walk. At night I dream of running, of climbing trees, of jumping over chasms, and then I feel the toughness of matter and strength in my nails. For me things are as muddy as clay, hard as stone, hot as fire, or wet as water; for you they are terracotta, Corinthian vases, Venuses, rockets, or H_2O. That's why I know he wants water when he's thirsty, that he wants joy when he's sad, that he wants to live when he speaks of ending everything."

"Yes; but when he's thirsty, I give him water."

"You? No; you only turn on the tap or work the handle on the pump; but it's from my palm that he drinks; water pours on me and I feel its coolness, its wetness, and hear the gurgling sound it makes in his throat, and know the pleasure he feels after he has quenched his thirst. You say you give him water when he's thirsty? No; all you give him is a glass. You even cast thirst in a form and fashion a style for drinking. You step in between him and nature, like a self-styled arbiter and censor, like a master of ceremonies; in fact, like a filter. Whatever wants to approach him must go through your fingers; you have to touch, feel, examine everything, you have to suit everything to your taste, whether it pleases him or not. You have to stamp your pretentious thumb, the seal of your taboo, on everything!"

"You don't expect him to graze, or gnaw the bark of the trees, do you? After all, nature doesn't pet him as it is."

"Of course I don't. And then you had to come along and 'vanquish' it for his benefit. You've 'leveled mountains' and 'tamed the waters' and 'captured thunderbolts,' and now you wield terrific forces with which, they say, you can destroy the world as easily as you can snap your fingers. The earth lies in your palm like a ball that you can throw out into the universe. Well, why don't you, Omnipotence? Throw the ball away among the stars to dissolve into dust? Why don't you consummate your Great Deed?

"I don't want to destroy the earth."

"How generous! Is there a century that you have not carved up with knives and riddled with bullets? It was not words, but your five fingers that were at work."

"There were words first."

"Yes, according to John the Baptist. But what would words have done if it hadn't been for you? Words would have quarreled, they would have clashed, the vanquished would have fallen, but no one would have been the worse."

"What about honor?"

"Honor? Whose honor? Define that chivalrous word. Your honor? When your palm itches, when your pulse quickens, when your fingers tremble and frantically seek the hilt of your dagger; when your finger is ready on the trigger, when you make the sign of the Cross and pray for God's blessing to alight upon the barrel of your gun, when your two fingers and thumb hold the pen that kills—is that what you mean by honor?"

"What pen?"

"The judge's fountain pen. Have you forgotten? The defendant was sitting in front of us because of some words. Not because of something his hands had done, but because of words. You didn't care to know what had made those words burst forth from his tongue; you simply took down the facts. He had said them and admitted them: that was all you wanted to know. He was pale, his lips were trembling as though he were freezing. He was counting his last seconds. . . . He stared at you with horror in his eyes, he followed every movement of your fingers, as though they could kill him. You were known as 'The Fist of Steel' and 'The Bloody Hand.' The iridium tip of your fountain pen was already thin with murder. That tiny speck of precious metal slid wearily along the paper, as though it were present at an uninteresting and tiring board meeting, and was doodling away its time drawing idyllic little houses with gardens and fences, and smoke rising out of the chimney. Your iridium tip, however, killed the idyllic little house with the garden and fence with a volley, and all that remained of the idyll was the smoke from the rifles. . . . You had already taken the pen between your ill-famed fingers and thumb and dropped resolutely to the paper. I jumped on you and, not knowing what to do, began to rub a smudge of ink off your forefinger. As I rubbed your forefinger with my thumb, I said, 'But he didn't do anything to you. Look how pale he is. He's trembling. Isn't that enough for you? He's listening to his last heartbeats and counting. . . . Don't stop him!' "

" 'Heartbeats, nonsense! He's fishing for pity with his pale look. That's an old ruse!'

" 'But your hand was like stone. Can't you shake instead of being so impassive, as though you were giving a pupil bad marks at an exam?'

" 'I've no reason to shake. I'm doing my duty.'

"Then you began to write your well-known D, the first letter of violent and criminal death, with slow, painstaking, calligraphic strokes. And then you added four more letters to your D to complete the word 'death.' And you didn't shake in the least. That same evening (you hadn't even washed) you tangled her silky hair and caressed her face, and your fingers trembled with love. Those fingers, that never trembled before death, trembled that night with love. Now, who can say that love is not stronger than death, especially that our love is not stronger than someone else's death?"

"How can you speak about love? You don't know what love is. That first touch, when the fingers grope for each other in the dark, and suddenly touching, tremble as though two electric poles charged with power had come together. . . .'"

"Yes, and a spark leaps: a short circuit and a blackout. And that's the end of love. What then? Duty? The gold pen dripping death?"

"You're erratic and crazy!"

"And I suppose you're rational and wise! That's the difference. Let me go!" and the left hand angrily endeavored to shake off the embrace of the right.

"What's come over you all of a sudden? Always behaving scandalously in the streets!"

"Don't touch me! Let me go! I won't have anything to do with you!"

"Whom are you going with then? The feet?"

"Even with the feet! At least they've got some idea of honor. They're at least noble as a horse. You're as cunning and venomous as a serpent."

"Yes, and they're as stupid as horses, too. All they do is walk and tug loads. You can't go with them. After all, you are a hand, you know!"

"I'm not a hand, and I won't be one! I'm ashamed of being a hand!"

"What do you want to be? A foreleg?"

"Anything, anything, only not a hand!"

"All the same, you're a hand like me."

"Like you? No! Let me go!"

And the left hand wrenched itself from the embrace of the right and crept into its own pocket, where it angrily rummaged about pretending to search for something. Finding nothing, it emerged, dropped defiantly to his side, and nervously twiddled its fingers.

The right hand remained a moment longer behind his back, empty and thoughtful. Then, snapping its thumb and dropping to his side, it fell in rhythm with the feet.

I watched the two hands, bad-tempered as they were, unable to believe my eyes. They were like two symbiotic animals or plants. The right hand was right: they were alike, they were both hands.

Two children were approaching them, a boy and a girl. They were holding hands and singing. But as they drew near, they dropped into silence, like crickets when someone is near, and separated. The girl passed the right hand, softly, as though she had done something wrong. It patted the girl's blond head. The girl returned the pat with a glance of gratitude.

The boy passed the left hand recklessly. He threw it an insolent stare, as though it were something lying in the road. It tweaked his nose awkwardly with its thumb and forefinger. The boy spat at it. It rose instinctively and made a playful feint over the boy's head as though driving flies away. But the right hand rose and slapped the boy. He yelled.

"Why did you strike the boy?" asked the left hand.

"Because he spat at you!"

"But he spat at me, not at you!"

"He shouldn't have spat!"

"It must have hurt him. I was clumsy . . ."

"You would be! . . . But still he shouldn't have spat. Disgusting!"

"To hit someone on the nose is the peak of refinement, I suppose!"

"You didn't hit him, you only tweaked his nose. That's not the same thing at all. Anyway, it isn't as if you had cut his nose off!"

"Why should I mind if he spat at me?"

"To spit at someone is an insult!"

"To one's dignity!"

"Yes, to one's dignity!" retorted the right hand, already at the end of its patience.

The boy was screaming about the resounding insult to his cheek.

In a moment two glistening streams flowed from his nostrils and dropped to his chin, where they reached flooding level.

"Look at the little rascal, what a row he's kicking up!" remarked the right hand, astonished at the row. Then it turned to the left hand. "Let me wipe you."

"It's all right, I've already done so."

"But you had to do it on his trousers!"

"No, I didn't. I wiped myself on his coat! Look, here comes the boy's father!"

The boy's father came rushing out of the house in his shirt sleeves. His white-collar hands with their blue, timid veins were delicate and pale.

"Why did you hit my son?" asked the father coldly, like a judge contemplating sentence.

"Because he's rude and impudent!" replied the right hand with a note of challenge in its voice.

"What did he do?" the father went on, now really offended.

"He spat at me!" said the right hand bitterly, almost believing he really had.

"He spat at me, not you," said the left hand in a tone of righteousness.

"It doesn't matter at whom he spat; the fact is that he spat," exclaimed the right firmly.

"Spat for no reason at all?" continued the father, now realizing he would have to fight.

"I didn't, Daddy! This hand hit me on the nose . . ." interrupted the boy tearfully.

"Only tweaked his nose playfully," said the right hand, "and he up and spat."

"Serves you right!" shouted the father in such a rage that a flood of fury seemed to burst from him. "I can spit too!" and he spat. "Murderers!" he shrieked.

The right hand rose and swung with all its strength. The boy's father, warding off the blow, swung his own fist and caught the right hand a cuff on the thumb. The right hand groaned.

Then the left hand went into action. It grabbed the boy's father by his shirt. The right hand acted as swiftly and, clenching its fingers into a fist, began to pummel his face.

Blood streamed from his nose onto the left hand, which was holding his shirt front. The right hand, which repeatedly struck the father's bloody face, was also a gory mess.

Seeing her father's blood dripping to the ground, the girl screamed and flew forward to catch the drops. The boy hurled himself into the fray, grabbed the left hand, and sank his teeth firmly into its forearm.

The left hand howled with pain and loosed its grip. The father took advantage of the momentary lull to take to his heels, a vanquished pulp, disgraced before his children.

The boy loosed his teeth from the left hand, which now struck him on the head. The boy received the blow hardily.

Then the legs, like obedient horses, started after the boy's father. The boy threw himself before them, not to implore mercy for his father, but to trip them up.

And, indeed, the left and the right hand suddenly found themselves in the dust.

"Oh-h-h!" groaned the right. Its thumb hurt.

. . . Two bloody hands on the asphalt. They lay in disgrace in the street, side by side, helpless, like cast-off gloves.

"The damned rascal!" muttered the left between its fingers as it got up.

"Serves you right for not giving him a good one!"

"But I did!"

"Yes, like a softy! Help me up. I think my thumb is broken."

"Does it hurt?"

"Terribly!"

The left hand was gentle, like a sister. . . .

They got up, leaving bloody blotches on the pavement. But they did not turn back to look at them; they rubbed each other, shaking in their desire for revenge.

Then the Face spat into their palms and wiped the blood and dirt off them.

Translated by Petar Mijušković

RANKO MARINKOVIĆ

Ashes

Of course he recognizes it, he really does! It is the round, correct *n* that reminds one of a seagull's wings. He had often warned her not to write it like *u* in his address. He is not Touko Jaukiu, a Japanese. He is Jankin, Tonko Jankin, and not a certain Touko Jau-kiu, Kiu-shu, Shu-shu, an invader of the Chinese province The-Devil-Knows-It! There is a stress on this *n*, a hint, something implied but unuttered. Ah, that *n*, the letter *n*—what memories!

I know you, madam, I recognize your handwriting in this *n!* But what do you now want of me, a clumsy, awkward fellow, a queer fish, a collector of old keys? With these same words you left me ten years ago, or rather, to be exact, eleven. Don't you remember it? Eleven years ago you got hysterical and burst into tears; you stamped your small feet on the pebbled path and screamed, "Why on earth do I need you with these old keys, you . . ." *Ah, how beautiful she was in those days, God!* Old Lucia, who was upstairs, heard you and asked me later, "Mr. Tonko, what was the matter with Miss Anne?" "Miss Anne?" I asked. "She was pricked by a palm leaf. . . ." "But she mentioned some keys," Lucia muttered, "that is why I'm asking you."

Old Lucia knew what the matter was, and she also knew it was neither because of the palm leaf nor because of the keys. I, too, was aware that it was not because of the keys. That I was a key collector, this you had known before—everybody knew that, the whole town knew it—and in spite of everything you became my fiancée. All the people in town sold interesting ancient keys to me, and so did you—you yourself, madam, gave me that beautiful Venetian-Gothic key as a gift—the treasure and paragon of my key collection! *Ah, Anne!*

No, indeed not, it was not because of the keys, fair lady, but because of a surveyor. Because of a surveyor who had come to measure our land. Because of a fellow comrade, Comrade Surveyor! This was the cause of your hysteria, tears, and stamping your foot on the ground! You even broke your heel, and then we had to send Lucia to a shoemaker to repair it so you could go home. You had to wait for Lucia to return with your little shoe *the tiny bare foot!*, and then you sat down on a bench amid the oleanders and, though irritated, you remained silent, you refused to say a single word to me. I felt guilty; what did I, the wretched one, know about the surveyor at that time? One could smell the oleanders around your head, but you were unaware of the scent. I even felt guilty because of that—that you could not smell the fascinating, love-inspiring smell that gives rise to sighs. I sighed, too, because of your silent anger, the scent, my own guilt, which was nonexistent *how cruel you were, Anne!*, and I fell to my knees in front of you and begged your forgiveness. I renounced the keys, I promised . . . and I wanted to kiss your toes, but you pushed me in the chest with that same untouched, unkissed little foot, and made me tumble onto the ground. Literally, I was rebuffed to make room for the surveyor.

Even today I do not know how he noticed you through his theodolite. But you were madly infatuated with him. You were not in the least ashamed of waiting for him, planning to meet him as though accidentally in the street *all this was talked about on all sides, and I was really ashamed of it, Anne,* and when he finished his job and left, you ran after him shamelessly. And later, when the war broke out, you even wanted to follow him to the forest! You wanted to wear slacks and become a woman Partisan!

When Lucia returned with the shoe, you went away, you left me without saying a single word, without even a handshake. I have never seen you since. When the war was over, Lucia told me that in spite of everything you married the surveyor. She told me that you found him dirty and exhausted *forgive me, Anne,* and dragged him into your bed *Ah, Anne, Anne, I cried for you then!,* and afterwards he registered you as his comrade mate.

And now this letter. What do you still want? With this *n* that looks like a seagull's wing? Are you, perhaps, trying to ridicule . . . surveying?

He sat on that same bench in the garden, near the path that was once, eleven years ago, covered with pure white pebbles and that was now dark, covered over with bare, muddy earth. The oleanders were in full bloom and smelled just as they did then, when she sat there. He sighed inwardly, plunging into his own memories.

You didn't even know, my lady, that after you had gone I became ill with a high fever and moaned your name, and called out for you. . . . I talked in my sleep and vowed that I would throw away all my keys except the one you had given me as a gift, the key to paradise. . . . Later, Lucia told me I had mentioned a key to paradise. She thought I was dying, that my soul was already in the other world at the gates of paradise talking to St. Peter. And I was really looking for a key to paradise, your key *you were paradise, Anne, my paradise,* with which I wanted to peep into your cruel, frightful soul. When I recovered, I called it the key to hell, and I hung it up there, on a hook under the window, where the canary cage had hung before, but the canary had died during my illness, neglected there below the window. Thus I hung it—the key to the door of hell—outside my house, so that the devil in you could come for it at night. . . . Every morning I went to see whether the key was still there under the window, and so, one night, the devil had taken it away.

I wanted to write to you, Anne, to tell you I had not returned the key myself and that the devil, your devil . . . forgive me, I did not know what to do. Later, Lucia told me I had sent the key to you myself, that she herself had taken it to the post office, but I can't remember that, I don't remember anything at all—my sadness practically drove me mad.

I waited for you—for two years I waited for you to come back. I even bought the recording "J'attendrai toujours . . ." and I played that record day and night, and, waiting for you, I cried as I played it. But you never came. Eleven years have passed, and you never came, and now what do you want with this letter?

He held the letter, still unopened. The light, white, tender weight on his palm seemed like the touch of Anne—pure, gentle, good Anne—as in the early days of their love. From his palm Anne seemed to smile at him—calm, obedient, submissive, as if she wanted, through that tired, exhausted handwriting, and this n that begged repentantly, "forgive me," to give herself to him as a gift, with all her fairness, sorrow, and disappointment. But still he could not get up strength enough to open the letter; the oleanders still smelled strongly of doubt, the old pain, hysteria. . . . And there was no key to paradise to unlock the heaven on his palm, that hell in his hand, that treacherous door to uncertainty. . . . The devil had taken away the key that night under the window.

He trembled all over excitedly. And he said, "Funny! She writes to me! Comical! Anne writes to me! How funny!" He wanted to imagine her disappointment, her unsuccessful marriage, her sadness, her longing for him and imploring, a direct, humble request to him to allow her to come back. . . . But as soon as his imagination began to work, a counterwind emerged, dispersing the enchanting clouds of a triumphant reunion. There was only a letter on his palm, an uncertain datum, a poor, ungrounded reason for such turmoil in him, an alarm that had startled him from the quiet dream of his tranquil life under an eleven-year thick layer of resignation.

When he heard the shuffling of Lucia's slippers walking along the corridor upstairs, he tucked the letter under his shirt. He jumped to his feet resolutely. The hard corner of the envelope pierced his chest and made him sigh. Nevertheless, he moved on. He went to his room and locked himself in, there to lament his new situation. The previous experience was taken out of his drawer of memories where it had become weary and worn away for eleven full years by the moths of oblivion, like an expensive Sunday suit that has never been put on. Then, all of a sudden, it comes out into the light, full of holes, oddly empty, but yet with a biting taste from the fragrance of the oleanders along the thorny path of the past from which the sands of time have washed all purity.

Anne had a fair complexion. She was a snow-white lady, as white as sugar, like cloud puffs, pale as a result of her illusions and delusions, pale because of his pure white devoted love. And then, all of a sudden, my lady, you melted away before my eyes. Only white spots, white holes, white fluttering memories have survived, waving farewell from a great distance with white handkerchiefs.

I waved my towel in greeting, the morning you left. I watched you through field glasses; I noticed you on the deck. You followed my waving, as you had done every morning after you got up and went to the window to accept my morning greetings and send your greetings to me in return. But then, aboard the ship, when you were about to leave forever, you did not answer my greetings. You took out a white handkerchief from your purse and wiped your nose. And this was how you parted from me.

Both the towel and the field glasses are still on the special shelf wrapped in white paper. And I have never ceased to wave at you, Anne, for the past eleven years. From my balcony I send you my greetings every morning *you are still my morning prayer,* but instead of you, your old foolish Aunt Rosa answers me from that same window.

He shut the windows that were struck by the heavy summer sunshine, pulled the shutters, and the room wrapped itself up into a mild, mourning twilight. In that twilight, as if opening a case containing photographic plates, he carefully tore the envelope and grasped the letter. It was too dark in the room to read it, and so he waited a little until his eyes got used to the darkness.

What does she want? I've returned her key, I do not have any of her belongings. Perhaps Comrade Surveyor wants something? Perhaps, through her mediation, Comrade Surveyor would like to make peace and beg my forgiveness for the happiness he has snatched away from me, and which he enjoys all by himself.

Good luck to you, Comrade Surveyor, just have a good time! I am not unhappy myself. On the contrary, you've done me . . . *forgive me, Anne, I'm only telling him this, that he would not laugh at me. You know how I feel* you've done me, Comrade . . .

"My dear Toni," the letter read, "it's even strange for me to write to you after all that has happened between us . . . and after such a long time. I've something to beg you, and I hope that you won't . . ."

His face beamed with generosity. *To refuse to do something for you, my dear Anne! Say, just say, what you want. . . .*

". . . After five years of vain waiting and after we had lost all hope, I have had a son!"

He read the sentence twice, but it was only after he had read it for the third time and had repeated it silently that he understood its meaning and translated the words into reality. Five years of waiting! Very well! Leaning on the window with your surveyor, you waited for the stork to come to you! Ah, is this what you call waiting?

He was malicious, cynical, and pleased with himself. He felt that an adequate grimace had twisted his face, and he went to look at himself in the mirror. It was a sad mask of disappointment forcibly covered over by irony; it was like a wrong glove, twisting his face oddly, as in a magic mirror. But he was satisfied. He thought this was the kind of smile that could destroy any adversary. He carefully dragged his grimace about the room, his head up in the air, like a juggler carrying a bottle on his nose.

Waiting, waiting . . . he muttered, visualizing to himself many bitter, offensive scenes. But let us see what the favor is.

"You know, Toni, how they are *I do—you mean comrades,* and I wouldn't like my child to remain without baptism. They only 'register'. . . . As for the marriage, I did not mind *we know that you did not, it was unnecessary for waiting,* we are adults, sensible people *this is questionable,* we know what we are doing *this is also questionable!,* but this innocent, small creature . . . if you could see what a funny small nose he's got! . . . What does that poor little one know of our politics? He could reproach me later. . . . And so I thought . . . here I have no one to turn to, just . . . you know *I do,* and you are still close and dear to me, like a brother *thank you, sister,* and so I've decided to unburden myself to you and ask you to be my little one's godfather. . . . Will you, Toni? *Hm . . .* My husband does not know anything about all this. The ceremony will take place in the morning, while my husband is at the office; I've already arranged everything with Father Vinko. And I've told my husband that you'd be coming to see us for a couple of days to see the little one, and he said, 'Let him come.' In fact, he has respect for you, and he also said, 'Although he's one of those, at least he didn't collaborate with the invaders. He has character!'

You see, politics is everything to him, and sometimes I'm fed up *don't say?*, but otherwise he's good and honest and wouldn't hurt a fly. The only thing is, it can't be helped *how? what?*, he spent four years in the forest, it takes time before he can adjust himself again to many things without which we cannot live. Please, Toni, don't reject my offer! *Hm* . . . If you accept my request, just send me a telegram to tell me when you are coming. Yours sincerely, Anne.

"P.S. Are you still collecting keys? I've a surprise for you!"

And I for you, he said aloud, and crushed the letter and flung it on the floor. A nasty smile was on his face. First this smile, like a little restless devil, hovered around his lips and nose, jumping from one side of his face to the other, prickling, shaking, and awakening those drawn features, those slumbering, sad wrinkles, those hanging, drooping bags; this smile stirred and created an uprising. The face was revived, it emerged from a dull, long passivity, it stretched itself, began to move, began to play, and the smile grew more and more vigorous and unrestrained; it had destroyed and abolished all obstacles and dams created by artificial, tensed grimaces, and brimmed over unrestrictedly and triumphantly, inundating his face like a flood. This pale, close-shaved mask was shaken by laughter, a genuine, vibrant laughter possessing the full force of fatal malice—a malice that destroyed all scruple and decency in him, all sentimentality and little pains out of which leak small streams of tiny tears. He laughed and cursed thunderingly and savagely, like a primitive, gluttonously grunting like a pig. Something revolting and inhuman, like dreadful, vindictive delight, was reflected in his laughter.

He rose to his feet, lifted the crumpled letter from the floor, smoothed it out carefully, and put it under a book. Then he called old Lucia and told her to go to the post office to send a telegram: "Arriving tomorrow—Tonko."

A ship glided smoothly on a calm sea as an old woman talked endlessly. She talked about her son who had been a Partisan and who had gotten married later and was now in Split "in a high position. . . ." She was going to pay him a visit. He also had a two-year-old son, my treasure, but the child, God forgive me, was not baptized! Ah, my dear Mr. Tonko, I'm afraid, God bless him, what will become of the unbaptized child if something should happen to him, God forgive me, please tell me, how would he face God? And what are these people like, and her son, too, though as good as bread? He is just the same as they are, always insists that everything is only nature, nature and nothing else. . . . And who created this world, this sun, both summer and winter, and this sea and those dolphins in the sea, you tell me, Mr. Tonko, how could that nature create all this, with everything in such perfect order and in the right place? Ah, me, I don't understand a thing, worried as I am, and I look at that child, my golden treasure, without grace, and tears stream from my eyes, my dear Mr. Tonko. . . .

Tonko said nothing. The seriousness with which the old woman spoke about the fateful importance of baptism plunged him into worry and contemplation. His decision to be a godfather wriggled in a net of confused thoughts that became even more entangled by the old woman's story. In spite of everything, these were sacred matters, and he did not want to interfere with them.

He began to tremble and regretted his having accepted the invitation. Nevertheless, the child would be baptized. He would not interfere with baptism. My full respect for baptism! Moreover, he would perform it behind the surveyor's back, silently, without being involved in any conflict, without much noise, with joy and ridicule in his heart. And what follows . . . has nothing to do with baptism.

He had settled the question of his conscience and again rejoiced at the deception. God would understand it and reward him. God was on his side. And Anne, too. God, he, and Anne against the surveyor—slyly, skillfully, silently, diplomatically, behind his back, and without any fuss or boisterous insult. Dip-

lomatically, he and Anne would baptize the surveyor's child.
. . . He laughed inwardly with pleasure.

He was flattered by Anne's confidence. She had asked him to
be an accomplice against her own husband. He dared to
see some hope in that fact. . . . She said that sometimes
she was fed up with him. A politician! Anne was, as before, his
own. Anne, involved in a secret agreement, in whispers, in secret
communications and a common secret. He imagined Anne in
that secret affair as in a dark room, shivering, excited, unresist-
ing, ready to give herself to him, whispering softly, inviting him
to embrace her. He shivered from bliss and shook, as if his
whole body had begun to sob.

"Death herself has missed you," said the old woman.

"What do you mean, death?" he asked harshly, awakened
from his daydreams.

"Yes, they say," said the old woman apologetically, "that
whenever someone shivers, death has just missed him. And who
knows whether or not this is correct?"

Death? He did not want the word to interfere with his present mood. His whole world was not big enough to hold the full
measure of the enjoyment that awaited him the next morning,
when the two of them would be alone, face to face, joined in
their conspiracy.

"Mr. Tonko, your gift is going to slip to the floor," the old
woman warned him, extending her arm to stop a small package
that had slipped from his knees. "What have you got there? A
gift?"

"Yes, it is," he said angrily, and pushed her hand away so that
she could not touch the little bundle; he caught it himself before it fell to the floor.

"I'm also taking these grapes to my son," the old woman
said, pointing at a small basket at her side. "But she, my
daughter-in-law, is going to eat more than he, my poor son. He
doesn't even have time to eat. He only rushes around."

Yes, it's a gift, he said silently as he made a wry face again, just as he had the day before, when he was in a turmoil and made that dreadful decision. A gift, or, rather, agitation—a bomb that would cause us, the three of us, to run in different directions, each in his own direction. If you only knew, he told the old woman in his mind, what dynamite is inside this package!

A small package, carefully wrapped in white tissue paper, tied with a wide red-ribbon bow *the color will appeal to the surveyor*, innocently rested between his knees like a loving baby in a cradle, submerged in a foam of silk and lace and adorned by the glowing redness of the ribbon. . . . The package was ready for baptism. He began to rock the dangerous loving thing on his knees and to baby-talk to him in his thoughts: wait, wait a little, little one, first we are going to satisfy your daddy, we'll baptize the little brother; then you'll lie down next to your little brother in his cradle, to cheer up Mama as well. . . . In fact, your mama will be pleased to see you again, and Daddy will jump for joy about the house as soon as he gets to know you. Finally, we will all begin to dance and be gay. . . .

"What have you got there as a gift, Mr. Tonko?" the old woman asked curiously.

"Ah, just trifles, things usually put in a child's cradle, to please both parents and child. Rattling toys, small rattles, and small bells, too."

"Small bells, that's fine. But my children played with matches, and would throw them around. . . ." Her voice was interrupted by a shrill whistle from the ship. The ship was about to enter port.

At the port the murmur of the crowd could be heard. Every time a ship arrived in port there was a small celebration, especially in postwar years, when people suddenly felt the need for some movement after four years of the restraints and restrictions under the occupation. People welcomed ships with inexplicable impatience and curiosity. Even these small ships coming from neighboring islands were awaited with excitement, as if they brought an unexpected encounter, a sudden joy that had been left behind somewhere and had now come back as a surprise.

He was excited. Among that throng at the port, among those heads that agitatedly turned, swung, and bustled as if a foolish wind had been joking with them, there was also her own pert and capricious head with certain thoughts in it. What thoughts? . . . Yet why had she invited him to come *just him!* to join in that conspiracy against the surveyor? Why had she involved him in this common secret and aroused a feeling within him—a feeling . . . that she was inviting him to some secret, isolated place where they would be completely alone and . . . whisper like conspirators? And he himself was planning his own conspiracy *his own, comprehensive, vindictive, that would be remembered!* with that infernal machine wrapped up in pure white tissue paper and ribbon, with that assassin's time bomb due to explode the morning after the baptism. . . . She'll be curious, she'll burn with impatience. . . . She'll unwrap the package, look at the godfather's gift *a godfather!* and—and the bomb will explode and the earth will quake with delight. . . .

He trembled for fear. Not because of the bomb, but because of Anne. He had some thoughts but they were only words, not thoughts, for the thoughts had shrunk, interwoven, trying to hide themselves from Anne.

Anne stood at the port waiting. She waited for him, an assassin, a treacherous murderer, with outstretched arms *Anne! Anne! Anne!* And with optimistic confidence and relief: he had accepted the invitation, Toni had accepted it! *Toni, spelled ni and not ui, but this time she pronounced his name, she did not write it out.* And, feeling guilty for being unfaithful to her husband, she expressed a tender sympathy for him, an assassin, and even showed a silent, frightened love that had been revived unconsciously within her after eleven years of sound, deadly slumber. Else why should she have invited him? Why? Perhaps the whole conspiracy was only an excuse. . . . Secretly he indulged in this possibility, and was on the brink of bursting happily into tears. And he carried a bomb as a gift for that incredible, unexpected happiness! Such ingratitude! Such foolishness! Were such foolishness and ingratitude possible?

He wanted to free himself, to discard the stupid, malicious burden that now suddenly weighed so heavily on his conscience: it was a perfidious and cynical man who stupidly and criminally roared from the package. But how could he do it discreetly and unobserved, avoiding any curious questionings or comments? Would it sink down? He put the gift at the very edge of the rail and left it there. It will drop down as soon as the ship jerks. He turned to the old woman to divert her attention from his own alleged absent-mindedness, but she was already saying something behind his back:

"Hey, Mr. Tonko, you've forgotten your gift!" the old woman screamed. "I just managed to seize it. It doesn't matter, I'll carry it for you—the way you feel now, you could even forget it on the ship! Ah, you learned people are like that! You forget everything! It doesn't matter, I'll carry it for you. . . . And would you, Mr. Tonko, do me a favor by carrying this small basket of grapes for me? Would you just carry it to the port? There are a lot of people, and I'm no longer firm on my feet. . . . Just to the port. . . ." Worriedly the old woman shielded the grapes with her skirt from the dashing passengers who had crowded to the portside of the ship. She held the package with the red ribbon in her hands.

He did not grab the package; he let it stay in the old woman's hands while he himself, with an obedient rage, lifted the basket of grapes up to his chin, as if he intended to throw it over the rail.

"Be careful, Mr. Tonko," the old woman screamed, worrying about her grapes. "Wait a while, they haven't yet set up the gangplank. You'll get tired. . . ."

But he did not put the basket down. He observed the port without even listening to the old woman. And what if she has come with her husband to meet me, he thought angrily . . .

and with the fruit of their vain waiting, he added treacherously, like an assassin ready to avenge himself.

A white handkerchief fluttered in the sun. Yes, she was there. Anne. Alone. She was surrounded by porters, militiamen, and a crowd of people, agitated, noisy, uninteresting. She was in a white sleeveless summer dress with a strange, low-cut square neck—naturally, he could see a lot of naked white flesh. *"Flesh?" he did not agree with that expression.* And on her head, a large panama sombrero with a fluttering blue ribbon—as blue as the sky and sea. . . . She was like summer herself, like the sky and sea, as white as a seagull, hovering over the crowd with her hat. . . .

"Let's go now," the old woman said, "slowly, Mr. Tonko."

He felt the weight of the basket in his hands, and it seemed stupid and cumbersome to him, full of fresh ripe grapes, like swollen grapes reminiscent of baby's cheeks and woman's breasts. . . . His thoughts changed and flew to the port, then slipped to the low-cut dress, entered the white, shivering valley . . . protruding under the dress, bulging, and full of milk. . . .

She seemed to have sensed his thought and glance and pulled up her dress, smiling perplexedly. He even saw her blush, and wondered whether she thought he was carrying the grapes to her as a gift. He did not even feel ashamed of this thought. On the contrary, he carried the basket with great care, as if many blessings were contained in it, he wanted to show her and all these people that he played the role of a man who had adjusted himself to the march of time, who had condescended to the mass level and had become equal with everything.

The old woman followed him as they crossed the gangplank and cautiously warned the passengers: "Get out of the way, make room for us to pass, for heaven's sake! Mr. Tonko, see that it doesn't get crushed. It's for him, the poor one." And then she grumbled to herself: "For him! Of course, she'll finish everything. The poor one doesn't even have time for a bite. He only dashes around until he gets sick, my poor darling. Make room.

Can't you see that we are carrying grapes?" she screamed angrily at some impatient passers-by; she was all prepared to start a quarrel.

"This way, Mr. Tonko, this way," she said, pulling to a side where there were fewer people. He had lost sight of Anne, who had disappeared among the crowds as he tried to push his way on the quay.

He was sweating profusely, the veins on his forehead and neck were bulging, he had pains in his back and arms, soft and unaccustomed to carrying a burden, and there was no room to put down the basket. Then he felt a light touch on his elbow: "Toni!"

He was startled, and he held the basket in front of him as his heart beat in his ears like the heavy march of a whole army parading in his head.

Her lips were glowing red and her teeth were white and transparent, and her eyes serene as the sky, ironical. She was ridiculing him.

He watched her for a long time like that, with the basket in his hands, and could not understand a thing. Nothing at all. A desperate, cruel, and hopeless paralysis had frozen his every motion, and it seemed as though he must remain in that position, eternally gazing at Anne. But the old woman reminded him to put the basket down, and he did so, automatically, idiotically, without lifting his eyes from her. Then, in the same mechanical manner, as if hypnotized, he took the extended, small round hand and bent down to kiss it, but the hand abruptly lowered itself downward, as if it were shyly escaping his kiss. He bent even more, following her hand, and tottered in a comic manner as if someone had struck him in the back. She smiled. She is ridiculing me, he thought, and straightened himself up, blushing and confused. One should not kiss the hand any more, it's forbidden. . . . She knew it. . . .

"You've grown old, Toni," she said, observing the gray hairs at his temples.

And what about her? I could hardly recognize her, she has changed so much, he revenged himself in his mind. Do you think you are still young? And here you behave like a young girl, a naughty young girl.

He did not know how to talk to her, as a friend or a stranger, and then he muttered something quite impersonal that sounded like an ironical compliment, which was lost forever in the confused hubbub of the port like pearls lost in mud.

He observed Anne's face and noticed how her former beauty was silently beginning to fade. The first wrinkles had emerged on her nose and around her eyes, black circles under her eyes. The skin on her neck was flabby, and farther down, in the décolleté dress *where earlier two solid balls were resolutely erected, and that beautiful, smooth fissure was like a dale between two waves, like an "ah" between two kisses!,* thick flesh had melted together. Old age had begun to nest there, he thought, and sadly diverted his eyes.

She was aware of this, and pulled her dress even farther upward and blushed slightly.

"Are you ready?" she gaily asked him then, and took him by the arm.

But the old woman had already been holding him from the back and confidently pulled his other arm.

"And what about the gift, Mr. Tonko?" she asked loudly, although she thought she had only whispered. "Have you forgotten it again?" She tucked the small package into his hand along with two very carefully selected bunches of grapes—swollen and round like a firm breast.

Once upon a time . . . a strange sorrow gripped his throat. Ah, Anne! His sorrow was mixed with the malice emanating from the small package like the outburst of a piled-up and compact rage: a gay, malicious fire had flared up within him and at the same time a sad, sorrowful rain was sprinkling it. The rain quenched the rage. He was sad.

The old woman resolutely refused to take back the grapes.

"But please, you've helped me a lot, Mr. Tonko. What would I, so wretched, have done without you?" She was about to burst into tears.

"And what shall I do with them? How can I carry them? . . . Thank you!"

He was cursing himself for his own courtesy. Anne turned away so that no one would involve her in the argument over the two bunches of grapes. She was ashamed.

"I've selected the two best bunches, just take a look at them. Please, won't you take them, Mr. Tonko? You've done me a great favor. Who'd have helped me had you not been handy? Take them or my feelings will be hurt," the old woman persisted.

"But how can I go downtown with grapes? Thank you very much."

"Ah, me, as if it's a shame to carry grapes. Grapes can be carried just like this, in one's hands, why not? Even the lady will tell you there's nothing to be ashamed of. Here's the lady, she can tell you herself."

Anne pretended not to hear anything. She had turned her back and was impatiently shifting her balance from one foot to the other.

He could not escape, and so he took the two bunches of grapes from the old woman and hooked them on his two fingers, the way fish is carried, by the gills. He left the old woman without even saying good-by.

Anne's face wore an ironical smile mixed with the conventional politeness extended to guests. He noticed both well, and as soon as they turned the first corner, he dropped the grapes furiously to the ground; they rolled all over the place like children's marbles.

She burst into laughter.

"What are you doing?"

"What the devil did she give them to me for?" he exploded. "Just for you to mock me."

"No, Toni, I'm not mocking you." But still she continued to laugh mockingly.

Wait a while, we'll see if you'll still be laughing tomorrow morning, he thought revengefully. Tomorrow, after the baptism. He felt the package under his fingers like a fearful weapon, and his decision was strengthened.

"It's so funny," she continued, "how much you've changed. You've given in, you're not a tyrant any more."

"A tyrant? I've never been one."

She did not reply. Of course, she had nothing to say. *I, a tyrant? It's impertinent, Anne. . . .*

They walked along the quiet coast, where there were many villas surrounded by gardens, where pines and palms rustled in the evening breeze that played with a small lock of her hair. Occasionally peeping at that thin lock of her hair fluttering around her ear, he realized how his courage was slowly leaving him, as if he were exposed to a dreadfully sentimental sun that was melting him away, as well as making him weak and drowsy. And so he yawned dreamily, like an exhausted man who needs much sleep.

"Of course, you must be tired," she said worriedly, looking at him almost sadly. "But here we are. That red roof." *Of course, a red one, That's your color.* "Can you see it? That's our villa."

"Your villa?" he thought, and then went on: "The one with a terrace?"

"Yes, that's it," she replied flirtatiously.

On the terrace, under a striped yellow and red awning, a spectacled man sat reading a newspaper.

The surveyor, he thought ironically. But that word, though uttered secretly in his mind, nevertheless frightened him; and he wanted Anne to believe he was worried.

"He's reading in twilight," he said to her reproachfully. "This is . . . not good. . . ."

"Yes, you're right. How many times have I told him," Anne added eagerly. She was obviously pleased with that care. "But

everything is in vain. You men are like that. He has already almost completely ruined his eyesight. . . ."

She whistled a melody from "Fra Diavolo" as a signal to her
husband, the same one she had previously used to call him,
Tonko. *Anne, Anne! His heart was torn into pieces.* The surveyor started and lifted his head as if surprised, then cheerfully
waved at them with his newspaper. Then he went into the house
to greet them.

"He's a nice man," Anne said hurriedly, "you'll see for yourself. I'm so sorry that this will be done behind his back. . . ."
She interrupted herself and sighed confusedly.

She was sorry! Again revenge began to nest within him—impatiently, restlessly, and greedy like a dog.

"Beware of the dog!" read the pre-war rusty tin sign at the
gate, while the dog in the garden uninterestedly dozed in front
of his hutch and did not even notice that a guest had come to
the house.

The surveyor was waiting for them at the door in a short-
sleeved summer shirt; tall, slim, sunburned, with his hands in
his pockets, like a cowboy. His oblong face, now without glasses,
with sensibly carved features as if he had designed them himself
from a model of cordiality and goodheartedness, smiled pleasantly and hospitably.

They shook hands. They knew each other "from that time,"
from pre-war days. But that time was never mentioned, it was
something shameful for them both.

Now he stood between them like an active, smiling link. She
wanted to bring them together, to make them friends, to bind
them through conversation, courtesies, small considerations that
would gradually develop into mutual appreciation.

In fact, the surveyor did not need her help. His kindness was
quite natural, his somewhat crude directness seemed completely
unaffected after the first few conventional words were exchanged; he began to slap Tonko on the back like an intimate
friend.

Forest manners. Tonko Jankin was insulted. He was hurt by this man's kindness, his crude frankness. Through the surveyor's clumsy gestures he saw fully emphasized the protective sympathy as well as the generosity of a victor. A two-fold victor.

"You need not be sorry for me," he wanted to tell him, "I'm not unhappy," and at that Tonko maliciously thought about the small package that he would ceremoniously drop into the child's cradle and put into the surveyor's hands tomorrow after the baptism. Then they would exchange their roles. In that case, I shall be the one who will be slapping you patronizingly, comrade . . . ha, ha. . . .

The surveyor and Anne competed in extending their kindnesses to see who could do more for him. Tonko was spoiled. "You are one of us, a member of the family . . . don't be at all shy . . ." This is what the surveyor said, and Anne added: 'Toni, make yourself at home. . . ."

He would have preferred a more reserved attitude, fewer familiarities, because as things stood, everything was indebting, a counterservice was expected too openly, and he was heading for a conspiracy. A twofold conspiracy. A twofold victor and a twofold traitor—this is the final summing-up of what everything amounts to! And she was the main culprit! Ah, Anne, why did you ask me to come?

He longed for his home, for his neglected garden, for his twilight behind the closed shutters, where only the hushed sound of Lucia's slippers shuffling along and the rattle of the keys hanging from her belt could be heard.

The keys. Little and big, and even those tiny keys for jewelry boxes and medallions, in which a lock of Anne's hair and confetti from the carnival of eleven years ago is still preserved. How much those old keys can tell him in his lonely days! About trembling, sweating, worried hands; about mean, vigilant, foolish, jealous hearts; about passions, fears, and dreadful sleepless nights; about the nightmares, doubts, and uncertainties of those locked in; about the anguish of those driven away from closed doors; about the suffering and longing in the face of everything that is locked, concealed, secret, unknown. . . . And the key to any anguish is simply a key, a simple tool having a tongue intelligible to everyone. Oh, if only he could now shut himself in with his old "polyglots," far away from this place and from everything going on here!

They took him to "his" room and wished him a good night's sleep.

After they left, he took off his clothes, piece by piece, and threw them aside scornfully. He had no pajamas, he had forgotten everything, left everything at home, even his toothbrush. He plunged himself on the bed and buried his head in the pillows, squirming and writhing like a crushed worm.

He touched something rustling and firm under his pillow. An oblong parcel wrapped in cellophane *red!* with a golden ribbon. A key was wrapped in cellophane—the key to paradise, which the devil himself had removed from his doorway eleven years before. And here it was, in hell itself! The key was now gilded *spoiled by this gilt, Anne!* with engraved numbers and letters. Its dented part was inscribed with the year 1937, and the Gothic filigree upper part with the year 1948. "To Toni" and 'From Anne" were the inscriptions on each of the two sides of the middle part of the key. So this was Anne's surprise that she had mentioned in her letter. "I've got a surprise for you." A gilded one. . . .

Nevertheless, he was touched by this gilding, by this consecration, by both the numbers and the letters, the names, his as well as hers, linked together like a noun and its preposition, the gentle kindness, like a tender, intimate touch, a kiss.

His naked body shuddered all over. Anne! Perspiration rolled down his back; he panted; the night was thick and hot, without the slightest breeze.

He went to the window.

A luminous full moon descended on the horizon and playfully extended its long yellow tongue to the surface of the transparent water, coming right up to where he was, right up to him as far as his windowsill, as though it were ridiculing him.

She wants to make fun of me with this gilded key, it dawned on him suddenly. Through these years and names, too. All in all, a plot conceived by these two.

He remembered them being there. . . . A tired, restful calm prevailed throughout the house now. He could hear only the sound of the silence buzzing in his ears, the sound of his disturbed beating blood, which was now sadly crawling along his veins and resignedly throbbing within him like a fearful, still dissatisfaction.

Perhaps all this does not exist, he thought. Perhaps, once more everything was nothing but a fever and a nightmare, as when Anne left eleven years ago. There was neither rhythm nor movement, only the aroused blood throbbing within him, brooding over his pleasant memories, singing a lullaby to his past.

Deep, deep within the house, far away in their room, the baby began to cry.

Cry, cry, my little one. . . . He moved his arms. Your dear . . . dear mother . . . He wanted to say something else, something that would spring up from his bitterness, revolting and cynical, but the baby became quiet at that moment . . . and he imagined the round, white breast she had offered the child through the opening of her nightgown. . . .

Funny, the baby will be baptized tomorrow secretly, without the surveyor's knowledge. He laughed at the thought with satisfaction because of his dark scheme. . . .

He sat on the bed and sighed heavily. The dilemma burdened him and he was still undecided: yes or no? No or yes?

He let his head droop majestically to his chest, like a tragic actor, and turned his depressed, aimless eyes to the floor.

He realized that one by one his nerves were giving way to something like an illness, the grippe, a weakness in his joints and tendons, and a sickness caused by his long naked skinny body and by his thinking, his fearful, malicious . . . This is where the explosive lies. From the side table he took the package in his hands. . . . I could completely destroy that marriage!

He was touched by the possibility of such theatrical pathos and suddenly, perhaps because of that feeling, he detected within himself an unexpected, lonely, almost a silly goodness. Silently he cried like a miserable man who had suddenly tasted the honor of making a chivalrous sacrifice.

He loosened the red ribbon, unwrapped the tissue paper, and took out a blue envelope from the pile of letters in the package. On the blue envelope *which can remind one of the blue sky, Anne!* was his address, spelled out in a beautiful handwriting in which the letter *n* was especially outstanding, with its softly accented lines and curves, as if the writer's hand was guided by a love never before recorded anywhere.

Falling to his knees, he kissed those rounded, soft letters and the hand that had written them and the soul that had felt that rounded, good, thoughtful love, which had persistently, tenderly, and carefully been transformed into those letters that made up his name. . . . The dear, my dear *n*, he stammered excitedly. As if you were engraved by those beautiful, full breasts: the breast—a gap—and another breast. Sweetheart!

He was in ecstacy. Afterward, when he began to read Anne's letters one by one chronologically, he realized that he was gradually more and more imbued by that sweet poison, the passionate fever of an unfinished, rudely interrupted dream; and now that he was infatuated by it once more, his intoxication came back to him again—its enchantment sensed but untasted, the never touched or experienced happiness. He bathed in the very foam of her words and washed his face with her sighs.

The town clock struck the time, but he did not hear it: all the hands of time had completely come to a stop for him. The moon had disappeared long ago. Dark and calm tranquillity prevailed outside. Only occasional timid, sad cricket chirps could be heard. . . . They made the night seem very dark and deep, fragrant and starry, and even his dreams were stirred up and sustained by the night itself. . . .

Then a cock in the neighborhood strikingly announced what time it was and blotted out the dreaming. Even the dog under the window was awakened by it and angrily howled a curse. And upstairs, the naked Tristan lay prone on the floor, buried under a pile of letters, floating on a cloud of dreams, and shuddering from the cold touch of reality.

But he refused to be dragged away from the clouds in that fashion and be thrown on the earth and simply abandoned on the floor forever. Could a life come to an end just like that: naked, lying on the floor, amidst a pile of old love letters? He himself insisted on an end to this story and to life itself. He therefore became aware of his naked buttocks touching the floor, and, desperately shuddering from this sensation, he rose to his feet like a man unaware of what he should do. . . .

On tiptoe, noiselessly, he went out into the corridor. . . .

Groping about in the dark, he came to a door behind which could be heard the strong-sounding sleep of a man who was breathing very deeply and heavily. Besides this healthy, rich breath of life itself, a melodious, gentle fluttering breath, like a noiseless breeze swaying airy mousseline curtains and rustling through a transparent, floating tissue, could also be heard. In utter stillness, as he stood in the dark corridor, he listened to those two very different and incompatible ways of breathing, nevertheless intertwined and embraced on the same night . . . and in the same bed. He tried to disentangle them, to separate them, and then to caress the fluttering one . . . like the breeze swishing through a silk curtain. . . . His lips kissed Anne's breath floating in the air and then he carefully approached the door and pressed his lips against it in an endless, passionate kiss, as though thereby he wanted to glue the damnation of his love to that door forever. Then he whispered, Farewell, Anne. . . .

On his way back through the corridor he spoke words of for-

giveness, and a false wish to die instigated within him a kind of
ponderous self-pity that created an almost pleasant feeling of being a true martyr. Who else felt as he did? Or, could anyone in
the world endure all this? He longed for a pistol, for some poison, for a skyscraper from which he could topple down majestically. . . .

In fact, he only searched the room, looking for a rather harmless medium, as though this were a matter of cleaning the house
and not of dying. He turned his eyes from everything that would
remind him of a knife, a rope, or great heights—all this was too
simple, too degrading. . . . Suddenly he realized that he still
held the silk ribbon that he had removed from the package containing Anne's letters. Of course it would not break, he lied to
himself. The grotesque symbolism of that somewhat poetic medium appealed to him, and when he tested its firmness with his
hands, the ribbon easily withstood the test. Then he made a
snare and put his head in it and tied the other end of the ribbon
to the window handle.

And now, farewell! . . . and may you all be forgiven. . . .
Turning his back to the window he suddenly crouched, letting
his legs slide along the polished, smooth parquet. . . .

BANG! The sound resounded throughout the whole house. All
of a sudden he was lying prone on the floor, amidst Anne's letters. First he felt something buzzing in his ears and a knock on
his head, and he remained like that, surprised and puzzled, with
a red ribbon around his neck like a frightened little dog who
had just fallen from a windowsill into the street.

Before he could pull himself together *and what was the use of
all this?* the door opened and the surveyor rushed into the room
rubbing his eyes because he found it very difficult to come to his
senses in view of the scene on the floor. A little while later Anne
also came running, wearing a dressing gown that she had put on
in a hurry and that was still unbuttoned so that her breasts were
visible.

"Toni, for heaven's sake!" she screamed. She was so frightened

that she did not even notice he was completely naked. The surveyor stood near the door and slowly began to realize what was
going on: he noticed a piece of the ribbon hanging from the
window and the rest of it tied to the man's neck. He linked
those two pieces together in his mind. Clear enough. A disdain-
ful sympathy twisted his face.

"Toni, what's the matter with you?" Anne asked, standing
over him without realizing a thing. She had not yet noticed that
he was naked. And he felt ashamed of his naked body on the
floor and began to bury himself under the letters as though they
were leaves, trying to hide from his shame, like Adam in the
Garden of Eden after his eyes had been opened and he realized
that he was naked, as Moses had written. Only after he had tried
to hide himself did she notice his nakedness, and at the same
time she realized that her breasts were exposed, and, screaming
bashfully, she covered them and closed her eyes. And he, he
stared at her bare feet trampling the letters that had been written by those very little hands up there . . . and he smiled
pointlessly and desperately, like a despondent man who sits on
the final border of his life and has nothing to look forward to.

The surveyor understood his glances as he scrutinized Anne's
bare legs. Standing above, he saw the beginning of one of the
letters: "My one and only one, Toni," as well as the wretched
smile of this naked, unfortunate man. Without saying a word,
he approached the wretched one, removed the ridiculous snare
from his neck, lifted him up like a child, and took him to his
bed.

The naked one yielded himself to that generous gesture like
a dead body removed from the gallows, and confidently whispered to the surveyor: "So you thought I was unhappy . . . and
that I would even . . . hang myself because of that? I played
a good joke on you, didn't I? Didn't I?"

Translated by Zora Depolo

IVAN DONČEVIĆ

The Insect Collector

My name is Marjan Lešnjak, but even while I was still in high school they gave me the nickname of Suleiman and today they still call me that although I've never had anything to do with the religion of the Turks. I don't mind the nickname, it's not an insulting one. What's more, when they call me Suleiman, they usually add "the Great," and this, it must be admitted, is not insulting at all. Apart from that, the Turks have always appealed to me, regardless of the "Turkish heel" and all the other things the blind bards sing about (but then I expose myself to the danger of having my patriotism questioned). Despite everything, I still say the religion of the Turks is the best, most beautiful, and most reasonable of all the religions I know. So I don't get at all angry about my nickname! But what does make me angry is my not being able to remember how I got it and what it was all about. So that I'm really only angry at myself, and that's allowed because I don't do anyone else any harm.

I'm angry because that's what my nature is like, a nature that is not at all simple. Anyway, who in this world is simple? It's quite clear to me that I'm not simple, but rather complicated—even very complicated; but for that very reason interesting and unusual, although the people around me don't think so. On the contrary, they think that I'm a sleepyhead, a mouse, a quiet simpleton who doesn't even know how to count to five, or something of the sort, and I let them think so and go on repeating to myself: "Just go on being silly, my friends, I know what I know and some day you'll have to reckon with me. . . ." I do know how to console myself, that's a fact. But alone with myself, in my room among my insects, I let my anger get the best of me; and a boundless anger it is, too. I look at myself in the mirror and see a terribly gloomy face with burning eyes—sometimes the look in those eyes frightens me. And that's when my insects take over. Bravo, insects! I have a wonderful collection of insects. I am no expert, no entomologist, but I've had this hobby of collecting insects as an amateur since I was a boy. My collection is neatly divided up into cardboard boxes of equal size with plastic covers that I make myself and the insects, stuck on their pins, can be seen through them. I am proud of this collection although there are no rare specimens in it like, for instance, the ones that live in underground caves and haven't even been given a name yet. No, my collection is made up of ordinary, or, should I say, domestic insects, from butterflies and houseflies of all sorts and sizes to wasps, hornets, grasshoppers, bumblebees, stag beetles, praying mantes, darning needles, cockroaches, ladybugs, horn bugs, spiders, stinkbugs, May bugs, cicadas, dung beetles, scarabs, and hundreds of others. But no matter how ordinary it is, to me it is a wonderful collection. What would I do without it? I spend all my free time with it, since I have no wife, no children, no sweetheart or friend. So I am committed to loneliness and to them, my insects. And when I get angry, when people insult and humiliate me, then the insects are the ones I vent my anger on and that makes it easier for me. For instance, the director of our company is a rude, hot-tempered man. He comes into the room where we're working, rolls his bulging, spectacled eyes around the room, and stops right behind me. "And you," he rasps right in my ear, "turn the page for a change, draw a line, add something, subtract something, make a mark on the page, do anything—but just do it, don't just sit there sleeping! What the devil were you doing last night?" He leaves. Actually, I was adding up figures in the ledger very industriously, I had become completely absorbed in my work, but am I to blame if my face always looks sleepy? What a beast that director is! But I'll get even with him. My time will come, and then he'll sing a different tune. Just you wait, brother, just you wait. But I have to go slowly and not do anything silly that would spoil everything ahead of time. At home I go to my collection and find the box with the hornets. The hornet is just like our director, sleek and yellow. Then I take an awl and say with the greatest pleasure that can be imagined: "Take this awl in the neck—and again in the neck—and again—and that's for saying I was sleeping when I wasn't sleeping, because I hate you, take this. . . ." After I finish, I quiet down. That's the way I lose my temper (and my temper is terrible) and that's the way my insects help me overcome my rage. I have every one of the people who ever insulted me, or made fun of me, or did anything bad to me, stuck on a pin and preserved in one of those boxes of mine. For instance, the janitor, a repulsive and malicious old crone, is the horsefly, and the lazy waiter in the restaurant where I eat is the dung beetle, and the head bookkeeper in our company is the scarab, while the chief of accounting is a stinkbug (he smokes the foulest tobacco imaginable). And so on down the line. Every one of them has felt the awl in his neck at least once.

How wrong people can be! They think I'm a quiet and timid fellow who bears all insults with resignation like the early Christians. They think I have no brains or strength and that I was born for them to make a monkey out of me. How wrong they are, how wrong they are! I have more brains and strength than all of them put together and enough passion to roast anything touching me if I'd only unleash it, but I go on smiling shyly, I withdraw; deliberately, intentionally I hold back, and because I hold back, people take it the wrong way. But the devil with them! It's better that way than if they saw through me and realized my intentions, which are really horrible, which. . . . But it's better not to say anything about that. That is my secret —a gruesome secret.

Not long ago I celebrated my fortieth birthday. I'm not superstitious, I don't believe in fortunetelling—that's all a lot of nonsense, as foreign to me as it is to any reasonable man who has seen for himself that only science can uncover life's secrets. But I am just as convinced, in contrast to most reasonable people, that the stars have an effect on man's character, and therefore on his destiny, and that this influence is not bunk, or mysticism, or superstition, but a scientific fact. Because astrology is a science like any other. What is more, in my opinion it is more exact than philosophy or political economy. I have consulted two astrologers in my life. One of them was a woman, even a very attractive woman, blond, plump, middle-aged. She had very intelligent, moist gray eyes and fine hands, and I fell a little in love with her. The second was an old man of dignified bearing with a beautiful gray beard, curly and cut off straight like those of the Assyrian kings. They drew up my horoscope on the basis of information they asked me for, and they did so independently of each other. They discovered strange things, quite identical. Not only did they describe my character with astonishing accuracy and explain certain things unknown even to me, but they described all the important events in my life that no one but I could have known about. I learned, for instance, that I was born under the sign of Cancer, that I was susceptible to rheumatism, circulatory diseases, and disorders of the liver, that I was timid in affairs of the heart, that my lucky number was seven, and my lucky day Monday. I also learned that I had chosen the wrong profession and should have been a pharmacist, male nurse, sailor, musician, or historian, and in no case a bookkeeper: this stupid occupation was probably the source of all my misfortunes. Then I learned—and this was the most important of all—that there would be a great turning point in my life after I had passed forty, a turning point that would be of decisive importance for me and for those around me. Forty years of age! Fearfully I waited for my fortieth birthday to come and finally, two weeks ago, on June 30th, to be exact, it came. What now? I was excited. What was going to happen in my life, what would happen to shake it to its very foundations, and would it now take a turn for the better? I hardly slept or ate for fear of the unknown, for unfortunately human knowledge is limited knowledge and even the wisdom of the astrologers sometimes cannot lay bare secrets. . . .

But the secret laid itself bare and very soon, too. One morning, just as I was leaving the house, it began to rain. It was still raining at about ten o'clock when I looked out the window. It was a cold, gray, drizzling rain, more like autumn than July. I had no umbrella and only canvas shoes on. The director came in and as usual stood next to my desk. I nervously turned a few pages of the ledger and dipped the pen squeakily into the inkwell. But he didn't say a word; just coughed and went on. A little later he called me to him. "A discharge," flashed through my mind; the doorknob to the director's office was wet with perspiration from my hand, I quaked in my trousers, and because of this I blushed like a schoolboy.

"Sit down," said the director, smiling and offering me a cigarette.

"Thank you, I don't smoke," I stammered, while he went on smiling and looking at me over his eyeglasses. Then he lit a cigarette and blew the smoke diagonally over my head.

"And I," said the director a bit later, blowing the smoke over my head a second time, "I have the idea of putting you up for our Management Board. What do you say to that?"

At first I didn't understand. Probably I just gaped. He then went on to explain his idea at length, but I no longer remember all the details he sketched out for me. But I do remember his saying that he had very strong reasons for choosing me. Since danger no longer threatened me, I began to pull myself together. Aha! He thought I wouldn't be a nuisance to him on the Management Board, that I would simply nod in agreement to all his proposals—those were the real reasons he had for suggesting me! His strong will was well known, lots of people in our company were already openly and loudly complaining about it! But we shall see! He's another one who will get a big shock about me when the time comes!

"Well?" he asked, raising his eyes over the spectacles.

I agreed, of course—why shouldn't I? The secretary hiccoughed two or three times and grew very pale when she saw how he escorted me to the door, slapped me on the shoulder, and extended his hand to me. Something like that had never happened before.

It is unbelievable how fast and how thoroughly many of my men and women colleagues changed their attitude toward me after this—precisely those who had been the worst, who had never stopped teasing me and insulting me by saying, for instance, that I had the nicest bald spot of all the baldies, that I was really a dangerous ladies' man but clever to hide it so well, that it was better to be born without a nose than without luck and that I had both to spare, that I was almost certainly very wealthy but keeping my money in a sock for a rainy day, and so on. The dogs never let up, not one opportunity did they pass up to take a stab at me, to humiliate me, and to make a laughing stock out of me. Now they kept quiet, putting their tails between their legs, the rats. Rats and cowards. Now all of a sudden they all behaved so nicely. Mr. Suleiman, they would say, said so-and-so! Did you see, they'd ask, how Mr. Suleiman frowned when they took his eraser from his desk without asking permission? He'd never do that to anyone! How strange it was, they'd say, how you could live with somebody for years, desk to desk, breathe the same air, and all at once you see what a fine and wonderful person he is, a whale of a fellow, and before that you never saw it at all! . . . That's the way they behave with me now, but I know why. I became a member of the Management Board at a critical moment. Our company, as everyone knows, turns out pencil boxes, pens of various kinds, and writing tablets. It is not a big company but it is a solid one, and moreover, it has a monopoly in the state and literally dictates the prices of its products. The buyers kick, but their kicking doesn't bother us one bit; our business dealings are fair and in keeping with sound economy. And since the company does business on these principles, we are often able to distribute bonuses—awards and such; but because of this, naturally we sometimes have arguments and dissatisfaction, which are quite typical of ordinary small men when it comes to handing out money. And it's because of this money, and only because of the money, that everyone is interested in being on good terms with members of the Management Board. And it was because of that cursed money that everyone's attitude toward me changed from the bottom up. But I'm not naïve, I can see through their hypocritical intentions and don't fall for that stuff at all; I only scorn them even more—actually they are repulsive to me, I hate them. And I'll get even with them, I'll bet anything that I'll get even with them, because my time has finally come. . . .

Crazy weather, it's raining again. Just a few minutes ago the sun was shining, but then a huge black cloud came, followed by a cloudburst. Again I had no umbrella and my canvas shoes on. I watched the rain pouring from the window, a muddy stream flowed down the street, people were taking cover in lobbies, and others who were in a hurry jumped funny little jumps over the puddles in the downpour; soaked to the skin, their clothes stuck to them; it was very interesting looking at the women. . . . But

the rain stopped soon and the deceitful sun came out from behind the clouds again. I was the last out of the office.

Down in the lobby I found a fellow employee, Irena, from the
commercial department, studying the sky and getting ready to
go. But when I appeared she smiled, showing all her fine teeth
in a face as shiny and freckled as a turkey's egg.

"I was just about to leave," she said, showing her teeth even
more.

I nodded to indicate I understood.

"I didn't want to ruin my pumps," she continued, putting out
a leg with a dark red shoe, too heavy-looking for my taste. But
the leg was very nice, strong and thickly grown with curly chestnut hair, but that did not detract from its looks. Funny I had
never noticed before what pretty legs Irena had.

"It's stopped," I said, stepping outside and raising my palm
upward. The sun shone brightly from a space between the
clouds.

"Actually, I don't usually go in this direction," said Irena as
soon as we had started off, "but today I have something to do
this way so I hope you don't mind if I go along with you?"

Of course I didn't mind. "What the devil," I thought, and stole
a glance at her sideways. She caught the glance and this embar-
rassed me, but she got very chummy and grabbed my arm. And
so we went arm in arm along the wet sidewalk. She was chatting
about this and that and smiling while I tried to break in with
something witty but didn't succeed. All at once she stopped and
asked, squinting: "Where are you going tomorrow?"

"Tomorrow is Sunday," I said, swallowing hard. "I'm going
to a soccer game."

"Fine," she said, pressing my arm. "I've got something to do
in the Maksimir Park district and I'll be finished at about the
same time the soccer game is over. Let's take a walk through
Maksimir Park—we can do that without people thinking anything, can't we? After all, we are co-workers."

Again I swallowed hard and of course I had nothing against our taking a little walk through the park after the game.

Afterwards, I felt very good during lunch in the restaurant I eat in (and which I otherwise hate). The waiter-dung beetle, a disgusting character, always unshaven, unwashed, with dirty hands and fingernails, a lazybones and spiteful creature who had it in for me and tortured me in the most underhanded way, making every mouthful I ate there bitter—even that waiter-dung beetle did not seem as impossible and unbearable as usual that day. I even smiled and said something pleasant to him when he pushed the plate of dishwater that is supposed to be soup under my nose while moistening his repulsive fingers in it. And I paid the cashier-wasp a compliment, telling her she had a lovely necklace. It was really a cheap thing from the bazaar, made of green glass beads and in very poor taste. With her long thin neck and the necklace, she really looked frightful, but I paid the woman a compliment anyway because of my own good disposition. She blushed and then paled with vanity and gave me such a sweet look that my conscience pricked me for the outright lie I had told. I even got scared that the lie might have some unpleasant consequences. But inside me, I sent the cashier and the consequences to the devil. At home I took out my boxes right away, pondered a long time selecting the one I wanted, and at long last chose the ladybug, or, as she is sometimes called, God's lambkin. That day Irena had been wearing a red dress with white polka dots so that the ladybug with its polka dots bore the closest resemblance to her. Sweet little ladybug! Tenderly I touched the round wings of the enchanting insect and as I did so I felt an unknown rapture fill my heart, while shivers of pleasure went up and down my spine as though from a wave of low voltage current. . . . And still there are people who say that astrologers are swindlers! And here my time was coming, coming with mathematical precision, all the signs said it was so. . . .

I felt wonderful at the soccer game, too. My club was not playing so that I wasn't too excited; the game was poorly played and uninteresting, but I felt wonderful nevertheless. Some bumpkin in a yellow outfit tripped up an opponent in a green outfit who fell and writhed in pain on the grass. I have a great feeling of fair play and yelled, "Dammit, that's the way butchers play. Damn!" A thick neck in front of me began to turn around. "If I show you how butchers play," he rasped from a pimply and unshaved snout that he stuck under my chin, "if I show you. . . ." His dull eyes squinted in the fat face, crawling over me as though looking for something. "Goal! Bravo, yellow! Get going, yellow!" the enthusiastic fans around me started yelling at just the right moment. Hats were thrown in the air, the snout in front of me disappeared, and I sighed with relief. But a little later, the greens got a goal, the thick neck began to turn around again, again the dull swinish eyes studied the lines of my face. "The damned butcher," I thought, sensing danger, "he's obviously looking for a fight." So I turned a little to the right as though speaking to the fellow next to me and said, "That goal the greens got is no goal at all. It's a crime! They got it from an offside position! And what kind of referee is that? Into the drink with him! It's a scandal!" That's the way I spoke, as though talking to my neighbor, and this, it seemed, softened up the butcher: his piggish eyes squinted and teared and I thought how his eyes would squint and tear in the same way if someone tickled their owner a little on the soles of his feet. The neck began to turn again, it turned for a long time, then went back again and finally stayed in its normal position. I felt wonderful because I had gotten the better of that devil. I felt wonderful because the greens won in the end anyway; the butcher was pale and downcast and mumbled something unintelligible to himself. I was feeling wonderful for other reasons, too.

Irena was already waiting for me. Some young men, muscular and sun-tanned, were rowing on the lake, showing off their skill and their biceps, which they strained more than was necessary

(I hate those addle-brained adolescents who ruffle their feathers in front of any skirt). Irena was standing under a tree, swinging her purse and probably stealing glances at the biceps. Although she had become attractive (or even dear) to me almost overnight, still I wasn't crazy enough to forget the real truth about women as the Bible describes them—that is, that woman is a deceitful creature, faithless and unclean, that she is capable of betraying her husband, friend, or lover at the first opportunity she gets. . . . But maybe I was being unjust to Irena? As soon as she noticed me coming, she looked so sincerely happy that she almost fell on my neck when I reached her, she did not even look at the young snots any more! I still say that women are what the Bible says they are, but I also say that there are honorable exceptions. And why shouldn't Irena be just such an honorable exception?

Well, the devil take me if she wasn't the cutest girl I knew! Where could my eyes have been that I hadn't noticed it before? She had the prettiest and most desirable body I had ever seen (with a dress on, naturally) and she was so slender and well built and lively and flexible, her luxuriant chestnut hair falling to her shoulders in a sort of old-fashioned style (but even that was nice), the skin of her bare hands the healthiest, softest, most velvety and cool skin I had ever touched. I had touched her unintentionally when we met, but she didn't get angry, just squinted a little and burst into laughter. I also noticed then that she had strange yellowish eyes (which probably shone in the dark) and that the freckles on her face were not at all a shortcoming but an advantage. They made her face resemble— if I may use a poetic expression—a fresh, dewy, reddish-yellow peach. "What the devil," I thought, greatly excited, "how nice that is: like a peach!"

We walked along the path between the oaks. Here and there on the benches couples sat, embracing. Evening falls in this park much earlier than it does on the street so that during their silly but nevertheless attractive love play the couples in the dusk were protected from the eyes of curiosity seekers and the malicious glances of promenaders.

"I love nature," chatted Irena ceaselessly, "I love nature, nature is my big weakness. Can you feel the smells coming out of the earth? Oh, that smell of decaying leaves and mushrooms! I don't like the decaying leaves, but I love mushrooms. Listen to the frogs." She pressed my arm firmly, we stopped, she leaned her head on my shoulder, and for a while we listened to the frogs croaking in the pond under the water lilies. "I like frogs too," she whispered softly as we left. "Are you sorry," she suddenly asked seriously, "are you sorry to be walking outdoors like this with me? No? Be honest, tell me what you think, because I only like honest people." Then she moved away from me a little. "I'm probably boring you . . . no, no! Don't deny it, I'm sure that I'm boring you to death with my blabbing. But what can I do?"

I assured her at length that I didn't find her boring—on the contrary, whatever she said was terribly interesting.

"All right, then, let's sit down on this bench," she said, and drew me down on a nice bench, half hidden by the bushes, "and let's turn the record on the other side. Have you ever been very much in love?" And she lit a cigarette.

"No, I haven't," I answered quick as a shot. "No, I've never been in love."

"That's interesting," she said.

"But maybe I will be," I continued, blushing as red as a beet, but she couldn't see that in the dark.

"Really interesting. Just go on."

"As I said, maybe I will be. All of us are bound to fall in love once in our lives."

"That's true. Just go on, I'm terribly curious."

"That's all there is," I burst out, and saw immediately that what I had said just wouldn't do, that I must seem awfully funny to her, and stupid as well. I felt ashamed but there was no help for it. That's the way I am, "timid in affairs of the heart"—that was it, and still there were idiots who dared say astrology was a swindle.

A stupid silence ensued. Irena tapped her foot nervously, inhaled quickly two or three times, then threw the cigarette away gloomily. The red tip of the cigarette described an arc in the dark and sizzled out. I didn't know what to do. I was clumsy, there it was; I stretched out my legs and clasped my hands behind my head; I was bathed in perspiration but I didn't know what to do. It's a funny thing with me. I notice everything around me, I can feel things that are not so obvious at first glance, I can tell precisely what people's intentions are no matter how they try to hide them, I see everything, I know everything, I guess everything, but I do everything wrong, completely wrong. There is no doubt, for instance, that this girl was offering herself to me, that she was after me openly; I can see that and it panders to my vanity that a young and pretty girl is after me and offers herself to me. So? So nothing. Instead of grasping the gift that offers itself to me, I perspire like an idiot, stretch my legs, clench my fists, and don't know what to do with myself or with her. Stupid, really stupid.

But fortunately Irena was not stupid. She was quiet for a time, probably offended, tapped her foot nervously, again lit a cigarette and again threw it away, and even sighed audibly two or three times. Then all at once she moved up very close to me— as though nothing had happened. She's wonderful. I adore her. Now she was talking about the ordinary things at the office.

"I don't like that office," she said simply and quietly, as though we had just been talking about it. "The people there aren't nice, they play all sorts of underhanded tricks on each other whenever they get a chance, they're all mad at one another, egotistic, envious, no character, but what can I do? You have to earn your living somehow. But I'd be happy if I were out of that place, any place, just not in that office."

"I don't like the people in our office either." I grabbed wildly at a subject in which I felt quite at home. And immediately I felt easier.

"I don't like politics, and today politics is all that counts," continued Irena. "I hear some bonuses are going to be given out, but I know that when they are, I'll get nothing at all."

"How can you be sure?" I wanted to console her.

"Like that," she replied, "I'm just sure of it. Because they don't look at the person, they look at his politics."

"That's true," I said, "but maybe it won't be like that."

"What do you mean?"

"Simply that. Maybe something has changed."

"I don't understand. Why should things have changed? And how have they changed? I'm sorry, but I really don't understand you."

"Leave that to me," I said finally.

"Oh!" she exclaimed.

We didn't talk about the office any longer. I felt exceptionally fine. I felt like a man who had become conscious of his power to do this or that, as he chose; the power was there, it was only necessary to exercise it. I'll eat my hat if I don't put up such a fuss in that Management Board tomorrow that those gentlemen will lose all desire to go on with their tricks. Enough of that business! Are we in the jungle? What had this poor girl done wrong? They were envious of her, that was it! She was young and pretty, and if she'd go to bed with them, then they'd sing a different tune. . . . I know them; I know them, those office bigwigs! But this is the death knell for their arrogance, I'll eat my hat if it isn't the end, and never again will this dear creature have to complain of their injustice. That's the way it is and that's the way it's going to be, I can tell you! It would have been better if they had drafted the most poisonous scorpion into that Management Board rather than me. . . . I felt wonderful; an invisible power and self-confidence and determination had flowed into me. And that poor girl drew even closer to me, she was so close that I felt the warmth of her breast at my left shoulder and the warmth made me dizzy, so dizzy I had to squint. Then she put her hand on my knee and . . . and what was I supposed to do? To grab that hand, to draw her near, to nestle my head in her breast that was rising and falling rapidly, to . . . Damn it! Time passed and I did nothing. The hand rested on my knee for a while and then trembled nervously, the fingers spreading and contracting (I heard her nails scratching dryly on the trouser material), then the hand slipped and withdrew. Finally the girl said in an unnaturally deep, hoarse voice: "It's already late, let's go!"

I stood up and we left. The whole way to the streetcar stop we didn't say a word. I was ashamed. But at the streetcar stop she put her sweet little face next to mine, her smiling, freckled, dear little face, a little paler than usual (probably from the night dampness), and said: "I have time tomorrow, too. If you want to, we can see each other again in the afternoon. . . ." The streetcar moved, she jumped up on the running board. "All right?" she yelled.

"Yes, yes, tomorrow. . . ." I waved. Then I waited for the next streetcar.

I was ashamed, it's true, but I consoled myself. Who says I'm a wax saint? That simply is not true. I'm not a wax saint, or a bungler, or a coward. I just don't have enough experience with women. And I am a bit too shy. But we'll see tomorrow, tomorrow. . . .

The next day the Management Board met in the afternoon. We were to discuss the bonuses; there had been gossip about it for some time. In a sleepy voice the director read out the names and after each name, the sum that was being proposed. For this one, so much, and so on. All right. Accepted. For that one, so much. All right. "It is a cinch," I thought to myself, "sitting on the Management Board and just nodding your head." My name came up too. "All right," the rest of the board said unanimously. "The money will come in handy," I thought. "I'll buy some summer slacks." The bookkeeper's name came next, followed by the accounting head, and then many others. Accepted! Then Irena's name came up. The director said that she did not deserve to get anything because she was neither industrious, nor disciplined, nor did she do her work specially well. He was sorry, personally, continued the director, because she was the only employee not on the bonus list, but taking all the aforementioned facts into consideration, it was only just that she receive nothing. But that was only his proposal, let the others say what they thought! The chief bookkeeper-scarab gave his opinion right away: "I agree with the director's proposal. The woman in question is lazy and indifferent. Apart from that, her private life leaves much to be desired. For the sake of the company's reputation, we ought to go into the matter of her personal life sometime. Perhaps the fact that she will not receive a bonus will have a salutary effect on her." Then the chief accountant-stinkbug took the floor and said: "If certain other things were in question,"—he put special emphasis on the "other things" and winked—"if certain other things were in question, then this young lady would surely get first prize. But let the young men hanging around on Zrinjevac Street and in front of the Dubrovnik Café have their say about that. We here are making decisions about specific jobs, isn't that so? Therefore," concluded the chief accountant, lighting a pipe that had gone out while he was talking, "I agree entirely with the director's proposal. Though," he added, "as far as any salutary effect is concerned, I really doubt it." Others then spoke up in the same vein. It was necessary for me to say what I thought. First I blushed profusely and then grew pale (something is wrong with my circulation, I've noticed for a long time), then I stammered something and nodded my head. "I must take care of myself," flashed through my mind, "I must avoid all excitement because, by nature, I am inclined toward diseases of the liver and circulation. Apart from that, it would not be a good thing to cause a scandal at my very first meeting. There's time for that! As a matter of fact, it would even be very stupid to create a scene at the very first meeting. . . ." Those present accepted my nod of approval and no one noticed anything. The meeting was soon over. But how surprised all these good-for-nothings would be some day! I was happy in advance at the thought of how I would fool them.

Irena was washing her hands in the hall sink and smiled at me from afar. Poor Irena! We hardly had time to make the appointment for the afternoon. . . . After that I sat at my desk, did nothing, and boiled with anger. The good-for-nothings! But they'll see who's boss some day when I get hold of them!

Again that afternoon she was at the appointed place ahead of time; I liked that particularly. Again she almost fell on my neck when she saw me, and I liked that too. We followed a stream through the woods and then another one over fields where women were harvesting wheat and tying it up into bundles. All the women down to the very last one had red bandanas on their heads and looked at us mockingly as we passed. Then we came to another stream and after that to the edge of a pine wood that stretched out along the plateau as far as the eye could see. In the twinkling of an eye Irena had found a half-hidden path through the undergrowth. For a time we went along with bent heads and then came breathless to a clearing. It was a beautiful clearing, shady and carpeted with grass as smooth as silk. Irena threw her bag on the ground and sat down.

"Isn't it beautiful here?" she asked, wiping the perspiration from her shiny, freckled face.

"It is beautiful," I replied.

"You might think I knew every bush, mightn't you?" she continued when she noticed my questioning glance stop at a suspicious-looking box (its color washed away by the rain), a crumpled bit of paper, a ribbon, and all sorts of other things people usually leave behind them. "But I've never been here before," she said, raising her voice. "I only love nature and that's why I find my way around in the woods so well. And this is the first time I've ever been here, my word of honor!"

If she said so, why shouldn't I believe her? Otherwise I really might get the idea that she had already stretched herself out in this nest before. . . .

She watched me from below: her mocking, bold glance seemed to say: here's the chance of a lifetime, and now let's see you do your stuff, brother, let's see what you're worth. . . . That's what women are like! The Bible has already had its say about them, but despite that my heart beats faster when I'm alone with her, with this very Irena, and I'm inclined to believe that she isn't one of the women the Bible is referring to.

"Sit down," she said, continuing to watch me from below with her mocking, bold glance.

I sat politely to one side.

"Sit over here," she said, pointing to the space next to her. "And talk to me. Yesterday you were in poor form."

She didn't have to make fun of me. And she didn't have to plant me so close to her. I tried to talk, but it just didn't work. I spoke disconnectedly about astrology, but I quickly perceived that the subject didn't interest her. Then I spoke about insects, about different kinds, about my insects. She opened her eyes wide, then drew her knees together and rested her chin on them, again squinting at me mockingly and boldly. A little later she stretched out on her back and dug her fingers into her hair. What should I do? My head was spinning. "But why?" I thought with my last bit of consciousness, "why did she plant me so close to her?" But my head was whirling around.

"Ah, bravo," exclaimed Irena suddenly, gently stopping my hand, which had at long last gotten a little courage and dropped to her knee. "Today was the meeting, wasn't it? And I completely forgot about it. Did I or didn't I get anything?"

"Those good-for-nothings," I mumbled casually, because I didn't want anything to obstruct me now that I had started.

"So I got nothing, eh?" she asked stubbornly, pushing away the hand that was getting more and more daring. "Tell me. Did I get anything?"

"Those swine, who . . ."

"So that's it!" she yelled, and sat up.

When I completely lost my head, when I tried to embrace her and sought her lips, mumbling words I'll never be able to repeat again, she pushed me away with all her might and jumped to her feet. I was taken aback. I was hurt. I was like a little dog that gets a kick for no reason at all.

"So, that's it!" she rasped, furiously shaking off bits of grass that clung to her skirt. "So that's it! So the gentlemen have done me in, have they! Lovely!" She seemed to be burning, to be smoking with rage. "They've done me in, by God!" Under her furious blows, her skirt whirled wildly above her head and without embarrassment she showed her legs all the way up to her stomach. (My God, she had lovely legs!)

A stupid situation. But maybe all was not lost.

"Irena," I whined, and licked the spittle from my lips, "Irena, I . . . of course . . . but . . ."

"What do you want?" She stood over me, her arms akimbo. "Look at the liberties you're allowing yourself! Is that the way to behave, eh? Look at him, will you, and he's supposed to be a fellow employee! He couldn't give me support when I needed it, and here . . ." It was only then she remembered to lower her skirt and tuck it between her knees. "Phooey. Shame on you."

Again I whined in a small voice: "Irena . . ."

"Shut up!" she shouted, and continued with revulsion, "You're bald and moldy. Look at the old devil, will you? Look at him, will you! I could be his daughter and he's acting like a hot old goat. Shame on you. Phooey!"

I looked at her wildly.

"And what more would you like to know? Such a handsome fellow, such strength, such a legendary hero! Suleiman the Great! Bah! And actually an insectologist, stinking and good-for-nothing! Go on, get out of here, you old monster, before I . . ." She wanted to say something very vulgar but thought better of it and added, "before I kick you out!"

That, then, was the way it ended. I collected myself slowly, the way a child collects his spilled marbles. I finally came to the conclusion that this dame was the worst bitch I'd ever met, that she had insulted me and humiliated me and mocked me more than anyone else had ever done. Horrible! But what did I do, what in God's name had I done to her that she had to mock me in such a rotten way? Nothing. Nothing at all. Despite all my efforts I couldn't remember a thing I had ever done wrong to her. That was a woman for you: a creature unclean, faithless, and underhanded. . . .

I came home and there was a ringing and roaring in my head. I took out my insects, the whole collection, and laid them out neatly on the table; but even my insects couldn't make me happy this time. I took the disgusting ladybug and pricked her to bits, cutting her up like a butcher: "There, take that in the back—and again in the back—and again—take that for playing around with me so shamelessly, take that for saying I'm bald and old and a monster, take that, you insatiable streetwalker, take that. . . ." I pricked her hard, tearing her to bits and pieces. Then I cleaned the pin and threw the pieces into the fire. But still I had no real peace. My anger was terrible, insatiable, my soul thirsted for revenge. How was it that I found no peace? "Is something wrong with my health?" I thought in panic. "Really, there must be something wrong because nothing like this has ever happened before. My circulation! My liver!" Before I fell asleep I decided that the next day I would go to see a doctor and let him examine that damned blood and liver once and for all so that I knew what was wrong with me.

I could not fall asleep. Damned liver! I thought and I thought and got sick of thinking; I threw up everything I had eaten that evening. What an unlucky fellow I was! I looked around at other men and women: they lived and had their troubles, perhaps worse than mine, and they bent under the blows of fate, struggled, fell back, and groaned, but nevertheless it seemed to me that these men and women had an easier time going through life than I did. How was that? I didn't know. Except that like this, in the night, when I am alone with myself, it is hard for me, terribly hard. . . . I'm tired, and I can't fall asleep. Through the window I see a piece of the clear sky between the dark walls of the apartment houses and on that sky a handful of wise, motionless, and ice-cold stars. Ah, stars! My only hope! Would the time ever come that would draw a sharp line between yesterday and today? . . . I'm tired, I'm terribly tired, and I can't fall asleep. Then I finally fell asleep, a sickly and broken sleep. I dreamed I sat in a big, cold, and severely furnished office turning the dial on the telephone, but turning the wrong numbers so that I had to begin all over again. Finally I succeeded in getting the number I wanted. "Hello," I yelled into the mute hollow of the receiver. "Hello! Hello!" From far off a voice as ghostly as a whisper said, "Who's calling?" "Mama, it's me, Marjan, your son! Do you hear me?" "I can hear you, son. What do you want?" "Mama, I feel bad, I feel awfully bad. They've insulted me so much. They've humiliated me and mocked me mercilessly. What should I do?" "Bear it!" said the voice like a whisper. "I know, but I can't bear it any more." "Bear it, when I tell you to. Therein lies your salvation." (My mother hasn't changed a bit. She's telling me the same things she said when she was alive, when at least they made some sense.)

"But, Mama, I can't stand it any more. Are you listening? I can't. I've come to the end of my rope. I must hit back. I must hit, scratch, choke, and if need be, kill. Do you understand, Mama? And kill." "You're crazy," whispered the voice, slightly angry. "I didn't give birth to you so that you should be crazy." "Quiet, Mama. Enough of your impossible advice! I want them to respect me, to fear me, to tremble before me. Do you hear? I want power." "Power is damnation, I've told you that so many times." "Damnation! And isn't this damnation, what they're doing to me now? There's a dame there, an ordinary tramp, and if you only knew what a bloody fool she made out of me!" "Take care with women, son! They also bring damnation,

I told you about that, too." "Damnation, damnation, damnation! What do I care about damnation? I want to live. I want to live at all costs . . . are you listening? . . . I want to live, even at the cost of killing." "Watch your tongue, you idiot, and pray to God to help you in your madness. Women and power are the worst whips in His all-powerful hand. In the name of the Father, the Son, and the Holy Ghost. Amen." I wanted to shout that what she was saying was stupid and that I didn't give a damn for that whip or that all-powerful hand, but the old lady probably was tired. I heard a yawn on the other end of the wire and then the click of the receiver being put on its hook. What was it she said? Power and women? Power and women? Ah! . . . I must have struck myself on the forehead with my fist (as people do when they remember something all of a sudden) and I woke up from the blow. . . .

I woke up. A piece of bright sky shone through the window— gray-green sky with stars growing pale before the dawn. Power and women! Of course! How could I ever have forgotten?

"Write down on this card what you want most in life!" Mama had said. I wrote: power and women. Everybody in the room—Mama, the postman's three daughters and their boy friends, the old fortuneteller, and some other people from the neighborhood—all gave one another knowing glances and laughed. "Look at the little devil, look what he's thinking of! Look at Suleiman the Great! He'll do great things in life!" They all laughed and they all called me Suleiman. And from then on, everybody called me Suleiman.

Suleiman! How had I forgotten? True, that was long ago —thirty-two years!

Something made me want to go out, out of the room. I dressed quickly. Outside, the dawn was coming up, on the street the milk-man's cans were toppling and banging against one another, the first streetcars could be heard. I went down the stairs easily and lightly, whistling At the bottom of the stairs stood the janitor-horsefly, a disgusting crone who couldn't stand me and whom I couldn't stand.

"Good morning, Granny," I shouted in passing, and she seemed to turn to stone at the sound of my voice. "How did we sleep, Granny, and what did we dream? Something nice, thank God. Me, too. At your service, Granny."

I felt wonderful. I didn't walk but danced, pirouetting, leaping, smiling blissfully to myself. "There, you see," I thought aloud, "I knew something would happen after all. Something extremely important. Something that would change my life from the bottom up, turn it in a more favorable direction! Life begins today! And from today onward, let those lice, those robbers and good-for-nothings, those whores and ne'er-do-wells watch out, because my time has finally come! Let them watch out! And people thought astrology was a swindle! Idiots, now they'll see. . . ." So I walked, dancing and leaping along the streets, the passers-by looking after me in panic.

In front of the office I met Irena.

"Maybe you think I'm afraid of you, eh?" Her eyes widened. "You think you got me down, don't you? Go on, you, you've done nothing at all to me, nothing, do you hear, nothing. . . ." She ran wildly upstairs.

And I stood downstairs, laughing as loudly as I could.

Translated by Cordia Kveder

Mr. Pink's Soliloquy

While I work I usually listen to my radio. Some people can't stand it while they're working. My colleague, Bermut, for instance, says he'd never be able to get any work done that way. On the contrary, it doesn't bother me a bit. I suppose I'm used to it. If the music interests me I work and listen at the same time; if it doesn't, I stop hearing it by automatically switching off my attention.

When I'm at home in the afternoon, I work till nightfall. It's rather tiring, so it's no wonder if I'm absent-minded in a way. They say one type of work is a rest from another. I'm a clerk at the Export Bank. I work there the whole morning, and at home I work for Continental the whole afternoon. Always the same old accountancy grind. They trust me, so they let me take my books home, especially if there's a two-day holiday. This usually happens when a feast day or national holiday comes next to a Sunday. Bands play in the streets, troops march by, but I sit at home engrossed in Continental's accounts, by way of resting up for the Export Bank. For a bachelor this is supposed to be recreation, but at times it fags me out completely.

Last Sunday, for instance, I worked at home the whole morning and afternoon for Continental. I wanted to get the work done at all costs. I went out to lunch at one, and when I got back I was astonished to hear my radio going full strength, so I hurried in to turn it down. You know how the neighbors yell their heads off and thump on the ceiling with their brooms for quiet when someone pounds the piano or plays the radio loudly at midday. I went on with my work till evening, when I went out again to have dinner and take a walk in the fresh air. Now, I remember distinctly taking special care to turn off the radio before I left. Being absent-minded, I delay a lot on my way out, fiddle about in the corridor in front of the door of my flat, and go over in my mind the things I might have forgotten to do. I see to the gas two or three times, the water tap, the electric light (especially the light in the lavatory, which is so easy to leave burning). There are times when I even return up the stairs to have a last look around. There's nothing easier than forgetting the electric cooker, especially if it is the kind with a covered-in top and you can't see the wires. A friend of mine once went off on a five-day trip for Easter with his wife, but when they were on the train they simply couldn't get it out of their heads that they had forgotten to turn off a small electric heater. Unable to stand it any longer, they hurried back after three days. Of course they hadn't forgotten the heater at all.

Well, anyway, before going out on Sunday evening I was careful to switch off my radio. And I'm quite sure I had switched it off. I might have left the gas on, I might have forgotten the cooker after making myself a cup of tea. I might even have left the door unlocked. (That's another reason why I often go upstairs again—sometimes even twice.) But I'm doubly sure I had switched off the radio. You will understand me when I say I was particularly careful to do so just because I had forgotten it at noon. To make certain, I remember trying to memorize the last words I heard before turning it off: "This disease used to play havoc with orchards. We now have many means with which to combat it, the most efficacious being . . ." —and at this point I had turned the knob, cutting the announcer's speech in half. As I was going down the stairs I repeated the words and asked myself what those most efficacious means might be. I should have listened at least till I had heard their name! And then something kept nagging at me for not having done so.

So you can imagine my surprise when, having got back home that evening, I found my radio on! I was going up the stairs when I heard the soft strains of a tango. Surely it isn't mine, I said to myself. I went in, trembling with apprehension. And indeed it was mine: from the small entry I saw its glowing indicator. It was playing a tango quite softly—but it was playing, all right.

I must say I felt uneasy. I searched the flat, looked into every corner, and even under the bed. What occurred to me was that someone had broken into my flat during my absence. The charwoman, who cleans for me twice a week, has the unfortunate habit of forgetting to lock the small balcony on which she keeps her brooms, mops, and other odds and ends, and a thief might easily slip in by that way—it's a perfect way for him to enter. But the door to the balcony was locked. Another idea: the thief might have found the door unlocked, entered the flat, and locked the door behind him. But there was no one in the flat: I searched again—nowhere a sign of anyone. If he had left by the same way, the door would have been unlocked. But the radio was playing! Softly, to be sure, but it was playing, all right. Then I thought that maybe there was something wrong with the control knob. I didn't feel much conviction in that idea. But I tried to reason it out: maybe the control knob was loose, maybe it switched off easily and then, when the current increases after housewives have finished cooking dinner (Is that what they call "tension"?—I must admit that physics is not my strong point), it attracts the control knob over to the "on" side. Anyway, I decided I'd call at the electrician's at the corner on my way to the office the next morning. I know him, and I always ask him to repair my cooker when the wire burns out. He's a nice man, a stout, good-natured fellow, and he always says "Good morning" to me as I pass. I switched off the radio and went to bed.

The next morning I dropped in at the electrician's. "Impossible!" he broke in on my explanation. Probably his other customers have often asked the same question. I don't know why, but the thought that I wasn't the only one was comforting.

There was no other explanation. I must have forgotten to turn off the control knob, that's all. Sometimes a man intends to do something and the intention slips out of his mind, and he's sure he has done what he intended to do. That is the only logical explanation. Maybe there are some other logical explanations too.

Being a bachelor and not given much to company, I often spend my time trying to get to the bottom of different problems, including problems that don't concern me, and working out different answers to them. And then sometimes I reflect over things that haven't really happened, but only might have. I see something in the street or hear something at the office, anything at all, about someone else's business, about an accident, a strange event, or something like that, and then I begin to think about it and go on thinking about it, imagining how it would develop. I imagine, for instance, a tiny detail being omitted, or a different course followed; and then I unwind the thread, deduce the consequences, and you simply can't believe what strange things occur, what unbelievable results are arrived at, what unexpected endings come out. Sometimes you only need to change an accidental and apparently negligible circumstance to bring about a terrible tragedy.

Chance can really contrive all sorts of strange things, so strange that human fancy is incapable of conceiving them. For instance, I heard the following story one day:

Three children were playing at home. Their mother had gone shopping, their father was looking for a job. Well, children being what they are, they climbed into an old-fashioned trunk with the intention, I suppose, of surprising their mother when she got back. They heard steps on the stairs and thought they were their mother's. They expected her to come in, stop in surprise at not finding them, look in all the rooms, hesitate wordless in the middle of the kitchen, and finally ask herself where they could have hidden. Then they would jump out of their hiding place like Indians and shout "Boo!" But by some accident it was not their mother climbing the stairs, but a lady from the third floor. By a further accident, the trunk was locked by one of those flaps with a slit in the middle that drops over a staple and is secured with a padlock when the lid is let down. Anyway, the children were as safely locked in the trunk as a mouse in a mousetrap. They screamed, frantic with fright; they pushed and pushed against the lid, but, of course, in vain. If, by chance, the lady next door had come in to borrow some salt (she was always borrowing something, and Mother was always saying things after she left), nothing would have happened; she would have come in (because the flat was not locked and it could be opened by turning the outside knob), she would have heard the children screaming and she would simply have unfastened the lid. The children would have climbed out wide-eyed with fright, perhaps they would have begged her not to say anything to Mother, and she would have promised not to, but would have told her anyway and begged her not to be hard on them. And anyway, in the future the children would always have been careful of the trunk and avoided it like the plague. But it happened that the lady next door didn't need any salt. . . . In short, anyone can picture the poor mother on finding her three children smothered in a trunk. It isn't hard to see her looking all over the house for them, imagining all sorts of things, including the impossible, but not the truth; searching everywhere, including the most absurd places, and altogether forgetting the one place she should look.

In fact it is hard to imagine her looking for them in the trunk at all, and that anything but chance should direct her footsteps toward it. Probably she would not look there till the following day, or even the day after.

Many things might have happened. The neighbors might have heard the children screaming and come to their rescue. Or their mother might have come back from shopping in time. Or by chance the flap might not have fallen over the staple, just as by chance it had. All these things might have happened; it was an accident that they hadn't. Almost everything that happens to us and around us depends entirely on small and insignificant details that might be imagined as happening differently. Possibilities simply teem all around us. We live a life of extreme peril. Everything—absolutely everything—depends on some trivial circumstance, on some negligible turn of our mind, on the minute electrical impulses in our brain cells. Everything hangs on a single thread! Our destiny, our very life, lies in the hand of blind chance. Just imagine that the life of three children, that the happiness and very survival of a whole family may depend on whether the mother remains shopping a few seconds longer (for instance, because the potatoes at the stall at which she bought her tomatoes are not of the best quality and she must go to another stall for better ones), or on whether the children decide upon their prank at nine twenty-three or at nine twenty-eight, or on whether they play it the day the lady next door needs salt or the day she doesn't, or even on whether the flap on great-grandmother's old-fashioned trunk is a little more rusty or a little less, and on whether it will drop over the staple at the smallest shock or not. Just as it was the working of blind chance that a slat was missing from the half-rotten back of the trunk through which sufficient air entered for the wretched children to breathe and survive till their mother returned from shopping. Anyway, that is another circumstance that equally might not have occurred—it was sheer chance that it had.

They say there is no such thing as accident, and I once heard a lengthy explanation to that effect. I remember, I was thoroughly convinced at the time. But now, to tell the truth, I no longer remember how it ran, but I do remember it was quite reasonable and that afterward I had laughed and laughed, assured that there is no such thing as accident. And indeed, there *is* no such thing as accident. But there is such a thing as our imagining a given circumstance in two, five, or even in a thousand different ways, and it is enough for one single, entirely negligible trifle out of this endless number to be this or that, and the consequence will be nothing at all or a tragedy. Whether the result will be according to one formula or another, we cannot say. This is quite clear to me and I think most people will agree on this point; but whether this implies that there is such a thing as accident or that there is no such thing, I cannot say.

Forgetfulness and absent-mindedness are also frequently the cause of "accident." As soon as a man is cautious, or the more cunning he becomes in his struggle with forgetfulness or absent-mindedness, the more cunning, the more deceitful, the keener, and the more artful become his forgetfulness or absent-mindedness. Their nets become all the easier to fall into, so that in the long run they win. Doctors say that it is often like this with illness: the more germs you kill, the more resistant the remaining ones become, and the time finally comes when penicillin or whatever it may be no longer works.

And then, what we often term forgetfulness or absent-mindedness is sometimes neither forgetfulness nor absent-mindedness in the true sense of the word, but merely something similar. Something that, when the matter is reconsidered, should rather be called thoughtlessness, criminal carelessness. But as a rule, we are all, without exception, guilty of carelessness every day. Carelessness, in fact, is quite a normal thing. Indeed, unless it has turned into tragedy it is not really carelessness and no one thinks of it as such. We calculate that we will get to the other side of the street before a car gets to us. If we calculate correctly, well and good. If not, we are guilty of carelessness, criminal carelessness, unpardonable carelessness, carelessness that even a car will not pardon us for.

I know of one such case. A young mother was bathing her baby in a large basin on the table. She noticed that the water was getting cold. "Baby will catch cold," she thought, and took the basin with the child in it and set it on the gas range, which was turned low. Perhaps she even felt a thrill of pride at her clever idea. Then someone rang the next-door neighbor's door-bell. She knew that the visitor was ringing in vain, as her neighbor had gone to the country to be by the side of her daughter, who was having a baby, and would be away a few days. The un-known visitor was persistent, like a man in an official cap with a sheaf of summonses and receipts in his hand and an indelible pencil stuck behind his ear, like the telegraph boy with a wire, an inspector who threatens to cut off the electricity, an official with a military summons. The unknown visitor kept ringing and ringing, as stubbornly as authority. The young mother hastened to the door for just a second, just long enough to tell him he was ringing in vain, that her neighbor was away from home, and no more. She ran to the door with her wet hands and opened it by pressing on the handle with her elbow. . . . When would the lady return? She didn't know, probably in a day or two, she'd gone to be with her daughter, who was having a baby. . . . And then—bang! a draft slammed the door shut.

A thing like that can happen. In fact, a thing like that often does happen; a thing we read of in comic books or see at the movies, a thing almost worn to shreds. I remember having read somewhere about someone who was just having a bath when a visitor rang his doorbell. And when the visitor finally gave up and was already halfway down the stairs, curiosity teased our bather and attracted him, all covered with soap suds, to take a look down the stairwell—and a little breeze slammed the door. I might even say there is no one who hasn't had a similar experi-ence. But sometimes it isn't funny. For instance, if that young mother had had a cherry pie in the oven, she would tell the story often and always give her guests a good laugh. In the matter of carelessness, as I have already said, the point is whether or not there will be any aftereffects. (But it isn't only a matter of carelessness; there is even something of the appeal of adventure, I tried to convince my colleagues at the bank. "Don't be a fool! No mother is going to risk her child's life because of the adventure!" "Now, don't be so obstinate; I know about these things better than you do," I'd retort heatedly.) So if the man in the official cap hadn't chanced to ring the doorbell, or if the neighbor's daughter hadn't chanced to be having a baby, there would have been nothing to accuse the young mother of. Or even if everything had happened as it did, but the wind—a quite imprudent, irresponsible fellow—hadn't slammed the door, no one, of course, would have had anything to say. Someone would have objected, though, if she had not gone to see who was ringing so persistently and to tell him no one was at home.

Fortunately, however, the young mother chanced to have the key of her flat in her apron pocket and unlocked the door, so nothing happened. Anyway, that evening, still half terrified, half exhilarated, she told her friend about her adventure, and she in turn told it to her husband, and he told it to me at the office the next day.

Well, that's how it is with carelessness. But forgetfulness and absent-mindedness are something different. I only know that every evening now, as I return home, I listen on the stairs for music coming from my flat. I listen with misgiving, as though it were my own voice, the voice of that other self of mine talking to itself inside, the voice of the detached, subconscious half of myself. And if by chance I do not hear it, I do not attribute this circumstance to myself, but to accident. It's clear enough: ghosts do not exist. The door to the balcony with the brooms is duly locked. As for the control knob, however loose it may be, there is no tension strong enough to turn the radio on. That's what the stout electrician at the corner said. Impossible! Therefore I alone must be the cause of its being turned on. The whole question is, did I forget to turn the knob off or, at a higher level of absent-mindedness, did I forget to forget this? And did I, confused as I am, think I had turned it off while in fact I hadn't, but only thought I had, or had I in fact done so, without having given a thought to doing so. And it might be that I really had turned it off and then unconsciously turned it on again. Because a man can force himself to remember what he has consciously and willingly done, but how can he remember what he has done unconsciously? And it is only toward evening, while going upstairs, that I get an answer to the question: I listen keenly for sounds coming from my flat; if the radio is playing, it means I didn't turn it off; if it is not playing, it means I did. And you can't imagine how this trivial unknown quantity that awaits me at the end of the day provokes me. In my lonely life it comes as a kind of entertainment—the only indefinite, uncertain thing in my monotonous life. The only unknown quantity, the only riddle in my life, the only thing that can constitute an uncertainty and a riddle is—myself. Often, as I leave the house, I turn back from the landing torn by doubt: Have I locked the door? And usually I find that in my absent-mindedness I have really locked it, quite mechanically. But I don't go back into my flat to see about the radio: if I did, I should be depriving myself of a small, provoking uncertainty, of a pleasant little surprise awaiting me at the end of the day, like a lump of sugar by my bed. But to find that I have indeed locked the door gives me pleasure, I must admit. It pleases me, as though I have cheated someone, and it flatters me, because it bears out my contention that if our absent-mindedness chances to turn out to our advantage, it is a virtue, we are normal, and everything is all right. But if it doesn't, we're like that wretched mother.

Occasionally, though, I ask myself, is it absent-mindedness or something else? I don't know, I can't say. At any rate, to look at it from a practical point of view, unless something disastrous happens, people will be inclined to believe it is absent-mindedness.

Of course! Ordinary absent-mindedness! Why worry your head about it? Things like that happen to me too, to everyone!

Still, I decided to see a doctor. (How strange, even in one's thoughts one is reluctant to call him by the name of his specialty: I say "a doctor" as though it were a case of bronchitis or heartburn.) But I didn't. And anyway, what could I say to him? "Doctor, sometimes I forget to turn off my radio"? He'd stare at me and say, "Well, what about it?" And he'd look me up and down in a funny sort of way. He'd be suspicious, not because I forget to turn my radio off, but because I came to see him about it. And he'd probably say to himself, "He's not quite right in the head."

No, no! It's better like this. So long as it's like this, I'm "quite right in the head."

Translated by Petar Mijušković

VLADAN DESNICA

The Tale of the Friar
with the Green Beard

This is quite a simple story; something like it could happen to anyone. It all depends on whether we set out in that direction; and then—the rest takes care of itself.

Let us imagine a man, quite an ordinary man, an average human like a million others, dreaming one night—and what may one not dream about, how many and varied are the things that come to man's mind in dreams! But is that reason enough to draw conclusions from them? Dreams are, after all, pure fantasy, there are no logical rules or laws about them. For example, a man dreams one night about a monk with a green beard. Or, if you will, a monk with a squint in his left eye. Or anything else —it doesn't matter. Anything at all! Because, in his dreams, a man sees such things as would take him more than a hundred years to envision in a waking state. He may dream, for instance, of a "man without buttons," that is, of a man who doesn't have a single button on his clothes. Not that his buttons have fallen off, and the bits of thread can still be seen where they were once sewn. This man just has no buttons, as though he had lived his whole life without them; he doesn't even have buttonholes. A thing, as one can see, not particularly unusual or fantastic and, while awake, not really awe-inspiring. But in dreams, such a buttonless man can acquire a certain similarity, a certain vague relationship with that aquatic animal which is usually called a "man-fish."

But let us not digress. Let us not lose the logical thread of our story. Let us remain with the "friar with the green beard," as long as we have chosen that example. Well, as we were saying, a man one night dreamed of a monk with a green beard. Very well. Throughout the whole of the following day he didn't give this a thought. But that night, just as he was peeling off his right sock before going to bed, it suddenly occurred to him that he might dream of the friar again. But the night went by without his dreaming of him. And the next morning, while going to the office, he thought: just imagine, I didn't dream of the friar with the green beard after all.

But matters need not take such a course. The opposite can happen: the man may not think of the friar during the day and yet dream of him that very night. These two cases are in fact identical; both the alternatives lead to the same result. But let us rather remain with the first possibility, since we have already set out in that direction. Well, then, that evening he thinks about the friar but fails to dream of him. And so on the next evening, and the third and the fourth. And every morning, while washing his face and shaving, he thinks: Well, last night I didn't dream of him again. He thinks of him familiarly. And such a thought gives him a quick little sense of pleasure. As though he were putting a saved-up coin into a small cashbox every morning. And then there came the morning when he did not think of the friar. But that was why on the following night he dreamed of

him again. Then, for some time, every day he either dreamed of
the friar or thought about him; and sometimes it was both.

And then a scandal broke in the office. Quite understandably,
in such a situation anyone would forget a score of things more
important than a mere friar! A huge embezzlement had been
discovered in his department and all the employees, including
himself, were subjected to questioning. That was the law. He,
however, was completely calm. From the tone of his questioners,
he realized from the very first moment that he was under no suspicion. Still, such things were always unpleasant. But that also
passed. And a week later (it was a fine, sunny day, and after
lunch he went for a walk in the zoo) he recalled with pleasure
that during the whole of the investigation at the office he had
neither thought of the friar nor dreamed of him. Even now he
would not have thought of him, had not a priest passed by him
along the way. True, this was a priest and not a friar; and the
priest did not have a beard, much less a green one. But that's
what our memories are like: sometimes we remember things by
association through similarity and sometimes through contrast.
More frequently through contrast. If, for example, we have a
small dog whose right eye has been knocked out, and somewhere we see another small dog whose left eye is missing, we
might cry out: Well, now, this one is missing an eye too! Only
mine is missing a right eye and this dog, a left one. And I firmly
believe that this small dog without a left eye will remind us no
less of the one we own without his right eye, than if this one,
too, were deprived of a right eye like our own dog. And, by this
same logic, when we see a cat without a left eye, we'll say: See,
this one is missing an eye, like my Tootsie, except that the cat
has no left eye and my doggie no right eye, and this is a cat,
while Tootsie is a dog. Also, if we see a dog that has no eyes
missing at all, we might say: See, just like poor Tootsie, except
that he has both eyes! And as all things are of necessity mutu-
ally similar or dissimilar, the conclusion might be drawn that

every object can remind us of every other object. All this brings me to the idea that those things which remind us of something else need not depend on similarity or dissimilarity, but on something quite different. On what, I don't know! But I'm sure it's something that, regardless of similarities and dissimilarities, lies deep under the ocean, like a cable.

Of course, that evening, while undressing, he again thought of the friar. And in the morning, while shaving, he said to himself: How strange, yesterday I thought so much about him, and yet I didn't dream of him! I might almost say that when I keep thinking of him all day long and expect surely to dream about him, I don't dream of him at all; but if, while I am awake, I don't even give him a thought, then, sure enough, he appears in my dreams! Very strange! Looks as though I must think about him quite intensely in the daytime so as not to dream of him at night!

"Nonsense," he said finally, with a wave of his hand. And when he arrived at the office he looked at his desk calendar, grasped a few random pages, turned over a fat sheaf of them onto a date in the distant future, and wrote the words "the Friar," in blue pencil. He did this because he recalled how in his childhood, after having recovered from an attack of influenza, a low, persistent fever had continued. Only a few degrees above normal, but still, there it was. His mother was beside herself with anxiety. How long will this last, doctor? . . . what shall we do, doctor? . . . were the words she addressed to the family physician, whereas he, an elderly and experienced man, thickset and short of breath, was not in the least perturbed. "Simply stop taking the child's temperature," he had advised phlegmatically. "Let the child go to school and let him play with the others. And then, when you take his temperature a few days later, you'll see how it will all be gone." And indeed, that's the way it was. So now he thought: That's how it's going to be. I'll stop taking the temperature!

And this really helped. At first he thought about the friar less and less frequently, until he finally dropped him entirely from his thoughts. Almost two months went by without his ever thinking of the friar, either asleep or awake. And then one morning, all unwittingly, he turned a page of his calendar—and there was the friar. From then on he kept recurring to him with growing frequency—if not all the time, at least whenever he glanced at the calendar. Everything the calendar stood for now seemed to be closely bound up with the friar: the former stuck to the latter like two caramels in a paper bag inside a warm pocket. Everything connected with the calendar now reminded him of the friar, and whatever had associations with the friar—such things as church, an altar, and the like—would remind him of the calendar and the friar. If he met a funeral procession, immediately the friar came to his mind! If he saw an agricultural calendar in a shop window of the Farmers' Co-operative—again the friar came to mind. If, while waiting in his boss's reception room to get his signature, his eyes chanced to fall on the calendar, or only on the wall clock, or even the barometer, his mind would immediately turn to the friar. True, in his dreams the friar appeared less frequently, but somehow at more regular, almost fixed intervals of time. And it seemed to him that now he could correctly foretell those nightly visits, that he knew exactly which was the "friar's day," just as one knows the charwoman's day or the day the rent collector is to call.

For some time all went well. But then logic came into play, that devilish logic which comes at the end to spoil all that which illogicality cannot undo: now in the mornings he no longer asked himself whether he had dreamed of the friar or not, nor did this give him the slightest pleasure any longer; it was, in fact, inconsequential. He realized that between the words "I dreamed of the friar" and "I did not dream of the friar" the whole difference lay in the "did" and "did not," but that in both cases the "friar" remained unchanging and permanent. He remembered how every morning while shaving he had naïvely enjoyed the thought: "Well, I didn't dream about him last night," or, "Well, I wasn't thinking of him today," and he smiled bitterly to himself, saying, "What a fool I was!" Did not thinking about how he didn't think of the friar really amount to thinking of him? And this critical thought at once demolished all others: it was only some kind of metastasis of the friar. So that, whichever way it was, asleep or awake, as a daytime visitor or nightly guest—the friar was there! And at once it struck him that during all that time, from the very beginning—during the investigation at the office, and all the while up to the fateful turning of the calendar's pages—the friar, invisible, had been there all the time, right behind the curtain. And one morning, while shaving, he stopped and groaned in the middle of the empty white bathroom: "Oh, if only I could forget . . . only forget . . ." He drew the razor down his cheek several times and again stopped short: "But what is forgetfulness? And can one ever be completely calm? Even if it settles upon you, how can one know if that is the real, final, genuine forgetfulness or only temporary oblivion? On what grounds could one reckon with certainty that one day some chance encounter, some small trifle, anything at all, would not unexpectedly, and thereby powerfully, reawaken the idea of the friar?" He lay the razor on the cold white porcelain shelf above the sink, looked at his haggard face and shadowed eyes in the mirror, and said aloud: "There is no salvation for me." His voice sent shivers down his spine.

But man is strong. Man is a resistant creature; a stubborn, wiry being. Man does not give in so easily. And he began trying to defend himself with the same weapon, that same "logical thought" that had ruined everything before. He began rationalizing: Actually, "to think of the friar" was not the same as "to think of one's thoughts about the friar"; although at first glance it did seem the same thing, it really wasn't! There was a small shade of difference here. In the first case, the friar is something that stands above me, something that tyrannizes me, something that governs and controls me; in this case he is the master, and I his slave; in the latter case, it is he who is subservient to me, he is my object: the object of my thoughts. In this, then, I am still the master. "Yes, I am the master," he said aloud in front of the mirror.

There, that was a possibility, another way out of the whole dilemma. Perhaps the only way. And this time the man really calmed down. Once again he found the will to live. On sunny afternoons he sometimes went for walks in the zoological gardens. He even gained a few pounds. This was obviously a good sign. From then on, he weighed himself regularly. Now he thought of the friar without anxiety, without any particular repercussions, almost nonchalantly. "In time, he'll completely disappear," he reassured himself. And the very fact that the friar became unimportant to him resulted in his thinking of him less and less frequently. It was like being in love: as soon as you got the first signs that she returned your love, you became cockier; you could afford the luxury of diverting your thoughts from her from time to time for the sake of a little change. It was like that in everything, the question always being, who is stronger, who is the master: you or she, you or the friar?

One Saturday, while he was sharpening his razor, he caught himself whistling. "It's been ages since I've whistled!" he said to himself. And then he went to the movies. It turned out to be stuff and nonsense. A silly, improbable love story fit only for tea-shop waitresses or young hairdressers. That evening, while undressing, something fell out of his pocket onto the small rug near his bed. He bent down to pick it up: it was the card that showed his latest weight. He reread the figures printed on it and once again rubbed his hands with satisfaction over the fact that he had gained. He smiled: "Looks as if I'm really rid of him at last."

But that very night he dreamed of the friar again. He seemed a bit thinner. He smiled sourly, winking his left eye and shaking his forefinger: "You are mistaken, my friend, sadly mistaken. Come what may, I'm inside you for good. Remember —you will never be able to drive me away."

And then—then there was really no more hope for him.

Translated by Olga Humo

MIODRAG BULATOVIĆ

The Lovers

"My flesh is clothed with worms and clods of dust; my skin is broken, and become loathsome.

My days are swifter than a weaver's shuttle, and are spent without hope."

JOB, VII, 5-6

The café was small and dingy. Olja and I sat in a corner, so that neither Ananije nor Fotije, who were sitting a table or two away, could see us, not to mention Sima and Nikifor, who were sitting behind the door. The café was dark, and but for its small windows you would have thought you were in a dugout rather than an inn on the outskirts of the town from which few people went out sober. Its dark-colored walls were very high, so that we could not see them properly; they towered above us, sheer as ramparts. Olja and I looked at each other. The people around us were whispering bits of cloth, murmuring or keeping silent over the tables. Olja whispered too, but I had nothing to say. The people looked gray, like clay or paper dolls, some suspended in mid-air, some not. Most of them were old men.

Olja asked me whether I was afraid. I looked calmly in the mirror. It was a tissue of smoke, spider webs, and glass. All the faces I saw in it were wrinkled and sick except mine. I had a birth mark on my cheekbone that improved my appearance. My eyes were particularly fine. They glowed darkly in the curves of my pale face; it was bound to be pale, for I was thinking about how to find something that would arouse my wonder and enthusiasm. Fotije told me that airplanes were a very strange invention, and that one ought to take an interest in them. I became very fond of them, with the enthusiasm of a child. I made them from paper and cardboard, wood and tin. I thought it would be the summit of my happiness when I took off from an airport. But I was disappointed. As soon as we left the ground I got sick. At that time I did not know either Olja or Ananije. Ananije was standing reflected in the mirror. As long as I had known him his face had been distorted and gloomy. He had a deformed foot that he dragged behind him, but I could not see it in the mirror for the smoke. Sima was standing stiffly beside him with a book. He was so tall that his shoulders broke through the frame of the mirror, and his head was somewhere above the glass. I was the only person who knew that Ananije and Fotije rehashed other people's poems and signed them with their own names. I found this out when they were drunk, but I never told anyone, as I always forgot. I used to write poems before I got interested in airplanes. Actually I am a born poet, with a natural talent, but I don't like this kind of lying. I had a special gift for making verses and devising new and unusual rhymes, but I had no interest in work of any kind. I looked in the mirror and saw Olja's head beside my shoulder. I laughed at Olja and Ananije for being sad. I did not know what it meant to be either gay or sad.

Even today I regard the world quite simply, as though I were looking at the most ordinary garden, though I am aware that I am better, wiser, and more handsome than all the people I know. Olja leaned her head on my shoulder.

Then I began to dream about boats. I lived in a world of shipwrecks, courageous captains, and sailors. I went to sea and embarked on a voyage. I did not come to my senses for nearly a month. When a mirror was held up to my face I saw that I looked like a skeleton. I grieved for the loss of my beauty. My eyes no longer had that fine, alluring gleam. I fled from the water and began to wander aimlessly about the world. I went from town to town, from country to country. To the Spaniards I presented myself as a persecuted nobleman, to the French as the son of the king of Serbia, to the Dutch as an ear, nose, and throat specialist, and to the Danes, Norwegians, and Swedes as the leader of the Yugoslav Communists. All this seemed dull and uninteresting, though people usually believed me and regarded me as a Serbian genius. Last year, after ten years of wandering about the world, I returned to Belgrade to the pubs beside the Sava, to my old acquaintances whose names I had already begun to forget. I celebrated my thirty-second birthday in my attic room, and as soon as I went out into the street I noticed Olja.

I saw my fine hands in the mirror. One was stretched out on the table and the other rested on Olja's shoulder. Her eyes were so gentle and sad that it seemed to me tears could pour forth from them at any moment. I couldn't look at them, and I cried out several times, asking her to smile. I could see in the mirror how she was clinging to me. This gave me neither pleasure nor amusement. Fotije and Ljubica came toward the mirror. He was small, and she was so tiny that you could harldy see her among the tables. I liked Fotije because when he was drunk he used to say strange things. I smoothed my hair with my hands. I passed my hand caressingly under my chin. It seemed to me that my blood passed from my fingers into my cheeks.

Olja asked me whether I was afraid. She was sitting with her hands on her knees, petrified, looking at me. I answered that I had nothing to be afraid of. She asked me:

"What would you do if a robber pointed his gun at you?"

"I should probably be frightened," I answered. "And you?"

"I should be frightened too."

She asked me again. I answered that it was practically all the same to me, but that I should be sorry to die, especially as I was so young. She said she would weep and beg them to spare her life. I told her I should probably do the same.

Since I returned from my wanderings I had become increasingly preoccupied with the fact that I must have an heir. I thought that this would calm me down and interest me more than planes and boats. Olja was whispering and looking in the mirror on the wall. She was a large girl with rosy cheeks, and I thought it would be a good idea to marry her. Ljubica went off with Fotije, and Sima with Ananije. A film came over my eyes. In the mirror I could see only smoke and an empty space around the frame. Then I asked Olja:

"Would you like to marry me?"

We were looking at each other. I remembered that Ivana had looked just like that when I put the same question to her. Ivana had consented and said she would bear me a daughter. I changed my mind and sent her back to her mother, unmarried. She cried bitterly at the station. I asked her why she was crying, though I knew that it was because it was hard to see me go away. She said I had ruined her future. I said that the future was just the present moment when we were looking at each other, and that there was therefore no need for her to cry. She looked at me. I promised to introduce her to Ananije, who would marry her at once, for women shunned him as though he were the devil. I told her that he would be pleased, because he was a virgin although he was old. She looked at me. At last she confessed that she was crying for me. I believed her. The train was ready to leave. I left her on the platform, wrapped in a cheap cloak and steam. Later I realized why I had fled from her. I wanted a son, and she had told me she would bear me a daughter. What's more, she had diseased, staring eyes.

Olja and I were looking at each other. Her expression reminded me so much of Ivana that I almost got up. There was something inconceivably dark in the hollows of her eyes, something that kept dripping down her eyelashes. Olja answered me:

"Am I worthy of you?"

Her answer pleased me. I embraced her and said quietly, "No, but I'll marry you in order to have a son, since you are healthy. I don't like small, thin women. I can't bear poor stock."

"But why do you want a son?"

"So that he may achieve all that I have been unable to achieve."

"Let it be as you say," she said.

Later I learned that Ivana had married a man who worked on the railroad. I didn't doubt this for a moment because her home was near a railway station. Ananije decided that her husband was hurt because her child was not his, but still he was in love with her. Fotije told me that they were always on the move from one end of the country to the other. He also told me that Ivana had suffered a great deal on my account. I believed this too, because a lot of them yearned for me. But I've never found out what causes suffering. I told Ananije that it simply didn't exist and that people had invented it. Fotije answered that it was one of the finest things in life. Ananije said that without suffering there was neither love, happiness, nor creative activity. Olja looked steadily into my eyes. Then I asked them both whether they would describe as suffering the feeling a man has when he is so hungry that he has pains in his stomach. They answered that this was only hunger and physical need. They explained to me that suffering was an accumulation of happiness, longing, and pain. I told them that I did not believe in anything in the world, least of all in theories that were sick fancies. I added that it would be better if they abandoned their poetry and took a look at the crawling gait of human skulls from an airplane; or sailed out to sea at least as far as Rijeka, to feel below them the fathomless deep and, around them, emptiness; or choose a healthy woman and breed children by her; any of these things would be better than this perpetual talk about the heart and human suffering, and about the future of poetry and the secrets of the universe.

"Why are you looking at me so long?" I asked her.

"I don't know," she whispered.

"Look somewhere else a little, not just at me. Look at the smoke."

"And what shall we do if it is a girl?"

"We'll both throw it in the river," I said, shaking with rage.

"In the river? What has come over you?"

"In the river, I say. Why are you looking at me like that? You and the child!"

She was clinging to my right side. I told her how I would teach my son right from his childhood to fly a plane, to sail the seas, to study people and to deceive them like a juggler. She asked me what would become of us. Nothing, I said. I promised her that I would take off her rags and buy her fine clothes if I had the money, but that I wouldn't do so if I hadn't, and that her best plan was to listen to me. She said that she liked someone to order her about.

Fotije and Ananije were the same age as I, but they looked about forty. Olja was sitting beside me. They looked at me enviously. I felt that they were talking about us, but I had no idea what they were saying. They were smiling. While Olja was whispering something beside my shoulder, I was thinking that Ivana had done well for herself to marry that railwayman who moved her around. I remembered that I had left a brass ring with her.

An old man stood beside Olja. He was tall and thin, with a beard pointed toward his breast. At his side he carried a bundle of shoelaces and dozens of other trifles. I watched him. He was weeping, but there were no tears in his eyes. He was quite an ordinary old man. He stretched his large wrinkled hand toward me. I continued to watch him. He said quietly:

"Give me something!"

He looked like Ivana's father, who was a watchman on the railroad. I think Ivana's father was an inch or two taller than this man, and, what's more, a thief; once my wallet and handkerchief disappeared from my pocket. I asked what he wanted me to give him. He repeated, in an ordinary, quiet voice:

"Just give me anything."

"Aren't you a poet?" I asked.

His voice was so quiet you could scarcely hear it. He went away. Then Ananije and Fotije came and told me that he was the most unhappy man in Serbia. They said he had been reduced to poverty and begging by love and suffering.

"Are you sure he wasn't a poet, Ananije?"

"He tried his hand at poetry, poor man," answered Fotije.

"Did he ever travel in an airplane? Did he ever swallow salt sea water?"

"The important thing is that he suffers, like any poet," said Ananije.

"But surely you aren't suffering, Ananije?"

"Yes, I am."

Ananije and Fotije were sitting in their old place. I thought what a pity it was that Belgrade and Serbia were so full of such daydreamers. There are fewer of them, I thought, in Montenegro and Macedonia. People are healthier there, because they really have to work for their bread. I didn't like this café scum— these people who sat in their tiny rooms and wrote poetry about love and social problems, and mysticism; these ragged, bearded painters who wandered about the cafés, got drunk, quarreled, and fought. I liked healthy people like football players, because they were ordinary. I asked Olja:

"Do you like football players?"

She made no reply. I asked her:

"Would you like me to take you to my home now? Do you want me to take you right now?"

She nodded.

The next day she became mine, and burst into tears.

I rarely dropped in to see Ananije and Fotije, my nearest neighbors, and still less to see Sima, Nikifor, and Akim, for I loathed poetry. I used to tell them that writing poems was not a healthy job, and that they ought to be sent to work on some building as manual laborers in order to learn about the real world. We all lived on Karageorge Street behind the cafés on the river bank. I told them that what they needed was to be healthy, and that they were just ordinary invalids—the kind that filled up the clinics.

I went to Ananije to complain about Olja. Since she had become mine, she had grown pale and withdrawn and looked at me very strangely. Ananije said that this was because she regretted her virginity. I asked him how she could regret her virginity after ten years of marriage. But Olja wept continually. Fotije told me that she was living through some difficult experience. I was interested to know what this was. Ananije said this was the fine, eternal Slavic suffering without which the very idea of an estimable person was inconceivable, especially if he were an artist. I told both him and Slavic suffering to go to the devil. Ananije and Fotije were surprised. I wanted a wife and son, and I had got illness and Slavic suffering. They looked at me. I said I would break her in two and throw her out of the house if she continued to be like this. Ananije said that Olja had a very deep feeling for poetry. I learned from Fotije that Ivana and her railwayman were in Aleksinac.

Olja wept constantly. I couldn't find any way to make her laugh. Circus and jugglers' tricks, with which I had conquered the world, didn't help me. We had a small attic room, like Ananije's. Some artists lived next door to us. I used to go out of the house so that I shouldn't see them. I found congenial company among magicians, hypnotists, and football players. Actually I had only one wish: to have an heir. Such was the pattern of my days. When I returned home I found Olja in a corner of the room. She stared at me for a long time and it seemed to me that she did not recognize me. I asked her what the matter was. She answered that nothing ailed her. We had nothing in the room but a table and a bed, which was quite enough for two healthy people.

We used to go out into the world for our daily bread, selling odds and ends. I stole whenever I could. Somewhere in Bosnia our hair began to turn gray. Olja asked me when we would go back home. I told her she was very ill. She asked me how much longer I would go on torturing her. I told her that she had dried up, and that I liked her better when she was plump. Someone had stolen the few possessions we carried in a bag and a bundle. She said:

"We are done for!"

"No, we aren't," I said. "I'll rob somebody."

"Isn't that wrong?"

"Why should it be?"

I often remembered Ivana. Sometimes I felt that it would have been better if I hadn't left her. Fotije told me that her daughter was like me, and that this particularly displeased her husband. I didn't believe that she had grieved for me very long, and that it was all the same to her whom she moved around with. But together with this memory came the thought of her weeping at the station, and then I at once turned to Olja. I told her all about it so as to arouse her jealousy.

Olja was growing more and more silent. My smile was still as beautiful as when I was younger. Wrinkles had improved my appearance and gray hairs made me look more serious. Finally Olja became almost dumb. She answered me only when I asked her whether she still loved me.

I soon saw that there was no hope of ever having a son. I came to the conclusion that it was foolish to want one. Later I realized that it was definitely a form of illness to want anything. My most foolish desire had been for an heir. I explained to Ananije that it was disgusting to see oneself in anyone else. He answered that it was a noble and lofty desire, and that he had suffered deeply because he had no son. I began to reflect about suffering, for I was constantly hearing about it. I wanted to experience it. I began to think about what I ought to do in order to suffer. I thought about suffering day and night, and decided that it must be a pleasant sensation. Olja refused to describe it to me. She even appeared not to have heard me when I asked her.

I went to Ananije, and he told me that suffering was like a rainbow above a river. I said to him:

"Tell me what I should do in order to suffer."

"Thrash Olja," he said.

"Hard, or just a little?" I asked.

"As hard as you can," he answered.

That morning I quarreled with the painters next door. They wanted to throw me out of the house. I went home and started to beat Olja. I watched her bend under my switch and spew out blood through her teeth. When I was tired I sat down, but still suffering had not come. I beat her some more. Olja made no protest.

I looked at a photograph of myself as a young man that was hanging on the wall. My head was leaning to one side, since Ivana's head had been beside it. I had cut it out before we parted at the station near the Morava. My eyes were large, dark, and gay, and smiled ruthlessly and self-confidently. I was unbelievably handsome.

Olja was lying on the floor. Her face was covered with blood. My picture had been enlarged and framed. I didn't want to have a picture of anyone else in the room. I gave Olja's to a man who had once been madly in love with her and used to write her letters and poems. He thanked me and burst into tears. He asked me whether she was happy. He was gray-haired and could not walk without a stick. Olja whispered a curse from the floor. I wanted to spit at her, since her cursing reminded me of Ivana, who had once knelt in front of me and cursed the hour she had met me and fallen in love with me. Olja tried to get up.

I beat her every day to see if it would make me unhappy. Fotije came up with another suggestion, but it was so distasteful that I cursed him. I told him that he was an incurable lunatic. He wasn't hurt. He really didn't know how to take offense. If I had said such things to Akim or Sima it would have led to a quarrel, or even to blows. Olja became more and more wizened and yellow.

For nearly two years I sought suffering, and as I didn't find it I decided to leave Olja and go off on my travels again. I wanted to wander through Serbia and Macedonia as a juggler. I had begun my life with juggling, and wanted to end it the same way. It seemed to me that it wasn't so bad to deceive others while one preserved one's own integrity. Just before my departure Olja said to me:

"You might at least wait until I die before you go."

"And what shall I do if you live a long time? You're tough, you'll live a long time." But I postponed my journey. For several days she was delirious constantly. She could not recognize me. I had many distasteful and unpleasant things to say to her. I remembered some of them only when her breath began to fail and a strange light appeared in her eyes. But they weren't unpleasant or distasteful things, just quite ordinary remarks. Olja held her hand to her throat. She kept clenching her fingers in agony and pressing them to her face.

Such scenes disgusted me. I was once sick when I saw a young man in his death throes. He stretched himself on the ground, crossed his hands on his chest, screamed with pain, and then died just like anybody else.

Olja lay motionless on the floor; only her lips moved. That night I didn't dream at all, but before I fell asleep I reflected for a long time in an absent-minded sort of way that I had made a mistake when I married Olja and not Ivana.

By dawn Olja was stiff. She looked quite as usual. One arm was lying by her head. Shrunken and yellow, it looked like a worm. Only her lips and eyelashes were visible above her scarf. I stood by the window and looked at her.

It was hard to believe that she wasn't awake. I thought about my trip to Macedonia. Olja looked peaceful lying there. I sang over her, quietly at first, then more and more loudly. I pretended to weep and lament. Only the elbow of her other arm peeped out from under the bedclothes. I threatened to kill myself and leave her to starve to death. She said nothing. I leaned against the door. I called out to her to wake up. Her eyelids were tightly shut and ridged like tiles on a roof. I remembered that old man who had sold odds and ends in the café.

The next day I called on Ananije and Fotije. They read me a lecture on suffering. I listened to them as usual. They persuaded me. I realized that I should begin to suffer only if I did something very unusual. I put Olja beside me on the bed. I caressed the top of her head. I tickled her under the arm. Her skin had begun to peel. When my fingers disappeared inside her it seemed to me that her ribs moved. Yet even when I possessed her, suffering did not come. I stood in front of the mirror; the only thing I noticed was that I was a little paler. My face had a wonderful beauty that comes only with age. Olja was lying with her hands on her throat.

I was frightened that I should die without experiencing suffering and sorrow. To take my mind off this, I began to perform my jugglers' tricks in front of the mirror. The only thing I had forgotten was how to mimic other people's voices. I started to cry, just so that I might hear something. It seemed to me that there was nothing finer than being in my room beside Olja. It was only when night fell that I went out for some food and brandy.

Two days later I called on Ananije. When Fotije and Ljubica had left I told him everything. Ananije looked pale. He trembled slightly as I told my story. I told the story in my usual voice. He said to me:

"You're a very strange and interesting man."

"What do you mean? Why strange? Why interesting?"

"If I were a prose writer, I should write a novel about you."

I told him he was a very sick man; and that I wanted to pass water. He was surprised, and an even sadder expression came on his face. I asked him:

"Why do all your poems have such gloomy, tragic endings? Why do you always write about death? It isn't the end of everything. You're old and experienced enough to know that—better than anyone else in view of the fact that you think yourself a poet."

"If I knew anything else, I'd write about it," said Ananije.

"Look a little more closely at life," I said, "it isn't all bad. Everything in the world is quite normal. But your poems are gloomy because you were born sick. Isn't it so? It is because you have a deformed foot. Perhaps there is some hereditary weakness. What do you think?"

He looked at me; he was pale. I asked him:

"And where on earth is the lavatory in this tenement of yours, my dear Ananije? I was going along the street wondering where to drop in, and in the end I dropped in on you."

While I was going downstairs from the attic room I noticed that I had forgotten half of my jugglers' tricks.

Olja was stiffer than ever. I packed for my journey. The darkness was weaving a curtain over the aperture of my window. Outside the door I heard a commotion.

"Who is there?" I called out.

"Your neighbors the painters."

"What do you want?"

"Can you lend us a few dinars to buy some bread?"

"I have some, but I'm not giving you any. You never pay your debts. I've been lending you money for years and you've never given me back a single dinar. You're a set of rotten swindlers, a thorough bad lot. I'm not such a fool as to feed such crazy gluttons."

I knew them well. They lived in attic rooms too. They were all in rags and smeared with paint. They wore beards, so that people laughed at them and asked them if by any chance they were priests. I avoided them like the plague, especially since I'd heard they were louse-ridden and liked to steal.

"Something stinks in your room."

"Get lost!" I said.

"It's such an awful smell that you can hardly walk along the corridor. This is what we wanted to tell you; we haven't fallen so low as to ask you for money."

"If you can smell something, I can't. Get out of here!"

"You must be rotting alive. Let us in! We want to paint you."

"Go to the devil," I said, "you haven't come because of the smell, but to throw me out. There's no smell here. You've imagined it, it's a sick man's fancy."

"And how is your wife?"

"She's ill. She's asleep. She's all right. What are you asking about her for?"

"Because she's likely to be in a bad way, living with a cretin like you."

For a long time they hammered on the door with their fists, threatening to break it down if I didn't open it. They got an ax and began to smash at the lock with its head. But when I took out my gun from under the bed and pushed a bullet into the barrel, they fled.

Olja was lying quite peacefully. A street car was rocketing down Karageorge Street. The car tracks shone in front of it, like two healthy thoughts lost in the night. Behind it, it left darkness and silence. It was too dark for me to see Olja. Under the boats the Sava was heaving. Toward it, peacefully, flowed the Danube. I stood at the window. I decided I had better take my gun with me on my journey.

I hurriedly wrapped Olja in a blanket and took her to the

cemetery. I buried her just before dawn. Beside a marble stone sleep overcame me. I didn't dream at all. When I awoke the sun was high above the graves. I wondered if I had forgotten anything. It seemed as if I had lost something. I felt in my pockets: all my usual things were there. I fell asleep again and woke up when the sun was slowly sinking toward the Sava.

The grass was growing over the grave and still I didn't go home. I made friends with the gravediggers. We started to steal food from the graves together. I completely forgot about my journey to Macedonia and my wish to end my days as a juggler. My only desire was that my conscience should prick me. This wish was present only in the morning, after I had slept. During the day all I wanted to do was to satisfy my hunger. Before I closed my eyes I would laugh at my naïve, childish desire for suffering. I realized that I had made a mistake in not having married Ivana. Many days passed, and I came to the conclusion that my desire for an uneasy conscience and a journey to Macedonia was a sick fancy. I started to think about airplanes and parachutes.

Ananije came to the cemetery. Fotije and Ljubica followed him. Ananije was tall and quite gray. He carried a stick and dragged his deformed, keylike foot behind him. Fotije was disturbed. Ananije said to me:

"I heard that you were here, so I came to see what you were doing."

"Nothing," I replied in my normal voice.

"What the devil are you looking for in a cemetery?" asked Fotije.

"I'm not looking for any devil," I answered. "Devils never come to the cemetery. Only vampires and bad poets come here."

"You will suffer from those vampires," said Ananije, "especially if you take food from graves; you're done for."

I told him that I could live without the food intended for the souls of the dead.

"You're in a bad way," said Ljubica.

They took me away. I could hardly stand on my feet, but I went off and looked around me as though everything were normal. The gravediggers waved to me. One of them whispered to me not to tell anyone that we had stolen food from the graves together. On the fence beside the gate I noticed some birds. They were fat and lazy, and weren't afraid of anybody. Ljubica talked to me about the painters, who had lost all sense of morality and social behavior; and Ananije talked about Akim and Nikifor, who had begun to flatter some leading lights among the politicians. I walked slowly and wondered if I could demean myself to ask them for a crust of bread.

The next day the painters turned me out of my flat. I went down to Serbia with a knapsack and a stick.

It's a long time since I saw you, Olja. Sometimes you come to me in a dream. You walk, but you don't say anything. Your blood trickles between your teeth. I run after you and ask you:

"How are you, Olja dear?"

You shake your head. I ask you:

"Do you still love me, Olja? Are you still madly in love with me?"

You weep, and ask me how long I shall torture you. I say:

"Wait, I want to look in your eyes. Turn around, I'm your husband. Perhaps I could come with you to the underworld?"

The sky is bloody above your head. And it seems to me that you hold in your hands, not shoelaces and odds and ends for sale, but a bundle of dead snakes.

As for me, I'm all right. I go about the world sightless and begging. I can tell night from day by human laughter. I cannot suffer, but a little well of pus forms in the hollows of my eyes when I remember how your lips rotted away.

Translated by E. D. Goy

About the Authors

IVO ANDRIĆ was born in 1892 in Travnik, Bosnia. He studied Slavic languages and literatures in Zagreb, Krakow, and Vienna, but because of his anti-Hapsburg and pro-Yugoslav convictions he was jailed by the Austrians in 1914 and kept in prison during most of the war. After the war he resumed his studies and received a doctorate in history from the University of Graz. With the creation of the Kingdom of Yugoslavia, he embarked upon a long diplomatic career. He was ambassador in Berlin when German-Yugoslav hostilities broke out in 1941.

Between the two world wars he published three collections of short stories. His major works, for which he was awarded the Nobel Prize for Literature in 1961, were written in Belgrade during the Nazi occupation and published in 1945: *The Bridge on the Drina, Bosnian Chronicle,* and *Miss.*

MIROSLAV KRLEŽA was born in 1893 in Zagreb. After graduating from the Budapest Military Academy in 1912, in an outburst of militant nationalism he asked to serve in the Serbian army; he placed high hopes in Serbia for the future of the Southern Slavs. But the Serbs believed him to be an Austro-Hungarian spy and sent him back to the Austria he loathed. During World War I, he served in the Austro-Hungarian army as a simple soldier. Between the two world wars he was strongly opposed to King Alexander's dictatorship. During the Fascist occupation of Croatia he stayed in hiding. In Tito's Yugoslavia he became Vice President of the Yugoslav Academy of Arts and Sciences and Editor in Chief of the Yugoslav Encyclopedia.

Krleža has published more than fifty volumes of poetry and prose. His trilogy, *The Glembays* (1929), *In Agony* (1928), and *Leda* (1930) is representative of the very best in modern Yugoslav drama.

In his novel *The Croatian God Mars* (1922), Krleža describes the tragic absurdity of the Croatian soldier, obliged to shed blood in the interests of Austria. In *The Return of Philip Latinovicz* (1932), a prodigal son returns to his native Croatian town after twenty-three years of exile.

Hodorlahomor the Great was written in 1919 and *The Love of Marcel Faber-Fabriczy for Miss Laura Warronigg*, in 1929. In the translation of *The Love of Marcel Faber-Fabriczy for Miss Laura Warronigg* for this collection, passages dealing with Marcel Faber-Fabriczy's genealogy have been omitted with the author's permission. The story belongs to a cycle of plays and stories constituting an organic whole, published under the title *The Glembays*.

PREŽIHOV VORANC, a pseudonym for Lovro Kuhar (1893-1950), was born in a small Slovenian village. His formal education ended with elementary school; a peasant's son, he was required to work the land. In the course of World War I, he was drafted into the multi-national Austro-Hungarian army. Believing Austria to be the Slovene's worst enemy, he deserted and joined the Italians who were posing as liberators of the oppressed Slavs. Paradoxically, the Italians put him in jail and from then on there seemed to be no end to the hardships he experienced, including several years of internment in Nazi concentration camps.

Prežihov Voranc's major works are two collections of short stories published in 1925 and 1931 and the novels *Doberdob* (1940) and *Jamnica* (1945). The time span in Prežihov Voranc's works encompasses the last years of Austria-Hungary, the events surrounding the Peace Conference in Paris, and the first years of the Yugoslav Kingdom up to 1929, when King Alexander established royal dictatorship.

CIRIL KOSMAČ was born in 1910 in a Slovenian region that was Austrian before World War I and Italian after it. In 1929, while still in high school, he was arrested by the Fascist police for membership in a secret anti-Fascist youth organization. He spent several months in prisons in Gorizia, Rome, and Trieste. Shortly after his release he escaped to Yugoslavia, where he lived for several years in Slovenia's capital, Ljubljana, before going to Paris on a French scholarship. When the Germans entered Paris in 1940 he left for Marseille and eventually arrived in London by way of Spain and Portugal. Via Egypt and Bari in 1944 he was able to join Tito's Partisans in Slovenia, where he became editor of a newspaper. A collection of short stories in 1946, *Happiness and Bread*, established his reputation as Slovenia's major modern writer. His novel *A Day in Spring*, published in England in 1959, deals with a writer's return home after fifteen years of exile.

MIHAILO LALIĆ, born in Montenegro in 1914, comes from a poor peasant family. He lost his mother when he was four and his father when he was seven and was brought up by his stepmother and uncle. While studying in Belgrade he worked as a milkman, a newspaper delivery boy and finally as a reporter for the daily paper *Pravda*. He graduated from the law school at the University of Belgrade shortly before World War II, during which he belonged to the Partisan Movement. After the war he returned to journalism, later becoming editor in a publishing house. He has published three collections of short stories: *The Reconnoiterers* (1948), *The First Snow* (1951), and *In the Moonlight* (1956). Two of his novels have won particular critical acclaim: *The Wedding* (1950) and *Leleja Mountain* (1962).

The Shepherdess was sketched in 1942 at the time when events similar to the one depicted were taking place. It was completed and published in 1948.

BRANKO ĆOPIĆ was born in 1915 in Bosnia. He graduated from the Faculty of Philosophy at the University of Belgrade. During World War II he was among the first to join Tito's Partisans. The titles of his poems, short stories, and novels published after 1947 bear the imprint of the war: *The Warrior's Springtime*, *The Dew on the Bayonets*, *The Fiery Birth of My Country*, *The Crash*, *Deaf Gunpowder*, *Fighters and Fugitives*, and *Don't Grieve, Sentry of Bronze*. His greatest successes: the prize-winning novel *The Crash* (1953) and the best-selling collection of short stories *The Adventures of Nikoletina Bursać*, published in Sarajevo in 1956.

RANKO MARINKOVIĆ was born on the Dalmatian island of Vis in 1913. He graduated from the Faculty of Philosophy at the University of Zagreb. His first published works appeared shortly before World War II. He is best known for his collections of short stories, of which *Hands* (1955) has brought him greatest recognition. Along with his steady output of short stories, he has written for and about the theater. Drama Director of the Croatian National Theater and Professor at the Academy of Theater Arts in Zagreb, he is the author of two successful plays (*Albatross* in 1939 and *Gloria* in 1955) and a volume of essays on the theater entitled *Gestures and Grimaces* (1951).

IVAN DONČEVIĆ was born into a Croatian farming family in 1909. After graduating from high school he studied agriculture briefly, but left college for writing and journalism. Critics have particularly praised his collection of short stories *People Without a Name* (1946) and his novel *The Peacemakers* (1953). At present Dončević directs the Zora Publishing Company in Zagreb.

The Insect Collector, written in 1953, renders much of the local color of Croatia's capital, Zagreb. Maksimir, the lovers' lane; Zrinjevac, the popular corso where high school and college students meet and walk together; the sidewalk in front of the Dubrovnik Café, favorite haunt of the bird and skirt watchers; and the inevitable Sunday soccer game at the end of a week's work in a socialistic-type business enterprise.

VLADAN DESNICA was born in 1905 in Zadar, a town on the Adriatic coast rich in cultural heritage. He comes from a family of wealthy landowners professionally oriented toward the practice of law. He studied philosophy and law in Zagreb and Paris and after graduating from law school in 1930 held a number of administrative posts. In 1948 he resigned from the Croatian Ministry of Finance to become a professional writer. A latecomer in the field, he has published three collections of short stories: *Derelicts in the Sun* (1952), *Springtime at Badrovac* (1955), *Here Just Beside Us* (1956), and a novel, *The Springtimes of Ivan Galeb* (1960) that has been hailed by critics as one of the finest Yugoslav literary achievements since World War II.

Mr. *Pink's Soliloquy* and *The Tale of the Friar with the Green Beard* were both written in 1954.

MIODRAG BULATOVIĆ was born in 1930 in a small village in the mountains of Montenegro. At sixteen he began wandering across an apocalyptic, war-torn Yugoslavia in search of food, shelter, and education. He has published two collections of short stories, *The Demons are Coming* (1956) and *Wolf and Bell* (1958). Since his 1959 novel *The Red Cock Flies to Heaven* became an international success, his wanderings have taken him all over Europe. He travels in a white German sports car from country to country, from one cosmopolitan outpost to another.